THE TEST

To Kerry! It is so important to share a SACRED SPACE together. Thank you for sharing this wonderful SACRED SPACE with me. Love Always! Tyrone T. Eure

T. S. Eure

authorHOUSE®

AuthorHouse™
1663 Liberty Drive
Bloomington, IN 47403
www.authorhouse.com
Phone: 1 (800) 839-8640

Published by AuthorHouse 11/03/2017

ISBN: 978-1-5462-1475-5 (sc)
ISBN: 978-1-5462-1476-2 (e)

Print information available on the last page.

Any book that draws emotions out of me is a great book! That's what happened to me when I read THE TEST. I connected to characters in every chapter. I laughed. I cried. I was in suspense, wondering what would happen next...a real page-turner.

So, for those of you existing on this journey called LIFE, I challenge you all to take THE TEST. You will not be disappointed.

Angela Perkins Jean, Editor In Chief.

About the Author

T.S. Eure was born in Omaha, Nebraska. At the age of 13, he had a life-altering event. He was sent to live with an elderly couple on their retired family farm in Iowa in order to distance himself from the trauma of inner city life. It was there, in the middle of Iowa, on this farm, while riding his bicycle through the sunlit cornfields, he heard the voice of God speaking to him. And through this experience, this inner voice has revealed itself to him throughout his entire life.

The Test is a powerful revelation given to heal the chaotic confusion that is in our world today. It is an attempt to awaken the soul to the loving vibration within us. Clearly saying, "Be not afraid, I shall love you forever!"

About the Book

It is morning. The sun is shining through your bedroom window. You hear the alarm clock ringing, and the birds are chirping outside. You try with all of your strength to move, but you are held in place upon your bed by a force you cannot explain. A voice is speaking to you in a faintly audible sound. You are terrified by what is happening, but you cannot move. The voice becomes louder until it is the only sound you can hear in the room. And then, suddenly, everything is swept away into blackness, and you can no longer see anything. You hear the voice again saying, "You have been assigned to take The Test."

Contents

~We called you here today~

We called you here today to speak to you personally. Our identity has been revealed to you many times. We have been called the, I Am, the Divine Consciousness, the Spiritual Awakening, the Inward Prayer, the Inward Voice, the All-Seeing Eye, the Everlasting Father. We are all of these things and much more. We watched you move through your life in a dormant, uninspired state. And it was so heartbreaking and troubling to see one of our best living creations dissolve into a disgusted and fallen attempt at living. And like a broken bicycle wheel, you have just limped along blaming everyone for your misery and constant whining.

We tried to speak to you this morning, hoping that you would finally pray, but you would not get out of the bed. Then we decided to speak to your spirit, but you shut down and said that you did not want to be bothered. So, we had to interrupt you today. We have rearranged your schedule so that you could take The Test. We have watched your anger and your insistence on blaming others...your wife, your husband, your children, your boss, and your friends for not advancing and moving you forward. For you decided that they were all holding you back, causing you to be miserable and irritated with life. You called out to us many times in anger, wanting to retry everything again. You even became angry at us for making such a terrible disaster of everything.

Now, you are lying in the bed with the alarm clock going off, but you cannot get up. Something is terribly wrong. Your outbursts, your temper, your total lack of compassion for others has caused us to keep you in the bed this morning. We know you cannot get up. You have been trying ever since the alarm clock went off. Well, you need to know the news before you realize it for yourself. You died last night in your sleep. We tried to stop you, but it was the continuum downward spiral that would cause you to do something so selfish and hate-driven that there was no turning back. You overdosed on the bottle of prescription pills that you shoved into your mouth because you were too drunk and angry or both to even care. And now we are deciding if we should wake you up.

Don't go pleading with us to come back. We heard everything you have said before. Like, it was only an accident and that you did not realize what you were doing. Right? Well, we don't buy that argument anymore. Just like the time you tried taking your life by working three jobs until you fell asleep behind the wheel of your car and drove off the Lake Manataka Bridge. That day we had one of our people there to save you. A young man who had just gotten his Lifeguard license, saw you go off the bridge. He dived into the murky water, brought up your lifeless body and revived you. With your first breaths, you started screaming and saying that you didn't want to live anymore. He tried praying with you, but you fought him off saying that you wanted nothing to do with that God nonsense.

And we remember when you bought the 45-caliber from the sporting goods store for the protection of your family you said. But we remember how you loaded it with live ammunition when you were alone and despondent. You convinced yourself that you were just playing as you turned the spindle around the chamber, pointing the barrel at your temple and pulled the trigger. But you did not know that we caused the gun to jam so that it would not go off. We have saved you many other countless times.

And now you want to come back and repeat the same miserable routine all over again. So, we decided that it was time for you to take The Test. The Test is given to those who have depleted themselves of compassion and concern for others. If you don't take this Test, you may never wake up and there would be no use in bringing you back. This Test is taken with your spirit. Even as you lay in the bed, you can answer and review all the questions that will be presented to you. You will see situations and people presented before you as if you were there. It will be like watching a movie being presented to you. But you will be powerless to interact or speak with anyone. And at the end of each situation, you will be given a series of questions to answer. Please be advised! These are real people on the earth right now that are going through these situations that you will be witnessing. And what you do with the situations that will be presented before you will have real-life outcomes. For everything is connected. You must know every merciful prayer creates a consciousness that can change even the physical world around you. So, the situations that will be presented before you are very real indeed. You will only be an observer. You will listen and watch the situations that will be presented before you. Like a movie that we control, we will stop and start it and allow you to make the ultimate decisions. What you do will have consequences good and bad that will affect the lives of people somewhere on the earth.

You will be given a Test at the end of each scenario. How you answer the questions will determine the impact that it will have upon others. Be careful how you answer for your choices will determine everything.

When you are ready to continue, please let us know. Or you can remain where you are, empty and lifeless, waiting for the alarm clock to stop and wake you up.

~Commitment ~ In Giving Service to Others~

Julie Ann Montclair stood in the enormous auditorium. Her large brown eyes appeared to be aglow, watching the graduates walking across the huge stage in the downtown city arena. She was preparing to graduate from the city's nursing college. It had been a most challenging task. Four long years that pushed her mind, body, and nerves to the point of breaking. But she had succeeded with the help of her mother, who was somewhere in the audience.

Her mother supported her and helped finance education. She worked two jobs. First, she worked as a waitress during the day. Then, she cleaned floors during the night in a large office building until her knees and legs swelled. Walking became extremely difficult and painful for her. Later, she was diagnosed with a progressing stage of multiple sclerosis that left her immobile, and consequently, in a wheelchair. So, when Julie walked across the large stage, even in this arena with hundreds of people seated, she still managed to spot her mother. Before accepting the coveted degree, she turned around and blew her a kiss as tears welled up in her eyes and blurred her vision.

In just a few more days she would be 26 years old. She had never been married and didn't have a life after deciding to become a nurse. She simply wanted to help others. It was this force of caring that had always been within her. Even as a child, she would find an injured bird in the park and bring it home to try her best to nurse it back to health. There was also the time that her mother found her in her bedroom where she had created a sick room for her dolls by bandaging them up and giving them tablespoons full of imaginary medicine.

When the Chancellor pronounced his last words, *"Ladies and Gentleman, I present to you the Nursing Class of Auburn University!"* a great roar erupted from the hallway that caused all the graduates to spontaneously throw their graduation caps into the air. It created a kaleidoscope of color in the arena as a final signal to the world that their hard work and the efforts of those that loved them had truly paid off. The crowd turned into mayhem after the graduation as thousands of cameras flashed all around the room. Elated families searched to embrace the new young nurses.

The lives of the nursing students have now been radically changed forever as they prepared to enter their new and exciting careers. As students, they had now become lifelong friends. So, they embraced while taking impromptu pictures together, holding their degrees in their hands, they yelled out, *"Yes we did it! We made it! They said we couldn't do it, but we did it!"* There were family members carrying flowers, gifts, and cards to bestow upon the graduates from every direction in the arena.

A group of noisy friends called out to her, *"Hey, Julie! We really did it! We are nurses!"* Tess, a young, pretty, brown-skinned African American girl, who had become best friends with her, was among them. Julie never had a friend like Tess before. She was brilliant and so beautiful that many young would-be Doctors begged to go out with her as she walked around the campus. But she, like herself, was too focused on her studies to have a life outside of school. Julie knew she would have given up and flunked out, if Tess had not burned the midnight oil with her. She made sure that she understood some of the most difficult questions dealing with the anatomy and medical terminology. Without Tess, she would not have walked across that stage with a newfound confidence and ability.

Julie's mother taught her to believe that all people are important and that the earth had no boundaries that the power of love could not cross. In nursing school, she began to understand those teachings from her mother. For she encountered people from every culture, race, and religion from many different countries. It was as if she was experiencing the classroom of the world, a sort of United Nations of humanity. They were all mostly young people like herself going forward, preparing to heal the hurt of others in some small manner, making a significant difference in the world. *"Hey, Julie, I want you to meet my Mom and Dad!"* Tess said, beaming like a lighthouse as her mother held her so tightly as if she thought she was going to disappear from her sight. *"This is my Mom and Dad. They are the greatest!"*, Tess said as her mother adjusted her long beautiful cornrows that fell down her neck. *"So, this is the young lady that I heard so much about. She is beautiful, Tess, just like you said!"* *"Well, if it wasn't for this doggone, long, red hair that makes me stand out like a street sign, I would be normal looking!"*, Julie said laughing. *"I am the only one in my family that has red hair. I don't know where this came from!"* She continued as she stood laughing with them. Tess's mother looked at her and then hugged her smiling, *"And you have the most beautiful freckles!"* *"Yeah, I know. I want to go back to the room where God was passing out body parts and tell him he did not have to give me the Orphan Annie look!"* Julie said laughing. *"On the serious side, I could not have made it in college without this young lady. She kept me going, drinking Starbucks, and pouring over books with me in the middle of the night. She will be my friend for life! And that's for sure! Nobody is going to break us up!"*

Julie then searched with a sense of urgency that suddenly now overwhelmed her because she had not found that one person who was so instrumental in helping her receive her degree. She made her meals and worked herself to the bone so that she could stand courageously on that stage. Then she finally saw her mother who looked at her from a distance with loving and tear-filled eyes. She quickly dismissed herself, but not before Tess whispered in her ear, *"You are going to the after party tonight, right? It is going to be bonkers! Those crazy doctors we met during ordination are going to be there. It is going to be the bomb! I will see you later."*

Julie finally found her mother. She was in her wheelchair unable to move. She ran towards her with her arms outstretched and tears streaming down her face. She had done it! She completed her degree and had already accepted a position at the Mount Vernon General

Hospital, in the city of Lakewood, California, where she would be starting in about a week. It was all working out flawlessly and according to plan. Everything was moving along perfectly, except her mother was not supposed to get sick like this and break down. It was wrong, so very wrong. She secretly blamed herself, wondering if she had not left home to attend college and earn her degree, perhaps she would have been alright. Deep inside, Julie was hurting. She could not let go of that feeling, even though she tried so very hard. Perhaps, even God was wrong, allowing her mother to become paralyzed and slowly lose her ability to move freely. She did not deserve this. God should not have allowed it. The hurt was overwhelming her at times. The doctors said that there was no cure. She wished that she could have stayed home now to spend more time with her. If it were not for the visiting nurse, she would have been in a more debilitating condition. That nurse helped her mother with her meals and did light exercises with her as well. This was something Julie believed that she was supposed to be doing. And now, Julie would have to leave her again, working at her new hospital job, and still not spending the quality time with her that she deserved. It just didn't seem right that a merciful God would allow something like this to happen to her.

Julie now ran to her, through the crowd, losing one of her high heels in the sea of people. She did not even go back to look for it. She ran towards her, falling on her knees, covering her wheelchair with her arms, weeping, saying, *"Mother we did it! We did it. I am a real nurse! Thank you so much!"* She held on to her for a long time while her Aunt Betty stood by the wheelchair, wiping away a few tears of her own. Finally, after calming down, everyone took a million pictures as she held up her Nursing degree, smiling like a Cheshire Cat. More cousins and uncles surrounded her, covering her with flowers, cards, and presents that overloaded her hands with their kindness. In the distance, she heard a voice from a group of nurses yelling out to her, *"Julie, aren't you coming to the after party tonight? Natalie's father bought her a brand-new convertible, so we are going to pile in right now! We are all going on a joy ride before we crash the doctors' party! You are going, aren't you? You don't want to waste a good time! It is about time we had some fun! And girl, we deserve it!"* Julie honestly wanted to go and told Tess that she was going. She felt that she had left her mother long enough. She simply wanted to spend some quality time with her. *"I don't know! I want to stay home tonight and be with my Mom. I just want to stay home and think about this beautiful moment with her! I will pass on the party tonight! Maybe another time!"*

Her Mother tried to stand up, pulling herself up in her wheelchair before sitting back down and rapidly jerking on her arm. *"You better go! It's about time you had some fun. I will be alright! I am a big girl and you know I can take care of myself! I will be waiting on you when you come home."* *"Mother, don't you stay up, alright! I will be alright. I want you to get a good night's sleep."* *"I am not an old woman in a nursing home yet! You go on with your friends. I will be waiting for you when you get home! And who knows, there might be a little surprise waiting for you."* *"It might be pretty late when I come home, so don't you stay up late!"* *"You deserve to have some fun in your life, Julie. You worked so hard. You are still a young woman! Tonight, is your night! So, go find those Doctors and bring one of them home!"* Her mother said laughing and playfully spanking her from the behind. Julie reached down and hugged her tightly, kissed her on the neck, and turned towards her laughing friends. *"Girls in a convertible sound dangerously fun to me!"* One of her giggling friends called back to her, *"Those crazy guys, who are studying to be doctors, have a pool in their rental house. It is going to be totally banging and the biggest outdoor bash of the year! You are coming aren't you, Julie?"* *"I am ready to have some fun!"*

The giggling nurses joined together and disappeared in a laughing group through the crowd of people. Betty reached down, hugged Emma, and said in a quiet voice, *"You did a great job raising that child of yours all by yourself. You should be so proud of yourself."* Emma reached up and hugged her tightly, and said, *"If you had not helped me after I got sick, I would not have made it! Julie always wanted to help people. God has given her the opportunity to do just that."* *"That child of yours is one determined person, just like her mother!"*, Betty said laughing as her eyes welled up with tears.

It was late when Julie came home, so she quietly tried to open the front door and sneaked in. She saw her mother sleeping in the front room in her wheelchair while the television was still on. It was a crazy party. It was almost 5am when she got home. But the party lived up to everything they said it would be, which included some of the would-be doctors swimming in the pool in their underwear, and in turn, pushing the other people in. The party eventually turned into a gigantic pool party with everyone dancing in the pool in their clothes. It was so much fun! Julie forgot all about the daily grind that she endured earning her degree, and for just a moment, life was indeed fun once again.

When she opened the door, she saw an assortment of cakes, cookies, and delicious looking sandwiches which had been prepared for her. In addition to that, taped up over the entrance of the room, was a large sign with streamers, and balloons hanging from it that read, *"Happy Graduation to the Nurse that is my Daughter!"* There was also a toy nurse's bag on the table with an assortment of gifts that were beautifully wrapped with her name on it. She tried so hard not to wake her mother up as she crept around the room, looking at the beautiful decorations.

Her heart fluttered after she stood looking at everything. She noticed that the room had a slight chill in it, so she found a blanket and gently wrapped it around her mother. Unexpectedly, her mother awakened and smiled sweetly at her. Julie reached over and stroked her hair, kissed her on the cheek, and said, *"You know you did not have to wait up for me all night. And look at what you did! I don't know how you walked around the room with your swollen knees and you know your body is going to start to ache tomorrow." "Well, I put a little something together."* She said smiling as a beacon of light lit all aglow over her. *"You know every time you use your walker, your legs start to ache!" "Well, I thought you were a nurse! People in my condition must keep moving. It's good for the circulation." "Well, I guess you are right about that! Everything does look delicious! And you know what? I sure am hungry!" "I thought you might be.",* she said chuckling to herself. *"I know it was very hard for you when Dad was killed in Afghanistan. I was merely a toddler and you became a single mom. I just want you to know how much I appreciate everything that you have done for me!" "I know you do, Honey! You know words cannot replace the love that is in my heart! For love knows no distance, no barrier, and it is always alive for you inside of me."* Julie reached over and hugged her tightly. Then she quickly wiped away a tear. *"Honey, I hope you had a good time last night."* Julie started laughing again, *"It was the wildest party that I had ever been to in my life!"* Then she turned around and started making herself a plate of the turkey, ham and cheese sandwiches that adorned the table. Munching on a handful of the oatmeal cookies, she went on to say, *"There was this want-to-be Doctor that picked me up and threw me into their backyard pool with all of my clothes on!"* *"Is that why you look like a wrinkled cat!"*, her mother said grinning. *"Yeah, that's why!"*, Julie said as she stood looking at herself, wringing her damp clothes. *"Well, I am glad you came home in one piece. The nerve of that young man, throwing my baby girl in a swimming pool with all of your clothes on too!"* *"Yeah, but I got him back, Mom! I pushed him in when he least expected it! And I must say, revenge was indeed sweet!"* *"Well, you should be ashamed too! But you know what? He deserved it!"* They both started laughing as they gave each other a high five. Julie started munching down all the treats that were on the table and opened a few gifts that consisted of sweaters, house shoes, makeup, and perfume. *"You know you really went all out! I hope you did not blow your budget."* *"I didn't, Honey! But this is a once in a lifetime event! And you have to splurge a little sometimes!"*

Julie looked around the room. The rooms looked so small as if everything had been reduced to some sort of miniature dollhouse. When she was growing up, she believed that her house was so enormous and the world was not big enough to fit into the rooms. And now she felt it more than ever. She would be moving away, leaving the old house. It was only a matter of time. Everything was becoming new. It was like she was passing through a time warp. She was changing inside and there was something more she needed to do. She did not know exactly what it was, but there was calling her to leave everything one day.

It was late in the afternoon when her mother entered her room, tickling her feet, saying, *"Hey, wake up sleepy head! Something arrived for you today. It looks like it's from some sort of volunteer nursing organization.*" She laid the letter on the front of her bed. Julie was just waking up and felt like she could have slept through the whole day, but she was glad that her mother had awakened her because she had many errands to run before she started her new job. As she looked at the letter, there appeared to be a dozen or more pictures of nurses helping children and sick people in Sudan in some sort of refugee camp. Printed on the flap of the envelope were the words, *"If you are looking for real rewards, this is it."* She opened the letter which began with the first sentence congratulating her for becoming a nurse. The letter continued to suggest that she needed to consider working as a volunteer in Sudan, helping people that needed emergency care. She read the letter. Dozens of pictures that fell out of it. The nurses in the photos seemed to be about her age. They appeared to be helping people with all kinds of sicknesses that required medical care. The condition seemed hopeless and desperate. There appeared to be thousands of people surrounding the medical volunteers in the dust and heat that formed a huge line of humanity, receiving some type of vaccinations. She took the photos, threw them off the bed, and said, *"Africa? Who is going there? Somebody must be out of their minds if they think I am going to Africa! I have enough to deal with trying to pay back my student loan debt and making ends meet. Who can afford to go to Africa?"* Laughing, she pulled the covers over her head and tried to get a little more sleep before she ran all the different errands that she had to do.

The first week at the Mount Vernon General Hospital was a lot harder than she would have ever imagined. The onslaught of trauma cases overloaded her sense of being disciplined and focused. A gang was having a clash in the city with a rival gang. Bodies started filling up the emergency room where she and Tess were working together. *"Girl, I have never seen anything like this before! There are so many young people in here tonight. I never thought that the first two weeks on the job would be so intense."* Tess said as she was running down the hallway with a plastic bag of blood. She continued since she only had a few seconds to talk with Julie, *"I never anticipated that I would see so many people practically dying in my arms. This is so sad. I talked to an older man and his wife in the emergency room. I didn't know how to tell them that their son had died only minutes before they arrived with a gunshot wound to his chest. I just never thought that the first two weeks on the job would be this intense!"* Wiping away tears and sweat from her face, she continued, *"I think I might quit. This is too much for me! I can't go on anymore. I am taking these problems home with me. They did not tell me all about this in school. I even had to pray with some family members. How can we not resist getting involved in these lives and not feel anything or internalize their pain? We are just human beings. This is too much for me!" "I know!"* Julie exclaimed. *I found myself bawling like a baby when a young man died the other day. He called out to me to help him, but it was too late. The family members embraced me as if I was a part of their family too! I feel like I need a break already, and I just got here. I didn't know what I signed up for. But I do know where we can go, Africa." "Where?"* Tess asked. *"Africa!"* Julie said laughing. *"Girl, I have enough problems right here in this hospital to deal with. There are enough people dying here that need my help! I wish they would stop sending those letters to me. But if you are planning on going, then I might have to change my mind."*, Tess replied. *"Look, I have worked too hard to get my degree to be working for free anywhere in the world! And I demand a certain level of comfort. I suffered enough with you, eating all those packets of Ramen Noodles in college trying to survive. And I need my hair done every other week. I am trying to make my life a little easier from now on! And besides, it costs a lot of money to keep this face looking exciting and fresh!"* Tess said laughing. *"Yeah, you're right about that! What a waste our lives would be eating bugs, rice, and living in a tent in the middle of nowhere. Do you want to know what I think? I think we should both go to Las Vegas for our first vacation. We can schedule it together and have a blast there!"*

As the weeks carried on, Julie could not stop thinking about Africa, especially when she started receiving letters from some of the people from the refugee camps in Sudan. The letters arrived in plain white envelopes with no forwarding address. They were written by someone that appeared to have problems writing in English. But the letters were legible. The letters started to arrive at the house on a weekly basis. The letters were disturbing and caused her to wonder how someone that she had never met knew so much about her. It must have been some kind of scam, she thought. How could the person, who was writing to her every week, know so many personal details about her? One of the letters read something like this:

Dear, Julie

My name is Raphael. I am one of the official guardians, appointed officer of the city. We are like your United Nations but on a higher level. We assist people in times of great need and disasters. Very few know we even exist. But we are here, moving secretly and sometimes even within the circumstances in the lives of the people. We exist only to do what we can. We reached out to you today because we know your heart. We felt your love for those that are hurting and sick, even though these people are thousands of miles away. Zuri and his wife Sheena had lived in one of the small settlements just outside the city of the Sudan. They loved each other greatly. Although they were but humble farmers, they could survive by growing crops and raising cattle. But a civil war has broken out that has affected their lives. The civil war has ravaged the city. Many have lost their very lives. No one can be safe living there anymore. The soldiers arrived the other day and immediately killed Zuri execution style. They searched through the house before burning it down, looking for more people that may have lived there. Sheena, the wife of Zuri, and their two children could escape because Zuri sacrificed his life. Sheena and her two children are currently in the desert plains, walking without food and water trying to reach the medical hospital mission some 300 miles away. Sheena's son Nafari is sick. He has been coughing and burning up with a terrible fever as he staggers in the blowing dust and heat. He also has a large gash on his leg. It has been bleeding profusely during most of the journey. Sheena wrapped the gash by tearing off a piece of her dress, trying her best to keep the blood from flowing down his leg. But he has lost so much blood, he might not be able to finish the journey. Her fragile one-year-old daughter Marla is lying in her arms bundled with rags in a sling draped over her neck. She doesn't cry anymore. She is too weak and malnourished to even raise her tiny head. She is barely breathing, and she doesn't have food or water. There is no certainty that she will survive either. They are still a long way off from reaching the medical hospital mission. Will you be there when they arrive? They are counting on you for their survival. Perhaps you and Tess can plan your vacation at another time. God will show you what he wants you to do. But I believe this is your purpose. You must come and help them. For delay, could mean certain death for all of them. Please, Julie. You must come to help. They need you, Julie. So many are waiting for you to help them.

Raphael

The letter devastated Julie. How did this person know so many personal details about she and Tess's vacation plans for Las Vegas? The letters always arrived in a plain vanilla envelope with no forwarding address, and with the same scribbly, elementary handwriting. The forwarding address simply said, Sudan. Julie told Tess about the letter. Tess couldn't believe that something like this could be happening. She suggested that Julie should contact the organization that sent the first letter that she received with the photos, inviting her to come to Africa. Tess was angry and worried about her own safety. She began explaining to Julie her own perception of what she believed was happening. *"Girl, this is some scary stuff! Someone is getting your information and then writing you these crazy letters. You better watch your back when you leave from work and be careful when you walk to your car in the parking lot. You don't want to run into some fruitcake out there lurking around! And if they are that bold to get your personal information, anything can happen!" "Yeah, you are so right Tess. In the letter, they mentioned you by name as well! I am contacting that refugee agency, the world mission or whatever they call themselves, and I am going to tell them to stop sending those letters to my house. And if they persist, then I will tell them that I am taking legal action.",* Julie said. *"You better do something! I don't want these people in my personal life either! I have never seen, nor heard anything like this before. How did they even know about our trip to Vegas?",* Tess asked.

During the following week, Julie called the director of the organization. She also mailed an official letter, drafted by an Attorney, insisting that they cease from sending her letters. Every week a letter would continue to arrive. Always, in the same fashion, a plain white envelope with no forwarding address with only one word, Sudan.

The letters were from someone that was living in the refugee camp, explaining intimate details about the terrible living conditions there. The letters would also include something personal about Julie that only she would know. This made her feel that she was constantly being watched. She became cautious whenever she spoke to people and very careful what she disclosed in her conversations at work and other public places when she was out with her friends. She did not tell anyone else about the letters she was receiving, only Tess.

One of the letters she read to Tess said,

Dear Julie,

We were so proud of you when you received your nursing degree. It was a tremendous event. We want you to know that we have been praying every day for God to give you the strength and endurance to work in the hospital, especially since you just started working there now for only eight weeks. We want to remind you to be very careful whenever you are scheduled to work

*in the emergency room. Be mindful there are hidden
dangers all around you. We foresee a dangerous event
coming your way. You must be careful.*

*But there is a makeshift hospital at the refugee
center in Sudan. People line up at the front doors of
this facility early every morning. This line of humanity
stretches for over a mile, all eager to receive medical
attention from a Doctor or a Nurse. The most extreme
cases are lying outside on mats in an area reserved
for five hundred or more covered tents. And at least
one hundred people are dying per day, due to lack
of food, clean water or unsanitary living conditions.
They could greatly benefit from your teaching them
the necessary skills for survival. We desperately need
you to come.*

*Julie, you need to stop worrying so much. We
have received some good news for you. Your mother
is going to be alright. We have received confirmation
that the swelling in her knees is going to go down and
everything will be alright. She will be walking soon.
You will see. You worry too much. You need to give it
all to God.*

Raphael

Julie was stunned that whoever wrote this letter knew that her
mother was sick and was in serious condition. What a horrible and cruel
joke she thought was being played on her. She took the letter in her
hands tore it up, and shouted, *"You have had your last laugh on me!
Don't you talk about my mother and make her a part of your cruel,
sick jokes! You creeps are going to pay for this! And I am going to
find out who you are!"*

Julie never told her mother about the letters that were arriving
because she did not want her to worry that there was a stalker prowling
into their private lives that could possibly hurt them. But she made
sure that she was extra cautious whenever her mother was home. She

closed the curtains throughout the house and was constantly double checking the doors, making sure they were all locked. And who was this Raphael character anyway, writing her the most upsetting letters. The whole thing was troubling and unsettling. This had been going on for almost two months now and Julie's nerves were at a breaking point. Julie repeatedly contacted the International World Mission Medical Society. She spoke frankly to one of the Directors of the organization that evaluated all their records. Her name was not on any register of being contacted by anyone in the organization or in Sudan. Julie screamed at the person on the other end of the phone, *"You are lying! You scamming creeps! If I get one more letter in the mail from you, I am going to the police!"*

After that, Tess visited her workstation inquiring, *"Are you still receiving more of those creepy letters! You should've gone to the police when all of this first happened! I'm afraid for you. You really need a break from all of this!"* *"Yeah, I know. And our work schedule is getting more bogged down. The trauma center in the emergency room is so overwhelming at times. It seems like we're practicing medicine in the wild, wild west!"*, Julie exclaimed. *"Well, we just have to hang in there. God is going to turn this whole situation around! My mother always said that I should just believe. When you have nothing left to give within yourself, put everything on auto-pilot and let God drive for a while!"* *"God?"*, Julie said mockingly. *"Where is he when I need him? He must be on vacation or something!"*

Yet something strange began to happen. Julie's mother started getting better. And even more bewildering, the swelling in her knees started to go down, just like the letter said. She had gotten so much better that she could walk short distances again. *"God is sure moving in a mighty way! Who would have believed that I could recover this miraculously! The doctors had pretty much written me off and had given me such a disheartening report. To be honest, I was afraid to tell you. But look at me, Julie! I am standing up and walking again! And you know what? I feel like dancing! This feels so wonderful!!"* *"Mother, please sit down! You're going to fall and hurt yourself! You know you shouldn't be moving around like this!"* *"Now you just shut your mouth, Julie! I know when I'm feeling better! And I have been thanking God every day that I am still alive! I am not going to let the rocks cry out for me!"*

Julie was holding one of the letters in her hands when her mother came over and tried to look at it. *"What are you so worried about? You have been shaky as a cat for weeks now, Honey. Tell me what's worrying you?" "Oh, nothing Mother, nothing at all." "And what are these plain white letters that are coming in the mail every week with your name on it, Honey?" "It's nothing but somebody just saying hello, that's all.",* Julie said as she quickly stuffed the letter inside of a book that was on her lap.

More letters continued to arrive as the mysterious writer Raphael spoke to her once again. But the letters were encouraging her, giving her hope as she started impatiently waiting for them to arrive in the mail every week.

Dear Julie,

You are such a hard and dedicated worker. Don't think we haven't observed your compassionate demeanor, your quick response in providing hope, and the way that you care for your patients in the hospital. For we know that light comes from the inner spirit, resonates from the release of compassion that can only be given by God. Your light is not only for you. It must be shared. For hope and compassion is the true medicine for all healings. We can find many other Doctors and Nurses, but we need you. You represent the greatest gift, which is hope. Hope is a key, unlocking the door, where all humanity is waiting to enter. It is the divine connection that gives humans strength to live. For hope is the breath of life when people are depressed and too powerless to breathe on their own. When there is nothing else, the energetic pulse of your heart can even help raise the dead. For God has no hands but your hands. God has no heart but your heart. God has no medicine on the earth but your touch and your powerful embrace. For we know without a doubt, God is working his miracles through you.

It was quite amazing watching you hold the hand of the older woman in room 334, sitting with her during a great portion of your shift, and even after your shift ended because she was afraid to be by herself, especially after her husband had just died. And the child who had gone through chemotherapy; you stayed with him, giving him hope and encouragement, even after he lost all his hair, including his eyebrows. And when his mother and father began to lose faith, being so overwhelmed with sorrow, you gave them determination and strength, reminding them that each day they have their son is a personal and daily miracle that they should cherish. You would make an amazing difference in the lives of the people of Sudan. The people are calling out to you now Julie. I am sent to you as their representative. And by the way, that little boy is now cancer free. All we ask of you is to believe.

Raphael

The letters were scary, but they were imparting strength into her. After reading the last letter from the mysterious Raphael, she quickly found the status update reports on the little boy who had cancer in his abdomen. It was true. He was cancer free! Raphael was right. Everything in the letters was coming to pass, just like he said. And the things that he said about her quality of care was also true. For patients were starting to talk about the wonderful young nurse that made everything just a little better, no matter what terrible illness was affecting them.

It was one of those nights, after an exhausting shift, that a distraught mother entered the hospital with two small children. Her face and arms were covered with cuts, welts, and bruises as if she had been severely beaten. She explained that her husband had just beaten her up and that she was in dire straits in fear for her life and for the lives of her children. Julie quickly called Security for assistance, just in case the woman's husband showed up looking for her. Security assured her that they were on their way. And as soon as she placed the phone back down on the receiver, a screaming, deranged man came through the automatic doors of the emergency room. *"You lousy, disgusting whore! You are going to die! You are not walking out of my life! I will break you in half if you ever think about leaving me! You are going to die if you think about leaving!"* She screamed in terror as her son, who appeared to be about five years old, also cried out, *"Daddy is going to kill us!"* The man pulled out a knife that was hidden underneath his shirt, and he lunged forward to stab her. Julie stepped between the woman and the blade of the knife as it went down deep into her chest. At that moment, the Hospital Security barged in, and yelled at the man, *"Drop the knife! Drop the knife!"* The man charged forward and went after the officers. The sound of gunfire filled the halls of the emergency room as the man's body laid motionless on the floor. Julie was still standing, bleeding profusely, and then tried to walk but only staggered a few feet, clutching her chest before falling to the floor. Another nurse ran towards her, shouting, *"Quick, we have to get her into surgery right now or she will die!"* It was a mad rush as a team of Doctors and Nurses appeared to materialize out of thin air, lifting her onto a stretcher. The lifeless body of the man, still laid on the floor with his eyes wide open, seemingly staring at the ceiling.

Julie was in surgery for more than an hour before they could stop the bleeding. Because she lost so much blood, she required a blood transfusion. The man that had attacked her had died from a bullet wound that went directly into his heart. When she finally came out of her drug induced coma, she saw Tess smiling at her, holding her hand with tears streaming down her face. Her smile was like sunlight, warming her up, and making her feel so much better. She tried to talk, *"My chest is hurting! What happened?"* *"Some crazy guy came into the trauma center and stabbed you! That's what happened!"* *"Oh yeah! That's what happened. I am starting to remember now!"* *"Girl you must have lost your mind! Who made you one of the Power*

Rangers? Who told you to stand between that knife and that maniac? You have this propensity for doing good, but it has gotten out of hand!" "I knew I had to do something, Tess. I did not want to see that woman get hurt; especially with her children there!" "Well, don't you do anything crazy like that again!", cried Tess as she laid on top of her lap sobbing. *"You know I have your back! I can't let anything like this happen to you again!"*

A few days later, Julie was discharged from the hospital and went home to completely recover. As the weeks went by, she was sleeping on the couch one day when her mother woke her up with some fresh baked oatmeal cookies and a glass of milk. She was shocked as she observed her mother walking, serving her the milk and cookies by herself! *"Hey, Julie! Look at me! I'm walking! I thought I would never see this day coming! I am almost as good as new! This is so wonderful! Don't you think so?" "Mother, what are you doing? You are walking by yourself. Does your doctor know about this?" "I got tired of using that old wheelchair! I don't need it anymore! I feel one hundred percent new! And as for that doctor, he can shove it! I can probably beat him in a footrace! Nothing is going to stop me now!"*

Julie stood up, looking at her mother while she munched on the delicious batch of oatmeal cookies. She started laughing in-between chewing. *"I thought I smelled something cooking. I knew you were baking something truly fantastic while I was trying to sleep!"* Her mother came closer towards her and grabbed her arms and said, *"I am glad you got some sleep this afternoon. I have been hearing you lately at night in your room. You sounded like you were tossing and turning all night long as if something was deeply troubling you! And last night I heard you crying out! Are you alright, Honey? Are you having nightmares about the man that stabbed you? God will give you peace about that man that stabbed you! He is off the earth and cannot hurt anybody else!" "Yes, Mom, I know. But that is not what is bothering me! It's something else! I see them at night, Mother. They show up around my bed. There are hundreds of them. "Who, Honey? Who is around your bed? What are you talking about?"* Julie was almost in tears as she blurted out, *"I see them, the people, the Africans. I am in Africa. and they surround me with their children.*

And the children are sick and dying all around me. I am afraid as I walk among them, knowing I cannot help them. They call out to me. And they call me by my name!" Tears were streaming down her face now as she tried to talk. *"I heard them, Mother. They speak to me in their native language, but somehow, I can understand what they are saying. One, by one they approach me saying things like, "My child is dying of cholera. Please can you help me!" or, "My child is dying of malnutrition! Can you please do something for her!" And then many more arrived, all standing around my bedside until the room is filled. Then I hear this voice calling out my name saying, "Julie, the children are dying in the village. A landmine has crippled many so they cannot walk. Can you please come and help us?"*

"I am only one person, Mother. Who are these people that surround my bed at night? I can't take this anymore! I am just one person." Julie sobbed holding her hands over her face. Her mother gently cradled her in her arms *"Looks like God might be calling you to do something else. You know what they say, God works in mysterious ways at times!" "And Mother, there is something else that I haven't told you yet. I am getting letters every week from a person in one of the refugee camps. The letters are from a person named Raphael. In the letters, he tells me what I am doing every week. It is frightening Mother because he knew you were sick and that you would get better. He also knew that I would get hurt. He even tried to warn me of the danger. I am afraid, Mother! I don't know what to do!" "It's alright, Julie. I just trust and believe God. I know we don't understand everything right now, but we have to just trust him!"*

Julie quickly dismissed herself, ran to her room and came back with a stack of letters. But when she showed them to her mother, there was nothing there but blank pages. *"These letters have been coming in the mail every week. This person, Raphael, has been writing to me, Mother. And now there is nothing there, but blank sheets of paper! What is happening to me Mother? What is going on? I can't believe that these pages are blank! There is nothing written on them! What's going on? Please, can you tell me?"* Julie's mother hugged her, held her close, and said, *"It will be alright. God is speaking to you. I don't know what is totally going on, but I do know that God will not force*

you to do anything. For he loves us too much to do anything like that!
Just listen to your heart, Julie. Listen well!"

It was just a few days later when the dreams stopped, completely. The letters didn't even come in the mail anymore. Julie would come home from work, go straight to her room and pray to God for direction. She never thought in a million years that she would be praying. But something amazing was beginning to happen. She believed that God was listening. She told Tess about her dreams. She told her about the people showing up around her bed at night telling her to come to Africa.

"Girl, you need a vacation for real! There is enough volunteer work to do in this city without going way over to Africa and risking your life in some little dirt pile to help people who can't even speak your language!" "I know. But you should see the way the people call out my name. They even bring their children to me. I'm going to consider the information about this organization and see what they are all about."

"Who made you Moses? I believe that Sudan place is dangerous! I have been reading up on the whole area. They have been in war over there for years. Look, there are enough people on the streets, and people that are on drugs out wandering all over this city that need somebody like you to help them. Look, I am not telling you what to do, but just give yourself some time before you jump into this." "I have been reading the information that I requested from the organization. They are a legit organization. They have been helping people for years. Next week, I have a meeting with some of the organization's representatives."

"Girl I think you have lost your mind! Well, good luck with going to Africa. I am staying home. I got too many soap operas to keep up with. And you know I worked too hard to give up what I have. I am trying to pay off my brand-new car, and the student loan people are on my back. This whole experience of going to Africa is too much for me! I suffered enough during college to even begin to think about giving it all up now." I am just in the learning process right now. I am just trying to feel my way through this Tess." "We are partners! How can you even think about leaving me? How can you even think

about going to Africa and joining a tribe? We are a team, Julie! You will stick out like a neon popsicle in Africa with that red hair of yours! All I'm saying is give yourself time on this, Julie!"

Julie did give herself time. She went to every seminar and attended all the classes to learn all that she could about the organization. She also learned about the people that appeared to her in her dreams. The people of Sudan had suffered for years with decades of war with colonialism, warlords and tribes fighting each other for territory. They fought until the people that once lived in the city and on their farms, were driven out until a city of refugees now materialized in the desert.

While lying in the bed one night, a little African girl came to Julie, and said, *"I have come to teach you a song. We sing this song when we are happy. During those times when we are not sick, and not overcome by war; we sing this song.*

We thank you for the day that has come. We thank God for the hour to love once again!" Julie sang along with the child and clapped her hands. She sang happily as the child sat on her bed throughout the night. They sang and laughed together until the morning.

Julie knew that if there was a God, he was truly speaking to her now. She knew that she would have to leave the hospital, find the people that talked to her at night and wrote her the letters. She met with the representatives of the World Relief Organization, began to take their classes and study the people of Sudan. She learned about their history, and the ongoing civil wars that were daily forcing thousands to live in the desert plains. Her training was very intense. It was as if she was back in college again. She attended a class on how to live without the modern conveniences that she was so accustomed to. She also learned how to help those who were diagnosed with malaria, and malnutrition. And she learned how to psychologically prepare herself to see people dying around her, daily.

It was too much for her at times. Tess thought that she had completely lost her mind. But the letters had now stopped, and there were no more people showing up around her bed at night, beating their drums, and calling out her name. And more importantly, there was a deeper understanding of knowing her purpose, and a consuming peace that moved without fear throughout her entire being.

She told the nursing staff and her supervisors about her decision to volunteer for a year, maybe two in Sudan. Everything was now moving so fast. This decision that she made, would be her attempt to respond to the voices that had called out to her by name.

The week before she left, Tess was so sad that her voice trembled. An agonizing look of fear came over her whenever she spoke with her. *"You take care over there. I still can't believe you are going to Africa. We are a team! You know this hospital is filled with so much drama in the emergency room. You should have taught me some of your Super Girl moves before you left so that I could survive in this place."* *"We are a team, Tess! We will always be a team! I will email you and text you every day to update you on what I am doing. Nothing will ever separate us from each other."* They hugged each other. Julie burst into tears as she whispered in her ear, *"I am afraid. Please pray for me every day."*

The large cargo supply plane flew over the bleak plains of Africa. It was a long, exhausting trip as the lush, green landscape gave way to a vast, endless, reddish-brown soil that appeared to be dusty and windblown. She finally arrived at the southern tip of Sudan. When she looked down, there appeared to be thousands of people looking upward at the plane. While the plane circled above them, they waved their hands in a friendly, welcoming gesture.

As she looked down at the scale of humanity, it was shocking to see so many people that were on the verge of dying, and most people in the world were still completely oblivious to what was happening there. Thousands of makeshift tents covered the landscapes. As the plane descended for landing, she could see people standing in long lines on both sides of the runway. The people surrounded the plane. Their faces were so hollow. They stared bleakly at Julie as her heart dropped down somewhere inside of her chest.

She started grabbing her luggage as a young Doctor introduced himself, *"Hello, I am Doctor Henry Phillips. I believe we talked briefly on the phone. Welcome! We are so happy you have arrived. We heard so many good things about you. You will be a great addition to our team of workers here!"* He held on to Julie as they navigated through the crowds of people.

As they walked through this immense sea of humanity, people began singing softly at first. Julie thought it was the wind, but then it turned into a beautiful humming that moved around her. It was as if the wind was hearing their joy, their pain, their survival. Many of them appeared to be so weak, and sick, yet they welcomed her with the only thing they had left which was the power of love inside of their hearts. It was as if the wind carried their song.

Consequently, her fears began to ease. It was a song that she had heard before. It was the same song that the little girl sang to her when she appeared by her bedside that night. Julie began singing the song along with them. They smiled at her in wonder and amazement at how quickly she picked up the song. Some of the sick found enough strength to clap their hands and whistled out their joy.

Doctor Phillips remarked, *"You must have heard this song before Julie!"* *"Yes, I did! It's beautiful. It is one of the reasons why I came to meet the person who taught that song to me! This is all so incredible! It's one thing to see it on television, but quite another to see the magnitude of the people that are gathered here."*

"And we are so happy that you have arrived. There are over one ten thousand people in this camp. And this is one of the smaller ones. There are others scattered across the entire southern region. We were in desperate need of medical staff. We thank you so much for coming. I hope you recognize that you have been given the opportunity to save lives."

As they continued to walk through the camp, Julie noticed that many of the people looked so weak, and thin as they stood in front of their makeshift tents, holding children that also appeared to be malnourished, and weak. *"You know Dr. Phillips, I dreamed about these people. They would wake me up in the middle of the night and call out to me to help them! And I guess that is why I am here! I had to learn their song of joy and survival before I felt worthy to come."* He looked at her, smiled sweetly and said, *"Yes, there is a calling to be in this place."*

As Julie looked around the camp, there appeared to be thousands of people; many lying lifeless as if they couldn't move. Dr. Phillips explained the reason why they appeared to be lifeless. He said, *"They are so exhausted from walking so many miles to arrive here. They were doing all that they could do to revitalize their bodies. That revitalization recovery does take time, and for some, just moving depletes all of their strength for the day."*

As Julie continued to look around, she noticed that there were many more women in the camp than men. Dr. Phillips explained that most of the men were killed during the civil war. And that many women lost their husbands and sons who were forced to enlist in the army. Julie also observed, thousands of women in line in front of the door of the large tent structure in the makeshift hospital. The women were holding babies that were so fragile looking. It was a miracle that they had survived at all.

Dr. Phillips also continued talking about the dangers that surrounded them. *"We are still in the middle of a civil war between the governmental forces, and the rebels that have taken over the area. And that does not include the fighting between the different tribes, and warlords all trying to challenge each other for power. Thankfully, we are so far away that there is nothing here that is valuable to any of them. Parasites, diseases, and sickness are not high on their priority list. So many people have been displaced, abandoned, and left to die without anyone to help. That is why we are here. We are an international group of Doctors, Nurses, and Medical Workers without boundaries. Our only mission is to help people. There are over ten thousand people in this camp. There are other camps that are even larger than this one, scattered throughout the desert. But we are volunteering our time to serve, and to save lives."*

As we walked near the daily food distribution tents, people appeared in a long, seamless, and endless line with all sorts of cups, pots, jugs, whatever they could find to receive water, a container of milk, bread, powdered eggs, and packages of the nutritious, vitamin-packed, peanut butter paste called Plumpy Nut. Dr. Phillips said, *"You will be working with a team of nurses in the critical care unit of the hospital. You are the last line of defense for many who are on the verge of certain death. Thank you for hearing the voices inside of you, and coming!"*

As we entered the critical care unit tent, there were hundreds of little cots that filled the room of a sea of people. He then introduced her to an older woman holding a small child in her arms while she was putting something in his mouth with an eyedropper. *"Hello Julie, my name is Amanda Middleton. I am one of the head nurses in the critical care unit here. We thank you so very much for coming! There are no words that can describe how much you are needed here!"* She hugged her and then gave her a welcome basket filled with fruit and flowers. Mrs. Middleton appeared to be in her late forties with streaks of gray hair mixed with some brown, and there also appeared to be some slight tiny age lines around her eyes. As she continued to talk, she watched carefully over the little baby that she was holding. *"Come on little fellow. You can make it. You can take some more. Come on little angel. You can do it. You know the babies that we take in here are so malnourished that it takes all of their little effort just to swallow."* She held the baby up and then gently patted it on her chest. *"I believe this little one just might make it. There are many more that don't survive you know. It is so hard on all of us, but we must keep our minds focused on helping those that do survive. I have heard so much about you, and your work in helping the people in the trauma center. What you did there was nothing short of amazing. The Sudanese and all of the medical workers here are grateful for your service." "I only did what I had to do. God does the real work in front of me. I just follow." "You are right Julie! I have seen God do some amazing things here with those whom we thought were going to die. They have survived and are still alive! When we have nothing left to give them, we are grateful for the intervention of the healing power of God.*

You will be working here with us, nursing the acutely malnourished. There are only three Doctors and seven Nurses that care for the medical needs of thousands. And with the little babies, we only have a small window of time to save them.", Mrs. Middleton said as she continued to gently rock the baby in her arms.

Julie looked at the vast number of people sleeping, lying on the cots. This scene was quite overwhelming. The nurses moved quickly between different patients. Julie's bags were taken to one of the small, secluded, staff tents. The tent had a few of the necessities of life. It had a small portable toilet, and a basin to keep fresh water to wash in. After more brief introductions with more of the nursing staff, Julie jumped right in, working alongside the rest of the staff. The day finally came to an end as she dragged herself into her little tent.

It was late into the night, and it had been an exhausting day when she walked out into the cool of the evening to look at the stars that hovered over the horizon. She called out to her mother, hoping that the wind would carry her voice in the air to her, *"Mother, look at your baby girl! You would have been so proud of me today."*

The next day, when she arrived at the critical care tent, there was already a group of people lying lifeless in front of the entrance. They were brought there before morning by a medical truck that was searching for wounded refugees wandering in the desert. One of the nurses lamented that when the truck arrived, there were over one hundred people or more that were carried in appearing to be lifeless, and completely emaciated. Julie didn't know if they were going to survive the next hour.

Julie's attention instinctively turned towards the women. Everything inside of her cried out as she observed the women holding their fragile children in their arms. The children appeared to be no more than living skeletons. The Medics quickly carried the children into the critical care tents. The Doctors and Nurses immediately surrounded them, and carefully placed their brittle, tiny bodies on cots. Tenderly, the nurses started IVs to replenish fluids, and nutrients essential for sustaining life. It took a considerable amount of time to find a vein to inject the needle to start the IV. Needles could break one of their bones if we weren't careful.

Julie was so grateful for the difficulties that she experienced at the hospital. That experience proved to be a good training ground for what she would encounter in Sudan. Now, she truly believed that God has a way of preparing us before we arrive into any situation that needs our uniqueness, and sacred intervention.

One of the women, who believed that her baby had already died, was screaming and crying hysterically when she came into the tent. The baby came back to life and opened his eyes, after responding to the intravenous liquids revitalizing his tiny body. The mother stood with tears of joy streaming down her face as she held her, the nursed back to health baby in her arms. Boldly, in the middle of the room, she began praying a blessing over our lives. She prayed for the angels to watch over us. Later that night, Julie thought about all the people that would have died, if she had not come; if she had not listened to the voices in the room that had called out to her.

The days turned into weeks, and then into months until Julie had been there for over six months. Yet Raphael, the one who wrote her the letters, was nowhere to be found. One day, she went throughout the crowd of humanity asking everyone if they knew someone by the name, Raphael, but no one had ever heard of him. Maybe, Raphael never existed. Maybe, he only lived because she instinctively wanted him to. Or maybe, it was her own thoughts that gave him life, importance, and a personality. For what if her own inner force, her inner thoughts created this being? He appeared to be someone watching over her. Someone she felt, but could not touch. Perhaps he was just her inner hurt, her inner loss of not having a father, who died many years ago. Because of that, she always felt abandoned, betrayed, and left out. And maybe, the letters were simply blank pieces of paper. Maybe she made the whole story up to give herself a sense of being needed. And what about the little girl that came to her, and sung at her bedside? She was sure it was the same song that the people sang when she arrived. There had to be some kind of connection or rational explanation for all of this.

The very next morning she prepared a package of the highly nutritious Plumpy Nut. With the utmost care, Julie took the tip of her finger, and put some of the peanut butter like paste on it, and let a malnourished infant suck on it while cradling the baby in her arms. It was a heartbreaking process. Once, one of the infants died in her arms. She cried for almost a week. Julie knew that they were becoming dangerously close to running out of their supplies. But Dr. Phillips assured everyone that a supply plane was on its way in just a few days. Julie sincerely hoped so because she could not face that vast sea of humanity without the means to help them. They still had to become agents of hope, no matter what. They had to maintain a sense of calm and assurance for hope was the greatest cure no matter what was lost.

Suddenly, there was a commotion in the camp as a truck came

rumbling through. The people surrounded it, believing it was a supply truck that had water, blankets, food, and other supplies. But when the truck was opened, it was filled with the bodies that a medical team was found on the plains, so the bodies were brought back for a decent burial. Nevertheless, a rush of panic spread throughout the camp, and the people started to believe that the government soldiers were on their way to kill all of them. Those who still had strength in their bodies began to run through the camp, crushing those who were too weak to move. It was turning into a danger zone as crowds of people began to trample over others. The medical tents were also in jeopardy of being torn down.

Dr. Phillips was also running through the groups of people, trying his best to reassure everyone that there were no soldiers coming to kill them. But it appeared to do little good as the crowd surged in every direction.

Julie placed the tiny baby back on the cot and went outside. She could see the mass confusion that had erupted all around the camp. And then she saw a little girl singing amid all the confusion. Moving her hands in a slow-motion, sign language type manner, she then pointed them upwards towards the sky. The song seemed to have penetrated the noise of the screaming as people ran came from every direction to surround the little girl.

Suddenly, it was as if they were being surrounded by this comforting song that was indeed a prayer. For it was a prayer for them to remind themselves of knowing the power of their inner strength. For it was a prayer for them to remember that they were a magnificent people, even amidst intolerable suffering. They were uniquely brilliant and had a divine purpose for their very existence to be upon the earth. And no matter how difficult it may become, they were given the power of determination to live and bless the world around them.

Julie watched the little girl as she imitated her slow-motion sign language and soft sounding song of prayer. And then, it was as if everyone in the camp instantly started to remember the power of the love that brought them this far. They began to embrace the consciousness of those thoughts, and slowed down their steps. One by one, they sat down with the little girl, imitating her hand gestures in slow-motion, and singing her soft, hymn-like prayer. Hundreds more stood still, and then thousands as they sat down, one by one, moving their hands slowly until they became like a wave, flowing in one continuous motion, an endless river of hands reaching upward towards the sky. As the commotion ended, and calm had returned to the camp, Julie searched for the little girl, running between the thousands of people, but she was gone.

This experience was just as terrifying as the letters she received from Raphael. Julie was afraid of all that had happened that day. But there was a deep level of calm within her. She now believed that Raphael, an*d his security forces, were always nearby.

A few days later, Julie received an urgent call from Betty, her mother's sister. She called to inform Julie that her mother had fallen down a flight of stairs in the house where she lived. Betty informed her that her mother was taken to the hospital for observation, but she was going to be alright. Julie was devastated when she heard that news. She was ready to leave Africa right away. But Betty reassured her that everything was alright. She let her know that her mother was getting her leg x-rayed to make sure that it wasn't broken. She also let Julie know that the hospital was going to keep her overnight and that she would call as soon as her mother was finished with all the examinations.

Julie was devastated. She returned to her tent and broke down, sobbing. She felt like she had abandoned her mother once again, when she needed her the most. She now wanted to leave Africa, leave everything behind. It was too much for her anyway. It was just too much to deal with. She began packing everything in her suitcases. She decided to tell Dr. Phillips that she was leaving right away. After all, she did what she could, and now, there was no more that she could give.

Finally, the phone rang. It was her mother. *"Mother, are you alright? What happened? Is your leg broken? Mother, please talk to me!" "Honey, girl, will you please calm down! Everything is fine! I am feeling so much better. I did take a nasty spill, but I am a lot more durable than what you might think."*, she said while laughing. *"Can you please just tell me what happened?" "Well, I was baking a batch of oatmeal cookies to send to you over there. I thought that I could take a quick nap, but then I woke up, realizing that I had left the cookies in the oven too long. So, I ran down the stairs rushing to take them out of the oven. Rushing, I twisted my knee and fell down the stairs. I managed to call Betty. She came right over; took the cookies out of the oven, and then called an ambulance to take me to the emergency room."*

"Well, I have decided to come home now anyway. I need to be there taking care of you. You need me now, more than ever. And anyway, I owe you, Mother! It's my turn to help you for all that you have done for me. So, I am leaving Africa as soon as possible. I need to be there by your side, helping you."

"Julie! You will do no such thing! You will not leave your work there to help me because I twisted my knee coming down some stairs. First of all, you have too much work yet to be done. God put you on the earth to do what you are doing. And he put me on the earth to help you get over there. You will not waste God's time and your abilities looking after me. And secondly, I am doing so much better! I was doing jumping jacks the other day before I fell. I think I pushed myself a little too hard."

Then Julie heard something emoting from her mother that caught her off guard. Her mother actually became angry at her for wanting to come home and care for her. *"Well, let me tell you something, young lady! I don't know if your letters or the voices that you heard when you were sleeping were real or not, but I do know this. I know that God got you over there for a reason. So, don't you come back home because you think you need to take care of me! If you don't want an old lady angry at you, don't you come back home! I believe there is something else you need to do. I don't know what it is. But you need to stay there, and let God show you what you need to do next!"*

That night, when Julie left her tent, the stars were out again. There were trillions of them that magnificently lit up the horizon. As she walked alone in the darkness, she felt angry at God for changing her life to come here. She said to herself, *"Besides I am way too young to be doing this. I could be having fun, just like other young women my age. And here I am, in the middle of nowhere, surrounded by people that can't even speak my language. I am totally alone now and just angry at God. Do you hear me, God? I am angry! And who am I to be doing this? I am nobody...just Julie Ann McClair, a small-town girl! I am not some Mother Teresa! I am just a plain, ordinary girl!"*

It was time for Julie to go back home. She was ready to leave and become ordinary, and normal once again. She wanted to return to her room where it was safe, and the world could not touch her. She wished that she had a plate of oatmeal cookies from her mother. A warm plate of her mother's cookies always made her feel safe and secure. *"God, I wish I was home! I'm tired, God. And I'm alone. Do you hear me? Do you hear me, God? Do you actually exist? What am I doing here in Africa, following behind some voices that I heard around my bed? I must be losing my mind!"*, Julie cried out.

And then suddenly, Julie heard voices in the wind surrounding her. There was wave after wave of voices. The Sudanese were walking on the plains that night as well. There were hundreds of them seemingly everywhere, lifting their hands towards the starry horizon. They were supposed to be too sick, and too malnourished to even walk this far away from the camp. What were they doing out here? But as she watched, there was something different about them. It appeared as if their feet were moving above the ground as they walked. It was as if they were being suspended in the air. It was all too surreal as their skin blushed, and illuminated with a glowing light. Who were these people surrounding her? There, they stood, encircling her with translucent, fluorescent wings appearing upon their bodies. They continued to sing and then leaped upward into the air.

Julie was speechless and stunned at what she was beholding. This couldn't be real. This was impossible! But they were all around her, laughing, and singing, trying to touch her hands. They did eventually grab her hands, lifting her up off her feet slightly above the ground. Julie found herself tiptoeing above the ground like an infant learning how to walk for the first time. She was afraid at first and cried out in fear. Somehow, she released herself and began to trust the hands of the beings that held her up. She found herself moving toward the sky, being lifted, off her feet, and trusting the hands that held her.

The next morning, she awakened on the dusty plains. Curled in a fetal position, she tried to focus, correcting her blurred vision. She touched the ground around her in a jumpy, panicky motion, attempting to restore her sense of normalcy and reality in the world around her. In the distance, she saw the medical camp and the thousands of people that were standing and assembling before the medical tents seeking help. She then noticed a brown paper bag lying next to her and a plain white envelope which simply had her name, Julie, written on it. She quickly opened the letter, trying to steady her trembling hands as she quickly read the note inside of the envelope out loud.

> *Dear Julie,*
>
> *I am Raphael. We have decided to give you a special treat. We sent one of our representatives to your Mother's house and we took the liberty of taking some of her oatmeal cookies to bring to you. Please enjoy.*
>
> *Sincerely,*
> *Raphael*

Julie quickly opened the bag of cookies. The cookies felt warm to her touch. She smelled them and held them in her hands as she inspected each one. And then she slowly put one of the cookies next to her lips, carefully bit off a tiny piece, and placed it in her mouth. She started to chew it and in a euphoric voice, she shouted, *"These are so wonderful! Mom could always make the best oatmeal cookies in the world!"* By the handful, she started stuffing the rest of the cookies into her mouth, laughing hysterically. *"What a wonderful surprise! A special delivery of oatmeal cookies! I am not alone! I will never be alone! For God, you are here with me!"* Tears streamed down her face as she happily ate the cookies.

Julie eventually arrived at the medical tent, ready for another day of trying to save those assigned to her care. Mrs. Middleton came running towards her. She was out of breath as she began to speak, *"Julie! We need your help right now! A cargo plane was approaching the camp. As the plane descended to land on the runway, it was reported that the plane had been shot at. It was also reported that there may be casualties onboard. Julie, I have been looking for you everywhere! I went to the tent looking for you this morning. When I couldn't find you there, I went to your quarters, and you were not there either. Where have you been?"*

"I had to talk to God last night, Mrs. Middleton. We had a great conversation. I'm ready. Ready to once again, roll up my sleeves, and get back to work. I just needed a little confirmation. So, God sent me a special delivery to let me know that he is still with me!" Surprisingly, Mrs. Middleton said in a sympathetic voice, *"I understand completely what you mean. In this kind of work, we all should take off and regroup. But please come with me now. Bring your medical bag and some supplies because we do not know what kind of casualties we might find when they land."*

As we ran towards the open flat plain, the cargo plane seemed to create an ocean of dust as its propellers rotated in a loud, cranking manner. The Doctors and Nurses stood by, ready to treat those that could be suffering from critical injuries. Julie could see that the plane had indeed been shot at. There was a line of bullet holes that ran horizontally along the side of the plane. There was also a bullet hole in the pilot's window.

More medical staff arrived to help the wounded. Other staff members started unloading the much-needed supplies for the camp. The pilot came out talking to everyone that had been assembled, revealing that they were shot at, but no one had been hurt from the isolated incident. More medical workers exited the plane to join the ecstatic doctors and nurses. There was one nurse, in particular, who was struggling to carry her bags. When Julie saw her, her eyes opened widely and she screamed so loud that everyone turned to see what was the commotion. *"TESSSSSSSS! TESSSSSSSSS!,* Julie exclaimed, *"FOR THE LOVE OF GOD GIRL WHAT ARE YOU DOING HERE?"* When Tess saw Julie, she ran in a mad dash towards her. They embraced, spun around, and tumbled onto the ground in a cloud of dust, laughing together. *"I THOUGHT I WOULD SURPRISE YOU! WELL GUESS WHAT.... SURPRISE! I BET YOU NEVER THOUGHT IN A MILLION YEARS I WOULD BE HERE!" "YOU*

DID SNEAK THIS ONE ON ME!" "BUT I AM SO HAPPY THAT YOU ARE HERE! IT IS TOO WONDERFUL TO BELIEVE!" They continued embracing and laughing on the ground. *"DO YOU REALLY THINK I AM GOING TO ALLOW YOU TO RUN AROUND AFRICA BY YOURSELF WITHOUT ME FINDING YOU?" "WELL, YOU DID SAY THAT YOU WANTED TO KEEP YOUR HAIR AND FINGERNAILS DONE EVERY DAY!" "WELL, I BROUGHT PLENTY OF EXTRA HAIR AND FINGERNAIL POLISH IN MY BAGS!"*

Tess walked with Julie through the camp. She was surrounded by a throng of people. Julie introduced Tess to some of her newly found friends she helped and cared for. When they arrived at her tent, Julie said, *"You will be bunking with me. There is an extra cot that they can bring in for you!" You must seriously miss me to come this far!" "Well, I did not want you to marry some African prince, take over his diamond and oil fields, and then come back to the states as a billionaire!" "Well, it's surely rough around here. Like nothing you would have ever anticipated. And yes, there are diamonds here, but they are inside of the people that we help!"*

"I am afraid! I want to go back home and hightail it out of here! You must help me to be strong, Julie! I don't know if I am up to this challenge!" "You will be alright! You're just like me when I first arrived! It was too much at times! But you may have to go somewhere alone and ask God to give you a little more strength, a little more motivation to see you through! And by the way, do you want to try some of the oatmeal cookies that arrived for me this morning? As Tess started to eat the cookies, she said, *"These are your mother's cookies! I would recognize these delicious tasting cookies anywhere. That was so nice of her to send them to you!"* Julie looked at her smiling, and said, *"It's the little extra things like this that will give you strength!"*

Throughout the day, Julie took her around and introduced her to all the people that she worked with, and those that she had cared for as well. They had become more than just people that she knew and cared for. They were now spiritually and consciously connected forever with her in love. For they had struggled together and healed each other together. Julie's strength was nourished and replenished by these people whom she thought had nothing to give to her. Julie understood that for love to be complete, it must be transcendent. It must be released and received at the same time.

During the following weeks, Tess and Julie worked together as a team of compassion. Gradually, the people were getting better. The death rate even began to decline. And sporadically, the unfamiliar sound of children laughing filled the camp. Julie believed the change was directly correlated to Tess's presence there. Tess would instigate spontaneous fun for the children. Crowds of children followed her wherever she went in the camp because she was the one who was always making up games. She also created imaginary stories and acted as the characters in those stories for the children. Amazingly, language was not a barrier to her.

Tess's skills as a nurse also proved to be highly valuable. She had an uncanny ability for helping the most critical recover when everyone else had given up on them. Before long, she was teaching other nurses more effective measures for treating the malnourished by preparing nutritious meals, rich in proteins to stimulate the body's immune system.

A light broke through the camp. An intense, glorified light filled everything with sound and the atmosphere with joy. Julie awakened one morning to the sound of hundreds of children near her tent. Tess started a huge game of kickball. The children were running, laughing, and appearing to be normal children once again. At that moment, Julie knew that the power of love is the greatest medicine. Healing must begin in the heart and then cover everything in its completeness. Only then, the spirit will revive and believe it is worthy to live.

The laughter in the camp was like a vibrating wave, a shaking force. The laughter became the sound of a church steeple's bell. Its sound caused everyone to stop for a moment, and come out of the medical tents. Even the critically ill, if for only just a moment, lifted themselves up to see the children playing and laughing. For the children believed in something greater than all our work. They believed in something greater than what we could achieve. Only the children had the capacity to release, and perpetuate the sound, the motion, and the power of life.

One morning, Dr. Phillips asked a group of nurses if they could accompany a small medical team to one of the outer refugee camps which were located two hundred miles away. That camp was in desperate need of nurses. It would only be a few days before additional medical staff would arrive to relieve them. It had been reported that great numbers of children were dying from malnutrition. So, Dr. Phillips issued an urgent plea for volunteers. He also added that due to the seriousness of the situation, the team would have to leave in less than an hour.

It totally surprised Julie to learn that Tess was one of the first to volunteer. She was so adamant in not wanting to come to Africa. Now she was volunteering to go to another refugee camp to help again. Julie wanted to go with her, so she volunteered as well, but Mrs. Middleton stressed how it would diminish the critical care unit where she worked at. Therefore, she decided it would be best for her to stay, and save the lives that were in her care. After all, she was committed to helping them.

Julie found Tess. Laughing, she said, *"Girl I can't believe you are leaving to help out! Incredible that a scaredy-cat like you, who was afraid to leave home, has now turned into a Super Girl, like Storm from the X-Men! Do I need to hold your cape or something before you fly off?" "Well, before I leave you, why don't you wash my cape and superhero tights, now that I think about it?"* They both started laughing. *"How long are you going to be gone?" "Well, Dr. Phillips said just for a few days. It's just a quick trip to cover their bases until reinforcements arrive." "Well, I guess somebody has to go. But what am I supposed to do when two hundred children come looking for me to play kickball tomorrow afternoon?" "I'm going to leave my Jordan's for you, Julie, but don't get them too scuffed up!"*

"I heard one of the Sudanese talking about how that place was attacked a few years ago." "I heard that too, but Dr. Phillips said that they have an International Police Force that patrols the area. And besides, the soldiers want nothing to do with us. We only have sickness and disease, nothing valuable at all! You know Julie, there is one problem that might occur when I am gone." "What is that, Tess?" "I don't want you trying to cheat those children when you are playing

kickball with them!" "Tess, you know I don't cheat! I only cheat when I play with you!" They both started laughing. Tess looked at her again as they embraced and held out her pinky ring. Julie extended hers. As they crossed each other's fingers, they shouted, *"Sisters for Life!"* Tess had a few bags and one suitcase when she boarded the little, rusty, mini-bus, and disappeared down the dusty, wind-blown road.

It was about three days later when a woman came through the camp in an extreme condition of starvation. Her bones were showing through her skin. Somehow, she managed to walk, holding a baby in her arms as she crossed the desert. Immediately, she was taken to the critical care tent. She told the medical staff that she had walked over three hundred miles for help. Her home had been burned, and her family all killed by the soldiers of the city. And by the grace of God, she lived long enough to bring her baby to the camp. She believed nothing mattered to her now, only that her child might survive. Julie never saw anyone in such deprivation. The woman was more like a skeleton than an actual human being. But somehow, she managed to walk by herself, still holding the tiny baby, covered in rags, draped in a sling around her neck.

The medical staff looked in bewilderment at the strength of this woman with nothing to survive as she walked by herself, across the desert floor, carrying her child, and only being nourished by her determination. The staff carefully removed the tiny baby from the sling around her neck. The baby was still alive, but barely as it hardly made any attempts to cry. A baby that did not cry was a terrible warning sign to the team of workers that it was on the verge of dying. In a whispering voice as if she was replaying the last, and haunting days of her life, she said, *"The soldiers came, and they started killing everyone in the village. My family, my friends are all gone!"*

There was something familiar about this woman. Julie had seen her before. For a moment, Julie was overcome with emotion. As if having a startling revelation, Julie then asked the woman, what was her name. She replied that her name was Sheena. She said that her husband's name was Zuri. She said her husband was killed by the soldiers when they first came into the village. She recounted how the soldiers gathered all the men together and killed the men that refused to join them first. She said that she also had a son. His name was Nafari, and that he had died from a leg injury during the escape, and bled to death as they walked through the treacherous desert. He was only nine years old, but she had little strength left to bury him, so she covered his body with small rocks. She also stated that she had nothing left from her family, but her baby daughter Marla. Sheena said that as she struggled through the desert, where there was no water. She said then she prayed to God for help and that an angel appeared, and water came up from the ground. She whispered, if it had not been for that water, she would have died along with her baby.

Julie asked her if the angel gave her his name. She said, ***"Yes, he said his name was Raphael."*** Julie now knew that she had to help this woman and her baby since there had to be a reason for them to still be alive. For she saw this woman in her night vision, standing around her bed, holding her baby in the sling of her arms asking for help. And this godly spectrum, this divine being, Raphael, was near too. But why was she chosen to help this woman and her child?

The woman then gathered what was left of her strength, and lifted herself off the cot, and touched Julie's arm as tears rolled down her cheeks. ***"I am going to die. I can feel it inside of me. But please, you must save my baby! The angel said that you would save her."*** Julie gently eased her back down, ***"We are going to do what we can to save the both of you. Everything is going to be alright. You will see."*** The woman laid back down on the small cot in a motionless position. And then her eyes became still and distant. Her breathing became slow. Julie quickly tried to take her pulse. It was faint and could hardly be detected.

Then Julie was startled as everyone in the tent reacted to the noise and loud shouts occurring outside. A nurse came in out of breath and in a state of panic *saying, **"The medical team just arrived back in the camp. There are people hurt, and there are also casualties!"*** A sense of dread and fear rushed through Julie's body as all she could think of was Tess. ***"What do you mean casualties? There are people dead? That area was supposed to be safe. What do you mean people have died! Tess, are you alright?"*** Julie immediately left the medical tent when she noticed that a large crowd had assembled around the mini-bus. As Julie pushed through the crowd of refugees and medical workers, she noticed that the bus had bullet holes on its side, and two in the windshield, and some in the back. Julie saw the medical staff taking the injured from out of the open doors in the back of the bus. Julie ran towards the back screaming, *"TESS! TESS! TESS! WHERE ARE YOU? TESS! TESS!"*

It was a chaotic scene as workers started to separate the living bodies from those that had been killed. Some of the bodies had been riddled with bullets, leaving no chance of survival. The driver of the bus was frantically talking in a hurried, panicked voice with words that you could hardly understand. He explained that the soldiers had descended upon the refugee camp, and started killing everyone. The driver indicated that he barely managed to drive out with some of the medical staff in a hail of bullets. And then he said something that frightened everyone, through the panicked, rambling of his words, he said that the soldiers were headed their way.

Julie was searching in a maddening state until she finally saw Tess on the floor holding her hands against her chest. Her clothing was drenched in blood. She was alive as Julie started sobbing loudly calling out her name *"TESS YOU ARE ALIVE! TESS, YOU ARE ALIVE! THANK GOD! YOU ARE ALIVE!"* A bullet had struck her in the chest. She was bleeding profusely when a doctor appeared to examine the wound and yelling to the medical team to prepare her for surgery. Julie ran over towards her, and placed her arms around her, calling out her name.

Tess was quickly picked up, and placed on a medical cot. They ran and prepared her for surgery. Julie ran with them towards the tent at a frantic pace as hundreds of the refugees followed, crying. While they worked on Tess, Julie stood praying asking God for help. *"She did not deserve this God. Please don't take her! Don't let her die, not like this. You said I would never be alone again!"*

It had been less than twenty minutes when Dr. Phillips came out with tears in his eyes, saying, *"The bullet, Julie, severed a major artery. We tried to repair it, but she is dying. There is little more that we can do."* Dr. Phillips collapsed on a medical cot, put his hands over his head and cried out in tears. *"NO TESS! NO TESS! TESSSSSSS!"*

Julie ran inside of the little room where a nurse was holding her hand as she draped herself over her. She was still alive. Faintly, she smiled for a second and tried to move her pinkie finger. Julie immediately understood, grabbed her hand, held it, and then crossed her pinkie finger with hers. Julie paused between her words as tears rained down her face, *"SISTERS IS WHAT WE ARE, FOREVER! I LOVE YOU ALWAYS!"* And when Julie let go of her hand, Tess breathed her last breath and was dead. Julie cried out in such a terrible scream that the refugees and their children that had assembled around the tent, understood the sound of the release of her pain, her sorrow. They knew Tess had died. The refugees also cried out in vibrating sounds that moved outward and then echoed across the plains.

Julie held Tess in her arms, gently lifted her, and carried her outside. With all of her strength, she walked outside amid the sea of Africans that surrounded her. She held her in her arms, sobbing as she walked across the desert floor where the dust and the wind blew all around her. Julie's body ached as she struggled to carry Tess's lifeless body in her arms to the place where she saw the angels. She finally found the place and laid Tess's body down in the dust. Thousands of the refugees surrounded her in an endless circle of humanity. Julie cried out, *"Angels, please come! Angels, please come help me! Angels, I need your help please. Angels, please help Tess! Angels! I know that you can hear me!"*

It was approaching late afternoon. Julie remained motionless, draped over the body of Tess. The refugees quietly watched her as they tried to absorb the desperation of her grief. Another lone figure now stood up and walked through the hundreds of refugees that had surrounded Julie. Dr. Phillips called out, *"Julie! Julie! Julie! Do you hear me? It is time to go back! People are dying, and they need you! Please, come back to us!"* Julie kissed Tess on her cheek and whispered in her ear, *"I will see you again!"*

A group of medical workers moved through the crowd with neatly folded cloths of linen in their hands. Julie took the cloths from the workers, and carefully folded them around Tess until her body was completely covered up. When Dr. Philips made a slight motion with his hand, the workers came forth and gently laid Tess's body on a cot, and carried her into the tent that served as the morgue area of the camp.

It was late in the day when the sun had turned into an orange ball that hung partially above the horizon. The wind started blowing through the camp in a dusty fog. Julie returned to the critical care unit, but she was drained as if the driving force of living had been taken away from her. She felt like she had lost everything; her reason for being there. For the vanishing light of hope that lived inside of Tess, had now been released. All things became empty, and hollow once again for the light of Tess could not penetrate the cloths that were draped around her in the morgue. There was nothing left to do now, but go home, escort Tess's body, and give her parents the sad news.

Then she remembered the mother that wanted to see her little baby live. Frantically, she began searching for the woman with the baby girl. She looked through all the medical rooms, and could not find her anywhere. Something had to survive. Something beautiful, and powerful still had to live. For some act of caring still had to blossom, and survive from the tears planted in the dust.

In a state of fearful panic, Julie ran through the tents, looking for the woman with the baby girl. She had to be there somewhere, she thought within herself. Then she started calling out, *"Where is she? Where is the woman with the baby? The woman that was brought in early, during the day. Where did she go?"* As she continued searching through the cots. One of the nurses, startled by her statement, responded, *"There are hundreds of patients here! And there are many mothers with children."* Julie replied, *"The woman with the baby that came in here this morning! I must see her, and let her know everything is going to be alright!"* She looked at her, searching for answers in Julie's face, said quietly, *"The mother died about an hour ago, however, the child is still alive. But I do not know for how long."*

Subsequently, Julie found the little baby girl, still struggling to live, so she carefully cradled her in her arms, and whispered in the baby's ear. *"You are all that is left from your family. You are the only survivor. You are in my care now. You are going to make it little girl. God be my witness. You are going to make it little girl!"*

Ok, let's just stop here for a minute, and pause everything, only for a moment.

I want you to answer just a few questions.

If you lost everything in your life, what would you hold on to? Let's say you lost your home, your family, and that one person in your whole world that was your source of stability, and strength. If all of that was suddenly taken away from you, what would be your source of strength to continue to live?

~~~~~~~~~~~This is a Warning! ~~~~~~~~~~~

You must answer these questions very honestly. Failure to not answer the questions honestly will cause you to flunk the whole test, immediately. And you will not wake up!

I think we should start playing the Jeopardy game show theme song.

Maybe then, you will realize how serious this is as you take this part of The Test.

1. *What would be your source to continue to survive, if you lost everything?*
2. *What would be the one thing that you could still hold on to that would make you believe that God is real? Can God's love be seen and demonstrated through tragedy and human failure? Do you have a personal example?*
3. *Tell us what would you do, if you were Julie? After working hard for your own goals, would you leave everything and go to Africa? How would you love people, if you never met them?*
4. *Tell us how you have seen the love of God in your own life, and in the lives of others, during a disaster. Have you ever been angry at God for losing something that was dear to you?*
5. *When someone you knew was going through great sorrow, and pain, how did you help console them?*
6. *What would you do now, if you were Julie when Tess was killed? Would you go home, now afraid for your own life?*
7. *Have you ever run away from a situation that God put you in?*

8. *And have you ever run away from a situation where you felt abandoned by God? Can you explain to us what happened?*

9. *When was the last time you helped someone, other than someone in your own family?*

10. *When was the last time you helped someone from another race, culture or religion?*

11. *When was the last time you prayed with someone that was hurting because they had gone through a tragic event?*

12. *Do you remember the last time you didn't care what happened in that situation?*

13. *Do you remember the last time someone needed your help, and you had the means and the power to help deliver them? What did you do?*

14. *What are the consequences of doing nothing when called by God?*

15. *Do you believe that there is someone that you met during the week, and we told you to help? Describe to us what you did? Describe the situation and how your intervention and connection made life better or worse for them.*

16. *And if you did nothing for them, what are the reasons why you refused to help?*

17. *Can you think of one time in your life when God called you to do something and you refused because you were afraid? Did you refuse because you thought it would cost you too much?*

18. *Can you think of a time when your fear caused you to angrily tell God to find someone else?*

19. *Do you think it is important to help people that are destroying themselves? Do you think there is a time to not help someone or to let them go through it?*

20. *Have you ever refused to help someone who was homeless when you heard our voice telling you to help them?*

21. *How do you define commitment?*

22. *List the things you are committed to? If you are committed to your family, and we told you to leave home and go another country to help others suffering in poverty, would you go?*

23. *Are you sure you have answered these questions truthfully?*

OUR OBSERVATIONS

Well, you did very poorly with your answers. How can you say that you ask? Well, we know you. And we know how you have tended to gloss over the truth. You have been living such a generic life for so long. You believe anything you tell yourself. But the reality is that you were never meant to be plain, generic, normal or to just fit in. Your problem is that you are trying to be somebody else. We have made you to be you. There is a uniqueness in you that can only be manifested and brought forth upon the earth by you alone. You were meant to open doors to discover new possibilities to improve your environment. You were created to touch and renew the people around you, on a life-changing, positive, intimate level. But you have ignored all your gifts, and you have decided not to open the gifts or your brilliance. For you are too possessed with your own pride and conceit to even care about others. And you have lived your life betraying your higher good and your higher purpose. So, you don't accept what we say.

And now we detect a little anger in you. Well what? Let's take a look at the correct answers.

If we asked you to go to Africa, what would you do? You would cry like a baby! You have always cried like a baby when things didn't go your way. For you cry in anger, in bitterness, in downright hatred of everything around you when life does not work out just right. Throughout your entire life, you have been crying like a baby. How can we say that? Well, we know you. We are not talking about Mother Teresa. It is you that we know. You have been a self-centered, spoiled rotten kid for your entire life. And you grew up the same way. It would take a lot for you to change now. Not only that, you have this taker mentality. This principle is embedded deeply within you. You have been a taker ever since you started walking, believing that it is your right to take the value away from others. You need to write a list, right now, of all the of the things that you have taken away from other people. And you need to recall what you would give back to them if given the same opportunity, and a second chance. We hear your inner thoughts. You are extremely upset now. You are even calling us names because we have you where we want you. You are immobile, and cannot storm away in anger like you always do when confronted with your own reality. We are controlling everything that is happening to you right now. I think we finally have your attention. You have ignored us many times before when we tried to talk to you. We heard your inner comments that you have spoken saying, "What have I taken from others? I worked hard for everything that I have. I had to live in the real world, and not some superficial dream world that you want me to exist in. And how can this make me into such a terrible person?"

"But what is the reality? Are we really talking to you right now? Have we put time, space, and circumstances together for you to hear us right now? Is this reality or not? Or is it a reality for you to work yourself into a chronic sickness, not knowing how to enjoy a single day of your life. For what is the reality when you are weak and unable to move as you lay on a hospital gurney with an irregular heartbeat from not knowing how to relax and trust? Our University has asked you to enroll. And you keep repeating the second level, making the same mistakes, over and over again. You have been flunking, and skipping class numerous times, after we tried to show you another way.

You were made to be brilliant, not to be dull, and not remain in the cubicle of the ordinary. If you don't wake up, your life will be over, and what will be the great accomplishment of your living? If everything you do is an act of frustration, what is the purpose of you being on this planet? You need a Second Life, a do-over strategy. If you are frustrated with your job or marriage, you need to launch a new level of possibilities.

The brilliance, the passion, the creativity within you has not ceased and has not ended. It is you, and you alone, that is stopping you from moving forward. For you have been tangled in the knots of your own creation, and the knots of your own destruction. Right now, you cannot move because we are holding you down because you are hurting inside. And that deep hurt inside of you has made everything around you toxic. It is time for you to give to all those that you have hurt. How have you hurt them you say? Well, let's see. You made it a lifelong practice, a principle to despise, betray, and ridicule anyone who would get close to you.

Now we have brought you close to our spirit. We are embracing you, something you never thought we would do. We will not let you go and return to the earth until you are ready to release your love in a magnificent, brilliant, fantastic manner. You have never gotten this close to us before. It is making you uncomfortable. Well, that is good because you have been lying on the bed of complacency for a long time. Let us sum up everything that we are trying to say. For you, unlike Julie, would continue to follow your own game plan, and that is to do nothing. For you will not love, you will not feel, you will not do anything.

When was the last time you truly cared about anything? Your answer should have been, "I have not seen the love of God because I really don't care." I know these words sound very harsh and may give the impression that we are giving an incomplete answer. But we can hear your inner spirit. And you are upset and angry. As a matter of fact, you are cursing right now. You are telling us to get out of your mind, just get out of your thoughts, and out of your spirit. You are creating a furious scene, a disturbing spectacle as you scold us saying, "Just leave me the hell alone! Just get out of my spirit! Stop talking to me now!" This sounds more like what you would say. Frankly, all your answers can be summed up by this statement. For you have seen us love you, even when you turned your back on us. You have been given many opportunities to exemplify the love of God when others have been faced with great tragedy and despair. And in most situations, just your presence, and your concern, would have been enough to help heal the hurt of others. People don't always need finances when they are hurting, but being a force of caring is a tremendous power that you ignored. But you always thought that someone was trying to take advantage of you. So, you withdrew yourself and made not getting involved your life philosophy. Therefore, your answer should have been "I have not seen God moving because I have been going through life with my eyes closed." Your answer should have been, "I do nothing but close my eyes."

If you had to make a list, of all the people, right now that you went out of your way to help improve the quality of their lives, how long would that list be? The list should consist of helping them spiritually, financially, through some great tragedy, and console them during a loss by just being there. And what about those people that you downright hated that we sent to you? We have watched how you treated the ones we sent to you. You remained silent when all they wanted was to just hear you say that you loved them. They came to you for instructions, blessings, care, and hope. But you remained uncaringly silent, programmed to a belief that the earth is void of goodness. We have given you many examples and situations where you had the ability and the gift to go beyond disbelief. But you were silent, not offering them a word of strength, neither releasing a prayer to empower their life, their faith, their journey. You could have reached out to them in their despair, and by the power of your caring, you could have brought them out. Your answer should have been, "I have done nothing."

If you were in Africa, you would have returned home. You would run like a rabbit! It would have been too much for you. You have always wanted a place of safety, a place to hide, a place not to be bothered by the problems of the world. That is why you have worked so many jobs. You are believing for a day in your life when you can stay home and not be bothered. But you did not come to the earth not to be bothered. You came to the earth to sacrifice to give up everything to give the world all your gifts, your talents, your abilities to repair and restore others around you. Did not our Son come and give everything? We have only asked for just a little from you. And you have given nothing, not in these years.

We know that you would not have gone to Africa; let alone, go somewhere that far to help the poor. The last time you did something meaningful, you thought, was when you tossed a coin in a Salvation Army kettle as a donation once on a Christmas Eve. You thought that you had totally changed the world. Well, don't you remember when they were there during the aftermath of that terrible storm that hit your neighborhood, causing the power lines and the trees to fall? There were people in your neighborhood that needed you. During all the confusion that was happening with all the power outages, yours was somehow still on. You didn't care what happened to anyone else that day. Consequently, there was an old lady that lived just a few doors down from you. You had seen her many times. She was afraid because some tree branches fell on the roof of her house. If you had simply knocked on her door, and asked her if she needed some help that would have made a world of difference in her life.

And the time you were driving home from work, and a young woman in the lane next to you had a flat tire and careened into a ditch. All you did was slow down, and look very smug at her. She appeared to be shaking and crying as you just drove on past her.

Or the time the homeless man came up to you in the grocery store parking lot, saying that he was hungry and that he was out of work. You looked at him in disgust, and gave him a crumpled-up dollar bill, and thought once again, you were saving the world.

Or the time when the young boy that was only nine years old, and growing up in the neighborhood without a father. You could have shaped his destiny, molded his mind, and prepared his attitude by just taking him to a movie or throwing a ball to him in the park.

Or the time you cursed at the young people because they were blocking your path. They were simply stopping vehicles to ask people if they could wash their cars for a church fundraiser to finance a trip out of town. When one of them accidentally splashed water on you, you thought for sure it was the end of the world and drove away cursing angrily.

You have been living in such a selfish, hollow box for so long. You believe it is the most acceptable way to live. For you have bought into the mindset of, "What's mine is mine, and what's yours is yours!"

And what about the time when the unemployed man asked to mow your lawn for a few dollars. You threatened to call the Police on him. When was the last time you listened to someone without talking over them? Without giving them a half-hearted response like, "I will get back with you on that." In effect, you said that to everyone who needed you. Those who needed your knowledge, your time, your concern or needed you just to be there. But you quickly ignored them, and gave them once again, a generic answer, and went happily on your way.

Well, we decided that you will be given the opportunity to improve your score, and you will be given a retest on this section. You will be given an opportunity to invite someone to your house of another race and culture to eat dinner with you and your family. You will be given the opportunity to help someone that will come to you in need. You will be given the opportunity to visit someone in a nursing home, prison, or a homeless shelter. We will be watching to see if you will respond in your same old manner. If you fail, you will once again return to your present state, waiting to get out of the bed. And we know how hard it is for you to care for someone other than yourself. But you must understand, your act of caring will change everything about you. You just wait and see. We hear your thoughts now. You are saying all this foolishness is not real. Well, you are listening to us right now. We have set this whole thing up for you to learn compassion. For love is the most real force on earth. Everything else is all make-believe.

This is the beginning of your new life. Things will be different for you after this after you wake. You will question, "Did we actually speak to you?" But you will see for yourself, all the things we talked about, and that is the second part of this test, the one you must demonstrate in your life. You must keep watching and learn before we wake you up. What you learn here is what you must apply. What you learn here, you must try. What you learn, you must live out before you die. You are borrowing this life from us. You are here as a visitor and a student. Even now, you are saying that you are going to run away, and we will not be able to find you when you wake up. We shall see if you can run away if you cannot wake up.

Let's consider your future. You are going to die alone. Your life will have been a terribly lonely experience with no joy or happiness. For in the same way you have treated others, it will be returned to you. You have the capacity to change right now. You have the capacity to renew your life's purpose and commit to a new life design. The nursing homes are filled with those waiting to die. Why wait to die when we have called you to live? You are angrily telling us to wake you. We can feel you moving in the bed trying to break free. As you continue to watch and go through The Test, we will feel your spirit. We will see your tears, and determine the activated strength of your love to commit to others. And if you do wake up, we will be sending people to you in the next few days. We will watch how you respond, and observe how much you have learned from The Test.

And lastly, you say you believe in safety. You have guns, and you have deadbolt locks. You have cameras. You have passwords and security over your computers. But your spirit has been locked.

The light that we have given you is faint. You are so afraid of people. You have failed to realize that we have created the people in your life so that you can uplift, encourage, heal, and restore them.

If you wake up, we will send you away from your home very shortly. It will be a directed pilgrimage, a mission journey that we will send you on. It will be something you have never experienced before. You may have to leave your house and your job. Is this too scary for you? You will be put into a situation where you must use everything within yourself to survive. And yet, you will still have something left within you to help someone else. You have never been so involved in anything like this. This is way over your head. For there will be nothing that you will be able to do but hold on, believe, and trust us for the outcome.

You will learn how to cry out to us. And this, in effect, will make you stronger. You will not like the things we are going to do to you. After you have been in the wilderness for many days without food and water, you will drink the sacred waters of your tears. And then, you will be able to speak clearly to us. You will have the ability to know how to pray and bring water up out of a rock.

Just by hearing these things we are telling you, everything will be different in your life, after The Test. You will understand what's yours, is not yours. What you keep, is what will be taken away. And what you give away, will be replaced a hundred times over. Our Son spoke these things. We thought we would just remind you. This is the first part of The Test. You have much to learn. You need to take your time now. Stop rushing through stuff. Our love is not a fast food or a happy meal for you to consume and move on. This is an eternal work that we are creating in you. You need to enjoy the ride. Sit back, put it on cruise control, and let us drive the wheel of your life now.

Julie wanted to hold on to the light that Tess transferred into her. She realized that light is not worth anything if it is not kept alive.

Always remember when you think you have failed and are lying on the ground in darkness, only then can you see the stars. This is only the first part of The Test. You have many more Tests to take, so be an attentive student. We are going to help you pass The Test together.

~Let us continue~

Julie looked at the little baby girl in her arms. She was beautiful as she reached her tiny fingers up, and held on to hers tightly. *"You have nothing left. Your whole family is all gone. You are alone in the world little baby girl. Yet, you are still here! You are still fighting for your life."* One of the nurses called out to her saying, *"Julie, it has only been a few days, and she is putting on weight! She is a fighter, that little one!"* Julie held the little baby against her chest and rocked her in her arms. *"Your mother wanted you to live. I have seen your mother before. She appeared before me in my bedroom back at home. She walked so far for you to be here, and for you to live."*

Suddenly, there was a dreadful commotion that occurred outside the tent. It sounded as if people were running. The sound of gunfire was heard throughout the camp. Julie peeked outside of the tent, and men dressed in military uniforms with rifles were jumping off trucks, shooting people as they ran by. Julie did not know what to do as she held the little baby girl in her arms. One of the nurses came into the tent, yelling in a terrified voice, *"Please, we must hide! The army has come, and they are killing everyone!"* At that moment, a stray bullet came through the tent and struck that nurse in the temple. She collapsed and was killed instantly.

Soldiers were jumping off trucks throughout the camp, and the sound of gunfire exploded. Julie heard people crying out, screaming as men went from tent to tent killing people. Some of the nurses started taking the babies off their little cots, and ran outside the tent, trying to run away.

It was a scene of total mayhem as the soldiers entered the medical tent, and started hurling the children, and babies off their cots. Julie ran with the baby girl in her arms as men with jeeps came driving through the camp, firing machine guns, and shooting people while they ran in every direction. As the people ran, the bullets from the soldiers shot them down, and dead bodies began to litter the camp.

Julie continued to run at a maddening pace, holding the little baby girl in her arms. A bullet grazed Julie's cheek as blood started to drip down her face. There were thousands of people running in this chaotic scene in fear and horror.

Julie saw a young man that was pointing at her, and calmly waving his arms, telling her to hide in a tent while he stood in the middle of the camp. Quickly, she went inside the tent. The floor was scattered with bodies. The sound of gunfire was all around. It would be just a matter of minutes before they found her, and killed the little baby and her. Then she saw the young man again. He stood before her. His dark skin appeared to be luminous and outlined in an aurora of light. He spoke calmly to her *"Julie lay down on top of the bodies, hold the baby underneath you, and you will be protected."*

Julie knew immediately who he was, and said, *"You are…You are… Raphael! You are the one who has been writing the letters to me." "Be not afraid! You were brought here for this moment to save the child in your arms. And by your great act of love, you shall save thousands!"*

Julie looked down at the bodies on the floor. She was afraid, but she hurriedly laid down on top of them, held the baby girl underneath her, and prayed that she would not cry out. When she looked back, the young man was suddenly gone. A group of soldiers immediately came through the tent, looking for people to kill. They looked at everyone on the ground. It was dark in the tent, and so Julie's red hair made her appear as if she was bleeding from a head wound, and was dead. One of the men was preparing to shoot the bodies on the ground when a soldier came forward and stopped him, angrily saying, *"These are already dead. Why waste your bullets shooting them?"* So, they took off.

Julie was amazed and grateful that the little baby did not cry out. The sound of gunfire had subsided, and everything was quiet once again. When Julie came out of hiding, there were groups of International Security Military forces that had arrived and had come to help the wounded. The rebels had fled before they arrived. One of the International Security Military Soldiers saw Julie kneeling on the ground in the middle of the camp. She was surrounded by a floor of bodies while rocking a little baby against her chest, weeping. He came quietly approached her, and said, *"Madam, how did you survive such a disaster?"* Julie answered him and said, *"My God sent an angel to help me. So, I was not alone."*

It was years later when a small plane flew over a large refugee camp. As Julie looked down from the plane, the little baby girl that she saved from death, many years ago, was now her adopted daughter. She had become a Doctor and was working with a team of doctors in the refugee camp below. They were developing new vaccines and methods for treating infectious diseases as well as developing new cures to combat the AIDS virus. And because of her work, many immune systems were radically improved and changed. Millions of lives were being saved.

When Julie's daughter saw the plane that was flying low over the sea of humanity, she began to cry out, waving her arms in a frantic pace, and calling out loudly, *"Mother! Mother! Mother! Mother!"* As she started to run through the boundless crowd, they were startled by her actions, and how quickly she was running. Julie's daughter ran towards the runway, and in her excitement and joy, one of her shoes came off, but she did not go back to get it. Her voice was even heard over the noise of the people that had surrounded the plane on the runway. When Julie boarded the plane, her daughter grabbed her and held on tightly. They were immediately surrounded by a vast sea of humanity that sung out to her in their language saying, *"FOR ONLY WHEN THE HEART IS OPEN, IT BECOMES A STAIRWAY FOR THE ANGELS TO COME THROUGH!"*

Julie's daughter stood before her with her dark skin illumining in her doctor's coat. As she kissed Julie on the cheek and patted her graying red hair, she said, *"Mother I love you so much! I am so glad you have come to see the work that I am doing!"*

OUR OBSERVATIONS

Julie saved one life, and through her act, a million other lives

---

were saved. We are all divinely connected to each other. Nothing we do is apart from each other. You are connected to all the experiences of your life through others. It is your awareness and belief in the power of love that is demonstrated through these experiences that we will give to you. For these experiences, will be the greatest joys of your life. The alarm clock is ringing, but it is your life that needs to wake up.

You will die tomorrow, and the opportunity to experience how great your life can be will pass by you. This is your last opportunity to take this test. The God of the Second Chance is speaking to you today. You must make a serious decision to step out farther than you have ever gone before. For you can lie in this unmovable state forever, hearing the alarm clock of your life, and be afraid to wake up. The ultimate decision is yours!

~Breaking the Cycle of Abuse~

Becky Austin Hamilton looked at her husband lying on the bed next to her. It was five thirty in the morning. He was supposed to be at work by six, so now he would be late if she did not wake him up. She nudged him as she laid next to him. She could smell the liquor reeking from his body. He had stayed up late during the night drinking and turning their small house into a tidal wave of destruction.

She turned and looked at the picture of the two of them that was taken when they were first married. Tom was very handsome back then. He was her high school sweetheart, and captain of the football team too. He was the dreamboat of all the girls at Westside High. His short blonde hair and his bright blue eyes made him look as if he was the perfect Ken doll, and she was his perfect Barbie. She knew as she laid in bed, listening to him snoring, and rancid from the smell of alcohol, that her high school image of him had been destroyed forever. It was not supposed to be like this. He was supposed to be the Prince of her Sleeping Beauty kingdom, and they would live in the magical castle with a happily ever after ending.

But nothing turned out like that at all. It was only a few weeks after they had first gotten married that he hit her. He was angry because he had to work overtime, and had promised some of the boys that they would go out drinking at the Sports bar with them. He struck her when she made the simple mistake of telling him to **"Suck It Up!"**, and then playfully began tickling him. He struck her so hard that one of her front teeth was loosened. She thought for sure that it might fall out. It did evidentially fall out while she was at work. It happened in the most embarrassing manner. It happened while she was waiting tables at her restaurant job. She found a fantastic dentist that could put in a new one so that you could not even tell that it was permanently gone.

Tom apologized to her many times over and begged her to stay with him. He promised that it would never happen again and that it was just an outburst of his rage, after putting in so many hours at his floor repair job. He also told her that he never meant to do that to her. But the fist imprint on her face would not go away. It left a lasting impression that was still visible every time she looked in the mirror and tried to cover it up with make-up.

But then there was the time when they attended their High School Class Reunion together. They met up with some old friends. A guy from her class who had a big crush on her when they were freshmen, made her laugh out loud when she saw him and heard him say, *"Becky, you still look amazing after all of these years!"* They shared a laugh together by the cake and punch bowl table, which made Tom go ballistic. In a violent rage, he punched the guy, whose name was Brad Decker in the face. He called Becky a whore and a slut. Then he grabbed her wrist and twisted it so hard that it almost felt as if it would snap. Humiliated, she cried out for help as he dragged her on the floor by one of her legs in front of all their former classmates. All the other males, from the class reunion, rushed in, and tackled Tom, and held him down as he continued screaming on the floor, trying, in a deranged manner to kick her as she fled shamefully away.

Becky was motionless as she laid next to him on the bed. She was thankful for any momentary periods of peace and quiet that had now filled the house. For Tom, had come home from work last night, after he had been out drinking again, and once more, he was in a drunken rage and totally out of control. He threw furniture around the house and screamed so loudly that she believed for certain that the neighbors would call the police. Now, she was lying in the bed with a man that she did not know anymore. She tried to get him to go to bed last night, but he cursed her and punched her in the arm, which left a large, swollen bruise. But she was just thankful that he did not hit her in the face, this time. That bruise was something that she could easily cover up, and hide from her co-workers, at her waitress job, at the pancake house.

But each day the bruises were now becoming increasingly more difficult to cover up. It was at the point where her whole body had become a mass of bruises that caused her joints to ache. She even developed a slight limp when she walked. She convinced herself that no one noticed how she wretched in pain when she walked. His fist had changed her princess looking image and created stress lines, and wrinkles on her face that she should have never had, at the age of twenty-eight.

As she looked around the room, she felt so small and insignificant as if she did not even exist. She had been reduced to an object in the house that cooked Tom's food and washed his clothes. But there was little left in the relationship that she could identify with him as being caring.

It was getting late when she nudged him on the side. He rolled over, almost on top of her, and angrily began choking her around the neck. He was screaming so loudly that she thought she could hear Tammy, their four-year-old daughter in her room crying. He shouted, *"Why didn't you wake me up sooner? You worthless woman! I am going to be late now because of you!"*

When he let go of his grip around her neck, she thought for sure she would pass out. The entire room had become a blur. Finally, she was able to catch her breath. Large imprints of his hands were visible around her neck. At that moment, Tammy came into the room, crying and holding her little stuffed Poo Bear, saying, *"Mama, I heard somebody crying! I'm afraid!" "It's going to be alright, baby. Please go back to your room. I will be in there in a few seconds to give you breakfast."*

Tom stumbled out of bed. He was still wearing his pants from falling into the bed drunk. He couldn't find his socks, so he ran out of the house, tucking only one side of his shirt into his pants. But before he left, he turned around and blurted something out. *"You look ugly as hell. I hope you fix your face before you go outside!"*

Becky started crying silently. She remained motionless in the bed. For there was nothing left for her to do but cry as she remained numb and motionless, afraid to move. She wished that she could die, and would not have to live in such a despairing manner. She whispered a prayer, *"God, I wish I was dead. I wish I could take Tammy and not have to come back to this house and be thought of something less than a servant girl."*

Becky had made up her mind that she would be leaving him in a week. It was too much for her to take any more. And if she did not leave, she believed her daughter could be killed by his daily acts of insanity. Becky got out of bed. Her body was aching so terribly, that when she stood up, she became dizzy. She almost lost her balance and fell. She quickly went to the mirror and saw the large handprints around her neck. And then, she looked at the latest bruise on her arm. It had already turned black. There were other bruises that had covered her entire body. She stood in front of the mirror, broke down, and started crying. She felt a tug on her nightgown. It was Tammy. *"Mommy, are you alright? What's wrong? Why are you crying, Mommy? "Everything is alright, Tammy! I was just picking some lint out of my eyes. Mommy is alright."* She bent down, hugged her real tight and kissed her forehead.

When Becky arrived at the restaurant, after dropping Tammy off at the Day Care, she was met with a large crowd of people from a baseball league's playoff series that had come into the restaurant for breakfast, and Rachel Henderson. Rachel was a tall striking brunette with hazel eyes, and cream colored skin that made some of the older men come into the restaurant, dressed up, just to flirt with her. Rachel had a sixth sense about things, which made it hard to hide anything from her. But since she started working there, for almost a year now, she managed to keep her secret away from Rachel.

Rachel looked at Becky as she walked past her, carrying an order to a table, and said, *"Girl, you look a mess, and you are ten minutes late! What were you doing last night making you come into work looking so disheveled? You must have had a wild night with your hair all muffled up, going in every direction. But I am so glad you are here! I have never seen so many people in this restaurant. We have college baseball teams from just about every state in the country wanting to eat breakfast. And we had to push some tables together* to accommodate all the people that are here today. *Mr. Milford was looking for you this morning. And boy he had such a sour look on his already prune-looking face. That little squirt of a man is bad news already. And you are giving the little Munchkin just what he needs to fire you! You better watch yourself or you will be out of here for sure." "Well, I am trying to get it together today!"* Becky replied as she placed a well-centered group of bobby pins on the top of her hair. She quickly put some lipstick on and looked at herself in a small mirror in her apron. *"I am going to do my best to look fresh, and ready for the day. I was a little late because my man had a bad night last night. I was trying to hold my family together, like any good woman. And then I had to feed my daughter, and I could not take her to the Day Care without getting a hot meal inside of her first."*

Rachel looked at her again, but this time her eyebrows rose as if she was sensing something that was altogether not right. *"Look, Becky, Honey, I don't know what is going on with you, but that little tyrant is gunning for you. He told me to tell you he wants to see you when you arrived." "Well, I will be ready for him!"* Becky said as she jetted away to take orders from all the many customers that were arriving, forming a long line outside the doors of the restaurant.

As the morning continued, she was cleaning up a stack of dishes from a table when Mr. Milford arrived. He was only three and a half feet tall, but Rachel always insisted that his nose made him appear to be taller. His nose hung down from his face as if it was a bamboo pole, and he was going fishing for bluegills. He was quirky. His eyes made him look like he had an ugly scrawl on his face. As he quickly approached her, looking the color of a beet, and out of breath, he yelled, *"Becky, where were you this morning? You were late again! You were thirty minutes and forty-seven seconds late and that is totally unacceptable! We had hungry people all over the restaurant, and I could not find you anywhere to take orders! I am putting you on probation again. Just one more screw up and you will be out of here! I am putting you on probation!"*

"Probation again? I just got off probation! You need to give me a break! Please cut me a little slack. Please, Mr. Milford. I had to take my daughter to school this morning, and I had a terrible night. And

you know I do more than my share of the work around here. I have handled, and served over thirty people since I arrived this morning" *"It does not matter!",* Mr. Milford snapped. *"You were not here this morning when I needed you. And not only that, your uniform always looks wrinkled, and you continue to groom yourself when you arrive. If you are late, one more time, I will have no choice but to terminate you for good!"*

It was at the end of an exhausting day when Becky was finally able to pick up Tammy from the Day Care. Her feet were aching, and she thought she had walked on coals of fire all-day. When she arrived home, Tom was sitting by the television watching a game. She could tell that he had already drunk six beers, and he just stared at her, silently. *"You are late again!",* he said with a sinister tone in his voice. It was the sound she had heard before when he was on the verge of going into a rage. But something had happened to him. There were papers scattered all around the room. Becky reached down and picked one of them up. It said, *"Evaluation Report!"* As she continued to read it, she put Tammy down near where she had a little desk, a box of crayons, some blocks, and a doll house. Then she saw the frightening words, circled in red, *"Termination."* He had been fired for drinking on the job, and for insubordination.

"What are we going to do, Tom? What are we going to do now? Without your income to pay the bills, we could lose everything that we worked for!" *"I don't care anymore! I don't care what happens! I am going to just sit here, and get stinking drunk. And then, I am going to get in that truck of mine, and take off! I still have some money left over from my pension, and I am going to spend every penny of it."* *"What about us, Tom! What about Tammy! How are we supposed to live? Have you figured that out?"* *"You have to figure that out for yourself! There is nothing more for me to do."*

Becky grabbed the bottle of gin Tom had turned upward into his mouth. *"You need to stop this drinking of yours! It is destroying your mind! It is destroying your life!"* Tom grabbed the bottle, slammed it down on the table, and backhanded her so hard that Becky thought that she heard something crack inside of her jaw. She tried getting away as he then pulled the back of her blonde ponytail, and dragged her across the room. She then broke free as she tried to run out of the room, she turned towards him and slashed her fingernails across his face. That was something she had never done before. Tom's face was scratched with lines that leaked a horizontal pattern of blood. She screamed in horror as he continued to drag her across the floor. He then turned and kicked her in the head with his boot. She could hear Tammy crying before she blacked out.

Becky awakened in the hospital. She did not know what had happened. She screamed out at first, still thinking she was on the floor receiving the terrible beating from Tom. When she came to herself, she saw Rachel standing over her wiping away tears from her eyes. *"I should have known you were getting the crap beat out of you every day. And I should have known when I saw all of those bruises all over your arms."* *"Where is Tammy?"* Becky asked excitedly. *"Where is my baby?"* *"Tammy is fine. She is with your sister, Emma. They had been here all day but you were heavily sedated because of your injuries. You should see the way you look! He beat you from an inch of taking away your life. Then he jumped in his truck, after almost killing you, and drove away like a madman. No one has seen him since. One of your next-door neighbors heard you crying out for help. When she investigated, your door was open, and Tammy was crying over you. She then called 911. There is an arrest warrant out for Tom, and the Police have been looking for him ever since. The Police Lieutenant said there is an all-out manhunt for him across three states."* *"Poor Tom."*, Becky whispered as tears streamed from her blackened eyes, and dark blue, bruised disfigured face. *"Girl, that man almost killed you, and all you can say is Poor Tom!"* Rachel said with a shocked expression. *"You must be out of your mind feeling sorry for that monster! You should see the way you look! You have a fractured jaw, four broken teeth, a busted lip, two black eyes, and a broken collarbone. If he ever comes around you again, I have something you can use."* She opened her purse and there was a black revolver. *"A Gun!"* Becky said hardly getting the words out. *"If he ever puts another hand on you again, I am going to shoot him for you myself! You have been through enough, and there is no way that you should have to suffer like this again!"* *"What about my job? Did I get fired?"*

Becky blurted out the words. *"Nope! That little troll must truly have a heart underneath that thick, scaly, calloused skin of his. He told me to tell you that he now understands what you have been going through. He also said that you can come back as soon as you are ready and that you will be paid for your time off as well."* "Well, that is something!" *"And he sent you a bouquet of flowers,"* Rachel said as her bottom lip smiled slightly. *"I decided that you can stay with me until you get better. I don't want that maniac showing up and beating you up again."*

As the months went by, Becky made a slow, but full recovery. With Rachel's help, Becky could return to work. She even found a part-time job as a Teacher's Assistant that paid for her education while she studied at night, trying to earn a Bachelor's Degree in education. She disciplined herself, and studied until she reached a new level of self-empowerment and self-determination that she had never experienced before, and throughout all the years of living with Tom. She would be graduating in less than a week with a degree in education. She was the first in her family to reach such an achievement. When school started, she would be the first-grade teacher at Thomas Jefferson Elementary School. She would be leaving the restaurant job in just a few days. She would miss not seeing Rachel, and she was so grateful to have such a good friend that passed on some of her guidance and strength. And if Rachel had not held her up, during her most difficult times, she would have collapsed.

She had not heard anything about Tom. One police detective said that they were given the description of a man, who looked like Tom, that was seen on a beach with an underage girl in San Diego. He went on to say, if that was true, more charges would be brought against him.

Becky was happy to see Tammy adjusting so well without Tom in her life. At last, she could sleep through the night without waking up in a panic, from all of Tom's drunken rages. Becky had moved out of the little shabby house and rented a lovely duplex that had a beautiful green backyard with enough room for Tammy to play in. And Tammy even found a group of young kids her age in the neighborhood, and instantly they struck up a friendship. Everything was moving extremely fast in her life, and with her divorce from Tom final, he was now only a terrible memory that she was trying to forget.

Becky only had two more days remaining of working at the restaurant, and then she would be starting her new teaching job. After the weekend, she would be starting fresh on Monday morning. Life was becoming a fantastic beautiful experience again because she became determined to succeed. Rachel gave her the revolver took her to a shooting range and told her to keep on practicing for protection. But she could not bring herself to the place to use it, let alone shoot and kill Tom. She kept the little, dangerous weapon inside of her purse. It frightened her to just look at it. But Tom was dangerous, and out of control. She could only imagine what new person he had in his life, that he was abusing. But all of that was behind her now.

There was no word from him for almost four years. He was now a ghost from her long, and distant past. And now finally, she was getting back on her feet, on a solid good ground. Although it was an exhausting comeback, she knew, that her future, which included raising Tammy, was becoming brighter every day. Tammy had just gotten her first report card. She received A's in every class. The Principal of the school wrote her a letter regarding promoting Tammy to a higher class for gifted students.

Becky felt good. Deep inside there was no shame, no hiding, and most of all, no fear. As she stood in front of a table, taking a final order before her shift was over, she noticed a man was sitting at the table with long hair and a shaggy beard. He appeared to be nervous as he kept looking around. It was Tom! He looked a wreck. He looked totally different as if he had not slept in days. His front teeth were missing, and dark black circles engulfed his eyes. *"Well, just don't stand there with your eyes bugging out of your head! Are you going to take my order or what?"* Becky's heart jumped when she saw him. She stood in a petrified stance as she tried to speak, but nothing came out of her mouth. He stared at her glaring in anger, and then he pushed over the table. *"I am going to make you suffer in the same way that you made me suffer. You have the police looking for me all over the country. You got me hiding like some wild animal. Yeah, you are going to take my order, and it will be the last time you take another order ever again!"* He rushed towards her and grabbed her by the neck. As people pushed each other out of the way in terror, someone yelled out, *"CALL THE POLICE! THERE IS A LUNATIC IN HERE! AND HE IS ATTACKING A YOUNG WOMAN!"*

Tom struggled, holding her from the back of her head. He had folded his forearm around her in a death grip. As Becky kicked furiously, it felt to her as if her windpipe was starting to crack and close shut. Tables were knocked over, and the sound of broken dishes cluttered the floor in an insane display of Tom's spontaneous rage. Then he dragged her by her blonde ponytail, across the floor, on top of the broken dishes. She could feel the glass cutting into her arms and wrists as he pulled her across the room. *"JUST LIKE OLD TIMES ISN'T IT! YOU DID'NT THINK I WOULD COME BACK! I COULD'NT LET YOU GO THAT EASY! I HAVE BEEN WAITING FOR A LONG TIME! YOU WILL NEVER BE RID OF ME! AND SINCE YOU HAVE GIVEN ME ONLY A LIFE OF HELL.....I AM GOING TO DRAG YOU TO HELL WITH ME!"*

Becky continued to struggle on the floor. In some sort of alternative universe, she felt the small revolver inside a little side pocket in her apron. Becky's arms were moving rapidly as she reached up trying to fight back. She dropped one of her hands on the floor. That is when Tom stomped down hard on it. Becky felt the bones breaking and crushing inside as the pain from the nerves shot up her arm. But with her other free hand, she quickly reached inside of her apron, pulled out the revolver, and pointed it directly up at Tom's crotch.

Now let's stop the story right here and take The Test.
1. *What should Becky do in this situation?*
2. *Is killing Tom the answer?*
3. *What are the consequences that Becky would experience after killing Tom?*
4. *After killing Tom, would she be free of him?*
5. *Have you ever abused another person? And if so, how?*
6. *Have you abused anyone close to you lately? Have you abused anyone last week, yesterday or today?*

OUR OBSERVATIONS

Well, let's look at your answers.

Yes, you are an abuser! If you answered yes, then that is the correct answer. You are doing well with your answers. We are so proud of you. I know you are saying that you have never abused anyone like this in your life. Let's take a look at your abusive history for a moment. You constantly devalue and give no appreciation to your wife or your husband for all the painstaking things they do for you to make your life easier, and happier. And if you don't have a spouse, you destroy the people around you with your condemning words. You constantly call them names that cut into their self-esteem and their self-worth. Let's look deeply at all the ways you hurt them. You call them stupid and dumb. And you say things like, "What a moron you are! What a dunderhead!" And you so easily allow these words to come out of your mouth. You make the most disgusting faces as you look at them as if your whole world has been destroyed. To make matters worse, you do not care if you are in a public venue like the grocery store or shopping at the mall. Others have heard you say things as well.

Hurtful words, you say things like: "For the life of me, why did I marry an idiot like you? For the life of me, why did I marry a worthless imbecile like you? I should have married someone else that made more money that made something more of themselves! You have gotten way too fat! Why do you eat so much? You look terrible! Being with you is a waste of my time. I don't love you anymore. I want a divorce. I hate everything about you. You cook your own food for now on. You wash your own clothes. I am not your servant. You are a slob! You are not sleeping with me. We need separate beds. We need separate rooms. I hate your family. I hate the way you look in the morning. I hate the way you style your hair. That dress looks ugly. Nothing fits right on you anymore. You are pathetic. You are a joke. You are a scum bag. You are a waste of my time!"

And let's not even look at the way you talk to your children. For example, you say these words to your children: "You will never amount to anything. You are dumb. You are a stupid little jerk. You better shut up and stop your whining. You don't know how to do anything right. You are flunking out of school; I can't believe you are that dumb. You will never amount to anything."

As a matter of fact, it has been a long time since you have spoken anything positive about anyone. We have watched you with that terrible scowl on your face. And you have such a disgusting view of life that has caused you to believe that everyone around you cannot measure up. Somehow you cannot see the destruction and the failure in your own life. You cannot see how terrible, lonely, and brokenhearted you would be if your spouse left you. And how empty you would be when you are old, bitter, and resentful. You cannot see how you are driving the ones that care for you away. You cannot see the destruction that you are unleashing upon your children, and how you are creating ruins of decay, low self-esteem, and resentment inside of them. You can't see how you are taking away their potential for growth and development. You are making them dysfunctional, fearful of expanding their minds and exploring their future. You are making them weak and terrified just like you. But you cannot see any of this. You believe that everything is hunky-dory in your world of living on your sofa in the front room, watching television, and believing you have a great relationship with the people in your life. For you have destroyed them because you have devalued their love. It is hard for you to be in any relationship without putting someone down. But you have been taught this from childhood, from watching your father and his relationship with your mother. How did that work out for you? You must be taught how to love, and then you must practice love daily in your life. And that is why you have been required to take this test.

If you awaken, you will be given the instructions to go a whole day without saying one negative word against anyone. And if you fail, you must repeat it again until The Test is passed. And then, you must tell us what you learned and what happened to the people that you encountered when you embraced them with the power of positive words.

Let us continue. Becky stood pointing the gun at Tom's crotch. For an instance, her mind flashed with a rush of thoughts, and images that flooded her being. She saw Tom screaming as she pulled the trigger of the revolver. She could not believe that she had actually shot him. As he fell over the table screaming, his face changed colors, and blood came out of his mouth. Rachel had gone to pick Tammy up from Day Care because she was working an extra hour. She saw Tammy coming into the restaurant screaming watching this terrible sight. Becky screamed out *"Tammy! Please! Leave Now! Please Go!"* She saw in an instance as her mind glanced at the newspaper's bold headlines, *"Woman kills her husband in the restaurant, shooting him in front of her child!"* Then she saw a reporter coming into the restaurant, interviewing her, and a crowd of people assembled around her. She saw her daughter, Tammy, crying on the television as she buried her head in her hands, listening to the newscast. She saw Tammy's friends laughing and teasing her at school saying, *"Your mother is a murderer! She killed your Daddy! Your mother is a murder!"*

And then Becky quickly snapped back into reality. She knew what she had to do. She whispered a prayer to God saying, *"Please help me, God! I need your help!"* Her hands were trembling as she held the gun pointed at Tom. Then she realized that the gun was never in her hand. It was still in her purse, secured in a locker in the back room of the restaurant. It was an open vision from a dream created by her own virtual reality. She was so grateful that she did not really have the gun. But she did see a fork on the floor, amidst the broken dishes and glass. So, she immediately took the fork and thrust it into Tom's genitals. Tom recoiled in pain as he reached for his crotch with a look of unbelievable shock and horror while he twisted and cried out on the floor.

A man was watching this scene unfold, but had been prevented from moving faster because of the crowd of people rushing towards the door. This man had just returned from being deployed, and he still proudly wore his military uniform as he ran towards Becky to help her out. The Soldier now leaped on Tom, knocking him down, straddled him between his knees, and proceeded to punch him repeatedly as he tried to wriggle and crawl away. The Soldier then dragged him by his legs as Tom continued to scream in front of a cheering crowd outside. The Soldier easily lifted him over his shoulders and flung him into a row of bushes. Shortly after, the police arrived, handcuffed Tom, and took him into custody. He was still crying saying, *"I was unjustly beaten up! I was unjustly beaten up! I am hurting so bad"* as he was put into a police car, and driven away to jail.

What are the steps in getting out of an abusive relationship? And do you know someone that is in a relationship that is abusive, and dangerous? And what can you do to help create an intervention to rescue that person that is being abused?

We really believe that you are coming into a place of awareness. You are developing a sense of what we call, "Spiritual Enlightenment." It is just a fancy way of saying that you are finally hearing our voice for the first time. But you are still asleep in your bed right now, and perhaps with more instructions, you can awaken to the possibility that your life can mean so much more.

~The Blue Bicycle~

~Learning to release fear is learning to release love~

Hector Carlton Winslow had always distrusted people. It was a long life principal that he had always espoused. Maybe it had something to do with the fact that he had his bicycle stolen when he was seven by a little brown-skinned boy with a round head, and was almost his same age. He had let that boy ride his bicycle without fully breaking it in himself. It was given to him for his seventh birthday, and he only had it for just one day. The little boy was so excited to ride the shiny new Schwinn bicycle while pedaling Hector's sparkly, blue birthday present around the park with a wide grin. The whole experience made Hector feel terrible that the kid was enjoying something that was meant for him. But the boy begged him to the point that he would have felt even worse if he did not let him ride it. Hector didn't even know the boy. He had never, ever seen him before. And now here he was, riding his beautiful blue bicycle. Hector believed that it would be alright, just a few laps around the duck pond, and the kid would have to find his own birthday present.

It was a beautiful Saturday morning, and the sun was shining brightly with a slight breeze that filled the park with weekend calmness. There were just a few people, along with their children, in the park that day. They were breaking off pieces of bread, feeding the excited ducks that were quacking noisily in large groups. The blue bicycle was the most beautiful thing that Hector had ever seen in his life. It had red and blue streamers that hung down from the handlebars. It also had reflectors on the spokes of the tires, along with a chrome mirror on the handlebars. And it even had a nifty looking small backpack underneath the seat for you to store your belongings.

The boy pleaded and pleaded with Hector and told him that he was only going to ride it a few times around the duck pond, and then give it right back. Hector was feeling good that he had such a wonderful birthday present, one that most of the kids in his neighborhood envied. So, Hector let the boy ride his birthday bicycle, but not before giving him a stern warning, saying, *"And you better not ride too close to the pond. I don't want any mud getting caught in the spokes of my tires or clogging up the chain!"* *"I will be extra careful!"* said the excited boy! *"I will make sure that nothing happens to it."* The boy stood looking at the marvelous machine and then said, *"It is a real beauty! I bet it can go over 100 miles an hour!"* *"That's nothing! I rode it downhill once, and I am quite sure I was going 200 miles an hour. I don't think anyone is ever going to beat my record!"* Hector said with confidence.

The boy hopped on the blue dream machine, smiling and showing all his teeth like a Cheshire cat. The boy started pumping the pedals amazingly fast, quickly gaining momentum, and speed. Hector called out to him *"BETTER BE EXTRA CAREFUL WITH IT! I DON'T WANT YOU TWISTING UP THE FRAME!"* The round head kid called out to him, *"I WILL TAKE CARE OF IT FOR YOU! AND MAKE SURE IT IS SAFE! AND WILL RETURN IT TO YOU AGAIN!"* The boy rode halfway around the duck pond. He turned around one time, looking at Hector, waving excitedly, and then verged off onto the main street. He started riding like he was never coming back. Hector felt tears welling up in his eyes as he looked at the startling events that were unfolding before his very eyes. Hector called out to the boy who appeared as though he did not hear him. *"HEY, YOU KID! YOU ARE GOING THE WRONG WAY! HEY! COME BACK WITH MY BICYCLE! YOU ARE GOING THE WRONG WAY! HEY, KID! COME BACK WITH MY BICYCLE!"* But the round head kid kept riding at a furious pace. The bicycle pedals turned almost into a blur as the boy disappeared from out of his sight.

Hector stood there crying with a face flushed with tears while screaming at the boy that disappeared with his brand-new birthday bicycle. When Hector arrived home, he was still crying. He tried to explain what had happened to his mother in a wail of tears that caused large drops to hit the floor. His mother explained to him that she could not go out and buy him another bicycle because she had saved all her extra money for an entire year to purchase the one that he had for his birthday.

Hector learned a valuable lesson that day. It was a lesson that he would never forget to practice for the rest of his life. He learned not to trust people. He kept this lesson with him in dealing with every individual that he met. After that terrible day, Hector distrusted everyone! There were no exceptions! And the boy who stole his bicycle was a little brown-skinned kid, so, from that day on, he had a deep resentment that turned into hatred for people of color. He did not see them anymore as people. Oftentimes, in his conversations, he would let words slip out like how 'those people' had no goals, and how 'they' had built their lives upon taking things from others. But as he grew older, he did his best to keep his true feelings hidden and kept them secret from others.

Throughout his high school years, he had no friends; a real loner who did not attend one football or basketball game. There was nothing for him to be excited about, and nothing to cheer about. He was an only child, raised by a mother that had little time for him. She tried her best to make ends meet. His father disappeared without a trace when Hector was only five years old. No one knew what happened to his father. So, Hector never got involved in any of the activities or clubs that he was interested in joining at school. He thought people were just users, and that they would eventually try to take something from him. Therefore, Hector stayed at home most of his life, alone in his room. He built model airplanes and hung them from his ceiling, believing he would fly them one day. However, he was terrified of heights and was afraid to leave his room. Hector was also afraid of people. He feared trying anything new. Yet, there was a girl at school that tried to be friends with him. Her name was Melissa Irvington. She would always smile at him whenever they passed each other in the hallway on their way to the next class. She was an extremely pretty girl, Hector thought. She had long black hair with amazing large brown eyes and a petite body. Once, Hector bumped into her in the hallway.

His books went flying into the air and embarrassingly onto the floor. Melissa was calm about the whole incident and helped Hector pick up his books. She even helped him adjust the thick glasses on his face. She looked at him and said, *"Hector, you are really smart! I am really impressed with all the A's you get on your math tests."* As she started to walk away, she turned around and Hector was quite sure she winked at him and smiled before leaving. Hector was stunned.

Melissa was downright gorgeous! From her long wavy hair to her cute little pink lips that excited him whenever she talked. Yet she had one terrible flaw that Hector could not overlook. She had that annoying brown skin! It could not be ignored. As much as he wanted to ask her out to the Spring Senior Prom, it was too much for him to disregard. She probably wanted something from him, he thought. He convinced himself that she was going to use him, eventually, he convinced himself. So, she could not be trusted either, and he could not afford to get involved.

So, he went through high school without any friends without one person writing in his yearbook. He had isolated himself from the world, and with that, he was just fine. But deep down inside, he wanted to go and find Melissa. He wanted to go out on a date with her, and perhaps hold her in his arms. But it was too much for him to break his lifelong principle of distrust. And Hector was not about to change now.

After high school, there was no use in going on to college. There were too many people there, and too many different personalities. He had enough of that in high school. Anyway, Hector believed that he had found the perfect job; a job at a telemarketing agency, harassing people to pay their bills. It was a job where he could assume another personality where he could speak up to people, and even yell and insult them, all while hiding behind the protection of the telephone. It was a thankless job that all the employees hated, but Hector truly enjoyed it. He worked in a room where it was his job to call people that were on the verge of foreclosure. He used tactics to frighten and manipulate them to make a balloon payment by borrowing the money in a desperate and often failed attempt to save their homes.

There was something emboldening about calling people and belittling them, which gave Hector a sense of power. He could almost scream at them over the phone, demeaning them as he called them out regarding their supposed irresponsibility. He hurled insults about how they had become a failure to their friends and family. Somehow, that made him feel a little better.

Hector called over one hundred people per day. He listened to customers plead with him to give them a little more time to come up with the money to save their home. On one particular day, there was one unusual client that Hector assumed was an elderly, Black lady that seemed to be sobbing, *"Please Mister, can you call back at another time? You have already called ten times today. My husband just died. We were together for over forty-five years. I am waiting for the mortician to come to take his body. Please. I will send the payment to you later. All I have is my Social Security payment, and I will send you that when it arrives. But please give me some rest from your continuous calling!"* Hector exploded at the elderly woman, *"Look you are the one that is trying to live for free! You probably don't even have the money to bury your old dead husband anyway! If you can't even afford to pay us, you certainly can't afford to bury him! You need to send the money! That is all we care about. You are going to be thrown out of your house. We are sending the Sheriff over there today and you will be on the street by nightfall. You are a disgrace to all of us trying to make an honest living! You deserve to be on the street!"* Hector did not feel any compassion or remorse. He had no sympathy for the elderly woman, sobbing on the other end of the phone. It did not matter to him that he was lying about sending a sheriff to her house.

Hector was quickly promoted, and in time, he became one of the most aggressive callers that the company had ever employed. He could traumatize his clients, upset them, and push them to the breaking point, where they would almost do anything to make a payment. And for the first time in his life, he truly believed that he was in control of his circumstances. He was finally achieving a sense of empowerment, and it did not matter to him that it was based on manipulation and fear.

One day, as he was making his calls from a random series of numbers that the phone dialed, he heard a pleasant voice on the other end of the phone. And before he had time to give his intimidating speech, the person spoke to him, *"Hello, is this Hector?" "Yes, it is. But how did you know it was me? This is a private number. How do you know my name? This is the number to a private business. How did you get my name?" "Well, Hector, we have been waiting for you to call for some time now to talk to us. It has been a long time since you talked to us." "Who is this? This must be some kind of prank call!" "Well, we can assure you it is not. It is someone you know but you have refused to acknowledge. It is your good friend…God." "What? Are you crazy?! Get off this phone or I will report you!"* He quickly hung up the phone and started laughing to himself saying, *"God is on the phone! Well isn't that something! God sounded like he was an elderly Black woman, maybe about in her late sixties. What a nut job! What a way to start my shift! I find all the mental cases!"*

He pressed the button on his phone. A series of random numbers came up on his computer screen, and then he answered the phone again. Before he had time to read the first part of his prewritten script, the same voice spoke to him again saying, *"Hector! Hector, is that you? You always were a stubborn kid. Real hard-headed, always wanting your way! We were waiting for you to call again. You have ignored us on many occasions. We were hoping that you might turn around. The conditions of your life are getting out of hand. You are about to die and you need our help!" "GET OFF THIS PHONE! I DON'T KNOW WHO YOU ARE! BUT YOU BETTER GET OFF MY PHONE!"* Hector shouted as he slammed the phone down, almost breaking the handle. All the other telemarketers stopped in the middle of their conversations to focus on the lunacy of Hector screaming on his phone. Hector was losing control. He was going outside of the procedures that he was taught by allowing the client to turn the tables on him. He was shaken up. He checked the phone and the receiver for any buttons that were not connected properly. He slowly picked up the receiver and held it to his ear, when the phone rang once again. Before he had time to say anything else, he recognized that It was the same voice of the elderly Black lady on the phone again, saying, *"Hector, it's us! You really think it would be that easy to get rid of God! You really have isolated yourself in your little world and you desperately need a new perspective on life." "Look, Lady, I don't know who you are, but you need to stop harassing me and get off this phone! I am going to have the authorities track you down and arrest you!" "Well, we have been arrested before; even executed, so it won't be the first time!"* The elderly woman stated while laughing. *"What are you? Some kind of lunatic that gets your kicks by calling people and saying that you are God?! You are truly sick and need help! Don't you call this number again!"*

This time, Hector tried to keep his composure, trying not to make a spectacle of himself in front of his coworkers. He looked around, making sure that no one was watching him as he checked the numbers on the phone, and all the connections before pressing the little button from his desk in his cubicle. He uttered a few foul words under his breath as a new number came up from a different state. He answered the call, saying, *"Hello, this is the New Horizon Banking Service. We are calling you today because we have not received your last payment."* And once again, the elderly Black woman spoke, saying, *"Is that you, Hector? We were waiting for you to call back! I wish you were here right now. I just cooked a delicious apple pie, sprinkled with graham cracker crumbs, and brown sugar. We know how much you loved this dessert. Your mother, Hazel, used to make this for you when she was alive. We know how much you loved her, and how her death drove you deeper into your shell. She wanted us to tell you that she really misses you too. She wants you to know that she is alright now and having the time of her life. She also told us to tell you not to worry. She said that you need to find a nice young lady, and stop living such a pitiful existence! For she raised you better than this; not to be treating people so mean. And she said something about how she really likes Melissa!"* Hector was furious this time as he screamed out so loudly that everyone stopped, paralyzed by his bizarre behavior. *"LOOK, I DON'T KNOW WHO YOU ARE? BUT YOU ARE GOING TO BE ARRESTED FOR HARASSMENT! DO YOU THINK THAT I AM STUPID? THAT I AM SUPPOSED TO BELIEVE THAT YOU ARE GOD! I AM NOT FALLING FOR THIS NONSENSE! AND HOW DO YOU KNOW ABOUT MY MOTHER? HOW DO YOU KNOW MY MOTHER'S NAME? YOU NEED TO GET OFF THIS PHONE OR I SWEAR I AM GOING TO CALL THE POLICE!"*

Everyone in the room halted their conversations to listen to Hector screaming at the old lady on the other end of his phone. *'YOU OLD DIZZY BAT! I DON'T KNOW WHO PUT YOU UP TO THIS! BUT ONCE I FIND OUT, YOU ARE GOING TO JAIL! NOW GET OFF MY PHONE!"* The old lady was now laughing hysterically on the other end of the phone. *"You always have been so selfish, never trusting, and could never really love. You have been wasting so much time hating people. You have destroyed all the beautiful things we have sent to you. You need to get out more, Hector. You are wasting your life! You are really losing it, Hector!"*

Hector's hand was now shaking as he held the phone when his supervisor came rushing over towards his desk. His supervisor quickly grabbed the phone away from Hector, and said, *"What has gotten into you today, Hector? You are acting like a complete idiot! You have lost track of all the procedures you learned from your training. You are letting the client get to you. And it sounds like you are chasing away a very important customer by having an emotional breakdown. If you keep up this troubling behavior, we will lose every customer that we have!"* The supervisor quickly got on the phone and switched it over to the speaker so that Hector could hear the conversation. Hector could hear the old lady crying on the phone saying, *"I was just speaking to the young man on the phone. He was so mean to me as if he did not care what I was trying to tell him. I will be sending the payment today, but he just refused to listen to me. I tried to reason with him, but he continued to shout during our conversation. I really think he needs to get out more!"* The supervisor continued to reassure the elderly lady, and let her know that Hector would be reprimanded. But before the elderly lady ended the conversation and hung up the phone, she spoke to Hector's Supervisor, saying, *"Please tell the young man that if he ever needed some hot apple pie to drop by my house."*

The supervisor spoke to Hector saying, *"You have been one of our best service representatives. Why are you losing control, and letting the client get next to you?"*

Hector wanted to explain to him that his last conversations had all been from the same person, claiming that she was God. Hector wanted to make him aware, according to her, God was on the other end of the phone and bugging the life out of him. But that would make him look even more stupid, and it was safer just to keep his mouth shut. So, Hector listened without interest as the supervisor went over the ten most important rules of not allowing the situation between you and the client to overwhelm you. Consequently, before he left, Hector's Supervisor gave him a stem warning about screaming and damaging the company's property by slamming the phone down on the console until it almost broke. The whole experience was completely humiliating, especially for someone who was supposed to be one of the best telemarketers in the entire company.

When Hector picked up the phone again, he took a deep breath and pressed the button. He waited as the phone went through a series of numbers on his computer screen. This time, a new name of a client came up. Hector heard someone on the other end of the phone. It was the voice of a man saying, *"Hello? Hello?"* Hector quickly commenced delivering his prewritten script saying, *"Hello, this is the New Horizon Banking Service. We are calling you today."* But before he had time to continue delivering his speech, he was interrupted by a person calling out to someone in the room, *"LUCILLE!! LUCILLE! LUCILLE! IT IS HECTOR CALLING BACK AGAIN!"* He could hear a woman in the background saying, *"Well you tell that boy that Gracie told me to say hello to him! He needs to get in touch with Gracie. She really wants him to pick up a piece of her apple pie, and let him know she has it all wrapped up for him to take!"* "Hey, Hector! My Man! This is June Bug Jones, and we have been waiting for you to call. You need to learn to chill my man! You really are stressing yourself out! You need to calm down, come over to the house, sit in the living room, put your feet up on my recliner, and watch a game or two with me. It has been a long time since we had a heart to heart talk. I will tell Lucille to cook you a plate of her famous black-eyed peas, and some of her melt in your mouth cornbread, and a plate of her fantastic greens. You can sit down with us, and just rest your feet. For Son, you are really stressing everyone out!"*

Hector exploded at the voice on the other end of the phone. He was so angry, the phone was shaking in his hand, *"I know what is going on with you people! Are trying to scam me? You are trying to play me for a fool. All of you must have your phones connected somehow! And you have the gall, the nerve to call me on my job! I read about people like you; groups of Nigerians scamming people. You, people, are nothing but thieves! You are nothing but scum! You can believe this! I am not giving you anything! YOU ARE NOT SCAMMING ME! AS A MATTER OF FACT, YOU NEED TO STOP HARASSING ME! YOU COLORED PEOPLE ARE WORTHLESS!"* Hector shouted as he slammed the phone down, again.

Everyone in the room stopped talking as they stared in silence at Hector, and his out of control behavior. Hector knew that he had gotten himself into some serious trouble. *"HECTOR!"* His supervisor called out to him, almost running towards his open cubicle," *WHAT ARE YOU DOING TODAY? I HEARD YOU CALLING THE CUSTOMER A NAME!"* The supervisor pulled the phone away from Hector's hand as he spoke to the customer on the other end. *"We are so sorry that you experienced such poor customer relations from us today!"* The voice on the other end of the phone spoke saying, *"Well, that young man of yours called me and Gracie a name! He needs a rest for a few days. I think a day off would help him a lot. He sounds like he is under such pressure. You need to give the young man a nice vacation. I think as soon as I pay off my account, I will have nothing to do with this business. Please tell him he needs to stop making personal judgments against people too. There are so many nice and caring people in the world. And can you tell him that Mercy, who lives next door, said if he wanted some Soul food, she will always have a plate ready for him if he ever comes over!"*, and then the phone went silent.

The supervisor was furious with Hector, almost shouting, *"You really are turning into a lunatic today! You are chasing away our client's customers, not following procedures, and disrupting the work of others! And not only that, you are intimidating some of our most valuable customers by calling them names. I am sending you home for a few days so you can recuperate!"*

Hector exploded at his supervisor, *"I WAS BEING SCAMMED! NO ONE IS GOING TO TAKE ANYTHING FROM ME AGAIN! I AM NOT GOING TO BE USED AGAIN! NOT BY A GROUP OF DIRTY SCAMMERS IN NIGERIA! I HAD ENOUGH OF BEING*

USED AND I AM NOT TAKING IT ANYMORE! I AM TIRED OF THESE PEOPLE STEALING FROM ME!" Everyone was looking at Hector as they tried to continue taking their calls. Hector was screaming so loudly, the supervisor angrily told him to get his things, and leave, and that his last paycheck would be mailed to him.

Hector gathered up all his things from his desk, left the building quickly, but not before smashing the frame, containing the certificate, naming him the best Customer Support Client Specialist of the year. Hector stormed out of the building saying, *"I bet it was a group of dirty Nigerians in Africa somewhere, working out of a dusty little office, trying to steal my money! You just can't trust those people! Nobody would believe my story anyway, even if I told them that these people were claiming that they were God, and called me on the phone trying to scam me! I am sick of that stupid job anyway! I need a change!"* Hector turned around, and yelled out in the room before leaving saying, *"GOOD RIDDANCE YOU LOSERS!"*

Hector did not know what he would do next. He was living in the same house when he was but a kid. His mother had died a few years ago, and the house was given to him since it was paid off. But he still had to eat, and pay his bills. It would now be a struggle for him to figure out a way to survive. But the phone calls he received were quite disturbing. How did they know his mother's name? And how did they know that his favorite dessert was apple pie? It was downright scary. Something deep inside of him questioned if God was calling him. He had never heard of God calling anybody else on the phone before. And surely God would not keep calling back masquerading as the personalities of other people. I guess it could be considered some sort of payback for all the people he tormented and hurt for the last three years without considering the damage he had inflicted on the other side of the phone.

As Hector drove away in his Mustang, he turned the radio on full blast to drown out the hurt that he was feeling. He started listening to some radio jock that was sending out music requests when suddenly, he heard him say, *"This one goes out to a young man that is confused and lost right now, drowning in his sorrow. This one is going out to Hector Winslow. Hey, good buddy! Hector, this is God. We seriously need to talk! Things are getting out of control in your life. You are scheduled for an appointment with me, and needless to say, you are not ready. You need to slow down good buddy, and pull over so we can have a little chat!"* Hector stopped the car to a screeching halt. He left skid marks on the street as he pulled over nervously on the side of the road. He started turning the dial on the radio in a frantic panic until he found an easy listening station. Hector was breathing hard as he nervously looked around wondering if 'he was being followed or if he was being set up again. He turned the music on full blast as he continued driving down the street. At that moment, an announcer came on the radio, interrupting the music, saying, *"This one is going out to Hector Winslow. This is God speaking to you! Hector, we need to talk. I can truly feel your emptiness, and it is overwhelming. You think that life is just a waste of time. And you believe that you have nothing left to live for. The way you are living, things are going to take a dangerous turn, if you don't watch out! Hector, you need to come back to a place of quiet and rest and listen to my voice. Hector, you need to pull your car over, take a break, and calm down! Hector, please! I am calling out to you! Please pull your car over now!"*

Hector reacted with more anger stepping on the gas pedal with full force, sending the Mustang rocketing through an intersection. He did not see the semi-truck that was barreling through that same intersection, and could not stop as it smashed into him from the other side. When Hector's Mustang was hit, he felt the metal of the side from the door crush, and cave in around him. He felt the long shafts of glass from the windshield piercing his skin as the crumbling pieces of the glass, flying through the air became flying scissors as Hector felt his body being lacerated. He felt his bones breaking as he tried to stay in the Mustang, but his seatbelt was not fastened, therefore, he was thrown forward. He felt shards of the glass impale his chest, and he saw his blood splattering the interior of his car. And then suddenly, everything stopped. All the broken pieces of the Mustang became suspended, silently, floating in the air around him. Hector watched the broken, crumbling pieces of glass from the windshield form a lethal crystal fountain that filled the interior of the Mustang.

Hector now had the inexplicable ability to be able to pass

through the glass and observe everything around him from a three-dimensional perspective. In a strange, and yet marvelous way, it was quite fascinating. But then without warning, in sudden shock, he unexpectedly found himself on the back of a bicycle being lifted airborne. In another startling moment, he appeared to be a boy again, maybe at the age of seven. The kid that stole his bicycle many years ago told him to hang on as he pedaled the bicycle so furiously that the bicycle chain below sparkled with light. Hector held on for dear life as they rode through what appeared to be a frightening thunderstorm. And the farther the round head boy pedaled the bicycle, the memory of the terrible trauma from the crash slowly subsided and faded from his memory while a consuming atmosphere of peace filled the space around him.

Hector immediately felt his chest and examined his arms and legs. There were no longer pieces of glass embedded in his skin. He carefully checked every part of his body for the flying shards of glass that pierced him and ripped away pieces of his skin. One large piece had passed through his chest, and he thought for sure it was still wedged deep inside. But there was not a trace of him being hurt at all. It was all so overwhelming. He tried to adjust himself as he now found himself on the back of his bicycle moving through a thunderstorm in utter darkness. But Hector was still angry. He started talking to himself, saying, ***"This is the same little boy who stole my bicycle! This stupid little thief has the nerve to show up again! And he is still riding my bicycle!"*** Then he remembered that he was a twenty-three-year-old man, and it should not matter about a bicycle that was stolen from him when he was just a kid. Hector ruminated on the strange events that had just happened to him. He recognized that God was talking to him on the phone at work, and through people that apparently knew everything about him. What in the world was going on? When the terrible crash occurred, he remembered being lifted, placed upon the bicycle seat, and cycled away by the round head brown-skinned kid.

The round head kid was pedaling like a maniac while Hector held on, hoping that he would not fall off. As they continued to ride through a howling thunderstorm, the round head kid continued to pedal insanely so that the metallic spindle of the bicycle escalated with heat, and changed into a fiery yellow color. Hector felt the glittering sparks burning through his tennis shoes from the fiery bicycle chain as he quickly tried to shake them off. They moved through the dark and menacing clouds that erupted with dazzling neon splinters of lightning, streaking across the sky. Hector cried out to the insane boy pedaling, ***"HEY, KID, SLOW DOWN! LET ME OFF! I WANT TO GO HOME! DO YOU HEAR ME, KID?! LET ME OFF THIS BICYCLE!"***

And yet, once more, the kid ignored him completely as Hector held on terrifyingly, hoping that he would not fall off and die. That is when Hector looked down and saw that they were in the air above the earth. He saw what appeared to be purple, green, and red colors of aurora lights that had illuminating waves, streaking across the atmosphere, flowing over the curvature of the earth. He looked and gasped in disbelief as he saw the sublime blue ethos of the earth below. Hector cried out louder, ***'WHAT ARE YOU DOING? ARE YOU TRYING TO GET US BOTH KILLED? DIDN'T I TELL YOU TO LET ME OFF THIS BICYCLE?"***

As the bicycle jerked upward, the force of the wind caused it to rattle and shake. Hector thought the thing would fall apart at any moment. The streamers of the bicycle were blowing so hard that one of them blew off, went flying into the air, and passed him. Then suddenly, everything became calm once more as a vast and brilliant universe lit up before them. Stars in unending circles, in crystal ribbons, having infinite canopies illuminated around them in a starry brilliance. And in the far distance of space, other stars were changing colors, twinkling before going into the supernova, leaving sparkling trails glistening like fireflies in the cosmic darkness. Hector tightened his grip around the round head kid as they appeared to be moving slowly, observing the quiet of the constellations unfolding in a seemingly precise and heavenly order. Evidently, a silent hand was the moving force orchestrating it all. This living animation was conducting and coordinating everything, even Hector and the boy floating in the darkness of space.

Hector reached out in fear as the bicycle started going down gradually. The pedals were moving so fast now that Hector had to lift his legs up, hoping that he would not be burned from the flying sparks that flew upward. Frightened, Hector looked down again. The wheels of the bicycle were skirting across the tops of mountain peaks. Hector could easily reach out and touch some of the freshly packed snow that the wheels of the bicycle bounced upon as he dragged his feet across a snow bank, cooling his tennis shoes from the flying sparks. He cried out in terror to the silent kid who looked like he was trying to control the descending bicycle as the front wheel started wobbling. *"HEY, KID CAN'T YOU CONTROL THIS BICYCLE ANY BETTER? WE ARE GOING DOWN TOO FAST! IT LOOKS LIKE WE MIGHT CRASH ANY MOMENT INTO THE SIDES OF ONE OF THESE MOUNTAINS!"*

The kid turned around and smiled at Hector. Then he took his hands off the handlebars and said in a soft voice, *"I am not steering it anymore."* The whole atmosphere was consumed with trailing auras of colors that streamed upward into the skies. Hector was immediately overtaken with a feeling of comfort, peace, and serenity. As he momentarily looked down, he could see the whole landscape, enshrined with enormous granite mountains, infused with a radiant light that formed a breathtaking mosaic natural sanctuary. A white glistening waterfall gushed from the top of one of the summits and formed a gigantic dark and still lake, which was only visible because of the stars that reflected from its surface. It appeared as if the lake was on an endless, horizontal plane that poured out into the nothingness of space. Hector could not see the end of the lake as it appeared to be black and without a distant shore.

The bicycle started bouncing up and down, vibrating with tremendous force as it sped dangerously downhill on one of the mountains. When they came closer towards the basin on the ground, the bicycle hit a series of large jagged rocks, causing the frame to fold in half. Tiers of the bicycle broke apart and rolled away. The round head kid and Hector flipped forward. They both went sailing through the air and tumbled upon a thick mattress of tall grass that lined the floor of a spacious field. Hector watched in shock and terror as the round head kid exploded into a ball of tumbling light, and then dissipated with just a few glittering embers that faded into the air until there was nothing left of him. The round head kid was gone. It was as if he had never existed. And once more, Hector was left alone with only pieces of his bicycle, now broken in half, and scattered across the field.

Hector arose from the carpet of grass and noticed that everywhere he moved, the grass moved along with him with waves of colors. Hector glided through the twilight and through the waves of colored grass. Hector realized that the round head kid had not only disappeared, but had also broken his bicycle into pieces. The pieces that were left in the grass no longer resembled a bicycle, but they had turned gray, and even began to rust until the pieces were almost beyond recognition. That blue bicycle was the last true joy that he had from all his living upon the earth, and now, it was destroyed. Hector's birthday bicycle was no longer blue and shiny, but it had turned into rust, and some of the parts melted and twisted because of the impact from exploding upon the ground. Hector cried out in anger as he desperately went about collecting the broken pieces, trying to reassemble it until he realized that it was beyond repair.

Hector blamed the round head kid for taking away his bicycle again, and everything that he had loved. Hector yelled out loudly at the round head kid that somehow fooled him and then disappeared. *"YOU DUMB KID! YOU THINK THAT YOU CAN FOOL ME AGAIN! YOU NOT ONLY STOLE MY BICYCLE, BUT YOU BROKE IT APART THIS TIME! AND YOU DIDN'T EVEN SAY THAT YOU WERE SORRY!"* Hector called out, now in the tranquil solitary atmosphere. His voice echoed, and trailed off into the distance, under the silent tapestry of stars. *"YOU BETTER NOT SHOW UP AGAIN or I WON'T BE SO NICE TO YOU NEXT TIME!"*

Hector then realized that he had transformed, once again. He was no longer a child, but he was now a grown man. So, he felt embarrassed for yelling out so loudly about a bicycle that was stolen from him when he was a kid.

Hector collected every piece of the bicycle and thought for sure there had to be a way to put it all back together again. In that moment, Hector looked up and saw what appeared to be planets in the distance, a cluster of stars and a large burning ball in space that must have been the sun. It was as if he had a seat inside of a planetarium. Halos of light, in various colors, surrounded the planets. The sky was a massive crystal cathedral, arranged in a boundless, endless, symmetry of stars. Then and there, he saw the earth. It was blue and it turned in whirls of hushed clouds. Hector felt a sense of sadness. He was no longer on the earth and had wasted so much of his life regretting incidents that transpired in his past. He wished that he had a second life; a second chance to go back and repair his sorrowful state. Hector strolled through the grass. It was bright, glistening in the twilight as he brushed his hand across the tips of the blades. He thought for sure that he heard music. It was music that came from the grass; the sounds of different tones and chimes that he heard as he touched the tips of the blades. It was a continuous sound of various notes, a smoothing relaxing sound that flowed through him and calmed his fears. He brushed his hand across the grass again as it changed into thousands of colors. When he stroked the blades, the sounds came together, forming songs that he could instantly recreate. Hector started playing songs with the tips of the blades of grass, just as though he was plucking the strings of a harp. Instinctively, the environment, the landscape, and everything around him responded to the mood and the song that he was creating. It was incredible and wonderful. His mind could not comprehend this impossible feat, but he was truly enjoying himself as he excitedly began to brush his hands across the tips of the grass, happily playing a variation of different songs.

Then Hector noticed that the songs that he played also connected with his inner spirit, stirring something deep and hidden inside of him. All of a sudden, he found himself singing. It was something that he had never done in his entire life. It was not a song of words, but it was a long low sound, somewhat of a groan that poured out of his being. For it was his very life force that had awakened and was responding to his joy, calming his inner fears. Hector could feel the musical notes that rushed out of him. And for the first time in his life, the regret that he felt, no longer chastised him. The hurt of being abandoned by his alcoholic father who disappeared without a trace; and without even saying goodbye, was finally being released from inside of him.

Hurt was always something that he kept hidden deep within. He kept it hidden during the growing pains of his childhood. When or if he failed at something, and needed a father, he hid the hurt so that life would not make him appear so awkward looking and different. He had to grow up; stumbling and making mistakes while his mother worked to the point of exhaustion. His mother had little time for him, so he isolated himself, safe in his fear. And now finally, the inner house of his soul was being swept clean, and he finally had the ability to release his emotions as he continued to sing even more loudly.

It was quite a shock to Hector as he noted tears flowing easily down his face. He had kept himself detached from experiencing the love of others, so he did not feel that it was important to have a personal relationship with a God that he had never met. In hindsight, even the way he felt about the little boy who stole his bicycle, seemed ridiculous, and downright hilarious now. Subsequently, Hector's countenance immediately changed into all-out laughter as he thought about how the little boy kept pedaling, and how ridiculously funny it all appeared to him now. Never had he experienced such emotions from all his living days on the earth.

As Hector brushed the blades of the grass, white opal carnations, burst open from the soil all around him. The white carnations activated a memory. He squatted down, touched them, and brought them up to his face. He could smell the pleasantness of their aroma. When he did that, he remembered how his mother loved white carnations. When she was dying in the hospital of cancer, he brought her a bouquet of the white carnations that she loved so much to her hospital room.

Hector noticed how the tears flowing down his face, illuminated and appeared as glowing crystals in the darkness. It was as if the environment was somehow speaking to him, sensing his hurt, and then allowing him to discover his inner truth. For it created a place of honesty within him where there was no more shame that he desperately tried to hide. Yet somehow, he started to understand that there were no mistakes, just missed opportunities to love.

Hector recalled the time when he didn't want to live anymore after his mother died. And even at her funeral, and in the subsequent days thereafter, he refused to cry. He choked down the tears and cursed them as they tried to surface. There he was, on an abandoned planet crying alone in the twilight. Now, it was all being released, pouring out of him like the opening of a floodgate. He could not stop the invisible force that was releasing it, for there was nothing he could do now but submit to the tearful cleansing that was pouring out of his heart. Just like the round head kid who tried to ride his bicycle when it was out of control, Hector now realized that he had taken his hands off the handlebars as well for he was no longer in control.

Hector walked further, surveying the environment in this amazing starry twilight that illuminated every rock, tree, and blade of grass. It seemed that the very energy of creation moved in everything. It was as if Hector became aware of a greater, personal love, and presence. He is here! God is here. Hector felt his incredible closeness. His spirit was flowing through him as he looked at the ethereal environment that surrounded him. But where was God? Hector believed he should have shown up by now; and that God should have introduced himself to him. He was quite sure God was there, on this marooned, twilight planet, and that he had brought him there for a reason. But where was God?

Apparently, there was no other life form there. Hector was alone on an isolated planet, somewhere in space. As he walked near the horizon, he saw waves of aurora lights streaming upward towards the sky that briefly illuminated the landscape. At that moment, he saw other individuals walking, unsure, like himself, not knowing where they were going, but seeking answers. There appeared to be thousands of people wearing the clothes of their ethnic cultures. It seemed as if they had been suddenly, and instantly transported to this place, like himself. They stumbled curiously about, confused, and lost; straining to hear the inner voice, directing each one of their steps. Hector noticed that he could see the inside of them. Every cell and organ, all illuminating and glowing as if their very bodies and life force were made transparent and radiated before him. Hector could hear their voices in the twilight crying out, *"God, are you here? God, please show yourself? God, why have you brought me here? God, have I died?"*

Hector watched as their living energy flashed within their bodies. It was as if he could see their living spirits, moving with activity. And then, like the light bulbs of an old 1930's camera, a great burst of light exploded inside of them. The great flashes of light appeared to be from their living spirits, exploding as the flashes lit up the landscape all around. Hector saw the brilliance of their bodies, creating waves of light, animating in the darkness. For the first time in his life, he felt the presence of God. It was all so overwhelming for Hector to experience the Creator of the universe, personally having a conversation with each one of the travelers.

The travelers walked curiously through the twilight, searching for answers when suddenly, Hector watched them frightfully lay prostrate on the ground, sobbing loudly as if they were being overtaken by a vision or a memory from their past. It was the same kind of circumstance that paralleled Hector's experience when the carnations came up out of the ground, and he was finally able to release his deep and terrible hurt. Hector could do nothing, but move through the memories, and be drenched with the tears of its cleansing. As Hector examined his body again, he realized that he was almost transparent. He had the thin outline of having human skin, but underneath he could see his own living spirit, moving with colorful waves of pulsating light. Then Hector saw a great burst of light erupt on the far distant side of the lake. That eruption of light created thousands of waves that lit up the darkness in a glaze of white, unfolding as a blinding sheet that traveled outward towards the shore, and moved up the sides of the mountains.

Suddenly, out of the darkness, an enormous, gigantic figure started to emerge from the lake. The image was spectacular and brilliant. Hector could not make out what it was. It slowly appeared to be floating across the water. The darkness of the lake intensified again. The light and all the waves shimmered together as the being moved closer towards the shore. Hector looked in amazement as it floated over the water, and appeared before all of them. It was a winged creature, which had a flowing white robe made entirely out of a mist that circulated and constantly reformed. It also had a face that changed from being tranquil and angelic, into a terrible lion looking beast that had a mouth filled with long sharp and curved teeth. The intensity of the light around the creature made it difficult to look at it directly. As Hector adjusted his eyes, he could see that the creature had more than one set of wings. The wings were embedded with precious looking jewels, which appeared to be diamonds, sapphires, and rubies that created a sparkling, geometric, mosaic design. As the light moved through the wings, it appeared as if the wings were made of stained glass. Hector looked fascinated by its misty robes that appeared as a solid piece of cloth, and then it transformed into a cloudy vapor that disintegrated into thin air.

Hector now believed that this being was an angel, which did not abide by the physical laws that he learned while living on earth. As Hector watched the angel, once again, its face transformed, and slowly changed into every ethnicity and people upon the earth. The angel's skin changed into many hues as though it was identifying with the struggle and the despair of every human being on the earth. Its voice was neither male, nor female, but a throng of voices moving together as if they were all crying out. Hector gazed at the angel's hair. It was composed of gold, silver, and bronze strands that were enlaced with braids, and beaded jewels. The winged creature moved before the wandering humans as they looked amazed at its gigantic body in the twilight.

After staring at the tiny humans, the angel spoke, saying, *"I am Michaela, one of the Arch Ambassadors, that you call angels assigned to all of you. For you have been taken, brought to our school, and saved from experiencing what you call, death. There are many classes here and experiences designed especially for your learning and development. Walking upon water is one of the classes that you will eventually learn. It is one of the courses that you will be assigned to take before you can leave."* When the creature laughed, the water shimmered nearby. *"Even those who were close to the Lord had difficulty with this class! I know all of this appears to be very mysterious and difficult to you. But God has brought you here to learn an extremely important lesson that you could only experience by leaving your earthly bodies. You have been brought to this university because God himself has enrolled you into this class. It has been obvious that your past existence was in such a pitiful decline that your eventual self-destruction was imminent. But the mercy of God is beyond our comprehension, at times. He is so willing to dig down into the junk pile and find the treasure that the earth had discarded. Be warned. If you fail this course, you cannot go back to the earth, and your past life. This class has been designed especially for you to succeed. Your first class is entitled, "How to Discover the Second*

Life!" In this class, you will discover how incredibly important your uniqueness and compassion is for the survival of those that God will send to you! For your living is so important, that many will give up on life if you are not there to inspire them with your patience and care!

For when your love is given, at the precise divine moment, its power can prevent the terrible act of suicide, and give someone that is on the brink of failure, the strength to move forward. For your love, can be a staircase, lifting those who are paralyzed and emptied on the floor of the memories of regret. For you have survived, and have not perished because of the pulse of love that still moves deeply in your spirit. And even as you wasted most of your days on earth, blaming others and cursing the light that has awakened you each, and every day. There was a faint glimmer of light that moved within you that would not dissipate. For the great microphone of the universe heard, and detected the faint cry of your prayer. And like a satellite sent into space, the message was received and translated by the stars. As you cried out to the sparkling ethereal light saying, "I know God. I can live a better way! Forgive me for belittling the miraculous power that you have sent to me!" For the brilliance of your life has not dimmed. The spark of creativity is a perpetual light of healing that is twinkling upon your fingertips. And what you could have achieved in this life, you have let rot in the trenches of criticism, sarcasm, and ridicule. In the past, criticism worked for you. You could stand on the sideline and look afar when someone you knew became homeless, broken, and lost. You could safely mock them for being weak, and not in control of their world. In the past, sarcasm worked for you. When someone needed you to hold them up as they went through their hurt, you used sarcasm to avoid exposing your real feelings; it was comfortable to hide in the uneasiness of your laughter. In the past, ridicule worked for you. It was easy to blame others when their lives teetered on the edge of failure. It was safe and comfortable to watch them from a distance, and not get involved. But now you are at the place where you have condemned others, and you find yourself on the edge of disaster, trying to maintain your balance. For love, does not graduate students in the classroom of isolation. You cannot love alone, and neither can you heal alone. For the real student of love recognizes that the light of their heart is there, not only to illuminate their path, but its purpose is to be a lighthouse, calling others to safety in the raging height of the storm. For it has been easy for you to deny your brilliance to dim its power and withdraw in the closet of blame and sorrow. But now it is your time. For only you have the divine key to the truth to unlock the chains to free yourself. Too long, you have guided your life and swayed and prodded along by what others thought and spoke about you. You have repeated second grade long enough! And as a scruffy scavenger, you have carried your sack of mistakes through the street, loudly shouting out your failures to everyone. God is now saying to you, "Come up higher and experience the power of a transforming love, prepared for you since the foundations of the world. Breathe in this new air. Lift up your hands, and climb upon the clouds!" For you have been so consumed with your failures that even when you prayed, there was no expectation that miracles would appear in your life. You have believed that your life was supposed to be painful, empty, and unhappy. And that there was nothing that you could do to change the pitiful state of your existence. But you should have known that your very breath was a divine act of love. All the living particles of the universe were activated and blessed at your arrival to the earth. But you were comfortable remaining stagnate, ignoring the immensity of the power of your gifts to repair the world for good. How long shall you be a mourner, following the corpse of your mistakes through the street, renting your garments, and throwing the dust from your dreams into the air? For by all the physical laws of earth, you should have died, and passed into the nothingness of existence, and be forgotten forever. But you are alive with an eternal spirit that is stronger than the earthly depression that constantly seeks to transform you into unhappiness. You are alive. Having not been defeated, shaking off the ashes of sorrow, believing that there is something greater in you that is still sparkling to live. No oppression, no sorrow, no sadness can overcome your joy to touch the sky. For you are presented daily with the new garment of grace to alleviate your pain and strengthen you during times of grief. This blessing has covered you with a grace that heals the mistakes of your past and breathes life into the bodies of your dreams. The dreams of heaven have come to you and stood by your bedside, but in the morning, the vision became blurred as you follow the procession of the real world, and accepted without the struggle of the fear of living. We are sending you a living spirit that shall appear unto you. This living spirit holds the passport papers to your Second Life. For like many that have come to our school, the guidelines to taking this test will make you only an observer. You will participate in a life and your life will merge with theirs. The memories of the individual, who once lived, will appear before you. For when the life force appears, you will instantly merge with their memories. And you will be able to see inside of their body and record their life. I know all of this is confusing, but please, be rest assured that God moves in precise order, and with divine connectivity. For nothing is out of order with God. Everything is in its place as it should be. Behold, it is coming. The living spirit is arriving for you! Please now, take a deep breath, close your eyes, and believe all things shall be made new!"

Hector closed his eyes and took a deep breath. And suddenly, everything became pitch black dark. Hector could no longer see his own hands before him. He tried reaching out in the darkness, attempting to grab hold on to anything to brace himself and maintain his balance. But everything was dark as if he was in a void of nothingness. Even more frightening, he could not feel his own body. It was as if he no longer existed. And then out of the darkness, another glistening figure emerged. The figure was translucent and had the appearance of crystal, having a living shell for a body. It also had the appearance of glass. As Hector looked at the being, he could see directly inside of it. He could see all its nerves and the veins illuminating with electrical pulses. He could see the movement of cells glowing brightly, and moving with rapid activity. Hector was shaken as he looked at the being. But he was awe-struck as he observed its life force. *"Could this be the animation of the human soul?"*, He said to himself. As he watched, he was enthralled and fascinated by the transparent activity of its life force. And then Hector looked. He could see himself. He had become as transparent as the being that stood before him. Hector understood what it meant to be human now as his body slowly vanished before him. It was all so overwhelming and frightful as he watched himself transforming into living energy.

As he stood before the transparent being, a compelling force began pulling him closer until he felt himself going directly inside of it. Hector tried to stop himself from moving directly into the creature's body, but it was nothing that he could do to stop it. While he was being pulled inside, Hector cried out, *"No I don't want to do this! Leave me alone! I don't want to merge myself with someone I don't even know anything about! Leave me alone, God! I don't want to do this! I do not want to become a part of the memories of someone else! This is too much for me! Please leave me alone! I did not sign up for this! I am sorry for being a selfish, rotten loner who hated people. I just want to go back home! Just take me back home to my own room. Please God, let me wake up again!"*

But it was too late. Hector was drawn closer towards the being until he could move directly inside of it. Hector tried crying out, but he could not speak. He was merely an observer inside the body of a being of another human. He watched snow banks and hills forming together as buildings emerged and formed, brick by brick. Roads and streets also appeared. Next, he saw people, living and working as they had done many years before. It was a cold day, and the streets still had a thin layer of ice on them, making every step a treacherous journey. Two small boys got off a large, bulky, yellow bus that appeared to be inching its way through the snowy, ice-covered streets. The boys were excitedly talking and laughing as white, fluffy flakes of snow continued to fall. Some of the snowflakes stuck to their clothing, but the boys were so excited, looking at the Christmas decorations around them, they hardly noticed. One of the boys was fully dressed to handle the cold and icy weather while the other boy walked shivering, trying to keep his hands in his pockets as the cold pierced his thin and skimpy jacket. The boys walked hurriedly through the downtown sidewalks of Omaha.

It was the day before Christmas in the year 1954. Unknown to them, one of the lives of the boys would be changed forever. It was Christmas time, and the city had gone all out to decorate the streets for the arrival of Santa Claus that would occur in less than a day. *"Hey, do you want to wear one of my coats? My Mom really dressed me before I left home as if I was going to the Antarctic!"* One of the boys said, who had a long plaid red scarf that draped around his head and dangled from his body. He also had on a large, floppy, rabbit fur-lined bombardier hat that had long ear flaps that hung down the sides of his face. He also wore a pair of long, black, rubber galoshes that fastened with silver large buckles extending all the way up to his knees. In addition, he had on two coats; a thick, wool, matted, bundled monstrosity, which made him appear just as though his chest was stuffed with hay. The bottoms of his pant legs were tucked inside of his boots, making his pant legs puff out from the sides. Furthermore, he had a pair of red mittens that were clipped to the edges of his jacket so that he would not lose them. While the other boy wore a jacket that was so lightweight that he tried to disguise his frigid expression to conceal that he was shivering and the cold was piercing through his clothes. *"Look I know you must be cold with that pint-sized, little coat that you are dressed in. It is still December out here, and it is starting to snow again!" "I will be all right! I am just fine!"* The other boy said as he became a little defensive, and agitated by his questioning. *"Well, it looks like you are shivering and cold to me. And your face looks terrible! It's blistering red!" "I told you I am just fine! It is just a little cold out here!" "Well if you need one of my coats, I will let you have it!" "Jacob, why don't you just shut your dumb mouth, and leave me alone? I told you I was not cold! If I was cold, I would have stayed home and would not have even come downtown tonight!" "Tommy, I was just trying to help you out! I have enough clothes on for you, and anyone else that needs an extra coat!" "Jacob, why don't you just leave me alone, and please just change the subject?" "Ok, I will! I was just trying to be helpful!" "I told you that I was alright!"*

Jacob and Tommy continued to walk together, taking in the gleeful atmosphere of the mad and frantic rush of shoppers that were crowding the downtown streets of the city, carrying their bundles of bags and packages, scavenging through the stores, making their last-minute purchases. The sound of the bell ringers from the Salvation Army commandeered every street corner. The ringing bells created a musical atmosphere in the entrances of the stores. And there, on one of the main street corners, was the largest store in the city, called Brandeis and Sons. It was a massive building that held every wonder known to delight and to amaze mankind. There was a two-page advertisement spread in the local newspaper that had a large and colorful photograph of the North Pole displayed, which brought every kid in the city on a pilgrimage to the store, during the week. Jacob and Tommy walked in, looking at all the colorful decorations. The street poles were transformed into candy canes, and decorated sleighs and reindeer arched over the city streets. Colorful Christmas lights were infused with all the decorations, changing the atmosphere into a festive pageantry of holiday fun. *"Wow...this is really something!"* The smaller blonde head kid said as a gust of wind whipped thru his hair from every direction, *"I sure am glad our moms let us come down here tonight by ourselves!"* The other kid was taller and appeared older. His skin was the color of smooth caramel. *"Yeah, we are almost grown-ups anyway! I can't believe how everything looks in Downtown tonight! I can't wait to see the Christmas display they set up in the Brandeis store! I know it will really be something!"* The blonde head kid with straw hair and wide blue eyes exclaimed as he glanced around, taking in everything around him.

Jacob Peterson and his best friend Tommy Henderson were, in a sense, the most unusual best of friends. From the day that Jacob met Tommy, he was being picked on by a group of boys at school, during recess. Jacob stood back and watched the scene being played out as a group of sixth graders surrounded Tommy, laughing at the way he was dressed, and calling him names. *"Tommy what are you wearing today? You look like you are part of a circus act!"*, one of the boys screamed out. Another pulled on his sweater, which had numerous holes in it. His pants also had holes in them, but those holes were covered up with large patches that were poorly sewn over them. *"Tommy, you look like a quilted blanket. Hey everyone! Let's look at all the holes in his clothes! And look at that moth-eaten sweater he has on! He really looks like a hoot!"* *"Where did your mother find those clothes that you are wearing? She must have looked at the bottom of the barrel to pull out your clothes from the bargain bin. Tommy, you look like a complete hoot!"*

The boys started pushing and laughing at him as Tommy started swinging wildly at them. Yet with him being so small, one of the boys just held his head and laughed at him trying to fight back. Jacob was not going to get involved, but when he saw two of the boys grabbing Tommy by his arms and legs, swinging him back and forth, like a wet little noodle, and then hurling him into a row of bushes. It was too much for him to ignore. Jacob charged into the boys, knocking one of them down. And then he hit the other boy in the face, giving him a bloody nose. The boy screamed, making a whimpering sound before scampering off to tell the teacher that he had been beaten up by Jacob.

Tommy respected Jacob and looked up to him as his mentor and even his as a big brother. After that day, no one dared to say anything mean to Tommy. Everyone knew that Jacob was like Tommy's personal guardian, and he would come quickly to rescue him.

The city had just recovered from a furious snowstorm that left most of the residents huddled in their homes for days, not knowing if they would have an opportunity to do any Christmas shopping, let alone leave their homes. Jacob looked at Tommy shivering, and he could tell that the cold was starting to affect him. For both of his cheeks had turned red, and he saw him shivering so hard that his hands were shaking. His blonde hair made him appear as if he was a scarecrow that was made of straw, freezing in the snow. Jacob took off his coat and put it around Tommy, who adamantly protested, at first, so he started to take it off. But the warmth of the coat immediately enveloped him, making him feel better. Tommy cried out in protest, trying to take the coat off. *"I was alright, you know! I was alright! I was not that cold, Jacob!"* But his protesting, and trying to take the coat off did little good because Jacob had already draped his large plaid scarf around his neck. And then he began tying it, making it difficult to take off.

As they continued walking down the street, Tommy could not stop thinking about how Jacob was almost like his personal guardian. Jacob would find Tommy at school, and he would know that he did not have any money to buy lunch in the cafeteria. Therefore, Jacob would give his allowance money to him so that he could eat lunch every day.

Tommy was poor, and not just poor, but dirt poor. There are levels of being poor. Tommy, along with his eight brothers and sisters were living at the very edge of a meager existence. Once, Jacob went over to Tommy's house. He lived outside of the city limits in a makeshift shack with his eight brothers and sisters. There was no running water, so Tommy, along with his brothers, had to carry water from a nearby creek, and then boil it to cook and clean with every day. The shack that he lived in was poorly constructed, built with ill-fitted boards that stuck out on every side. There was also a porch that was crudely constructed. The wood looked so old; it was amazing that the whole thing did not crumble to the ground. There was an outhouse in the back of the shack since there was no indoor plumbing. Also, there was no electricity, so they used kerosene lamps to see at night. During the night, when they became cold, the whole family huddled around a potbelly stove to keep warm. Tommy's mother was always on the old porch, rocking one of her babies in her arms, looking with such sad eyes. It was hard for Jacob to look her in the face without sensing her deep hurt and regret for having her children live in such squalor. Tommy told Jacob that once a week, the government assistance truck would arrive with a sack of beans and rice, and lecture his mother about providing for her family until she would be reduced to tears. Tommy's father was an alcoholic that would show up for a few days, and then disappear again for weeks at a time.

Everyone at school knew how poorly Tommy was living. They avoided him, along with his brothers and sisters as if they had the plague. But none of that mattered to Jacob. No one at school dared to call Tommy names now. Even the most feared kids at school did not tease or humiliate Tommy anymore. For now, Tommy had a personal angel that watched over him. That angel was Jacob. And it did not matter to Jacob that he was poor or skinny or that his clothes had holes in them or that he was a different color. All that mattered to Jacob was that they were the best of friends.

Tommy had cut an advertisement out the Sunday newspaper and kept it in his front jean pocket. He tried to pull it out from the bundle of clothing that he was wearing as they approached the entrance of the store. Tommy almost screamed in delight as they walked through the door, *"We're here Jacob, and everything really looks like what they said it would!'* *"Tommy, don't go pulling out that newspaper ad to show me again! We are at the store now and all we have to do is find the Christmas North Pole display."* But somehow, Tommy dug through the bundle of clothes that he was wearing and pulled out the newspaper advertisement again and excitedly said, *"See, I told you, Jacob! They have all the latest trains and bicycles at the Christmas North Pole station on the tenth floor!"*

As they approached the entrance, they saw the window display in the front of the store that had a running electric red train. The whole window display was turned into a miniaturized Christmas village. There were two Lionel black locomotive trains with towering smokestacks that blew out puffs of smoke and whistled loudly as it followed a series of tracks through tunnels, miniaturized towns, and over snow-capped mountains, arriving at a tiny post office with a sign that read, The North Pole. In the cargo boxes of the train, there were tiny letters, candy canes, and gumdrops. The miniaturized Christmas village took up the entire window display of the department store.

Tommy was mesmerized as he stared, looking at the display. And for one magical moment, he had been transported away from his poverty, the cold outside, and the reality of hunger; since he had hardly eaten anything that day. Tommy stood, looking at the display. His fingers spread wide apart as if his hands were stuck to the glass. *"JACOB! JACOB! LOOK AT THIS! THIS IS REALLY SOMETHING! WOW! THIS IS REALLY SOMETHING! JACOB! JACOB! LOOK AT THIS TRAIN! WOW! LET'S GO FIND THE NORTH POLE CHRISTMAS DISPLAY! IT IS ON THE TENTH FLOOR JUST LIKE THE NEWSPAPER SAID!"* Once again, Tommy pulled out the newspaper ad that he secretly kept in his pocket. There was a sign that was over the toy village that said, *"COME TO THE TENTH FLOOR AND SEE SANTA'S CASTLE!"*

Tommy pulled hard on the front doors of the department store. He moved quickly through the crowded room of people amassed around cash registers, which were ringing loudly as people were making their purchases. Jacob had a hard time trying to keep up with Tommy, who was walking so fast that it turned into a brisk trot. So, Jacob lost Tommy from his view for a few seconds. *"Hey, Tommy, wait up for me! Hey, Tommy, wait up!"* Jacob started laughing at Tommy as he scurried through the crowd, trying to find the elevators that led to the tenth floor. *"You were moving awful fast for a little person! You look like a tiny mouse moving through a maze!"* Jacob chuckled. *"You better shut up and learn to keep up! I can't help that you got those big feet of yours! That makes you move as if you got arthritis or something! Plus, it was cold outside, and I was tired of freezing! And I wanted to make sure I was not going to get trampled by the crowd of people trying to get in!" "Ok, but I am sure that you still believe in Santa Claus!" "You must be kidding me! I came in here to look for that beautiful blue bicycle that was advertised in the newspaper! You see, I got a picture here, somewhere in my pocket!"* Tommy exclaimed as he reached down, and pulled it out. *"How much stuff have you got crammed in those pockets of yours?"* Jacob asked. *"I have been looking at this bicycle advertised for a long time now. And I told my Mom to tell Santa that I want one for Christmas! And I believe that Santa is going to bring me one! I just believe it is going to happen!" "Are you kidding me? You still believe in Santa Claus.!"* Jacob replied as he started laughing.

Jacob and Tommy stood in front of the large gold elevators that were designed in an art deco style, a real piece of art in itself. They crowded inside of the iron-gated elevator with a large group of shoppers, alongside a small woman, wearing a gold-colored uniform that was trimmed in blue on the sleeves and the lapels with the words, **"Customer Service Attendant"** stitched into the material above a front shirt pocket. She pushed a series of levels as the elevator moved like a humming rocket upward into the air creating a smooth vibrating noise. The Elevator Operator called out to everyone in the elevator with a Nebraska dead drawl in her voice as if it was the most uninteresting thing that she had ever done in her life. She also called the names of the products that were on each of the floors. Jacob and Tommy caught glimpses of the activities of the shoppers as the elevator zipped upward. It was quite an entertaining show. Tommy looked at her calling out to everyone in the elevator, saying, *"Second Floor! Beds towels, sheets, pillows, housewares, and appliances! Third Floor! Furnishings, tables, sofas, recliners, and lamps!"*

Groups of people shuffled off the elevator to the different floors until Jacob and Tommy were left alone with the Elevator Operator. She looked at them and said, *"I bet I know where you guys want to go. You two want to go to the tenth floor, Santa's Castle."* Tommy was awe-struck by the elevator, and by all the dials that she turned and pulled to operate the wonderful machine. Finally, the doors of the elevator opened. The room was engulfed in a mystic aura of blue. Large boxes that were decorated as ice cubes, resembling Santa's castle became visible in the distance. There were mammoth candy canes that hung down from the ceiling. Others that stood upright and formed a column that led to a shrine where Santa Claus was seated in a large red velvet and gold chair. There was also a long, seemingly infinite line of noisy kids waiting with their impatient parents for Santa. Tommy was virtually jumping up and down for joy when he saw the store attendants passing out large red stockings filled with a variety of candies, an apple, an orange, and a small toy airplane and car inside.

Tommy ran behind a group of kids that were just as excited as he was. He stood in the line smiling from ear-to-ear. One of the store attendants, dressed as an elf, gave him a large stocking that he held with both hands, smiling happily. Jacob caught up with Tommy, and said, *"I thought you didn't believe in Santa Claus anymore Tommy!"* *"Well, they are giving away free candy. I wanted to get mine before they are all gone!"* *"Well, I am not going up there to see no Santa Claus! I will wait for you right here"* Tommy stood in line for a long time sucking on a candy cane he found in the stocking, believing that his whole existence would be unfulfilled if he did not talk to the man in the red suit. Tommy knew he was too big to actually sit on his lap, but he still thought it would be a good thing to make a connection with the big man, even if he had to stand. Jacob was not too far away, so he heard what Tommy said, *"I did not want to give you a big list. I just want only one thing. Santa, my family don't have much! They can hardly afford anything. And every year I haven't gotten anything nice. But if you can make a way, I want this right here!"* He pulled out a picture of the blue bicycle that he kept in his pocket. *"This is what I want right here! It is blue and beautiful! I really want this!"* Jacob heard his conversation with Santa Claus, and a tear formed in the corner of his eye. The man in the costume looked at him, paused for a second, and appeared to be quite taken by surprise by his words. Then he smiled and gave him a big hug and said, *"We will do what we can! You know miracles do happen this time of the year! I can't promise you everything you want! But one thing I know for sure, if you have a family that loves you, then that is the best Christmas you will ever have!"* Then Santa gave him another hug and winked at him.

As they were preparing to leave, the Elves loaded them down with all kinds of advertisements of the after-Christmas sales. Then Tommy did something that caused Jacob to take notice, he begged for three more of the red stockings. He said almost choking on his words as a tear fell from his eyes, *"My little brothers and sisters will really be happy if they can only get something like this for Christmas under the tree! Please! I am not asking for myself, but for them."* And without hesitation or even saying a word, smiling in silence, they gave him four more of the red stockings which Jacob had to help him carry.

Walking towards the elevator as they were leaving the tenth-floor, Tommy looked up at the ceiling, and then he saw it, the blue bicycle. It was suspended and outlined in Christmas lights. Tommy cried out, *"Jacob there it is, the blue bicycle! It looks just like the advertisement in the newspaper!"* There was a sign underneath it that read, *"Christmas is coming, so put this under your tree!"* Tommy looked at the bicycle, and then he quietly said, *"It's never going to happen. I have been asking for this bicycle every year. I still get nothing!"* Then he tore up the newspaper clipping of the bicycle that he had in his pocket as large tears fell from his eyes, and dropped onto the floor. *"None of this is real! I am getting nothing for Christmas! I never get anything! We are just too darn poor! There is no Santa Claus! There is nothing! I hate Christmas! I hate everything! I wish I was dead. I just wish I was dead!"*

Jacob watched Tommy. At first, he did not know what to do. So, he decided that it would be best if he did not say anything at all. On the other hand, he wanted Tommy to know that he would always be his friend, but words just seemed insufficient, insincere, and inadequate to heal his deep hurt. And he knew just being there would be the best thing that he could do. *"Don't worry about it, Tommy. I am your friend."* Jacob said, in a moving whisper. *"And I will be with you no matter what happens!"*

Tommy munched on his apple and snacked on some of the colored candy from his stocking while they were walking back to catch the bus. As they were preparing to go their separate ways, Tommy suggested that Jacob should come by and see some of the decorations that he made at school to put on his Christmas tree. *"If you can come home with me, I will show you the really neat stuff that I made at school to put on my Christmas tree!"* *"Ok I will come over, but I can't stay too long. My mom told me to be home by a certain time. I will be in real trouble if I am not there by eight o' clock."*

It was a cold and dark trip to Tommy's house. Tommy lived on the outskirts of town, on a dirt road, where the houses were in an area that the city did not feel was worth their effort to develop. There were no street lights to be found, and most of the houses were just shacks, nailed together with boards. They approached the front door, which was not a door, but a large piece of a board that covered the front entrance. There was a rotted front porch and an assortment of boards that covered the house on all sides. The porch was so weak and fragile that Jacob thought that the weight of his foot would cause him to crash through it at any given moment. *"Tommy, you better shut that door! You are letting all the warm air out of the house! You should reposition those boards just right to keep the wind out Tommy! I can't have these kids getting sick again! And where have you been? I told you don't stay out too late! You need to help with finding some more wood so we can keep the fire going in the stove!"*

Jacob looked inside the house. It was the worst living conditions that he had ever seen. There were six children, all gathered under blankets in front of a large black potbellied stove. The stove had a series of rickety looking pipes that went upward into the ceiling, and then outside. The floor was a set of nailed boards that were assembled together in an uneven state, causing you to watch your step as you walked around the room. Tommy's mother was rocking a baby, and holding it next to her breast as she spoke, *"Tommy I need you to watch some of the little ones that are getting out of hand around here! And how did you pay for your bus ticket downtown? You know we don't have money like that! Where did you get it from?" "Yes, Mama, I came home as soon as I could! Jacob bought my bus ticket downtown! And look what I brought home for everyone!"*

A group of dirty-faced children came out of a tattered blanket. They stood with wide grins, looking at the sacks of candy stockings that Tommy brought home. *"Give me some candy! Give me some candy Tommy! Please, Tommy, give me an apple!"*, they shrieked as they crowded excitedly around Tommy with their hands held out. *"Please, Tommy, tell your friend to take a seat. He is more than welcome in our house!"*, said Tommy's mother.

Tommy found a box that was covered with some kind of cloth and gave it to Jacob to sit down. Jacob stared in disbelief as he looked at the dismal way Tommy was living. Tommy stood in front of a little Christmas tree that was bent over and hardly resembled a tree at all. It was more like a broken pine branch. There were no electric lights on the tree, but it was covered with the paper decorations that Tommy made at school. *"See I told you, Jacob! I really made some neat stuff at school this week!"* There was a string of paper loops and rings that were colored by Tommy that said, *"Happy Christmas!"* There was also a series of drawings of Santa Claus and the reindeer that were also drawn by him and taped on the walls by the little broken Christmas tree.

Jacob tried his best to act excited, and force a smile as he looked at the little dingy decor in Tommy's house. Some of Tommy's brothers and sisters appeared to be between the ages three and six. They hardly had any clothes on as they huddled together under a dirty blanket, and they only came out from underneath the blanket to take a piece of candy from out of the stocking that Tommy brought home and placed under the tree. There was a small group of bags placed beneath the tree. And they were wrapped with a flimsy type of tissue paper. Tommy looked down at the presents, and said, *"This is the same stuff I get every year. It's from the Goodwill. I can tell you what it is."* He picked up several of the small boxes and said, *"This is a box of crayons. This is a coloring book, and this is a pair of socks; all from the Goodwill, and all from their donation box."* Tommy threw everything down onto the floor, and then a sad look took over his face that he quickly tried to disguise.

Jacob looked at all the drawings that Tommy had taped on the walls of the shack. Then Tommy's mother spoke saying, *"You need to let me cut up those apples and oranges that you got from the store tonight, and we can give them to your little brothers and sisters."* It was a heart-wrenching scene to behold as the apples and oranges from the store's Christmas display, now became their evening supper. Jacob was so filled with empathy by what he saw that he felt sorry for them, and gave them his stocking of candy and his apple as well.

A gust of wind momentarily whistled through the shack. Everything turned into a bone-chilling cold before the potbellied stove was set ablaze and warmed everything up again. But it was only for a few seconds, and then the shack returned to the numbing cold. There was no running water in the house, but there was a creek nearby. Tommy told Jacob that he had to break off pieces of ice from the frozen creek and let it thaw out so they could have water to drink. Then they had to use the remainder of the water to take cloth baths.

But now it was Christmas time, which was one of those times when Tommy's poverty would come to suffocate him. Tommy was good at hiding how poor he was. Even at school, the kids knew he didn't have much, but they did not know he had nothing. Christmas came into his world. It brought him into a place where he dreamed again. It brought him to a place where his fingers pressed against the glass display window, but he could not pass through it because his father was an alcoholic, and his mother was surviving from day to day. Tommy's life, during Christmas, was just another day that brought him to a reality that he was outside, in the cold, looking at the magic of the world around him.

It was getting late when Jacob said, *"I better be getting home. My mom is going to be blazing mad at me for taking so long. Tommy, I have to go. You have a Merry Christmas! I will see you after Christmas!"* *"Yeah, I will see you after Christmas! Thanks Jacob for taking me downtown with you tonight. That was really fun!"* As Jacob was getting ready to leave, Tommy reached in his pocket and taped up another picture of the blue bicycle to the wall near the Christmas tree. He had saved another picture of the blue bicycle that he had torn from an ad at the department store. Jacob knew that would be the closest that Tommy would ever get to the blue bicycle that he wanted so desperately to have.

Jacob walked home and arrived at his house. He could see the large Christmas tree standing in his front room window, blinking cheerfully along with the other houses in the neighborhood that were decorated with festive lights. Jacob lived in the middle-class section of the Colored area of the city. It was an area where the teachers lived, the Pullman Porters, and where even preachers had built their houses. Christmas time was a time for people to show off their influence in the community. As Jacob looked at the red brick houses, and the decorations all around, he could not help but feel the hurt from Tommy's family. He was reminded of how Tommy's whole family was gathered around an old potbelly stove, shivering under a tattered blanket.

When he opened the front door of his own home, he could see his mother and his little sister, sitting on the sofa, wrapping the last of the presents that they would give to their relatives who would be gathering at their home Christmas day. In the dining room, there was a table which had a large baked turkey that had been slow-cooked all day. The table was also covered with an assortment of other foods, such as ham, sweet potato pies, cakes, and special dishes that had been prepared by Jacob's mother for the big celebration tomorrow. There were bowls of apples, oranges, and candy that were in the special silver bowls that his mother always brought out for Christmas. There was the special white tablecloth that had an engraved pattern that was put out only during the holidays. The Christmas tree they had was over six feet tall and it had so many decorations that it appeared to shimmer as the lights blinked upon it. When he opened the door, his little sister Tiffany, who was seven, excitedly told him how she had baked a fresh batch of Christmas cookies by herself. *"Look at what I made, Jacob! I made these cookies all by myself! Mama only helped just a little. Why don't you taste one to see what you think?"* Jacob took one of the little cookies and started munching on it. *"You did a pretty good job with these. I remember the last time you tried to cook something, and you could have burned down the house. And the way you made that cake last time, it tasted like sandpaper, I could have choked to death.”* He started chuckling. *“Jacob don't be teasing your sister! She is just learning to cook! And I told you, boy, to be home by eight! What took you so long to come home? Where were you at all of this time?” “I was with Tommy. I stopped by his house after we left downtown.” “You mean that little boy who wears those terrible looking clothes with the holes in them? Where does he live anyway?” “He lives down past the Basin area.” “You mean that group of shacks where the transits live?” “Yes, Mama.” “You don't need to go down there by yourself! It is too dangerous down there at this time of the night. Your father would be upset with you if he knew that you were down there after dark. You go upstairs and wash your hands and eat your dinner. I am not going to warm up your food again. And then you need to help Tiffany with all of the presents we still have to wrap before everyone comes over here tomorrow!” “Is Aunt Brittany coming over tomorrow too?” “Yes, she always comes over on Christmas!” “Mama, I don't like her. She always sucks her teeth when she eats and it is disgusting!” “She does not suck her teeth! And what has gotten into you, talking about your Aunt Brittany like that?! She does not suck her teeth when she eats!” “Yes, she does and it is the most horrible sound. It sounds something like this.”* Jacob started imitating the noises she makes when she eats. *“You stop that right now! If you say anything to her to tomorrow when she comes over, you will be grounded for weeks! Do you hear me, young man?” “Yes, Mama. I was just saying it would be nice if she just stayed home this year, and I would not have to hear that disgusting sound.”*

Then the door opened, and Jacob's father came in. Tiffany ran towards him and hugged him around his neck. *“Hey, Honey! How was work today?” “It was ok. They gave me an extra twenty dollars as a Christmas bonus that I really appreciate! It looks like it might snow again.” “I hope not.”,* Jacob's mother said looking out the window. *“We had enough snow that will last us for the next year. I don't know what we are going to do if we get anymore.” “Hey, are you kids ready for Christmas in the morning!” “Yes, Dad! I have been waiting for this all year! I can't wait any longer. I want to open my presents now!" "Did you and Mom get the list and everything that I asked for?" "What are you talking about? We have nothing to do with it. It is all left up to Santa Claus. He is the man that is working behind the scenes. We just work for him."*

Tiffany sat on her father's lap, put her head under his chin as if she was going to fall asleep, and then said, *"I don't care what Jacob says about Santa Claus. I am still leaving him milk and cookies, just like I did last year!"* She quickly turned around and stuck her tongue out at Jacob. Jacob frowned, and just said, *"Little kids are weird!"*

Then Jacob's mother said, *"Jacob has something he wants to tell you! He wants to tell you about where he went today after dark." "Do I have to tell him now?" "Yes, you do!" "I went down to the Basin with Tommy Henderson today to see his Christmas tree. There are some seriously poor folks down there. A lot of people are really struggling and hurting you know." "What were you doing down there anyway? And who told you that you could go?" "I was walking with my friend Tommy to see his Christmas tree like I said. And Dad, they are so poor that I really feel sad for him." "I know son. Something must be done to help people like Tommy. But it does not look like too many people are willing to step forward and commit themselves. But I am glad you did not get hurt going down there. It is just so unsafe." "It was alright. He does not live too deep in the Basin, just right outside of it. Just cross the railroad tracks is where his house is at. You can almost see it if from the school playground." "Next time you ask me or your Mother before you go venturing off like that!" "Ok, I will next time."*

Jacob went upstairs, washed his hands, returned and sat down to eat a hefty dinner. He spent the rest of the night being annoyed by his little sister, who was trying her best to wrap presents for the relatives that were coming over. But her wrapping skills were worse than her cooking. So, she started turning everything she wrapped into bundles of papers. *"Mama, Tiffany is just wasting paper! Look at the way she is wrapping up the presents!" "Tiffany, you have to take your time, and wrap the presents the way I showed you." "Yes, Mama! Can you please tell Jacob just to leave me alone? I don't want to be bothered by him!" "Jacob, please stop teasing your sister!" "I am not doing anything to her! She is bothering me! She is the wrapping paper*

monster of the house. Somebody is going to have to rewrap all of her presents!"

The old, large, wooden dial radio was in the living room. Jacob's father was smoking a pipe and had his slippers on while he listening to **"Jack Benny"**. He wanted a black and white television and he was hoping to get one for Christmas. It was the new rage that everyone was talking about. It was a long night. Jacob thought he had wrapped too many presents which were making him tired. He and Tiffany were falling asleep on the sofa. He vaguely remembered his father picking both of them up, and carrying them to their bedrooms until they fell asleep under a thick covering of warm blankets.

Jacob thought he overheard the sound of his mother and father working during the night. And during his stirring dream state, he thought he heard his father talking and saying ***"Do you have the directions on how to put it together? How much more do we have to do? I am ready to go to bed. It is getting late."***

Tommy was shivering underneath his blanket with his brothers and sisters. It was cold in the shack and the fire from the potbelly stove diminished into a small, flickering flame, causing the house to be converted into a tomb of ice. Tommy and his brothers huddled together beneath a pile of raggedy coats and socks, and his mother slept on the large stuffy chair with her three-year-old nestled towards her breast. Christmas was now over for Tommy's family. The children had quickly gone through the Goodwill presents of coloring books and socks. And someone had even given them hats this year that helped keep the cold air out. But now, there was nothing left to eat. The apples and oranges were all gone. Tommy knew that he would have to go out to the grocery stores and beg for the day-old bread or food they could not sell anymore.

The whole experience of Christmas exhausted him. He wished that he could have given his brothers and sisters something more for Christmas to make them feel happy. He had sung songs to them and made up stories to help them make it through the night. But Christmas morning was coming, and they would wake up cold, hungry, empty, and hurt as they had done every year. It would all be over soon, and he would go into his world of hiding once more; hiding at school, hiding when he walked down the street. He tried his best to appear normal and to make it seem as if he was like everyone else. For no one would see his inner room of shame that haunted him every day.

The light of the morning was creeping over the city. The atmosphere would be consumed in the laughter of holiday families gathering together, and quickly tearing into presents. But something deeper and more powerful was occurring. It was the eternal moment. The eternal moment is the power to believe, the power to continue, the power to go forward no matter what circumstance is trying to destroy the sacredness of your existence. And even in the midst of cold and desperation, you go forward, determined to stand together in love. Tommy knew this eternal truth as he shivered in the darkness under the blankets with his brothers and sisters that were sleeping right underneath him. He was glad they were sleeping. Perhaps the sunlight would warm up the house in the morning; he quietly prayed under the covers in a whisper.

He peeked out from underneath the covers of the blankets, and he saw the picture of the blue bicycle in the dim light of the room taped on the wall. And for a brief moment, he saw himself riding it down the street. He was pedaling it around the neighborhood while all the kids watched and waved with delight. Then he saw the bicycle under the Christmas tree in the house. The little tree transformed before his eyes and illuminated with decorations, and with presents for everyone in the house. And then quickly the vision vanished before him and everything was gone. There was just the sound of the cold wind pushing up against the boards of the house and a faint light coming from the potbellied stove in the room. Even the collection of wood that they had for the stove was almost gone and he would have to go out into the countryside in the morning to look for more wood. But in the quiet of the night, Tommy did have something that caused him to smile. Jeffery who was barely five, briefly awakened under Tommy's arms, and whispered before falling back to sleep saying, *"Tommy, is it Christmas yet?"* Tommy then said, *"Yes, it is Christmas. Now, go back to sleep!"* *"Merry Christmas, Tommy! We are going to have some fun in the morning!"* *"We always have fun on Christmas day. You know that! Now go back to sleep!"*

On the other side of town, the light of the morning was creeping through the darkness and filling the spaces of the rooms with a seemingly glowing light of the splendor of Christmas day. Tiffany was already up knocking on Jacob's bedroom door. *"Jacob! Wake up! It's Christmas! It's here! What are you waiting for? Get up out of the bed!"*

Jacob was happy it was Christmas, but the blankets felt so good that he did not want to leave, so he stayed buried under the warmth, just to take in more of the comfort. Then he felt all the blankets being quickly pulled off him. It was Tiffany. She had pulled the blankets off his bed. He tried to cover up into a ball, but she started pulling on his pajamas as well. *"Jacob get up! Jacob, it's Christmas! Get up! What's wrong with you! Get up out of the bed!"* *"I am Tiffany! Just give me a few more seconds. It's cold, and I want to get some more sleep."* *"Have you lost your senses? If you don't get out of this bed this moment, then I am going to do something to you that you won't like!"* *"And what is that Tiffany?"* She then started tickling his feet and pulling on his toes while Jacob started twisting and turning and laughing until the top sheet was pulled away from the mattress. He then quickly rose up and said, *"I know it's Christmas! Let's go downstairs! What are you waiting for Tiffany?"* *"What am I waiting for? I am waiting for you to get moving! What do you think, you oversize sack of potatoes!"* She started laughing and tried to tickle him again. As they started to creep down the wooden stairs, they heard their mother's voice from their parents' bedroom, shouting out to them, *"Jacob! Tiffany! Don't you go downstairs until we get up!"* *"Alright, Mother, we will wait for you!"* Jacob heard his father's voice in the dim light of the stairway, *"Do we have to get up now?"* *"The kids are already up, and it's Christmas! Come on, Honey. The kids are ready to get up!"* *"It is awful early in the morning!"* Can't they wait until another hour or two to get up?"* *"It's Christmas morning, Honey, and they are ready to get up!"* *"Alright, I will get up!"* As the door opened, Mother came out of the bedroom. Her hair was covered with a head full of rollers, smiling brightly at Jacob and Tiffany. *"Are you ready for Christmas?"* *"YES!"* *"What is taking Father so long to get up? Mother, we want* *to go downstairs!"* Jacob said in an excited voice. *"He's coming! He sure is taking his time!"* Tiffany shouted out.

Father came out of the bedroom looking disheveled. His hair was out of place, and shooting out in every direction. He looked just as wrinkled as his pajamas. *"Do we have to get up now? How about if the kids waited another hour or two, and we can all get up about nine o'clock?" "Today is Christmas, Honey! They want to see their presents now!" "Daddy! How can you say such a thing? Today is Christmas!"*, Tiffany said almost on the verge of tears. *"Alright, let's all go downstairs and see what we all got!"* Together, they all walked down the creaking stairs of the house. The Christmas tree was still lit, and the lights from it created a fantasy atmosphere in the darkened room. In the distance, around the tree, Jacob and Tiffany could see large wrapped boxes with their names neatly printed on them. Tiffany screamed out in delight saying, *"Look at what Santa brought me for Christmas! Look! I see it! A cooking set!"* Tiffany bolted from the sleepy group and ran towards a large box that had a variety of aluminum cookware and packages of little cake mixes. She tore open the package, and cried out happily, *"Jacob look I can make a real cake now!"* She started separating everything and examined each little cooking utensil as if she was getting ready to cook a full-course Christmas dinner.

Jacob saw a large train set on a silver track that was shaped like the figure eight. After staring at it for a long time, he scurried quickly and began examining all the cars. He found a small black box with a switch connected to the tracks, and when he turned it on, the train rapidly went around the track, whistling and blowing out white puffs of smoke in the air from the engine. There was even a tunnel and a few miniature buildings with tiny people that surrounded the train creating the facsimile of a city. This is just like the window display at the Brandeis store. *"I GOT IT! I REALLY GOT IT! THIS IS FANTASTIC!"*, screamed out Tiffany again in delight. Tiffany saw a large doll that said, *Betsey McCall.* *"I got the Betsey McCall doll and it came with a box of beautiful looking clothes too! Just look how beautiful she looks Mommy!"*, she exclaimed, embracing the doll as she began putting on the different hats and coats on it. Then she noticed a tall dollhouse with a vast collection of miniature furniture that filled each room. She quickly scurried towards it as her face lit up once more, *"Father, Mother! Oh My Gosh! Look! I have the doll house that I wanted! And look at all the furniture that came with it! I have my very own doll house! It's so beautiful!"*

Jacob then saw a package with his name on it that he quickly tore open. It was the ***Buck Rogers Sonic Ray Gun.*** He had been asking for it almost every day. And as he ripped it away from its box, he found a package of batteries that was taped alongside it. He carefully inserted the batteries and then pulled the trigger of the gun. It made a loud buzzing sound that could be heard throughout the house.

The noise from the toy gun irritated Jacob's father as he held his hand against his ears saying, *"I guess we have to hear that thing blasting all day long now!"* *"Honey, it's Christmas! It's alright for the kids to make some noise today! That's what Christmas is all about!"* *"You are right. I need to stop acting like a Scrooge!"* *"Well, I have something for you that you really wanted. It just came out on the market! It is the latest thing!"* Mother dug around the Christmas tree and then pulled out a tiny box with his name on it. She then smiled happily before planting a light kiss on the side of his cheek as she placed it in his hands. *"You really helped Santa last night. You worked so hard helping him put everything together!"* *"You are right. My back is still hurting from bending over and reading all of those instructions!"* Father tore away the wrapping paper and opened the small box. He appeared wide-eyed and motionless for a moment as he held it in his hands. And then examined it, moving his fingers on the small dials, he whispered, *"Isn't this something! Wow, Honey! You knew what I wanted. Everybody is talking about this! What will they think of next? A portable transistor radio! Wow, this is unbelievable! How did you know I wanted one of these?"* *"Well, you know Santa does know everything!"* He found a little battery inside of the box and carefully inserted it. And then he turned the dial as some Christmas songs from ***Johnny Mathis*** started playing. *"Can you believe this? I have a portable music player that I can carry wherever I go. This is amazing! Thank you, Honey! This is the best Christmas present ever! This must have really cost a mint."* *"Not really I have been saving up* *all year to buy this for you!"* He bent down, lifted her up off her feet, and twirled her around laughing and kissing her on the cheeks saying, *"You are the Greatest!"* The room erupted into waves of laughter.

After that, Jacob's Father stooped down under the tree and brought out a variety of beautifully wrapped boxes and presented them all to her. His mother carefully tore away the paper from the boxes. There was an array of earrings, bracelets, house shoes, perfume, and a new bathrobe. And there was a beautiful mahogany jewelry box that could fit everything inside with her name engraved on it. *"This is way too much stuff, Honey! How could you afford to buy all of this?" "You know Santa Claus does not reveal all of his secrets!"* He said laughing and hugging her tightly once more.

Tiffany screamed out again when she saw a small sewing machine with a foot pedal and a collection of sewing patterns. Then Tiffany screamed again after Jacob spoke out, saying, *"Do you have to scream in my ears, Tiffany! You are really getting annoying!"* Jacob pointed the ray gun at her and it erupted into a buzzing noise. *"Jacob, look! I can make my own dresses now! This is going to be so fun!"*

Then Jacob saw another large box with a bow with his name on it. When he tore away the paper, he read the large words printed on the box that said, *"GIANT ERECTOR SET! Now you can build a working electric Ferris Wheel!" "THIS IS GREAT! A REAL ELECTRIC FERRIS WHEEL! DAD, CAN YOU HELP ME PUT THIS TOGETHER TODAY?" "I thought we could work on it together! It will be fun for the both of us!"* Jacob's father laughed a little looking at him pulling out the pieces, along with the large instruction manual that he unfolded and spread out on the floor.

Next, Jacob noticed something silver and shiny on the side of the Christmas tree. There were two bicycles, one for Tiffany, and one for him. Jacob just started looking at it like it was not in the room. It was the same bicycle that was suspended from the ceiling of the Brandeis North Pole display. Jacob stood up and moved unhurriedly towards it and then screamed out, *"BICYCLES! TIFFANY, WE HAVE BRAND NEW BICYCLES! OH, MY GOSH!"* It was an almost surreal experience. Jacob wondered why he did not notice them before now. Maybe he believed, deep down in his heart that his father and mother would not get the bicycle for him. It was something that everyone wanted. But he knew the cost would be too much for them to afford. But here it was, in his front room, all shiny and blue. The beautiful blue bicycle that he wanted. *"TIFFANY LOOK! TIFFANY LOOK! SANTA BROUGHT US SOME BICYCLES!"* Tiffany cried out *"I thought you did not believe in Santa anymore!"*

Jacob timidly approached the blue bicycle. He was almost afraid to touch it. It was the exact same kind that was in the store. It had red and blue streamers that hung down from the handlebars and cool little mirrors on both sides. The tires were trimmed with white walls and there was a neat little storage bin under the seat. Jacob positioned his foot, moved the kickstand upward, and carefully rolled it out from behind the tree. Tiffany ran towards her bicycle as well. It was a lot smaller with two little training wheels on the back. *"Mother, I don't know how to ride a bicycle yet!"* *"That's what the training wheels are for. They will help you keep your balance."* Jacob stared at it for a while, and then jumped on the seat and yelled out, *"YAHOOOOOOOOOOOOO! IT LOOKS JUST LIKE THE ONE AT THE STORE! THIS IS UNBELIEVABLE! I GOT THE BLUE BICYCLE, JUST LIKE ONE AT THE STORE! THANK YOU, DAD AND MOM! YOU GUYS ARE THE GREATEST!"*

Jacob remained seated on the bicycle for a long time, pretending he was in a great race with others, going down a winding hill as he steered the bicycle from one side to the other. Then he cried out saying, *"I WON! I WON! THE FIRST-PLACE TROPHY!"* Tiffany cried out *"Jacob, you are getting too loud!"*, covering her ears. Jacob's father walked back upstairs, still holding the transistor radio in his hands, *"They really came up with some neat new inventions!"* Jacob looked outside, and he called to his Mother, saying, *"Can I ride my bicycle outside? It did not snow last night, and the streets look dry; not too much ice."* *"It is still way too cold out there for you to be riding a bicycle outside Jacob! I am not letting you ride that bicycle outside young man! It is way too cold out there. It will be the death of you!"* *"Please! I will be careful. I will not be out there that long! I just want to break it in. I will bring it right back!"* *"Jacob, it is way too early in the morning to be riding a bicycle around in the cold!"* *"Mom, I am just going to ride it around the neighborhood a few times and bring it right back in the house! You can watch me from the porch if you want!" "I don't like you riding the bicycle by yourself this time of morning. If you promise me, Jacob, that you are not going to be out there no more than ten minutes, then I will let you ride it." "I promise, Mom. I will bring it right back!" "Ok, but you better not hurt yourself, and you better be right back in this house or your father will be hearing about this for sure! And you better not hurt yourself. So, you better be careful!"* Jacob's Mother dressed him as if he was going snow wrestling with the Abominable Snowman! He was wrapped so tightly with three different layers of clothing. He wondered how he could move at all.

It was cold like his mother said. And he could feel it cutting through his clothes when he opened the front door of the house. Jacob was glad that it did not snow again. He loved seeing the snow on Christmas, but it had been such a deluge of snow that he thought it would be alright with him if he never saw another snowflake again for the rest of his life. The wind was slightly blowing as the streamers of the blue bicycle started to fly upward. There was no one outside of their homes. So, he quickly started pedaling in front of his house, doing magnificent figure eights in the middle of the deserted street. Jacob's mother watched him. She slightly cracked the door open to make sure he was safe.

It was cold outside. *"Mother was right."*, Jacob said to himself as he pedaled in subliminal, silent joy. Since he was now grateful for the way she had dressed him as the cold wind whipped around him. Jacob noticed that there were still some slippery patches of ice frozen on the street that he avoided with caution. Jacob thought to himself, saying *"It would be such a terrible accident for me to slide the bicycle on a patch of ice and then come into the house with a scraped and bleeding knee. She would never let me outside of the house by myself again; not in a million years!"*

His mother kept a watchful eye on him as he pedaled, watching the streamers flying in the air in front of him. The light of the sun was moving over the housetops, causing the streets to take on a glowing brilliance that could only be experienced if you were up early enough to witness it. He went around the block a few times before coming back, cycling effortlessly into his marvelous pattern of figure eights. Then he heard his mother's voice calling out to him. Her voice sounded as if it filled the air around him, *"Jacob you only got a few more minutes to stay out there, then you come into this house!" "Yes, Mama! I will! Just a few more rides!"*

The beautiful blue bicycle was the dream machine; the main item that every kid wanted for Christmas that year. Jacob knew that he was lucky enough to have one of his own. As he started riding around on the noiseless street, he could see a vision of Tommy waking up on Christmas morning with nothing more than a paper picture of the blue bicycle taped on the wall of his dingy and drab shack. While riding his blue bicycle, Jacob continued to see Tommy's sad face, shivering underneath his little blanket. Somehow, Jacob knew that Tommy never had a real Christmas. And then he remembered how Tommy looked when all the kids returned to school after Christmas, talking excitedly about all the presents they received. Jacob could see Tommy moving sadly and quietly among them, not saying anything, but he knew how deeply inside Tommy was hurting.

Jacob continued to ride his bicycle around in slow figure eights, thinking about what to do when he heard his mother's voice piercing his compendium of thoughts about Tommy. *"Jacob! You bring that bicycle back into this house right now! It is too cold for you to be out there! You need to come back into this house right now!" "Yes, Mama, I will be in the house in just a minute! I just need a little more time!" "Didn't I tell you to bring the bicycle into this house right now? And don't you give me no back talk!" "I will be there in just a few more minutes!" "I am not asking you, Jacob! I am telling you! You bring that bicycle into this house right now!"*

Jacob's mother had stepped outside of the house and was standing in her bathrobe, now demanding him to come in. Jacob knew that she now meant business by the sound of her voice. He had pushed her as far as he could. And then Jacob looked at his mother and said, *"Mama, there is something I have to do! I will be back!" "Jacob, you bring the bicycle into this house right now young man! Do you hear me?" "I will be back Mama, there is something I have to do now!"*

Jacob took off like a flash! Speeding down the empty street as if the bicycle was being propelled by angels, maybe Christmas angels! The bicycle trekked through the neighborhood, gliding, and wheeling forward as the pedals twirled with an otherworldly speed. He held on, hoping that he would not fall off. He could see the brief glimpses of Christmas celebrations in the front room windows of the houses of the neighborhoods that he wheeled by. He peeked in their windows as the bicycle sailed by. There were numerous people standing in front of their Christmas trees, opening presents, like he had done, all with smiling faces.

Jacob approached the Basin as a large freight train was approaching the only entrance into where Tommy lived. The train was enormous, so he knew that it might be more than an hour before all the cars of the train passed by the small entrance. Therefore, Jacob saw that he only had one option to be in front of Tommy's house for Christmas, and he was not turning back now.

Jacob started turning the pedals of the bicycle as fast as he could to try to beat the train that was approaching the entrance of the Basin. Jacob was moving with so much speed and force that he thought for a moment the chain and the pedals of the bicycle had turned into a bright gold hue, and there appeared to be glimmering sparks flying off them. That's impossible; Jacob reasoned within himself. It had to be the sunlight of the morning reflecting off the chain, and the spinning pedals moving in such an erratic state. Christmas morning would be over soon and Jacob was now determined to be in front of Tommy's house before it was over.

The train engineer saw Jacob moving closer towards the open road that led to the Basin. The guardrail was slowly coming down as Jacob approached the barren road. The train's engineer started blowing his horn in a furious sound when he saw Jacob approaching the track, trying to ride across the closed entrance. It was no turning back now. As Jacob pressed forward, the train's horn was blowing so loudly that it caused him to become deaf to everything around him. Jacob pedaled with supernatural speed. The bicycle pedals turned into a blur as he crossed the tracks. But it still was not enough. The train hit him and the bicycle exploded into pieces. Jacob was left crushed by the force of the train. His tiny body was almost beyond recognition when the ambulance and the medical workers found him lying face down, smashed into a ditch on the side of the road.

And now you must take The Test.
1. *What is the lesson that Hector will learn from the death of Jacob?*
2. *If given the chance, would you stop Jacob from going on such a dangerous ride?*
3. *Do you think love is so important that your life is the requirement for its survival?*
4. *Can you think of a time when you believed that love was so important that you would give your life so that someone else could live?*
5. *Did you help anyone in need last Christmas?*
6. *Do you know a child that is poor and wants a bicycle for Christmas? Do you know a poor child who is having a birthday soon and their parents cannot afford to give them a present? And what did you do to help? What did you do last year when someone needed your help at Christmas?*
9. *Have the circumstances and events in life put you in a situation with a person you never met before of a different race and culture, and you found yourself being with them, and sharing a life bonding sacred experience? How did this experience change your view of other people not like yourself? Have you ever eaten at someone else's house for dinner? Or have you prayed with someone of a different race or culture? And how did that experience change you?*

OUR OBSERVATIONS

For when the true awakening occurs, it instantly unites all humanity having the commonality to accept this sacred invitation. This invitation transcends all colors and cultures for it will only ask for you to believe that the survival of humanity is our ability to connect with the divine in each of us.

For if you crush the flower the seed will remember the blossoming.

For the flower, will give up the essence of its nature in the pollen, and a bee will make something sweet and wonderful in the honey that will last for a thousand years. For even a tree records the rings of its living. For each moment is a sacred experience for love is not forgotten.

For this body of dust and perishable fragment cannot compass the infinite power of the soul. For this existence is not contained only in your flesh. For there is a vast God inside of you that personally touches and holds the DNA of your molecules together with His grace. For your physical body may be wrapped in the grave clothes of the earth and death may appear to be so completely final. But by the power of the infinite touch of a living Christ, your grave clothes, like the grave clothes of Lazarus, shall be ripped away for the love of God in you is perpetual and everlasting. It cannot be destroyed.

For there is a place where death can no longer terrorize you. It is a place where people are left in the plains of the Sudan without anything. But they can still find comfort by holding their hands in the wind and hearing the heartbeat of God. It is a place where refugees are trapped in the middle of the ocean, not knowing if their small boat is going to capsize. But they hold on to the belief that if they live or if they die, there is a loving God that will walk on the water, and embrace them with His love.

For the true story of Christmas, and the true story of love can only be completed by an act of love. So, in a moment of supreme love, an angel was dispatched to Jacob. In a blinding flash of speed and light as the bicycle moved in front of the train, and unknowingly to Jacob, Raphael was there and swept the bicycle upward into the air in a powerful gust of the wind with the descending force of his wings. He hurled the bicycle forward as the train heaved, moving in a sturdy stride, missing Jacob by inches.

The bicycle rolled into a ditch. Jacob remained face down. His tiny body appeared lifeless, still, dead, and unrecognizable. Yet, even though the laws of time and space, death and physics that are so precise and irrevocable, they too can be altered, reconstructed, and changed when touched by the compassionate power of a loving and merciful God.

Jacob moved his tiny body. In an instant, life returned to him. He breathed and moaned when he looked at the hole in his pants leg and the skin that was pulled off his knee. Jacob looked for the bicycle, hoping that it was not damaged. When he saw the bicycle, a sense of relief fell upon him. The bicycle appeared just as new. But he had a large gaping hole in his pants leg, and there was blood trickling down through an open hole. *"I am in big trouble now! Mama is going to get me for this! And wait until she tells dad! I am in big trouble for sure! At least the bicycle is not destroyed! That train was moving awful fast! I could have gotten killed. But the bicycle is not broken! No pieces have fallen off. Thank God!"* Jacob wiped the wet dirt and icy snow off his pants and jacket. He painstakingly walked the bicycle from out of the ditch, hopped back on, and looked at the train in the distance. The way the engineer was still blowing his horn, Jacob could sense his anger. *"Boy, that was a close call! But I am glad I am alright! Just a few more inches and that train could have killed me!"*

Jacob continued riding his bicycle along the ragged streets of the Basin. He traveled through a row of shacks. Everything was silent and still as the sun now appeared to ascend a little above the tops of the trees. It was almost morning. He had made it to Tommy's house before morning. Jacob hopped off the bicycle and crept up the rickety porch. He leaned the bicycle on the side of the front wall of the house. His hands were cold as he pounded on the boards that were placed in front of the entrance of the door. Jacob could not hear anyone moving inside. He found a large broken board on the porch and started beating on the door. When he did that, he heard a weak voice that sounded like Tommy, saying, *"Who is out there? Who is there? What do you want?"* Then Jacob heard what sounded like Tommy's mother calling out to him. *"Tommy, will you go out there and see who is at the door?" "Who would be coming over at this time of the morning Mama?" "I don't know, but you be careful! And remember where you placed those boards. I don't want too much cold wind coming through the house." "Yes, Mama! I will be careful!" "Who is out there? What do you want?"* Jacob moved back and ran like a wild cat into a deep row of bushes. There, he laid down quietly so that he could see what was going to happen next.

It was cold. Jacob was hiding behind a snow bank as he watched Tommy coming outside. He saw Tommy looking at the bicycle, and then he saw him jumping up and down like he could not believe what he was seeing. He heard Tommy crying out, *"I WAS NOT FORGOTTEN THIS YEAR! LOOK! I HAVE A BRAND-NEW BICYCLE! JUST LIKE THE ONE AT THE STORE! MAMA COME OUT HERE! I HAVE A BRAND-NEW BICYCLE! I WAS NOT FORGOTTEN THIS YEAR!"*

Jacob had never heard Tommy cry out like that in his entire life. He watched Tommy running back into the shack, and then coming back outside, wearing the coat that Jacob had given him. Tommy jumped on the bicycle and started speeding down the street, smiling, laughing, riding, and then gliding, creating joyful figure eights.

Jacob was almost frostbitten when he arrived home an hour later. His hands were like ice. His knee was hurting so bad. He thought it was swollen as he walked with a slight limp. Jacob knew he was in big trouble. He could feel his father and mother's wrath surrounding him. He knew a severe punishment was coming to him. He had returned an hour later and had given away his beautiful blue Christmas bicycle. It had been a long time since his father had given him a whipping. The last time, he remembered, was when he stole some candy from the nickel and dime store with some of his friends from school. He was in the third grade back then. But now, he was in the sixth grade and did not know what punishment he would receive for this.

When he arrived home, his mother was still at the door waiting for him. His father had left the house looking for him. His mother saw his bleeding knee and saw that his bicycle was gone. Jacob began explaining to his mother that he had given away the bicycle to Tommy because he was poor and never received anything good for Christmas. He added that all Tommy had was a taped-up picture of the bicycle that he wanted on the wall in the front room of his house next to his Christmas tree. Jacob started sobbing as he tried to explain to her what he had done. He was sad because Tommy had nothing for Christmas. His mother held his head against her shoulder, and then whispered to him as she kissed his cheeks saying, *"I knew that you were going to help Tommy! I am so proud of you! We all are so proud of you!"* Jacob whispered back to her with a face drenched in tears, *"Mama this is the best Christmas ever!"*

Later that afternoon, a large group of people drove to Tommy's shack. All the children inside of the shack looked outside through the cracks of the boards, frightened, wondering what was taking place. It was Jacob's mother who made the first phone call to one of the neighbors sharing how a little boy and his family had nothing to eat on Christmas day. She also told them that the shack that they were living in was cold without any presents or food. And in a moment of divine connection, they all saw Tommy hungry and holding his little brothers and sisters shivering under a dingy thin blanket.

A group of cars started arriving. People got out of their cars, smiling, carrying boxes that were placed near the front of Tommy's boarded door. Inside of the boxes was an assortment of delicious holiday treats. Tommy's mother looked inside of the boxes and started crying as they contained fully cooked turkeys, roasted chickens, pans of sweet potato dishes, mashed potatoes, and cornbread dressing with cranberry sauce. Additionally, there were desserts from every palate, from chocolate cakes, pound cakes, lemon meringue pies, apple pies, and oatmeal cookies and sugar cookies in the shapes of tiny angels and Christmas trees. The food items were all taken directly from their own Christmas dinner tables to help the little boy and his family who they all knew was hungry and cold.

The boxes were placed on the porch of the shack. Tommy looked inside and cried out, *"Mama, we got food to eat! We got real food to eat!"* And still, other people arrived surrounding the tiny, boarded shack with their vehicles, carrying blankets, hats, gloves, new shoes, coats and scarves for each one of the children. One woman had a beautiful red warm wool coat that she was carrying and placed it in Tommy's mother's arms. *"I have so many coats and I think this one just might fit you!"*, she said as she wiped away a tear while embracing her.

Then a group of men arrived in a truck singing Christmas songs, carrying tools and large pieces of wooden boards. They quickly began working on the shack. With their hammers and nails, they pounded and measured into place, the pieces of new wood until a new door was created. They worked, building a new porch and insulated every crack that they could find so that the wind could no longer be felt sweeping inside. Next, they unloaded stacks of cut wood and placed them in the back of the shack for the potbelly stove. Tommy knew that it was enough wood to last through the winter, and the next winter as well.

Yet, and still more people arrived with their children, all of them carrying decorated Christmas gifts. Each of the children gave up one of their most valued, precious toys to give to Tommy and his sisters and brothers. It was the most unbelievable spontaneous phenomenon that ever occurred in the city before. It was later, during that day, Jacob came over, and they both started riding the blue bicycle, happily, and not even feeling the cold around them. Tommy held onto Jacob from the little back seat as they sung Christmas songs, and rode down the street together.

Then Hector saw a rapid life progression of Jacob's life. He saw Jacob's life as he grew into adulthood. The experience of the blue bicycle transformed his belief as he continued to make small, yet powerful differences in the lives of the people around him. For Jacob understood that the act of love was not measured by the applause of those around you, but by the power to move forward, even when no one was around, even when it was difficult to move forward, even when it stretches your faith and sacrifices your comfort. He watched as Jacob went to college, and received a law degree because Jacob wanted to help those that had no representation, giving them the right to maintain their dignity and to live and preserve their human rights.

After college, Jacob joined a group of dedicated students building homes in a village in Nigeria. He also helped the villagers dig wells that were desperately in need of clean drinking water. And this is where he met his wife, MaryAnn, who also had just graduated from college with a law degree. They soon married and opened a law office that was dedicated to helping the poor and those who could not afford legal representation. Shortly after having children, they started a pantry to help the homeless and starving families that were struggling in their community. And every year, Jacob would make sure that he would buy blue bicycles for all the poor families with children that wanted a bicycle for Christmas.

Next, Hector watched Jacob celebrating his fiftieth birthday with his wife, children, and grandchildren. It had been a most wonderful and pleasant day with all his children and their families, including all the people he had ever helped. All of them convened at his house to help celebrate his special day. They all came over to watch Jacob blow out the candles on a cake that had so many candles that Jacob thought he would never be able to blow them all out. It was the most fantastic day of his life! People from all over the community came to his birthday party.

Later during the afternoon, after everyone had left, Jacob decided to take a walk to the park. He just wanted to be alone. He wanted to talk to God. He had not told his wife, but during his last physical examination, the doctor found an inoperable tumor in his brain. Subsequently, he received a dreadful report. He was told that he only had a few weeks to live. But he knew before he died and left the earth, there was still something that he had to do. But he did not know what.

As Jacob crossed Decatur and 84th Street, a small boy riding a blue bicycle appeared and said, *"Hey Mister do you want a ride!"* *"What?"* *"I SAID, DO YOU WANT A RIDE?"* *"WHAT ARE YOU TALKING ABOUT KID? GET OUT OF THE STREET!"* *"YOU ARE GOING TO NEED A RIDE MISTER! HOP ON!"* Jacob knew that the boy should not have been in the middle of the street with so much traffic going through the intersection. Jacob pleaded with the boy to get out of the middle of the street saying, *"PLEASE, KID! GET OUT OF THE STREET! IT IS TOO DANGEROUS FOR YOU TO BE RIDING A BICYCLE OUT HERE! PLEASE, KID, GET OUT OF THE STREET!"*

Jacob did not see the orange Mustang that ran a red light and then went spinning out of control after being hit on the passenger side by a large truck. The force of the truck hitting the Mustang pushed the car forward on its side. When Jacob crossed the street, he was immediately hit, forced backward, slammed against a wall, and crushed by the impact. In a matter of minutes, Jacob was dead. Then Hector realized that the person who was driving the Mustang was himself. If there was a way to cry inside of a spirit body, Hector was now crying as tears flowed out of his eyes. *"HOW COULD THIS HAPPEN? I KILLED JACOB! I KILLED HIM! I KILLED HIM! I*

WAS DRIVING RECKLESSLY! I WAS ONLY THINKING ABOUT MYSELF! I WAS SO UPSET! I WAS NOT LOOKING WHEN I RAN THROUGH THE RED LIGHT! I WAS IN MY SELFISH WORLD ONCE AGAIN! AND I KILLED JACOB! I KILLED JACOB! OH GOD! PLEASE FORGIVE ME!" Hector screamed out as he continued to watch the events unfold before him.

Hector now spoke in a whisper. It was as if he had become like the wind without a living body. He no longer wanted to live. He wanted to disappear. He was ashamed of his life, and how stupidly he had lived. As he looked at the terrible accident, he spoke saying, *"Oh God! What have I done? I have been so terrible! I hated people! I hated people who were good, and people who helped others! I killed Jacob! I killed Jacob, a good man. I crushed him with my Mustang in one terrible act of rage! I should have slowed down! I should have listened to you, God! I should have listened. I took Jacob's life away!"*

Hector now realized why he was placed inside the consciousness of Jacob. God wanted him to see what he had done. For he needed to understand how everything in life is divinely connected to everything else, nothing exists apart from itself. For all the elements in the universe exist within our very breath. He had to see how stupid it was to hate people and assume things about others as if their lives were not important as if their lives did not matter.

And more importantly, Hector understood how he was divinely connected with all humanity in every experience of his life. Hector felt himself being released from out of the body of Jacob. He watched as he saw a translucent form of himself, stepping out from Jacob's body. And then, in a slow-moving procession of ethereal animation, he watched skin materialize on his body as he transformed into a human being once again. The flesh and tissues all emerged and came together, creating a marvelous uniqueness. Hector and Jacob were able to look at each other face to face. They stood quietly at first, just looking at each other for a few moments, and then Hector came forward, extended his hands and then embraced him saying, *"Please forgive me for taking your life. I did not know. I did not know that I killed someone during the accident. I thought that I was the only one that was hurt. I took everything away from you. I took away your family, your children, only because I did not want to accept other people that were different than me!"*

Jacob held him, kissed him on the cheek and said, *"You were forgiven when I felt your tears coming out of my eyes. I only have one favor to ask of you. When you return to the earth, please tell my wife and my children that I love them so very much and that we will all be together again one day soon. Let them know that I will be waiting for their coming with open arms!" "I will!"* Hector exclaimed. *"I will keep your promise! I will let them know!"* He continued as tears sparkled in his eyes, and flowed down his face like drops of light. *"Also, it has been passed on to you!"* Jacob said. *"What has been passed on to me? What has been passed on?"* Hector asked in a trembling voice. *"The blue bicycle. It is now your responsibility to deliver it to whomever God will tell you. In time, you will be sent to give it to someone that needs your help."*

Hector continued to hold on to Jacob, crying when he realized that Jacob was changing. The composition of his body, his skin, his very being was shifting and transforming as he tried to hold him tightly. And then in a burst of spectacular colors, Jacob changed into a dense cloud of Monarch butterflies that flew apart from out of Hector's embrace and scattered ascending into the sky and then disappeared.

Hector looked around. He was alone again. The darkness of the beautiful world around him shimmered. Hector walked farther towards the endless lake and the splattering of stars upon the horizon when he saw the large gigantic figure of Michaela, beckoning him to come forward. Her skin, body, hair, and wings were flowing with waves of light into the darkness. Hector believed that Michaela represented the glory of the wonderful world that she had descended from.

As Hector looked around, there were others with him, hundreds of people, all standing by the shore in the darkness at the lake. All of them were assembled by the edge of the shore. Each of them had blue bicycles as if they were ready to ride them. Hector saw the little round head kid holding his bicycle. The round head kid appeared to be waiting for Hector when he said, *"I am sorry for taking away your bicycle that day, but you would have died! You would have been hit by a truck as soon as you left the park. I am the Archangel Raphael.*

I was sent to help you." Hector looked at the kid and smiled. The small round head kid spoke again saying, *"I have returned what you lost. And you have found what you needed; your love for God."*

Hector looked at the bicycle. It appeared to be brand new once again. The angel boy then said, *"Always remember that which is given in love is never truly taken away. God can make all things new again!"* Hector started weeping as he held the small boy in his arms. The angel boy continued, saying, *"I was waiting a long time until you were ready to ride it again!"*

Michaela then spoke to all of them smiling, saying, "*You have all passed one of the courses of the University of the Second Life. What a wonderful experience God has given each one of you. The next part of The Test is for you to go back to earth, and deliver the bicycle you have received to someone in desperate need. You did remember that I did tell you that you would have to walk across the water to complete your first semester here. Didn't I? Well, I should have told you that it is a little more difficult than that. You have to ride your bicycle across the water of the lake to return to the earth!"* She said smiling. *"Now you must all go for there is someone on the earth that needs a ride on your bicycle!"*

As they moved their bicycles towards the edge of the black waters of the lake, a canopy of stars appeared around them, shimmering off the solitary waters. Jacob could see what appeared to be the earth, rotating in a slow blue crystal of clouds. Each one of them moved their bicycles cautiously towards the edge of the darkened waters. In a flurry of joy, and fear, they began pedaling their bicycles with tremendous speed over the waters, and surprisingly, they found themselves gliding across, not sinking down into the dark waters below.

Now it was Hector's turn to go and ride his bicycle across the waters. How are the wheels going to stay up? It's impossible! He thought. But he knew that the impossible could be achieved here with enough faith. Hector took a deep breath, pushed off onto the shore and started pedaling, fearing that he might go down into the dark waters at any moment. Yet the bicycle started moving as if it was suspended in air, bouncing across the water. Hector was pedaling as fast as he could. He could feel the water splashing under his feet while he kept looking at the earth in the distance. Something within him spoke to his spirit that if he had stopped, he would swiftly go down into the depths of the waters, and never reach the earth. Now, this was a test of his determination, and his ability to keep going forward, no matter what ominous circumstance threatened him. For with the fear of uncertainty behind him, he pedaled forward with all his might, believing that he would not sink if he continued to trust in God. Hector knew that this was the only way for him to return to the earth; a most unlikely form of transportation, he thought. Why didn't God just zap him back to the earth? That would have been so fast, and most convenient. But he had to return in a total act of faith, not knowing what to do, but pedal his bicycle over the darkness below.

When Hector looked around, there was a caravan of other riders with him, marveling at the gliding speed that they were traveling in. They were all riding upon the waves as the stars glistened in the heavens above. And in one humorous moment, while they were all pedaling together, they spontaneously began laughing. It was like they were in the final moments of a graduation; during the last part of a great commencement exercise for together, they had successfully completed this class. They all pedaled towards the earth. It was truly a graduation as they all laughed together.

As they continued riding together, someone called to Hector saying, *"WHERE ARE YOU FROM?"* Hector shouted back, *"I AM FROM OMAHA!"* *"OMAHA? WHERE IS OMAHA? WHAT DO THEY HAVE THERE, COWS AND CHICKENS?!"* He said laughing. *"I AM FROM NEW YORK CITY!"* He shouted to Hector. Hector shouted back, *"THAT IS A BIG PLACE! WHO IS GOING TO BELIEVE WHAT HAPPENED TO US? NO ONE WILL EVER BELIEVE US!"* *"I KNOW! BUT IT'S ALRIGHT! BECAUSE WE ALL HAVE SOMETHING TO DO WHEN WE GET BACK HOME!"* Then immediately, all the bicycle riders felt their handlebars turning by themselves, moving upward into the air. Hector cried out, *"WHOAAAAAAAA! THE BICYCLE IS STEERING ITSELF!"* Another one of the riders called out to Hector, *"YOU BETTER HANG ON!"* The group of riders went upward through the air, turning and twisting as if navigating the cosmic wind flowing around them. Hector looked down below. He could see the mountains encrusted with light and the glowing figure of Michaela. Her large wings had transformed again into a shimmering cloud of mist that moved upon the darkened waters. *"I SEE IT! WE ARE GETTING CLOSER! I SEE THE EARTH!"* Hector called out. *"WE ARE GETTING CLOSER. THIS IS REALLY SCARY!" "YOU BETTER HANG ON IF YOU DON'T WANT TO GO BACK!"* Someone called out to Hector as he held on tightly to the shaking bicycle handlebars. Hector gripped the bicycle handlebars tighter, looking in amazement at the beautiful blue glow of the earth below. Then suddenly, all the riders began to move through a sun-filled maze of clouds and light streaming around them. Hector knew they were getting closer towards the earth. It felt good, once again to feel the sunlight on his skin. He started laughing when he extended his hands and touched the white clouds as he passed through them. For a moment, he almost lost his balance and fell off the bicycle, so he tightened his grip on the handlebars.

Hector suddenly felt air being forced into his lungs. He took a deep breath and he felt a stinging, deep pain in his chest. He saw himself inside of his Mustang, and he thought he heard someone calling out, *"Hey, he is still alive inside of here! Somebody call the fire department! He is trapped inside! They need something to pry him out!"*

Hector found himself covered with pieces of glass. He looked down, and a large piece of glass was embedded in his chest. He knew that he was dying. He could feel his breath and his spirit clinging to his body. His mind was in a haze. Everything had happened so fast. He saw everything in a blur of moving images of himself. He remembered riding the blue bicycle in the air, discovering an isolated planet, meeting a beautiful angel, and seeing the life experiences of a man named Jacob. It all appeared to be so surreal. Everything had happened to him in a flash of a moment. He wanted to get out of the car, but the steel and glass were cutting into him from every side. Then firemen arrived, surrounding the car, and completely cutting the door in half. He was placed on a stretcher, put into an ambulance, and raced towards the nearest hospital of the city. As the ambulance hurried down the street with its siren blaring, Hector started laughing which amazed the paramedics. He was remembering how much fun he had riding the blue bicycle.

It was a day later, they said when he had awakened. He was groggy and was in a daze when he looked around the room and felt the soft fingertips of a nurse stroking his forehead. *"We almost lost you! It is truly a miracle that you are still alive!"* Hector touched his chest because it was hurting, making it hard for him to breathe. Then he saw the clear tubes that were protruding from out of his chest, connected to some sort of machine that appeared to be monitoring his vital signs. Hector ached all over. His body was sore, and his chest hurt so bad that he thought there were still pieces of glass from the windshield of his car still embedded within him.

The nurse dashed off into a hallway nearby and called out the name of a doctor. Hector heard footsteps drawing closer towards his room, and the voice of the nurse saying, *"Doctor Reynolds we need you right away! Mr. Winslow has awakened!"* A tall older man with a head sprinkled with graying hair approached him. His bifocals balanced on his nose as he held a chart in his hand. He carefully touched and examined the clear tubes protruding out of Hector's chest. Hector felt a surge of pain flow through him. The doctor peeked at him from over his bifocals and said, *"Hello, I am so glad you made it this far. I am Doctor Reynolds. I was your surgeon. It is a miracle that you are still here, Mr. Winslow. You were involved in a very serious accident. A pedestrian was killed while walking across the street. An intoxicated truck driver hit you from the passenger side, and your vehicle slid through a red light pinning you against a wall, striking the pedestrian. Because the truck driver had been drinking and was intoxicated, he was taken into custody. Your heart, however, was damaged beyond repair when a long shard of glass pierced it and severed it completely. We had to quickly give you a heart transplant. There was no other way for you to survive. The family of the man who died in the accident, whose heart that you have now is here, outside of your room, and they would like to meet you."* Hector nodded his head in agreement. As a tear dropped from his eye, he softly said, *"Yes! I would like that too."* A few minutes later, a middle-aged woman with dark brown skin, along with her two adult children, came quietly into his room, smiling, and then said, *"My name is MaryAnn. My husband's name was Jacob. He would have been happy to know that you are alive because you were given his heart."*

Are you ready to take The Test?

Shall we play some more of the Jeopardy game show music for you again?
We hope that this will relax you.
Ok let us change up the music this time while you are taking The Test. What about if we played something soft and relaxing that will calm you down? Your nerves are going berserk right now! Take some deep breaths. Everything is going to be alright. We promise you. What about if we played a Sam Cook song for you? What about if we played that song entitled "You send me!" Do you remember the first time you saw your sweetheart, and how on that day, your life changed forever? Now that was something! We only gave you the best. You are starting to calm down now. You know life can be a beautiful experience, if you would just listen to us sometimes, and stop being so headstrong, and convinced that everything is going to fail, and not work out. There is so much beauty, and yes even fun that you have not experienced in your life yet.

~Now let's take The Test! ~

1. *Can you think of a time when you had no control of the situations and the events in your life? And all that you could do was to hold on to the handlebars of your bicycle like Hector did with your feet dangling in the air. And you knew that you had to trust God to bring you through the most painful situation you had ever experienced.*
2. *Are you living an empty life right now? What are the things in your life that give you true meaning? Can you create a list of the things that give you meaning and purpose in your life? And tell us why are you living without doing these things?*
3. *What do you think Hector will do now with the rest of his life?*

4. *How will Hector now think of people from a different color or culture?*

OUR OBSERVATIONS

What can you do to overcome the daily emptiness and the dissatisfaction you have with life?

It is this inward battle you must overcome. It is the emptiness that overtakes you when you believe that your life is not important. And you have assigned yourself to the classroom of fear and disbelief. But you should know that the power of your living affects everything!

Have we not spoken to you every day of your life? Our inward voice has attempted to reach you many times on how to design and create a blueprint for the daily struggle for successful living. But you have cursed us, and pulled the blankets of "I don't care!" over your head. For we have attempted to wake you before, many times. We did not want to take this drastic action. But in too many of your dreams, you have slain in daylight because of the fear of doing something unknown and the fear that you might fail. You have cursed and blamed everyone around for your inability to move with determination and act.

Your purpose and the powerful instructions on how to guide your life have always been with you. It speaks to you when you awake in the morning, and it is there when you wrap your blankets around yourself and fall asleep at night. It is there to comfort you and to calm you and give you direction. If you would only listen to your inner voice, we will be there to direct you into all divine truth, into a peaceful awakening.

For truly there is nothing causing you not to wake up. But the lies that you have isolated your life with have caused you to believe that you are not worthy to live. For you were worthy when we dreamed you into existence, knowing your mistakes and failing, knowing that your power to love would be the most awe-inspiring force upon the earth. For in truth, we cannot wake you up. Only you have this ability to look at the world through our eyes. For only you can make this powerful decision to ignore the miracles and the opportunities that we have presented to you. Or you can continue to go through the routine that the world does not need your gifts to survive. And why should you do anything to help? But this gift was never yours to waste. We brought you into this world to magnify light in places that have caused many to stumble in a self-created void. It is your time, and your challenge to do something different to be a better version of yourself. We have given you dominion, not to sit in your room, afraid of the new day. We have given you the power to shake the earth wherever you walk, creating destiny.

For the vision that we have given you terrified you so that when you awakened, you did not want to believe that your life could be better. And it was better not to get involved, you believed. For it was better, you said to let others work in the homeless shelter. It was better for others to counsel drug addicts. It was better for someone else to mentor children with absent parents. And if you could just come home from work, get paid, put your feet up on the sofa, fall asleep, and watch another game, you could justify your life by saying that it is not your responsibility to get involved. Everything would be hunky dory in your world, if you could just be left alone with the television remote in your hand, just changing the channels as you willfully desire. Then everything would truly be wonderful in your life. But you do not know that you died this morning. When you did not show up for work, and when your neighbors had not seen you for days, was when everyone began to worry. The paramedics arrived and broke down your door. They found you sprawled out on the bed with your eyes staring wide-open in a state of disbelief, wanting to come back to the earth and try it all over again. But it was too late. And yes, we heard you pleading asking to come back to the earth again so that you could make another attempt to try it again, but this time with a new heart. Your name appeared, like so many thousands before you in the obituary section of the newspaper. We can show it to you if you like? It will be over soon if you don't wake up! If you don't act now, and if you don't love, you will continue, like so many to sleep in The Void.

This is the reason we have contacted you. It is of the utmost importance that you finish taking The Test.

~The Challenge Assignment for the upcoming weeks~

And you, like Hector, must now view all things differently. You are starting to have a new awareness that somehow the world is more than a place for you to eat, sleep, and work. It is an opportunity and a gift given to love. We will send someone to you this week, and you will go to their home and share a dinner with them. There is something profoundly sacred about sharing bread together. Someone you have never met before of a different skin color, culture, and community. We want you to experience the commonality that you have with others that you didn't know. We want you to laugh with them, talk, eat, and pray with them, for all things are possible for them that believe. When that experience is over, we want you to take some quiet time with us. We will reveal and teach you all the wonderful things that you have learned. And we will speak to you about all the broken things you are now healed from through that experience.

~The Angel with One Wing~

~Traveling on the road to destruction~

Zach stood on the dusty highway on a road somewhere between the border of Texas and Mexico waiting as the wind blew powdery dirt into his mouth. He started spitting it out along with the bitter taste of tobacco. He knew something was wrong, something terrible had gone wrong because he was tasting the wad of tobacco that he had put inside of his mouth. It was strong and bitter and he could hardly keep it inside of his mouth before he spat it out. Frowning in disgust, he said, *"So this is what tobacco actually taste like? How can they stand it? And this is supposed to be something enjoyable!"*

Perhaps they did not know he had the power of taste. This had never happened before, not in all his one thousand one hundred and four assignments. He could not tell, though, if he was tasting tobacco or dirt because he never tasted either one before. He picked up a handful of dirt and put some in his mouth, and said, *"This is even worse!"* As he quickly spat it out. He rubbed his hand across the rough whiskers that had grown on the sides of his face. It was like touching a hard piece of sandpaper, and it felt as if the tips of his fingers would be pricked. *"This stuff is hard and prickly! Why would anybody grow this on their face?"* He said feeling his newfound facial hair growth.

Zach had been waiting on the road now for a long time. He was waiting for someone to come along on the road. The note card he received said someone would be coming soon. He looked up and down the dusty road. There was a beat-up gas station that had not pumped any gas since the 1930's. *"What a miserable place."* He said to himself as he looked down the dirt road while the wind was blowing, and creating a twirling mini-storm before him. He saw tumbleweed blowing near him, hopping along the desolate landscape. In the distance, flat plains with reddish colored boulders that jettisoned out of the soil and appeared as forgotten temples from a prehistoric time. There was an assortment of cactus that covered the ground. Tall, hulky ones that had arms with long sharp needles, threatening the very atmosphere to come near them. There was also little fat cactus that barely came out of the ground that could easily pierce through a shoe or a boot and leave a nasty stinging scar. *"This is a good place, if you are an outlaw or a bandit or if you are just trying to hide from something or someone."* He said, wiping his lips from the dust that constantly powdered them. *"What a terrible and miserable place for someone of my status to be reduced to, a farmhand. I wonder how long I have to wait on this road before this loser comes to pick me up!"* Zach murmured as he took his cowboy hat off, which had a broken front ridge and was stained from months of sweat. He took off the hat and beat out the dust on his faded jeans. Then he folded some creases into his hat before tilting it sideways on his head. *"Somebody really screwed up royally this time!"* He said as a small grin appeared on the side of his cracked lips. *"I can actually feel stuff! That has never happened before!"*

Zach wanted to run around like a lunatic touching, smelling, and tasting everything in his sight. But he knew that would cause too much suspicion. And he knew, above all else, that he had to remain in character. On the ground, near his shoe, there was a tiny, fat, stubby cactus growing between two rocks. On top of it, there was a small opal colored flower that had opened with amazing beauty. He reached down to pluck it off and smell its aroma against his nose. But when he did, one of its long, dagger needles broke off, and pierced the tip of his index finger, causing an inkling of blood to shoot out of it. He jerked back, holding his finger, he dislodged the needle from the tip of his finger. *"God that was painful! That shot all the way through my body!"* He examined the blood on his finger, and then wiped it off on his pants leg. *"Pain and beauty all mixed together. I see why they get so caught up in things that can destroy them."* Zach said as he looked at the flower in admiration and caution. *"I am still adjusting and discovering new things. Even the little things are still new to me."*

Yet as Zach stood in this tremendous world of feelings, it all still felt like a test ride to him. There was no way he should have been there, after standing against the malicious attack from the terrorists in a small town in eastern Europe. Terrorists had assembled a bunch of school kids together, preparing to mow them all down with their machines guns in one horrifying, gruesome moment. But he used his lightning speed, and his impenetrable wings to stretch out, and prevent the bullets from touching them. To the human eye, the bullets appeared to be bouncing off them. When one of the terrorists saw this frightening sight, he declared that the village was cursed, and was too frightened to ever return.

Analyzing the beat-up clothes that he wore, and the dust that covered them, he said in disgust, *"Why would they do something like this to me! They had the gall to let me stay down here powerless! And look at this; I am sweating!"* He lamented as he wiped off some streaming drops of sweat that had rolled down his face. *"And now, I am supposed to remain down here as a dusty, powerless, weakling. What a disgrace that they would do something like this to me. After I stood before that Ebola Virus Creature, I unfolded my wings until a curtain of fire prevented the creature from destroying any more people in that village in the Congo. I stood there, unflinching as the Virus Creature screamed and cursed me through his rotten teeth and smothering body. The creature recoiled in pain as it appeared with an oblong head with long, black, wiry strands that covered it. It had white, clouded, milky, glaucoma, oval eyes, and rows of blackened broken teeth that sneered at me, after it was singed by the curtain of fire that I created to prevent it from passing through to infect the village. Then the creature cursed me in its contempt, and with his decayed teeth as his body recoiled and withered in pain, saying, "How much do you love God? Can you lose that which you love the most for him?"* Zachary cried out in response, *"I would lose it all for God!"*

Then the creature screamed and laughed in a wicked response before disappearing, leaving only the grass burned where he once stood.

Zachary continued to re-live the story of his decline as his inner soul narrated the events. *"For I believe at that moment it happened to me! After the fight with the creature, everything changed. Something was sucked out of me. Some of the power of virtue was taken away from me. I had passed out, blacked out. The Africans found me in the field in front of their village with no clothes on, and having some sort of a shell of a body, barely breathing and on the verge of death. Some of the Elders in the village talked about my transformation. They saw the skin return and mutate around my body. Hair, skin, and color appeared over the skinless form that they salvaged from the fields. The Elders of the tribe said they saw something else, a demonic creature reappearing after I had passed out, and then ripping something from off my body that looked like a wing. And they were so very right. I only have one frayed wing now. But I still have some limited abilities. But they are really limited. I can still pull out the disgraced limp and broken wing from out of my body. But why should I, it is just a sorry reminder of my failure.*

I was fortunate. For the compassion of the African tribesmen, patiently nursed me back to health. But I had to find a way back to the states; I didn't know what else to do. I had to survive. I found a job working as a deckhand on a cargo freighter, moving oil and natural minerals back to the states as it traversed across the ocean. It was hard adjusting from having been a being of divine light to a deckhand on an old freighter, washing down the decks. I had to learn and make quick adjustments. I had to find a way back. I had to find a way back to recover my glory. I had to find a way back to God. And that is how I became depleted, empty and filled with the rage of the creature that defeated me. But why did you allow it, God? I did nothing wrong. How could you allow that disgusting Virus creature do this to me? And God, how could you forsake me now? For you have left me alone in this terrible world. How could you? How could you do this to me?"

His eyes started to water up. So, he quickly wiped the tears away. As hurt, and then hate filled his being, he wanted to run away. Zachary wanted to go find one of the old buildings on the road he saw when he was on the bus, and just hide out and be left alone. He started to breathe slowly and dropped his head for a moment, and then he looked skyward and then said, *"You have failed me, God. I am alone down here. Now you want me to help others. But, how can I?"* And in a sign of defiance, he took his hand and started pulling something out of his chest that looked like a frayed and broken white wing. *"This is all I have left! This one broken wing that I am too ashamed to even look at."*

Zachary continued to recall the events that led to his disgrace. *"The Africans found the discarded shell of my celestial body that somehow separated from me. They brought the broken and charred pieces to me while I desperately tried with painstaking patience to assemble the hollow shell back together. But as I tried, it crumpled, and then deteriorated, destroying forever my last chance to recover my past again. And now I must accept this body and adjust to wearing these stale earthly clothes, having required only the power to sweat and taste and feel pain. When I returned to the states, there was nothing left for me to do, but drift and work a little, and then ride the Greyhound Bus. That is what I have been doing now. I continually ride the bus. As I ride on the bus, going from state to state, trying to find peace and solitude, I discovered that there were still traces of the glory, some final memory residue that had not dissipated entirely within me. There were very small traces, yet nevertheless, traces that still lingered.*

I took a dishwasher job in a little diner somewhere in the middle of a dust bowl in Reno. I was washing dishes, and picking up dinner plates while the waitress Ellen was busy taking orders from the different buses that made their way through the middle of the desert, traveling to the bigger cities. The tired and hungry travelers would arrive wanting a hot meal before departing to their different destinations. The restaurant was crowded that day. We became overwhelmed by a barrage of buses that arrived going to a church convention. I was exhausted picking up the dishes from the constant flow of humanity coming in and out of the restaurant. I was carrying a huge stack of dishes in my hands when a group of bikers arrived. Their motorcycle engines disturbed the normal restaurant sounds when a group of ten or more bikers barged through the door. The frayed blue jean vests that they wore had decals and drawings that said, "Hell's Angels". As I walked nervously down the aisle, one of them pushed me aside. I stumbled and the stack of dishes that I was carrying wobbled, sending broken dishes all over the floor. I ran, now frightened, and began sweeping up the dishes, not wanting to make a spectacle of myself. And I was hoping that I would not be fired for not keeping them balanced. Ellen, who was a waitress, came over and helped me sweep up the broken dishes, and reassured me that everything would be alright.

The bikers crowded around several tables, putting their feet on top of them. One of them took a water glass and poured the water out onto the floor. They started yelling very loudly, demanding to be waited on. Ellen, who left me to finish sweeping up the remaining broken dishes, made a mad dash towards them, and then gingerly took out her little notebook from her pink apron and said, "Gentlemen, what can we serve you today? One of them reached out and grabbed Ellen's wrist and swung her around and forced her to sit on his lap. She got up, playfully laughed it off and said, "Please, no touching the merchandise." She straightened out her dress, and said, "Ok, let's try this again. What do you want from our menu today that's reasonably priced? And because there are so many of you here today, you will get a ten percent discount." She was swung around again and her wrist was twisted by one of them until she wretched in pain. "Why don't you, little lady, forget about the order for today and give us a little dance!" All the rest of the bikers started to laugh and clap their hands as she was forced again to sit on another biker's lap. She finally broke free and started running when she ran into a table, knocking it over and the dinner plates to the floor from a family from the church group that was seated together. The biker caught her as she struggled to run away. He dragged her by one of her legs until she kicked him in the face. She stood up again and tried to run, but he grabbed her, and ripped away a part of her dress. There was a slight struggle that occurred when Ellen slapped him across the face and dug a few fingernails into his skin as she fought to escape. The customers that were seated, bolted in terror, moving quickly from every direction in the restaurant, heading for the door. The bikers proceeded to tear off more of Ellen's dress as she pleaded with them to let her go while they held her down by both of her arms on the floor. The customers began running and shouting as they watched the shocking events unfold. Some of the bikers started throwing chairs and overturned tables while they continued to hold Ellen down on the floor, tearing off the front of her dress, and exposing her bra. I had to do something, so I took one of the plates that I was holding, and smashed them on the floor. Then I cried out, saying, "Leave her alone! Or something, I promise, will happen to you! Something that you will not like!" They all stopped momentarily and started laughing, saying, "Let's break every bone in the little man's body!" Perhaps I still had some Warrior Fury still left in me or maybe it was just foolishness, for I was weak and helpless and on the verge of getting pummeled to death. I started backing up, now terrified as they came rushing towards me! Then automatically as if some cosmic switch was turned on, I start vibrating, like I was having a seizure for everything in the restaurant started to break and explode. All the dishes and the glasses began erupting with micro-explosions like someone had released a bomb inside the restaurant. Everything started to break apart! Even the tables lifted off the floor and chairs went flying mid-air across the room.

The bikers fought each other, trying to leave, tripping over one another as they tried to get out of the restaurant. As one of them scrambled on the floor, trying to get to the door, he found himself lifted off the floor and thrown through one of the front glass windows. The bikers raced towards their motorcycles, falling once more upon each other, looking for somewhere to escape and run for cover. They quickly jumped on their motorcycles, screaming about how the Death Angel had been following them on the road as they left in a terrified cloud of dust.

Needless to say, I had to leave that job until I found work as a ranch hand, mending fences. I became a wanderer, seeking my own peace, and my own existence without God. I started traveling on the bus for months with nowhere in particular to go. I was about to get off the bus as I was approaching my destination when I noticed a man who had been traveling, seated in the back of the bus with a long white trench coat. He had pale albino skin and hair, and he wore dark sunglasses. Abruptly, he approached me and handed me a small note card. The note card read that when I exited the bus, I should wait on the side of the road because redemption was coming to pick me up.

What a lousy and terrible joke! There are so many weirdos that ride the bus. But I had become one of them, just traveling on the bus, trying to find myself once again. Well, I had to try to do something anyway. I had nothing to lose. I had already lost everything. And now, I am standing in the middle of nowhere with dust blowing into my mouth. This was the last hope from my failure.

Zachary had thought many times that he could just forget this whole idea of trying to save the humans anymore. They cared nothing for themselves, so why should he care. He put another wad of tobacco in his mouth and said, *"There is something about this horrible taste that kind of grows on you. I should enjoy these human perks. I have already lost my glory. I am too defeated to help anybody! I could easily hide among the humans; no one knows my past. There is nothing wrong with living for myself! I paid my dues, and I got nothing out of it! I am just as weak and helpless as the ones I am supposed to help!"*

His finger was still stinging as he looked at it. *"How long is this thing going to hurt?"* It was all so confusing and humiliating to be stripped of his gold metallic raiment and to wear the dirty clothes of a ranch hand. His mind quickly recalled the time when he was once on the bus, sitting next to an old lady, and he made the mistake of telling her that he was a fallen angel. She thought he was crazy, and patted him on the hand, saying that everything would be alright, and asked him did he take his medication.

He heard his soul and thoughts speaking again saying within himself. *"I wonder if God knows how I've changed or how my body could now interact with this environment. We were never supposed to feel anything during our assignments. Now I have changed completely and was starting to enjoy this fallen human experience. And here I am in the middle of nowhere, waiting for someone to come along. What a waste of my time and abilities."* Zachary said, still feeling the stinging pain in his finger.

He looked at his red flannel shirt and his faded jeans, which were faded and had a few rips and holes in them. He kicked some dust off his old brown worn out cowboy boots, which were cracked as if they had a story to tell by themselves. He wished he had a larger hat to cover his suntanned face. His identity was completely concealed, even down to the crow's feet around his eyes, and the tobacco stains on his teeth. He could not believe what had happened to him as he wiped the dust off his lips and brushed some more off his shirt and pants. *"Well at least I look the part!"* He said laughing to himself. *"It is really amazing how I have a completely new identity."*

This had to be one of the best identities he had ever seen before. He took on the name, Russell Crowfeet, and he gave himself a history. He was now Russell Crowfeet, half Indian, half Irish, hard drinking, hard fighting, cattle driver, ranch hand, an alcoholic drifter, looking for a friend. The story was so complete that he gave himself, he was able to muster up and release some celestial powers to download a phony memory about himself into the minds of certain people that he met in bars or on the jobs he worked.

So, Russell Crowfeet existed, even though he was never born. Russell looked skyward towards the heavens as the desert sun blazed down on him. He whispered to himself saying, *"When will this heat ever let up? God, what did I do to you to deserve this humiliating state?"* He had studied his target and knew about the crazy middle-aged man that was coming and having a mid-life crisis. The back of the note card gave him some information about the man he was waiting on. *"I sure pulled a loony assignment this time. But if it takes this to get back to glory, and the possibility of being a celestial once again, I am going to take it!"*

It just did not seem right that the great legendary Zachary, the demon fighter, was now reduced to this degrading life, and job, and was forced to transform to defeat evil without his long, ten-foot sword that he carried into battle on his belt. Even when the demonic hordes that he had fought in the past, spat out the poisons of hell, he was always covered with the shield of light that surrounded him. And now, he was depleted of even that. There was nothing left to protect him from being overtaken by evil. And many cities on the earth would have long been destroyed or overrun by evil, if he had not stood against them. So, it was such a blow for him to be rewarded like this to be transformed, and to have nothing to protect himself, but his faith. *"Now I have to fight the demonic hordes by only using faith. They must be out of their celestial minds! It had been months since I heard from them and now they show up, giving me instructions, saying I must fight evil with only faith. They have taken away all of my weapons, and put me on a back road in the middle of nowhere, waiting for a loser that is about to commit suicide. How am I supposed to defend him from the Spirit of Suicide? This is one of the nastiest and deadliest creatures that I have ever heard about roaming the earth. And I have nothing to defeat him with, but a human body. God, this must be some kind of terrible joke to fight evil with just faith. This is insane!"*

The sun was beating down on him as he waited, wondering what was going to happen next. Then he saw a red, custom-made, four-door convertible Chevrolet Camaro Z28 with a white racing stripe in the front flying up the road, kicking up a dust storm as it fishtailed from side to side. The man behind the driver's wheel was driving like a lunatic and appeared to be driving well over 100 miles per hour, breaking the speed limit. But with no police around, who really cared? He was driving as if he was trying to escape something. Russell stuck his thumb out, trying to catch a ride from the man driving the shiny, new-looking convertible like a lunatic. He drove right by him at first, covering him with a cloud of dust. Russell started waving his arms back and forth, and then took out a blue handkerchief from out of his back pocket to flag him down. He did not even think he was going to stop at first, but he did. He backed up the glossy, red convertible and opened the door for Russell. Russell extended his hand, and said, *"I am Russell Crowfeet and I just need a ride anywhere!" "That is actually where I'm going!"* The man said smiling with a set of amazing dental work.

Russell looked at the man. He was obviously wearing a fake-looking toupee and had on a neon, bright-colored, Hawaiian shirt that had drawings of colorful birds on it. The collar of his shirt was open almost to the middle of his chest, and there was a crop of gray hairs that shot out of it. He also wore three gold chains that looped around his neck as if he had just come back from a time machine from the 1980's. His face was tanned as if he had spent way too much time in a tanning booth. He also had a small suitcase that was handcuffed to the dashboard of the convertible, and he would adjust his toupee as the wind moved it slightly to one side. He wore large, goggle, Ray-ban, silver sunglasses; like the kind Elvis used to wear. Then he took out a tiny comb and methodically stroked his mustache, licked the tips of his fingers, and pressed down on his mustache as he grinned looking at himself in the rear-view mirror. *"A lot of people say I don't look my age. I guess I have good genes. I don't know why I have not aged like all the people I went to school with. You know I saw them not long ago during my class reunion, and they looked awfully old."* He said as he started chuckling to himself and continued, *"Yes, it's just good genes, I guess."* Russell looked at him and said, *"They used to say the same thing about me. If I told you how old I am, you would not believe it. But unfortunately, these days, I am starting to look my age."* *"Yeah, I know what you're talking about!"* The man said still grinning while driving and taking glances at himself in the rear-view mirror. *"Yeah, stress is a killer. That stuff can make you look awfully old."* *"Yeah, it's a killer."*, Russell said as he moved his cowboy hat to deflect some of the wind blowing over the windshield. It seemed like the man was breaking the sound barrier with his driving. *"You know I've really been through something in the last few days. Life can really take you for a loop. You start to go in one direction, and then you end up in another."* It appeared as if a teardrop formed in one eye before he quickly reached up and wiped it away. *"Yeah, I feel you on that."*, Russell said.

Russell appeared to genuinely like this guy; they seemed to connect. *"You know I worked for this company, and they threw me out like a piece of trash. Just like that, I was nothing. And just like that, thirty years was gone in an instant."* The man said driving as he frowned, and then he forced a grin. *"I know what you are talking about. I had everything too. I was thrown out of my company, and given a lesser job. It is a trip."* Russell said. *"This is a really nice car. And I love the red color."* Russell continued. *"Well, I had to give myself a nice little present. You know life is short. You should have a little*

148

fun and reward yourself. Nobody else is going to do it for you." "I need to reward myself also.", Russell said.

This guy was really cool. Russell thought that he didn't need any help from him. He wondered why he was sent to him. *"I have only had my car now for two days. I left my job, raided my retirement fund, and rewarded myself. Oh, what the hell! It is time to have some fun!"* The man said as he started looking in the mirror again. *"You are right! I really want to have some fun in my life. I am tired of living through other people."* Russell said, nodding his head in agreement. *"I really have been through some terrible things in my life in the last few days. But I am going to have some fun now. I say it is about me now!",* said the man as he shifted the convertible into another gear.

Russell felt that he had entered a rocket ship, and he also was leaving everything behind with his new-found friend. *"Hey, you want something to drink? I got a cold six pack in the back. It's hotter than hell out here!"* Russell paused for a moment; he never drank beer before. But it didn't matter now, for it was scorching hot out in the open, and he was reduced to a human that was hot and thirsty. He reached in the back, popped open a container, and started drinking it. As it cooled him down, it gave him a feeling of wheezy satisfaction. He didn't realize that he had drunk the whole can of beer in one continuous swallow while the man looked at him saying, *"You really must have been thirsty!",* the man said laughing. Russell wiped his mouth and started laughing as well. *"Yeah, I really was thirsty!" "There is nothing like a little beer and chips when you are going on a long trip.",* the man said laughing.

If this was the way for him to return, he already failed a test since he drank a can of beer and enjoyed it. He knew that when celestial beings participated in human failure, it diminished their ability to transform and use The Brilliance as a weapon. But it did not matter. He was kicked out of the celestial club a while ago, and he's operating on his own.

As they rode a little farther, he promptly asked him for another beer. He popped open the can's lid, and quickly drank the beer down in one great long swallow. *"Ahhhh, that is really good! It hits the spot on a day like this."* Russell said as he belched rather loudly to his surprise. *"Good God Man, you really can drink!"* The man said as the car accelerated through a dusty cloud. *"Yeah, I am going to go for the gold this time. I am tired of people pushing me around."*

Russell said as he closed his eyes and allowed his senses to enjoy the beer. Russell knew that his human transformation was almost complete for there was no adverse physical reaction from him drinking beer. Perhaps he was more human now than celestial. He put another wad of the tobacco in his mouth and decided to sit back and enjoy the ride of the lunatic driver. *"Well, being human was not that bad of a setback after all.",* Russell lamented.

The man slid in a CD, and pushed a button while they both cruised down the one-way dusty road singing along with Frank Sinatra the song, *"I Did It My Way!" "I guess things just work out if you just relax and go with the flow." "Hey! You never really asked me my name?",* the man said, taking off his sunglasses and adjusting his eyes to the sunlight before putting them back on. He then extended his hand saying, *"My name is Strickland, Charlie Strickland. I used to be one of the best stock traders for America Great Trading Company. I was one of their sinister stars. I made a lot of money for those bloodsuckers, and I got nothing out of it but kicked out of the door. I had my whole future plotted out, and what I planned to do, after I retired, but none of it worked out that way. Not the way I had planned."* He hit his hand against the steering wheel one time which caused the little convertible to almost go off the road as it hit a small sand dune and bounced upward. *"God, they did me wrong!",* he said. *"WHOA MAN! STAY FOCUSED ON THE ROAD!"* Russell nervously said as the car jumped, and found the dirt road once again.

"Your story is just like mine. I was kicked out, rather forced out would be a better term. They left me without anything! That is why I am in the state that I am in right now." "I am glad I picked you up, Russell. You got a good head on your shoulders. You understand life, just like me." Charlie continued to talk as he angrily remembered what happened to him. *"You know, everything was going as I had planned, then it all just went out of control. I just started to lose everything, one thing after another. It was all taken away from me. You know, life can be a total trip sometimes. I am just sick of the whole rat race.*

I just want to live my life now and have me some fun before they put that dirt on top of me." Charlie said, stroking his mustache a few times, and looking at himself in the rearview mirror. *"Hey, can I have another one of those cold beers you got back there?"* Russell asked. *"Go for it! Drink as much as you want! I have a trunk full in the back covered with dry ice."*

Russell really felt comfortable with Charlie. He had been kicked around by life, just like him. Charlie was determined to live for himself now and have some fun before it was all over. Russell grinned, and then said to himself, *"This has to be the best assignment I ever had. Who can complain when you are drinking cold beer, and listening to some nice sounds with a cool friend? Well, where are we are going?"* Russell inquired. *"Well I heard there is a Casino up ahead about one hundred miles from here. If I push it a little faster, we can make it there before nightfall."* Charlie started to sing along with Sinatra. *"If you push this thing any faster, it is going to transform and grow wings."* Russell said laughing as he comfortably kicked his boots up and let them lean on the side of the door of the convertible, watching the scenery as they drove by. Russell thought perhaps his luck would now change. And perhaps, this was the beginning of a new winning streak, and he was ready for a little nightlife from that Casino. That might be really fun and the very thing he needed the most right now, he thought.

As the two men continued traveling down the road, more life information started being exchanged. Russell told Charlie how he worked for a boss that had no more feeling for him anymore, even after he did the most dangerous jobs that no one else would do. *"And what did I get out of it? A demotion, and a thankless job that nobody else wanted?!"* *"Yeah Charlie, you are right! It is time to enjoy ourselves!"*

"You know Russell, I was the top trader, and they treated me like dirt! I was given a demotion as well. When I lost one of our main accounts, all the bigwigs blamed me. They forgot about all the other money that I made for them in the past. They forget everything that you have ever done. I am just sick of living anymore for other people. I am sick of the whole rotten rat race. Occasionally, I feel like checking out. It's just too overwhelming sometimes!" Russell nodded his head in agreement. Then he asked Charlie if he had a cigarette. *"I*

guess you don't want to live long." He said as he reached into his front pocket and pulled out a cigarette. Russell quickly lit the cigarette took a deep drag and said, *"I see what I have been missing out on! I can actually taste this! It is really relaxing!"* *"What in the world are you talking about?"* Charlie gave him a sideways glance as they continued down the road. *"This is a weird road. There is nobody on it but us. Where do you think we are?"* Russell inquired as he continued to look around as the sun was setting and large shadows were appearing on the landscape. *"I think we are at the edge of Texas, and near the border of Mexico.",* Charlie said. *"Well, this road does not have a sign on it.",* Russell replied.

Russell felt something deep within him; it was a voice that was telling him that this man needed God. He needed the love of God desperately, but Russell turned the voice off. He reached in the back and grabbed another beer and started sipping it, enjoying every drop. Then Russell noticed something that made him drop the beer on his lap, creating a small puddle on the seat. *"Hey, Russell, what are you doing? This is a brand-new car! Don't destroy the interior before I have time to break it in!",* Charlie said looking at Russell in frustration for what he had done. *"Oh, I am so sorry that happened, clumsy fingers I guess!",* Russell said. But what frightened Russell, was that all his fingernails had changed colors. They had all turned menacingly black. And that was a sure sign that he was changing into something that he did not even want to think about.

Then out of nowhere, a wild dog jumped on the hood of the speeding car, and then leaped between the two men. The dog had wild yellow eyes, and saliva dripping from out of its mouth. Russell was dazed from drinking the beers. So, he took off his hat to protect himself from its jaws. The dog's fur was a mass of matted hair and tangled knots that stuck out everywhere. Its tail was bent as if it was broken, and its bones were protruding out of its fur like it hadn't eaten for many days, and was scavenging the desert for food.

The dog turned in frustration because it was not having any luck from the hat that Russell used to protect himself with. He tried to bite Charlie, snapping at him a few times before he picked up the suitcase that he had handcuffed to his dashboard. With one hand on the steering wheel, he started protecting himself from its snapping jaws. Russell quickly took off one of his boots, and he knocked the dog out of the seat onto the road. *"DID YOU SEE THAT THING?! IT WAS HORRIBLE!"* Charlie said, trying to take control once again of the zigzagging convertible. *"IT CAME JUST INCHES AWAY FROM MY FACE! IF IT WAS NOT FOR MY HAT, THAT DOG WOULD HAVE TAKEN A CHUNK OUT OF ME!"* Russell said excitedly while breathing hard. *"I HAVE NEVER SEEN ANYTHING LIKE THAT BEFORE IN MY LIFE!"*

Charlie's hand was shaking as he steered the convertible. He noticed that his toupee was on sideways, and he quickly adjusted it while looking a little embarrassed. Russell then said, *"That dog's eyes were yellow. It must have had some kind of disease. It's a good thing he did not bite either one of us!"* They continued to drive as the dog looked at them in the distance, and sneered. And then, standing on its hind legs in a vertical position, its bones snapped, pushed upward, and its legs became long. The tangled, knotted fur disappeared, and human skin covered the crouching animal. And a dirty, naked man emerged from out of the injured dog. The man had merged with the dust and the shadows, and he appeared almost camouflaged in the desert landscape. He crouched down, sniffing the road, and looking at the speeding convertible in the distance. Then excitedly, he started to howl wildly. *"God that thing was ugly! Did you see its eyes? They were yellow, and it had nasty looking stuff coming from out its mouth! That thing was disgusting looking! I never saw anything like that before!"* Charlie said looking around the landscape of the desert. *"I don't know where it came from, and I hope you killed that slobbering mutt."*

Russell found another beer. He wiped off the top of the can, then said, *"The hell with that dog, turn up the music, and let me get back into the groove!" "That would be a hell of a payback to get bitten to death by some desert dog, and then bleed to death! This is supposed to be the trip and the vacation of my life! To get bitten by an infected dog in the middle of nowhere and die would have been some kind of payback."* Charlie exclaimed. Russell put his hat back on his head sideways and said, *"Maybe I should just take a nap, and ease my nerves; too much excitement for a ranch hand like me. Charlie what* are you talking about being paid back?" "Oh, it was about something that happened to me! It is now my past life; it doesn't matter now." "Well, it might do some good to get it out of you anyway. It is just me, and you, and we got all night, so spill the beans man! And let it go!" Russell said. "Yeah, that would be some kind of payback." Charlie said as he continued to speak. "It all started when my wife found out about Jenny. My wife came into my office on an unexpected visit while at the same time, Jenny was there, and we were engaged in some extraordinary office work right on top of my desk." He tried to grin a few times, but a huge frown appeared as he continued to talk. "Jenny was every man's dream. She was about twenty-six with baby blonde hair, deep blue eyes, and soft bouncy breasts that stood up like the Statue of Liberty. She started working for me as an Intern, and she started to really understand what I was going through. I was working hard every day with all of the pressure of meeting the deadlines. There was nothing appealing that excited me about Mildred anymore. She had become just a dead weight, something I was just living with and had gotten sick and tired of. It was the most chaotic day of my life when Mildred arrived in my office that day. We were on top of my desk, half-dressed when that dumb secretary of mine let her walk into my office without even notifying me. She must have suspected something. Mildred had been so quiet and passive during our marriage. But she created a scene that is still being gossiped about in the lunch room during break times to this day, I suppose. Mildred turned into a hurricane, an unstoppable storm of my destruction. She started throwing my office furniture out of the window down to the street below. My office was located on the executive level of the tenth floor, so it was just a miracle that no one was hurt from everything flying out of the window down to the street below. I did my best to try to calm her down by telling her to show some class and dignity, but she was not having any of it. For thirty-four years of our marriage, she never acted out in an outrageous manner. She was a housewife, and she handled all the matters of the house. She had never ever visited my office before. Then she tore into Jenny! She ripped off her blouse as Jenny ran out of the office for her life. Jenny left the office terrified, holding up her broken bra straps, but she turned around screaming at *me saying, "YOU LIED! YOU SAID THAT SHE LEFT YOU YEARS AGO! YOU LIER!" Mildred was also screaming, and was just saying the word, "BETRAYAL, BETRAYAL, BETRAYAL!" She also took a black marker, and wrote in large letters all over the walls in my office the word, "CHEATER!" Mildred then found the pot of coffee that Jenny had made for me right before our interlude. She then poured all the coffee all over my important papers. She poured the coffee over all the weeks it took to compile the statistics and the figures of the percentages of the company's net worth, and the projections that I had calculated. All of it was neatly stacked on a small side desk in the office, but she destroyed it, along with the computer that she unplugged, and hurled through the window. You know things just started getting worse for me that day. My supervisor walked in on all the mayhem and even brought the head of the company with him for me to meet. Mr. Arthur Jacobs Fulbright, the head of America Funds, was paying all the top executives an impromptu visit that day. Mildred, in her rage, tore off half of my shirt and was pulling on my tie, clocking me when they arrived through the door. My supervisor quickly rushed Mr. Fulbright out of the office and yelled at me to have some discretion and get the quarterly figures together for Mr. Fulbright because he wanted to see them immediately. But how could I show him anything now? Mildred made sure that everything in the office was wrecked. Mildred even ran to other offices, kicking my co-worker's computers, and knocking over their potted plants. Someone had called the police, and you could hear the sirens coming in the distance. Mildred, then hearing the police sirens, quickly ran out of the office, and disappeared as she drove down the street in an erratic manner. The whole scandal made the front-page news and my career, my job, my life, everything was instantly over. I did not stay around for any of the fallout. I depleted my bank accounts before Mildred got to them with her team of lawyers, and then I just disappeared from the face of the earth. I can't be totally blamed for my situation. Maybe I was working too hard, and I needed a break, and Jenny was the right stimulus to keep me going. This right here, is my life savings, everything I got in the world, along with this car.*

Charlie opened the suitcase while he kept his hand on the steering wheel. His suitcase was packed tightly with one hundred dollar bills. *"One hundred thousand dollars is in there; everything that I have in the world. I have nothing to live for anymore. After I spend all this money, who knows what I might do. I might just kill myself and get it over with. Now that would be a plan!"*

Russell looked at him, lifted the brim of his cowboy hat off his eyes and said, *"You know you are not alone." "WHO ELSE IS DOWN HERE WITH ME IN THIS ROTTEN WORLD?"* Charlie said almost screaming as an ocean of tears flooded his eyes and blew out into the wind. *"God is with you, Charlie!"*, Russell said in a solemn, almost whispered voice. *"YOU HAVE TO BE KIDDING ME!"*, Charlie said angrily. *"God is still with you, Charlie."* Russell said again as he looked down the road. *"THEN WHERE IS HE AT? WHERE IS HE AT? I LOST EVERYTHING BUT MY LIFE! I LOST EVERYTHING! HE IS THE ONE THAT MUST BE LOST BECAUSE I SURE IN THE HELL CANNOT FIND HIM! AND IT LOOKS LIKE HE CAN'T BE FOUND ANYWHERE AROUND HERE!"*

Russell wanted to tell him to pull over, grab his hands to pray, and tell him that God is not lost. We are the ones in the middle of nowhere, running, trying to escape stuff that will eventually find us. Russell wanted to reach over, put his hand over his heart, and tell him God is right here waiting for you to come to him. But an overwhelming feeling of self-pity inundated him, so he put his hat back over his eyes, and said, *"Maybe, if you keep driving, perhaps both of us will find something that will save us!" "I don't know. We have been driving for hours, and there is nothing but darkness up ahead."* Charlie said looking concerned.

Russell had finished a beer and wanted to take a little nap when he felt something blowing out of his mouth. He spat it out and noticed that his lap was covered with feathers. Without warning, in one tremulous burst, thousands of feathers started shooting out of Russell's chest. They started to cover the car so thick that Charlie had trouble seeing as the convertible started to go off the road. The feathers filled the convertible so that it covered them completely until it spun around in a circle, almost overturning on its side. *"WHAT IN GOD'S NAME IS GOING ON? WHERE DID ALL OF THESE FEATHERS COME*

FROM?", Charlie said angrily, looking around. Russell was choking as the feathers kept flying out of his mouth. Charlie looked at the spectacular sight, wondering what was happening to him. The feathers covered the car and even covered parts of the road that they were on. *"Where, in the love of God, did these feathers come from?"*, Charlie said looking around amazed. Russell was still choking. Finally, he pulled out one extremely long feather from out of his throat. Charlie continued looking around saying, *"We must be near a chicken farm, factory or something for those things to blow all over the car like this! And some of them must have blown into your mouth! Russell! Man, are you alright? Do we need to take you to a doctor or something?"* *"I'm alright. Some of them got into my mouth, that's all."* Russell replied while spitting feathers out. They stopped, and got out of the convertible, sweeping out the feathers that covered the interior, and filled up the backseat. *"These feathers are everywhere! I have never seen anything like this before! And I almost ran into a sand dune, if I hadn't stopped. I have never been through a feather storm before in my life."*, Charlie said as he jumped back into the convertible laughing. *"Who is going to believe us? Russell my man, we just went through a feather storm! Feathers falling all over, from out of the skies, now that was something!"*

Russell knew what happened. It was the adverse reaction of the beers that he drank. For these kinds of reactions occurred with celestial beings sent on an assignment, who began to fail, and lose their brilliance. They always suffered some kind of consequence when they started to lose parts of their brilliance. Russell knew that this was the first sign of failure for he was losing the last particles of his celestial power, which was called, The Brilliance. Once the Brilliance was completely gone, you either went crazy or found yourself transformed into some sort of outer darkness creature. Russell looked at his hands. They had turned dark green, and his nails had become long and black. But he was still on a sacred mission, even if he was only now half Celestial. Charlie looked at him with concern saying, *"It looks like you could use another beer."* Russell quickly hid his gross looking hands, and he stumbled a little with his words before speaking, *"No thank you. I had enough for one night."*

Nightfall descended as they moved through the eerie darkness. Charlie flipped on his bright headlights, saying *"God! It really is super dark out here! I would not want to be stranded in this place!"* As they drove a little further, they saw what appeared to be a woman in the distance, standing outside her car with her hazard lights blinking off and on. *"Hey, look Russell! Wake up! There is a vehicle up ahead, and it looks like it is having some kind of engine trouble!"* Russell had put his hat over his eyes so that he could pray and ask God for direction. He did not want Charlie looking at him. Russell looked up, and said, *"It looks like a woman that is on the road. And her car broke down for sure! Pull over Charlie. She is going to need our help!"*

They both noticed that the car was an expensive, top of the line BMW that was now blowing clouds of white smoke out from underneath the hood, almost smoldering the car completely. She was bent over, looking under the hood, oblivious to the fact that someone had pulled over and was behind her. She had on a red miniskirt with black stilettos which had straps that wrapped around her ankles perfectly. Her long shapely legs and the smooth form of her body molded a perfect fit around her dress. She wore black fishnet stockings that accented her red dress. Her petite and innocent Barbie doll face hid her many facelifts and the reality that she was way over forty. Her lipstick was cherry red, and she had powdered her face so white that Snow White looked pale in comparison. But she understood that her face was her meal ticket. It was the door to a way of life that she treasured, and she would do anything to keep it. She had long blonde hair that was thick and full and hung down her back to the center of her shoulders, and even in the darkness, her beauty stunned them as they stared in awe. But underneath her made-up exterior, she made her living studying men until their very life force was depleted, leaving them broken, empty, a financial shell. There were large rings that sparkled on her fingers. The rings appeared to be diamonds, rubies, and sapphires that sparkled in the darkness from all her romantic encounters. And she had dozens of gold chains that draped around her neck, making her appear even more dazzling as the headlights from the convertible shone on her.

When Charlie and Russell got out of the convertible, they were flooded with the strong smell of her perfume that consumed the desert air with the pleasant aroma of rose buds. Charlie tried to catch his breath as he started breathing extra hard while Russell started to grin, appearing like an excited dog that wanted to play catch. When she saw them, she continued to flip her hair around and tried frustratingly to talk on her little jewel covered phone angrily. *"Hello, is anyone there? Hello, is anyone there? This is Miss Honey Creek! Why am I only picking up static from my phone? I wonder why this thing is not working! Hello! Hello! God, this makes me so mad! Nothing is working tonight!"* She slammed the cell phone case shut, and put her hands on her hips. Looking at the smoke rising from her BMW, she then put her hands to her eyes and burst into tears.

Charlie approached her, and softly spoke, *"If you need help, we can help you. We saw your hazard lights blinking, and we have come to assist, and we will do whatever we can."* She finally turned around as she spoke with a soft musical tonal quality, *"I have been calling on my cell phone since it broke down, and I am getting nothing but a busy signal. It must be dead or something."* *"My name is Russell Crowfeet. Madam, I learned how to fix certain things because I once worked on a cargo ship. Stuff used to break down all the time. If you will allow me, I will look under the hood and see what needs to be done."* *"Oh please, that would be so kind of you. Do what you can to fix it!"*, she exuberantly said.

They both were overwhelmed by her perfume, the glaze on her lips, the tiny diamonds that were even glued around her eyelids, and on the tips of her fingernails. Charlie spoke again saying, *"My phone is out too! It's been out since I have been traveling in this area. We must be in some kind of dead zone where the connections are out."* As Russell was examining the engine underneath the hood, and wiping away the smoke with one hand, saying, *"This thing is not going anywhere! There was some sort of electrical fire!"* Russel said as he held up a group of wires that were black and charred. *"Yep, it is fried to a crisp. Lucky, you got out when you did. Who knows? The whole thing could have caught fire and went up in flames."* *"Wait until I see that dealer! I am going to let him have it! This is a brand-new car, and I paid good money for it. This shouldn't have ever happened! This is their top of the line vehicle, and I am on the road lost, like some common hussy! This is so humiliating and embarrassing." "Well Madam, if you need help, we can assist, and take you to the next gas station or Kwik Shop",* Russell said wiping some black oil and grease on a rag that he had in his back pocket. *"I just can't believe this! Nothing is working out for me tonight."*

As she started walking towards the back of the vehicle to retrieve her Louis Vuitton handbag, the heel of her shoe broke. She started crying once again, and then took the broken shoe and started beating the top of her car. *"This is unbelievable! This is unbelievable! My shoe has even broken! I can't stand it anymore! I deserve better than this! This is unbelievable!"* She screamed as she took her other shoe off and threw it into the darkness. Russell came over quickly, gently grabbed her elbow and escorted her to the back of the convertible saying, *"Madam, everything is going to be alright. Just sit in the back, behind the driver's seat, and enjoy the view."* Then Russell opened the trunk of the convertible and found the cold beer that Charlie said was there. He brought one to her and said, *"Don't worry about anything. We will take you back to civilization, and everything will be put back into place."* She sipped the beer while sitting in the backseat of the convertible and then gave him a slight wink of the eye as the two men pushed her car off the road and slammed the hood. Then all of them took off down the road. While driving, Charlie spoke up saying, *"I did not introduce myself. I am Charlie Strickland. I was in the stock market business, and now I am on a permanent vacation."* "Well, Mr. Strickland, you really do have a nice and lovely car. You know what? Red is my favorite color. I want to thank you for rescuing me on the road. You guys are really my angels tonight."* Then Russell interjected, saying, *"I bet you never met an angel like me before!"*

Ignoring Russell's comment, she continued. *"I can't believe that my cell phone is dead. Everything has been going wrong for me lately!"* "Yeah, I know what you are saying, Miss. I'm sorry, I didn't get your name.",* Russell said. *"Oh, I am so sorry. I am Miss Clementine Honey Creek!"* She said smiling as she took out a compact mirror and put some glaze around the bottom of her lower lip. *"Wait until I get back to civilization. I am buying a new car. They should be* *ashamed of themselves for selling that terrible machine. I am suing that whole company. I cannot believe this! That was a brand-new BMW that overheated and broke down.*

Well, would you like to hear how I got stranded in the middle of the desert with just a few clothes on my back? I was a trophy wife; married to a man that just could not appreciate a woman like me. He was so overly protective. I just got all my things and left him. I had to leave him. He was too abusive and too controlling. And then, he got sick. I just had to get away and be free. He was very old, but also very rich. It was when I was taking care of him. He died, suddenly. Everyone started blaming me. At the end of the day, I found myself being investigated by the police. It was just too stressful and humiliating, so I had to leave quickly. I had to escape from that terrible situation. It had become too demeaning for me to stay. So, I took what I could and left. I headed out on the open road, trying to start a new life. But I don't know if the police or any other law enforcement officials are still looking for me. So, you have to help me hide and help me get away. I think that his estate has hired a hit man to take me out. I am so afraid for my life. Please! Can you help me hide? I am so afraid of what might happen to me!" She cried, covering her face with her hands. *"Please, I need your help to hide! I don't know what else to do now, but hide!"*

Russell turned around and started to pat her on her hands to comfort her. *"Miss Honey Creek, everything is going to be alright. We will take care of you, and take you wherever you want to go."* *"Mr. Russell, you appear to be such a big strong man with such a kind, gentle spirit. You must be married or your girlfriend must be extremely jealous everywhere you go. I wish I had a real man in my life like you Mr. Russell to protect me."* *"I am not married, and really don't have anyone in my life.",* Russell replied modestly.

"Hey, beautiful young lady, I am single and available! And I would love to take you out on the town! It's a big world out there, and it is good to have a good friend that can help you and then show you the best of what this world can offer!" Charlie said, rehearsing one of his lines that he had practiced on many occasions when he wanted to meet someone new. *"Well, I don't know Mr. Strickland.*

I do like men with real hair.", she replied, snickering. Charlie turned another shade of red. He was so frustrated. When he looked in the mirror, an expression of shock and then horror fell on his face. *"I think I am looking for a real man in my life right now. I lived a long time with that old mouse face, squeak of a man. Yes, it is true. He did have money. But after he died, he did not leave me one single dime. I worked my fingers to the bone for that old rusted screw. I helped prepare all his meals, along with the catering staff. The mansion that I lived in was just a nightmare with me caring for him as he constantly called out my name as he tottered along with his two-wheel squeaky walker. He was driving me crazy! I thought after the old crust bucket died, I would inherit something. I deserved it! I was his wife! But that old coot left me with nothing. I do admit that I did go through his safe, his bank accounts, and got what I could before I left, before the police came and started to make accusations. Everyone started blaming me for his death! Even the catering staff, the cleaning people, all started to make me feel so guilty and afraid, Mr. Russell! I need a real man in my life that will protect me. Please, can you sit with me in the back, Mr. Russell? I really need a friend right now."*

Russell unbuckled his seat belt, climbed over the seats, and started to sit near Miss Honey Creek. Miss Honey Creek put her head under Russell's chin. Her perfume caused his thoughts to float as his body started to tingle. He was hoping that the feathers would not start exploding out of him again. It would have been a most embarrassing and unexplainable situation if an outburst of feathers would fill up the car and cover everything. He had never been that close to a human in his life; not like this, and it felt good. Russell put his hand on her legs and started breathing deeply while he looked at her deep blue eyes.

Apparently, Charlie was still frustrated about the comment she made about his hair because when he shifted the convertible, it jerked wildly as she was pushed even closer to him. Russell then found himself stroking her legs. They were soft to his touch. But suddenly, she looked frighteningly at him saying, *"Mr. Russell what is wrong with your hands? They are so rough, and your fingernails are so long, green, and black! Those things are creepy looking!"* She screeched as she pulled away from him. Russell now knew that he was in trouble. He didn't know what to do. He stumbled over his words, and then he started to lie. *"Well, you know I have been in the oil business for such a long time now. And sometimes, when you are part owner of the Shell Petroleum Company and own a few thousand head of cattle, and a few dozen ranches, the business leaves a permanent scar on your hands. It is just the hazard of the business that I'm in."* *"You are in the oil business?"* Miss Honey Creek said as her eyes became wide and bright as she licked her lips a few times. *"I knew you came from wealth! I just knew it!"* *"Well, my father owns a thousand head of cattle on a thousand hills.",* Russell said with a gleaming smile. *"God that has to be the perfect line!"* He thought laughing to himself. Miss Honey Creek scooted closer to him and laid her head on his chest underneath his chin again.

As she sat in the backseat of the convertible, the night began to fall with a wonderful sky that was lit up from a spectacular canapé of stars. *"This has to be the best assignment of all."* Russell thought as he took the beer from her hand, and began drinking some of it. She started to rub her hand across his chest, causing Russell to believe that being human really did have some perks to it. *"I don't know why they warned me, saying this has to be one of the most dangerous assignments of all of my missions. What a piece of cake!"* He said. Miss Honey Creek heard him and said, *"I am so sorry, but I don't have any cake, but I am sweet as a Honey Creek."* *"Yes, you are!"* Russell said as he got even closer to her. She started to nibble on his neck, leaving her pink lipstick on his chin and neck. She took her finger and started to play with his bottom lip. Russell started to choke, and began to panic, clutching his chest as if he was in pain. *"Are you alright, Mr. Russell?",* Miss Honey Creek said sweetly? *"I'm fine!"* Russell said as he examined his body to make sure that he had not lost any of his brilliance.

Then Miss Honey Creek asked him, *"How did you get here, in the middle of nowhere, with the rest of us common people?"* *"Well, it's a long story. I was going to a board meeting to check on the productivity of my staff when I decided to fly over my oil fields to make sure that my assets were up and running, and still in place. I had boarded my small private plane, and everything was going along well when I began to lose power in one of the engines. As the plane dipped and started to descend, I took evasive action. I had to make a quick decision, so I found this flat area, and I was fortunate to glide my plane down safely. There was no real damage to me or my plane. I am thankful to find such a perfect place to land my plane. It happened so fast that it was just so unbelievable!"* Charlie looked at Russell seated in the back from his rearview mirror, and called him out saying, *"Yeah, it's all unbelievable!"* Russell continued, *"And that is when I launched the GPS from my computer. They were able to locate me, and they sent Mr. Strickland to pick me up and take me to another airport where my staff would be waiting for another private plane to retrieve me."*

Charlie jerked the car to the side, and both slid to one side, causing the convertible to buckle. *"Oh, I am so sorry Mr. Crowfeet! Next time we will fly a plane directly to you. You know we have such excellent service."*

"I knew you were the kind of man that was waiting for a real woman like me." Miss Honey Creek started to stroke his face with her fingernails. As her perfume filled the air, she arose and started kissing him with her soft red lips. It was like Russell was airborne as he floated happily with feelings of desire. He was journeying on a fun, accelerating rocket, strapped in, and losing everything he was originally sent to the earth to accomplish.

Suddenly he cried out as a sharp pain pierced his chest. He then began shaking and smacking his lips in a crude manner as he nervously and quickly pulled back from the kiss. Then Miss Honey Creek started choking and coughing while grabbing her throat with both of her hands as if something was stuck inside of her mouth. She cried out to Russell, but he could do nothing but watch as she pleaded in agony. She reached out to Russell grabbing his shirt and almost ripping it off as she shuddered, coughed, and pleaded for help from him. She then stood up in the moving car, and she almost tumbled out of it before Russell caught her, and pushed her back down. She started pleading with Charlie, *"STOP THE CAR! STOP THE CAR! FOR THE LOVE OF GOD! STOP THE CAR! I'M DYING! PLEASE STOP THE CAR!"* She reached forward and grabbed the steering wheel. The convertible weaved back and forth like it was going to tip over on its side. Charlie hit the brakes as the convertible spun around in a half circle in a cloud of dust. As everyone came to an abrupt stop, Miss Honey Creek opened the door of the convertible, almost leaping out screaming, *"THERE IS SOMETHING IN MY THROAT! THERE IS SOMETHING IN MY THROAT! SOMETHING HORRIBLE IS IN MY THROAT! HELP ME PLEASE!"* She kneeled on her knees, choking and coughing until she reached in her mouth and pulled out a long white feather. *"What in God's name is this? What did you do to me, Russell? What kind of freak are you? I don't know how you got that thing in my mouth, but you stay away from me!"* Charlie started smiling, looking at the spectacle saying, *"Russell got a thing for feathers!"* *"You will never get that close to me again Russell! Do you hear me?! Stay away from me!"* Russell tried to come near her to extend an arm of comfort, but she screamed at him. *"DON'T YOU COME NEAR ME AGAIN! DON'T YOU EVER COME NEAR ME!"* She climbed back into the car and sat with her arms folded, staring at him in contempt. Next, she took out her compact mirror and began to powder her face with so much powder that she was creating a white cloud as they drove down the road. Russell wanted to explain to her that the thing that was happening to him was out of his control, but nevertheless, he was developing feelings for her. He felt his arms and they were tingling and burning as green and purple veins broke out all over his body. *"You look like you are sick Russell! You need to go find a doctor. And you had the gall to kiss me! I will be glad to get away from the both of you two freaks!"*

Soon after, she noticed something else about Russell. As she looked at him awkwardly, there was something wrong with his face, and the top of his head had changed. Russell slowly reached up. The shape of his head had changed dramatically, and out of his skull protruded two small eruptions that resembled two small curved horns that had formed. *"What is wrong with you Russell? My God, you are sick looking!"* Miss Honey Creek cried out in alarm. Russell's eyes also had become wide. His pupils morphed into a black color, and there was a cloudy film that covered both eyes that made them look fluorescent as if he was going blind. His nose had shriveled up until there was only a flap of skin, where the two holes that were supposed to resemble his nostrils. Russell touched his face and gasped in horror.

He knew that the transformation had taken place. He had failed this last assignment. It was all over. He would be totally transformed soon. There was nothing left for him to do but put his cowboy hat over his face. He looked at Miss Honey Creek and said, *"It never really would have worked out anyway. I am not parcel to dish colored blondes. I think I will just take a nap."* Then Russell said to himself, *"It's starting. I am losing my Brilliance."*

Russell was afraid now of how he would transform. It was always dangerous to be around any fallen being of light that was going through the last stages of the withdrawal from the brilliance. He recalled one incident that still frightened him. Once, he arrived with an Angelic team that tried to save a Celestial that had fallen and was in the last stages of releasing The Brilliance. It was a dangerous situation. The Celestial was going through the withdrawal. He appeared to be in agonizing torment. For those individuals that were in the last stages of losing The Brilliance, would do anything they could to try to stop the horrible transformation of being instantly swept into the darkness of oblivion. It was a heart-wrenching scene that occurred as the rescue mission tried to help the Celestial maintain his Brilliance before being swept away. The Celestial had been living in a fallen human state for years, ignoring any attempts to save him as he became increasingly ruthless and diabolical in his behavior and physical appearance. As the last particles of The Brilliance were departing from him, a terrible struggle occurred when he tried to stop the total transformation.

As soon as Russell and the team arrived at the condemned warehouse where the Celestial was living, he had almost lost all his human characteristics. His eyes were large, black inky wells that had no pupils. His skin also looked like it was covered with second and third-degree burns as if he was experiencing instantaneous, internal combustion while flames appeared and then burst out of his skin. He pleaded in anguish for Russell to save him as his long black fingernails dug into the wooden floor as he tried to keep himself from being lifted and pulled into the screaming vacuum of darkness. The darkness became a gravity-defying, screaming sinkhole; a collapsing cavern, pulling everything into it. For everything in the room was being pulled into a gigantic wind storm. The dining room tables, lamps, oriental rugs, picture frames, dishes, and silverware became airborne and flew out of the cabinets, and were pulled off the walls until they crashed onto the floor and were then pulled into the opening of the screaming darkness. The tremendous force was like that of a hurricane that had been released. Russell and his comrades would have been blown off their feet, sucked into it and disappeared into the oblivion, had they not tied themselves down with anointed ropes before entering the room. The Celestial was in a traumatic state of demonic psychological shock as he, at first, pleaded with Russell to help save him. *"PLEASE HELP ME BEFORE IT'S TOO LATE! PLEASE SAVE ME BEFORE IT'S TOO LATE! I NEED YOUR HELP! I CANNOT DO THIS ON MY OWN! I NEED YOUR HELP! IT WILL BE OVER SOON! I WILL BE TOTALLY TRANSFORMED AND NO ONE WILL BE ABLE TO HELP ME THEN!"* And then instantly with an insane personality shift, he began to fight against Russell and the rest of the rescue team while spitting out wads of acid from his mouth. Russell and the rescue team made several attempts to tie him down with the anointed ropes, but he bit and chewed through them like he was a wild and savage dog. Russell watched him, screaming and cursing them as his long rows of sharp teeth hung down the sides of his mouth as he sneered and hissed at them saying, *"Leave me alone! You stupid fools serving the God of Heaven! Why have you come to save me? I need no saving! Leave me alone! Leave me alone! There is power in the darkness! I have felt it! I need no saving from you!"* He sneered again and lunged at them, attempting to bite them with his vicious teeth before uttering a final word, and leaping gleefully into the screaming darkness. *"SAVE YOURSELVES! I DON'T NEED YOUR GOD ANYMORE!"* Russell watched him for a second, screaming ferociously before being pulled apart until there was nothing left of him, but the traces of his long fingernails that were left on the wooden floor of the warehouse.

Miss Honey Creek was still furious at Russell. *"Mr. Russell, you must be some kind of old freak, preying on beautiful women such as myself. I don't know where that feather came from, and how you could put it in my mouth. But you stay away from me! You are just a plain sick freak!"* Charlie added, *"Russell do you want another beer? You have made this woman totally delusional. That is a sure sign of love!"*

"Nawwww I'm fine Charlie! I am just going to sit here and enjoy the ride." Charlie then said, *"You know, we must be near a chicken farm for those feathers to be flying all over the place. I was driving once through Oklahoma, and I got caught in a grasshopper storm. Those little critters were hopping all around the car. And they even went inside the interior of the car, just like those feathers. I couldn't even see, and I almost wrecked my car. Those hoppers had covered the windshield completely! And if it was not for that rainstorm that blew them off, I would have been dead for sure!"* *"This is such an interesting conversation. The only thing you two can talk about is chicken coops and grasshoppers."* Miss Honey Creek said in defiance as she looked at them in disgust. And then she folded her arms against her chest, and turned her head away, looking at the darkness of the desert landscape as they drove by. Agitated, she continued. *"I think you lied to me, Mr. Russell! I think that you are nothing more than a dirt-poor drifter. You should have never even touched a woman of my stature and beauty. And you had the gall to put those filthy, black and green hands on me!"* Russell was still mumbling to himself, *"I cannot stop the process; it may be already too late. It may be too late for all of us!"* Charlie yelled at him saying, *"Russell man, I think you lost your mind! I am talking to you! Do you hear me? Are you alright, or what?"* *"Oh, I am alright. I am just back here thinking!"* *"Well don't worry about it, we are going to have some fun tonight!"* Charlie said while looking in the mirror, adjusting his perfect dental work.

Russell thought about the man dressed in white on the bus, and the instructions that he had given him about how Charlie would be trying to kill himself in just a few hours, and that he was his last chance to stop him. Russell thought how he could help him, but he was in such a fallen and broken state that he could not even stop himself from holding on to the last traces of his own Brilliance. Lowering his cowboy hat over his eyes once more, he wanted to forget everything. He thought about Miss Honey Creek. He thought about how she really needed a life makeover because she was spinning out of control and he had only made things worst.

While Charlie was driving, he began playing some Frank Sinatra music again. He fine-tuned the dial of his speaker and started singing,

"The summer wind comes rolling in from across the street. It lingers there to touch her hair to talk with me!" *"I didn't know you could sing so well, Mr. Strickland."* Miss Honey Creek said with a soft musical tone in her voice. *"Well, I enjoy good music and having a good time. But good times are getting harder and harder to find these days!".* *"I was just wondering what you got in that briefcase of yours. Why do you have it handcuffed to your dashboard? It must be something really important for you to do something like that."* *"Oh, it's just a little traveling money. I don't want to go this far without a little pocket change."* He took his free hand from the sterling wheel, and popped open the case." He picked up a stack of bills, all tightly held together by a rubber band. *"It's just a few one hundred dollar bills, that's all!"* Miss Honey Creek instantly came alive from her depression. She leaned forward. While Charlie drove, she started to sing the words of the song along with him. Then she playfully started nibbling on his ear. *"This is what I had been looking for all along, a man that knows how to take the wheel of the situation."* She started to move her fingers up and down his ears and gently straightened out his toupee. *"You know I love a man that can reinvent himself."* She softly spoke as she started to kiss his neck, and take her fingers and stroke his chest. She started playing with the gold chains that looped around his neck. At one point, the convertible swerved to one side, and moved off the road, hit a sand dune, and jumped upward. Russell lifted up his cowboy hat and said, *"Charlie, how am I going to have a good time if I'm dead. Keep your eyes on the road man!"* He pushed his cowboy hat down on his face again, ignoring Miss Honey Creek and Charlie. When she reached down to pick up one of the stacks of hundreds out of the case, Charlie jerked the case back from her hand, *"Take your little grubby hands off of my loot! I don't want an old trophy wife. I am looking for some young action. I had an old trophy wife before!"* *"What kind of prize are you? Where is the horse that died so you can keep your head warm? Both of you are losers! I am looking for a man that can create an adventure, a man that is a leader in business, and that will appreciate having a beautiful woman on his arms! I am looking for a man to escort me to his social and wealthy circles, knowing that I signify success. Mr. Strickland, you are a loser that*

is having a flashback from the 1980's. There is a price for a woman like me, and you two losers cannot even make it to the qualification trials!" Charlie was clearly agitated as he turned completely red, and angrily turned towards her saying, *"If you touch my money again, you will be walking in the middle of the desert with your cheap high heels!"* Miss Honey Creek started chuckling, *"Your little money is too small for me to be excited about. I wonder what else is small on you little man." "You better shut your mouth or I swear you will be on this road walking in the middle of nowhere! Look Miss Honey Creeper! Or whatever your name is! You are yesterday's oatmeal, and I know a facelift queen when I see one. I like them a lot younger than you. You are an old crusty potpie that has been left out way too long on the serving line. Look Miss Honey Creeper, you are an item on the dollar menu!"* Miss Honey Creek started powdering her face again, ignoring his comments. Even Russell started laughing under his cowboy hat at what Charlie had said.

It was annoyingly quiet when Miss Honey Creek lifted Russell's hat and started staring at him and said, *"What in the hell is wrong with your face Russell? Are you wearing prosthetics to hide what you really look like? You are truly a strange one. Stop this car and let me out! It is just too scary being with the both of you!"* Russell held his hat down again, covered up his face, and said, *"Can a man take a little nap if he wants too? Just let me be!"*

As the convertible traveled quietly in the darkness along the deserted road, they saw someone walking, carrying a tattered suitcase. He was dressed in a gray plaid suit and tie that was ripped from every side with holes in it. He also appeared to be just as dusty as the road that he was walking on. The soles of his shoes were frayed in the front, so some of his toes were hanging out. As Charlie drove by the man, he yelled out, waving his arms frantically *"HEY, YOU! HEY, PLEASE! I NEED A RIDE! I NEED A RIDE! HEY, CAN YOU GIVE ME A RIDE!"* The convertible came to a sliding stop as a cloud of dust surrounded it. The man ran towards them carrying his battered-looking suitcase. He looked as if he had not showered in weeks. He was also missing some of his front teeth, and his hair resembled a windblown haystack. Charlie called out to him as he approached the convertible, *"I will pop open the trunk so you can put your suitcase inside it!" "Thanks! I appreciate your kindness!"* He extended his hand towards Charlie, shaking his hand so many times that Charlie thought that he was trying to pull it out of its socket. *"You can sit up here with me and let the two lovebirds sit by themselves.",* Charlie said. The dirty man said that he had just come from Las Vegas where he had lost everything. *"You know Lady Luck betrayed me. That woman broke my heart. I was on a winning streak when everything came to a complete halt. Everything just went haywire! I was winning big time, living the high life, and then everything started falling apart. It is a dirty rotten shame!" "Yeah, I know what you're talking about.",* Charlie said in a muffled voice. He took off his dusty shoes and started to shake them as a cloud of dust floated over the backseat. Miss Honey Creek screamed in anger, *"Can you shake those dirty shoes out somewhere else? That dust is flying into my hair!" "Oh, I am so sorry Miss! But I had a lot of dirt in these shoes. I have been walking a long time, trying to find something in the desert. I have been looking for a Casino they said is somewhere around here. I have been walking trying to find it. They say that people are winning there, big time! They are taking in so much money that they can retire! That is where I'm going!" "Today must be your lucky day because that is exactly where we are heading.",* Charlie said.

The man took out a large eight-page colorful brochure from the inside of his suit jacket. *"Isn't that something? This brochure tells everything about it."* He also found a roll of coupons from the inside pocket of his dusty jacket that said, *"Free Play"* on them. Furthermore, he said, *"And every new customer gets fifty-five free plays on their slot machines! You cannot beat a deal like that! I must find that place! I'm going to get my winning streak back, once and for all!" "Where did you get that from?"* Charlie asked. *"It was sent to me in the mail, along with a bus ticket. The bus let me off about ten miles ago before it could no longer travel any further, and I have been walking ever since. I have been walking in the dark now, trying to find the place, and it appears to be just a dead end. I'm sorry! I should have introduced myself. I am Lucky Jewels Diamond Jenkins. I am a professional slot machine player! I have played the slots from Atlantic City, New Jersey to Las Vegas, Nevada. I have won big, and lost big!" "Looks like you lost more than you won, Honey!"* Miss Honey Creek said smiling.

Charlie reached in his pocket, and he pulled out a colorful brochure, just like the one Diamond Jenkins was holding. Miss Honey Creek appeared stunned. Her hand was shaking as she reached inside of her purse, and pulled out a similar brochure that described the fun and excitement at the *"End of the Trail Casino and Resort." "I was looking for this place when my BMW broke down. I figured it would be a nice little getaway. And besides, they sent me a 7-day free complimentary room and buffet ticket."* Charlie, in turn, spoke up saying, *"I received a free complimentary admission to the Show Girl Night Club Palace and Performance with all the drinks I want for free! And I also get a special V.I.P room with a private dancer! I have been selected to be part of their Elite Membership! This is the place that I have been looking for too!"*

Russell then spoke out, lifting his cowboy hat a little above his eyes, *"Mr. Jenkins, you did not explain anything about your life, and how you got here with just a suitcase, walking alone in the dark and in the desert."* Diamond Jenkins smiled with a mouth that only had a few teeth that were chipped, and stained brown and said, *"Lady Luck can be so changeable. She will love you one day, and will leave you cold and empty the next."* Russell then turned his head, gave a side-eye glance to Miss Honey Creek, and said, *"I know exactly what you mean." "It all happened when I was playing the slots. I put in my last ten-dollar bill, and then, all of a sudden...BAM! Just like that! The machines started ringing like crazy! The alarms started going off, and then the three diamonds appeared all in a row on the screen. People surrounded me, and then the manager came over and said that I had won the One Hundred Thousand Dollar Prize! I have never had money like that before. And the very next day, I quit my job at the Super-Mart as the store stocker manager. I was on a winning streak. I knew it, and I could not stop now. I went back to the casino the very next day and won five thousand more. God, it was unbelievable! I started to live in the casino. I spent all my time on the crap tables and at the slot machines, winning and losing. I started drinking heavily and living in the casino weeks and months at a time. I lost track of time. I spent very little time at home and saw my wife occasionally during this time of my life. I paid what bills I could, but as I won more, I disappeared again into the casino until it all started to fall apart. I started losing consciousness of the time of day and night. I was determined to recover what I had lost. I had turned into a maniac, a wild man, and I went for days without sleeping, eating or even changing my clothes. I lived for the slot machines and even fell asleep on them while playing them day after day until I was exhausted. My appearance also changed dramatically as I started going without sleep. I became delirious. I started playing with large sums of money, losing my sense of reality. I had played the slot machine so much until my fingers started to cramp and my arms became sore from pulling down the levers. Until one day, I could not pay for my room in the casino where I was staying. Then I started borrowing large sums of money and even started borrowing money from a notorious gangster that controlled the operation in the casino. I was sure that I would be able to cover all my expenses, up until the day that I had spent everything. There was nothing left. And to make matters worse, the gangsters came looking for me because I defaulted on my loan. I went home looking for my wife to help me out of this desperate situation. But when I came home, there was an eviction notice on the door and a letter underneath the door from my wife saying that she had left me with the kid. I had to leave the city if I wanted to live since the gangster had put a hit out on me. That's when everything changed for me. I started traveling by freight trains, scavenging bus tickets, and begging for rides as I traveled across the country, going to different casinos, trying to jumpstart my winning streak. Yes, I want to touch her again! Have her kiss me upon my lips and embrace me with her magical touch. "Yesssssss Sirrrrrrreeeee! It is going to happen! It's just a matter of time. I am going home with a big win. I am going back to my family once again. It is going to be so wonderful! Given that I have been saving these coupons in my pocket for a long time. I have fifty-five free plays on the one-hundred-dollar machine. This has to be the deal of a lifetime. I'm telling you Lucky Diamond Jenkins is going to kiss Lady Luck in her fat little face again! And I am coming back to sit on top of the world once again!"*

"The dirty man with the rotten teeth has nothing but a pocket filled with broken dreams." Miss Honey Creek said laughing. *"Well, at least he's got dreams. All of yours have been made by a plastic surgeon!"* Charlie said grinning. *"At least he has some hair! All of your hair is either made by Lassie or Roy Roger's horse Trigger!"* Miss Honey Creek retorted laughing in a sinister crackling voice.

Russell looked at them, wiped some lipstick off his face. He found a beer on the floor, popped it open and took a swig. *"It is too late for all of us anyway. It does not matter anymore. Nothing matters anymore! You should know. We are all on the road to damnation. And we are being chased by the Demon of Suicide! I am quite sure of it now."* *"You are a crazy sick drifter Russell! And your 1980's disco wearing clothes friend should have never picked me up! You might be some kind of dangerous lunatic, psycho freak that needs to be kicked out of this car!"* Miss Honey Creek said angrily. *"Hey, Russell, why don't you just shut your fool mouth and drink your beer? You are getting too whacked out!"* Charlie said. *"It's dark as hell out here, and I don't want to hear anybody talking about some Suicide Demon stalking us in the desert. I can hardly drive this car in this darkness. I don't need you trying to scare the hell out of me! So, Russell man, just shut your fool mouth up!"*

Diamond Jenkins spoke, stuttering as his eyes looked around trying to pierce through the darkness that consumed the convertible from every direction. *"Well, there is nothing out here but darkness. There is no Suicide Demon chasing anybody. Russell, you need to stop frightening everyone!'* Charlie demanded. *"Hey, this is supposed to be a fun trip!"* Miss Honey Creek blurted out. Russell then quietly spoke in a hardly audible whisper as everyone suddenly became quiet, *"Well, I have seen the Demon of Suicide once. It was during one of my last visits to the earth. That is one time that I don't ever want to repeat again."* *"Your last earthly visit? Are you for real Russell? How many times have you been to the earth?"* Diamond Jenkins said in a jittery, almost laughing, shaking voice. *"This is just really getting unnerving!"* Miss Honey Creek said as she started powdering her face erratically with a cotton ball. *"It was a brief encounter but I remember it all too well. And I still remember what it looked like. The creature was downright ugly! The ugliest thing I had ever seen! It was downright scary!"*, Russell said as he sipped his beer, closed his eyes, and pulled his cowboy hat back down over his face. *"You got all of our attention! You might as well finish your story, Russell."*, Miss Honey Creek said as she started laughing, still powdering her face with the cotton ball, nervously glancing around. *"I was working with this rescue team; a celestial rescue party sent down to the earth to help."* *"Well, are we supposed to believe you are some kind of angel or something?"* Miss Honey Creek said, frowning at Russell, looking disgusted. *"We were sent down to save people that were involved in suicidal and traumatic situations to hopefully deliver them."*, Russell said as he tipped his cowboy hat upward a little over his eyes. *"Russell man you are really getting strange."*, Charlie said with a tone of concern in his voice. *"You might have to get out of my car at the next Kwik Shop. You have just gotten too weird for me!"*

"When we arrived, it was a chaotic situation that was taking place. It was a prestigious office building in the downtown area of a major metropolitan city. Everyone in the building was screaming about the man that was on the rooftop, standing on the ledge, threatening to jump off. He was determined to kill himself. He had somehow short-circuited all of the elevators. So, the only way to the roof was to use the stairs." *"I thought you were some kind of an angel! Why do angels have to use the stairs? If you were an angel, you could have just flown up to the rooftop."* Diamond Jenkins said as he peeked over the top of his brochure, looking at Russell, blinking and squinting his eyes. *"There was a force of depression and heaviness mixed with sorrow that clouded the atmosphere around the building. And that prevented us from using our powers of flight."* *"Boy, this is really getting complicated!"*, Diamond Jenkins said, still clutching his colorful brochure, excitedly examining the pages. *"All of his co-workers were devastated by his actions. For one moment, he sat calmly at his desk working as if it was just another ordinary working day. He was typing on the computer at his desk, checking documents and expenditures for the company. Everything appeared routine. Then in a shocking, eruptive manner, he began screaming as he untied his tie, and ripped opened his shirt. It appeared as if he was being dragged, and pulled*

over his desktop in the room. It was as if something had attached itself to him, and he was powerless to stop himself from being pulled along. He began screaming at everyone in the office with a horrible, terrifying-sounding voice, "IT HURTS SO BAD! IT HURTS SO BAD! THE CHAINS, THE FLAMING CHAINS ARE CONNECTED TO MY CHEST! PLEASE HELP ME PULL THEM OUT! The chains are connected to my chest! Someone help me pull the chains out of my chest! My heart is on fire! Help me pull the flaming chains out of my heart." But there was nothing that anyone could see, at least not with human eyes. He continued to scream, and he started pulling on his chest, puncturing holes in his skin and angrily pulling off pieces of his flesh. He continued screaming like a madman, trying to find a way out of a nightmare. And then suddenly, his hands caught on fire as large blisters broke out on them and sizzled with heat as smoke rose from them. At that moment, he cried out even louder, begging for someone to help him. I can still hear him saying, "My hands are burning! My hands are burning! Help me! Please, for the love of God! Pull the chains out of my chest! Help me pull the chains out of my chest!"

The frightened co-workers could now see that his hands were indeed burning and black clouds of smoke began to fill up the room. Someone called the police and the fire department reporting that he had set himself on fire. They reported that he was now threatening to jump off the roof of the building. When we arrived, we instantly transformed ourselves into policemen and firemen and moved freely through the panicky crowd. Celestials can assume any human appearance in a matter of seconds. His co-workers were fleeing out of the building overtaken by fear while the office turned into chaos as they scrambled for safety. They cried out to us saying, "He has gone utterly insane! He is on the roof! He is cutting himself and tearing his skin apart!" When the rescue team arrived, he was standing on the ledge of the building, threatening to jump. We could see that the skin of his hands and his chest had been charred black. And there was black smoke coming from his blistering hands, and from out of a hole in his chest. He then cried out insanely saying, "He is pulling me off the edge! I cannot stop myself! Please help me! I don't want to die! I don't want to go to oblivion! I am afraid! Help me!" We watched him as he pulled on his chest, tearing his flesh apart, and then crying out, "My hands are on fire! The chains are on fire! They are burning my hands! I have tried to pull them out of my chest, but the chains are on fire! And there is nothing that I can do now, but die the way I choose!"

His hands continued to shake as smoke rose from them while he tried to pull at something invisible that was protruding out of his chest. Everyone from his office believed that he had gone completely mad as they looked up at him teetering on a ledge on the roof of the building. He was now just inches away from falling to his death. He lifted one of his legs forward and then tried to go backward. He cried out to us, "Please help me! I am not ready to be consumed by the darkness! Help me! Please pull me back to the roof!" I then opened my jacket, pulled out the sword of the Arc of Light, and I ran towards the screaming man, wielding the sword around him, hoping that it was destroying the evil that had possessed him. I could hear the sound of chains falling off him as he was able to free himself and inch closer away from the edge of the ledge. And now, black smoke emitted from out of his chest and hands and clouded the air. The Arc of Light, the holiest weapon that the Celestials can wield in battle, can destroy the deadliest of the dark creatures. For even a simple glance upon its light, could send them screaming back into The Void. Then I noticed that something was terribly wrong. The Arc of Light was changing colors. It started to dim and flicker as if it was losing its power. This had never happened before in all my interceptions of rescuing a fallen Celestial. Then a hand appeared out of the ethereality of the air. It was diseased and covered with terrible looking sores. It touched the Arc of Light and snapped it in two. I gasped in horror at what had just happened. I felt weak and dizzy as if I was depleted of my supernatural might. And then the man screamed out again. As he was being pulled closer towards the ledge, he cried out saying, "LET ME DIE NOW! I HAVE LOST EVERYTHING! I HAVE NOTHING LEFT TO LIVE FOR ANYMORE! PLEASE JUST LET ME DIE!" His mind was confused his thoughts were being manipulated. I heard another voice speaking along with his. "I HAVE NOTHING TO LIVE FOR ANYMORE! MY WIFE LEFT ME, AND I AM ON THE VERGE OF

FORECLOSURE! AND IN THE PROCESS OF LIVING, I HAVE BECOME SO ADDICTED TO DRUGS! I CANNOT FUNCTION OR LIVE IN THIS WORLD ANYMORE!"

The rescue team recognized that they were dealing with one of the higher principalities; one of the elites who was able to block the searing sword of the Arc of Light. All at once, the Demon of Suicide revealed himself to us. He stood on the ledge of the building. His body was completely covered with hideous sores. He screamed at us saying, "WHY DO YOU STUPID BEINGS OF LIGHT STILL WORSHIP A GOD! IN THE DARKENED VOID, YOU BECOME A GOD!" Whenever he opened his mouth, a mass of slithering chains having the movements of pythons recoiling, would then quickly leap out, trying to reattach themselves to the screaming man's chest. Then I saw that the chains burst into flames, attaching themselves to his arms and legs. The Spirit of Suicide is the most sickening creature that I had ever faced in all my hundreds of encounters upon the earth. His hair was wiry and moved erratically upon the top of his head. Then I noticed that his hair was alive and composed of thousands of tiny black snakes as if he was Medusa's apprentice. The snakes on his head hissed and screamed terrible insults at us. Suddenly, we were overtaken with fear. Our focus became distorted as we stumbled backward, consumed with panic and dread. The creature's face and skin was pale and covered with black veins and black open sores. His eyes were off centered. One of them was on the side of his twisted face, and the other moved rapidly around without a pupil. The creature had black wings that unfolded like an umbrella that appeared to have a wingspan of over eight feet in width as he leaped off the building, hovering as he continued to pull on the chains that were attached to the screaming man. The wings cast a cold dark shadow over the ground below. Some of his co-workers lost their sense of empathy and began to hold their cameras upward, waiting for the man to jump. The office workers that stared at the man on the ledge, failed to see the chains that were dangling from out of his chest. Then the creature spoke again pleading to the man to end his life. "You died many years ago! You died in your loneliness, in your bitterness, in your hatred for everyone! You died in your contempt for living. You *died in your anger, in your distrust, in your hurt, in your emptiness, in your sorrow, in your pity, in your distrust. For there is no one that wants to love you. Don't you know how truly empty you are? Don't you know how dead you are? I can restore your power back to you again! Make you believe you are worth something!"* He then pulled harder on the chains as the man jerked forward almost falling to his death while struggling, fighting to maintain his balance. We knew we had to move fast. He was just seconds away from falling. I rushed towards the man, grabbing one of the fiery chains when it snapped and broke. The creature started howling with a terrible laughter as the man leaped forward crying out in a most pitiful voice, *"DON'T YOU KNOW I AM ALREADY DEAAAAAAAAD!"* He leaped off the ledge of the building and plunged to his death below. We had failed miserably that day! Our rescue attempts were distorted by pride, by arrogance, by the importance of our abilities. We had failed because we had forgotten about God. Now I am struggling again, afraid that I will lose again. I am afraid I will fail at another rescue attempt. I am afraid of being a failure! I am just plain afraid. And I want to be left alone!"*

"Well, that was some story Russell. Do you have any other scary bedtime stories to tell us before you put all the children to bed tonight?", Miss Honey Creek said laughing out loud. But she was nervous. She attempted to apply her lipstick and missed her top lip because it smeared across the side of her cheek. *"Mr. Crowfeet you are some storyteller. How are we supposed to believe all of this stuff is true?"* Diamond Jenkins said as he could not stop his hands from shaking while holding on to his casino brochure. *"When I pulled on one of the chains of the Demon of Suicide, I received his mark upon me. It is a permanent mark of my failure. It is the mark that he will come for me next! For Celestials that are on the verge of transforming into the emptiness will begin to mutate for they are gradually being pulled into the utter Void."* Russell held out one of his hands and it instantly caught on fire. As a flickering flame appeared, covering his skin, he grimaced in pain and cried out. He jerked his hand back quickly and put the flame out as he eased his hand back into his jacket. *"This is not supposed to happen to Celestials! I am already near The Void!"*

Everyone in the convertible started screaming as the car swerved out of control and came to a silent stop. Everyone just stared at Russell in shock and fear while he held his hand inside of his coat, seemingly in excruciating pain. *"I don't know how you did that, Russell? I don't know what the hell you are? But I swear, you better shut up or I am putting you out of my car! I have had enough of your creepy nonsense for tonight. This is the vacation of a lifetime for me, and you better not mess it up, Russell! Do you hear me, Russell? You better shut up now! Or you will be in the middle of nowhere, walking home, if you ever had a home!"* "Yeah, nowhere. *That is where we are going, in the dark, in The Void. We are all going to a place called nowhere."*, Russell said as he put his cowboy hat over his face and closed his eyes.

As the convertible traveled in the timeless darkness, nothing appeared but the surface of the road before them. All the conversations in the convertible had now stopped. An eerily strange, frightening silence fell over everyone. Russell quickly chewed on a wad of tobacco and quietly kept pushing his hat down over his face, trying to keep it from blowing off. Then Diamond Jenkins spoke up, stuttering, saying, *"Hey.... Hey......Hey......Mr..... Mr. Russell...Crowfeet, when did you go on your last mission? And why aren't you with the rest of your angel friends? What happened to you?"* "I began to tick them off I guess. I don't know. Maybe it was just my attitude. Maybe I became arrogant. I thought I was doing it all. I didn't realize how weak I was. I guess I just messed up everything."* Russell conceded. *"I guess that sums it up for all of us."*, Diamond Jenkins said as he stared in shame while shuffling a pack of cards in his hands.

Another hour had gone by as the convertible was still speeding in the darkness with a cluster of stars as the only visible light. Then shockingly, a dilapidated old shack appeared suddenly out of the darkness. It was a small-scale wooden building that had some of the boards falling off its frame. And on the top of the building was a crooked sign that was blinking off and on with some of the letters missing that said, *"The End of the Trail Casino!"* Diamond Jenkins became overjoyed, laughing uncontrollably with a mouth of dark stained broken teeth saying, *"THIS IS THE PLACE! THIS IS THE PLACE! THE END OF THE TRAIL CASINO! THE END OF THE*

*TRAIL CASINO! JUST LIKE THE BROCHURE SAID! THIS IS
THE PLACE! I FINALLY FOUND IT!"* *"Oh, my! What a dump!"*
Miss Honey Creek snarled. *"We came this far for a shack! What a
waste of my time?!"* Next, Charlie spoke out. *"This was supposed to
be the best time of my life. Now, look where we're at, a shack, on a
deserted road, in the middle of a desert. What a terrible joke someone
played on all of us!"*

The shack was covered with old weather-beaten rotten wood.
Charlie slowed the convertible to a stop. They exited the car cautiously,
observing an old man rocking in a chair as he sat there motionless,
on the porch of the shack. *"He looks like he is dead!"*, Diamond
Jenkins exclaimed. He slowly walked up to the motionless corpse and
examined him as he sat in the rocking chair. His skin looked as wrinkled
as his clothes. His face was pale, dried, and covered with dust as if he
had become dehydrated while sitting silently in his rocking chair. It was
as if the graveyard was missing one of its residents. His eyes stared
blankly into nothingness as the rocking chair appeared to move by
itself. *"I...I...I... think that he is dead for sure!"* Diamond Jenkins
said as he pulled out his brochure and sadly looked around, *"There is
nothing about him in this brochure. What a complete letdown!"*

The man appeared to be about ninety years old with large dark age
spots covering the top of his bald head that had wispy gray strands of
hair that fluffed out on the sides. He seemed like he was an old farmer
that had died in his chair without anyone even knowing or perhaps
even caring. He wore faded jean overalls and brown cracked work
boots. Everyone crept onto the porch and quietly stared at him. Then
Charlie approached him and poked him with his finger to see if he was
really dead. Then suddenly, his eyes flashed. He blinked his eyes for a
few seconds and spoke in a squeaky, excited voice, *"Hello, folks! We
are always open! We have been waiting for you! We are always open!
Go right in! You will have the time of your life, guaranteed! Hello,
folks! We are always open! Go right in! And you will have the time of
your life! Hello, folks! We are always open!"*

The old wooden front door opened by itself. There appeared to
be nothing inside but darkness. *"I don't understand how all of us
were fooled! There is nothing here but a rundown shack and an*

old man with dementia talking out of his brain.", Miss Honey Creek cried out in disappointment. *"And all this time I have been carrying this brochure around in my hands, believing this would be the place where I would win big, come back financially secure and finally be in the good graces of Lady Luck once again! This must be the most terrible humiliation of my life! I believed this place really existed. I believed everything in this brochure. What a letdown. It is just a dusty, broken-down shack."*, Diamond Jenkins said angrily, stuffing his brochure inside of his torn, dirty jacket. His eyes became glassy and moistened with tears. *"Maybe if I leave now, I can catch a freight train and be in Atlantic City tomorrow morning. I always wanted to play the slots there anyway!"*, Diamond Jenkins added as a terrible emptiness rushed through him.

"You know, one of my husbands died just like this, sitting down in a chair. He was at the breakfast table. I had just made him a bowl of oatmeal. The next moment, he died, and his face fell right into that bowl of oatmeal. It was a hilarious sight!", Miss Honey Creek said as she started snickering which eerily turned into a sinister laugh. *"The only thing tragic about it was that he left all of his assets to charity, the Cheapskate! The Rusty Screw left me with nothing! If I had my way, he would have been buried up to his neck in that oatmeal!"*, She remarked looking at the old man in the chair, still laughing.

"This place is dangerous! I can feel a thick atmosphere of sorrow. Don't you feel it? It is cold and empty here! We must leave now before it is too late!" *"Calm down Russell my man! I didn't come this far not to look around! Why don't you push your cowboy hat down over your pie hole and shut the hell up! I have to take a leak anyway while I am here!"* Charlie said. *"I have no powers left to fight the darkness. If they decide to attack, we can be overtaken! It is cold! The cold is a terrible sign that we are very close to the opening. It is the opening of The Void! Can you feel it? The loneliness, it is here. It has found us!"* *"You are a complete looney, Russell! You are a traveling psycho! You need some serious help, my dear Mr. Russell!"* Miss Honey Creek chided. *"Please believe me!"*, Russell said in a quivering voice. Russell then started choking as he desperately tried to breathe. He held his hands around his throat, and then pulled out a long white feather

from his mouth. *"You are disgusting!"* Miss Honey Creek said as she stared at him with contempt. When she placed her hands on her hips, her red fingernail polish appeared to eerily glow in the darkness. *"You are completely disgusting! Get away from me, Russell! Or I swear I will slap that silly cowboy hat off your face!"* Then she took her hand, wiped the lipstick off her lips saying, *"And you had the gall to kiss me! You worthless dog!"*

"I am mutating, losing the last of my brilliance and this place is expediting the process. We are going to die if we don't leave now!" *"THAT'S IT, RUSSELL! I DON'T GIVE A HOOT IF YOU HAVE TO WALK BACK HOME! YOU ARE NOT GETTING IN MY CONVERTIBLE! YOU ARE SICK, MAN! AND YOU NEED HELP! You have been drinking beers and chewing on that loco weed all night! But you have gone too crazy to get back in my car! Russell, you find your own way back home tonight!"*, Charlie angrily said as his toupee moved somewhat on the top of his head.

"None of you understand that you are going to die tonight, all of you! We have been marked. The Demon of Suicide is near. The coldness is all around us. I cannot take it anymore! I am afraid! I have lost before! And I have nothing left to fight it again!", Russell cried in a solemn voice.

"I cannot take listening to his foolishness anymore. There has to be an outhouse or somewhere for a fellow to take a leak.", Charlie said as he looked around the shack, peeking through one of the windows. *"Russell, My God, Man! You are losing your mind! I don't know if it is the beers you drank or that loco weed that you have been chewing on. But you need to calm down! This is a good place to take a break. I have been driving all night. There might be an old outhouse somewhere around where I can take a leak."* *"The front door is open. I wonder if we should just go in."*, Diamond Jenkins said forcing a worried smile as he pushed the door back further.

"Let's take a look-see and poke around what we can dig up in this little shack. We might find a few old pots and pans that we can rattle around. I need a little fun tonight!" Miss Honey Creek said as she walked through the door. Charlie followed behind Miss Honey Creek through the pitch blackness and disappeared. Diamond Jenkins was

totally confused on what he should do next. He pulled out his long row of coupons and stretched them out in his hands. *"I have been carrying these coupons in my hands for a long time. I want to get my free plays! It doesn't matter what I have lost!"* He walked through the darkness singing, *"Luck Be a Lady tonight!"*

Russell was the only one left on the porch looking at the mumbling old man as he kept repeating the same thing over and over again. *"Don't you have anything else to say, old man?"* As Russell approached the door and proceeded to enter into the darkness, the old man began mumbling something new, *"All who enter lose all hope! You lose all hope! You lose! You lose! You lose!"*

As they wandered through the darkness, the skin on their bodies started stretching out of place. They felt diabolical hands tearing inside of them pushing outward. Their hidden pain of loss and the sorrow that stalked their lives took shape and form, becoming animated inside of them. Russell could hear Diamond Jenkins scream for help as his clothes were being ripped and shredded from off his body. Diamond Jenkins watched as horrid, dark, green hands come out of his chest and grab his precious roll of free-play coupons that were hidden inside of his jacket. Terrified, he frightfully, but desperately tried to hold on to them.

Miss Honey Creek's long blonde hair turned into a thicket of prickly thorns. She took out her compact case and tried powdering her face as her skin started peeling away. Charlie continued to hold on to his suitcase until his fingers became like the roots of a tree as his fingers wrapped around the case. He then began to scream when he saw that his hand and arm had become as brittle as rotten wood and snapped in half.

Each one of the travelers found themselves in a conscious state of regret and sorrow, reliving the pains from their past lives. As the sorrow overtook them, they began to repeat their failures, reciting their loss and emptiness. And in a similar manner, they were like the old man rocking on the porch of the shack, empty and lost.

Russell heard a compilation of voices, crying out in The Void. *"My life was a complete waste! I was married and divorced three times, and I have nothing to show for it!" "I tried hard to be successful! I worked two jobs, and I am still so very far behind. This is not the place I thought I would be! I wanted to be successful just like my friends, who moved on to important jobs and exorbitant salaries. And where am I in life? And look what I have accomplished! Absolutely nothing! I have nothing to show for my life. I am such a failure! I am such a failure! I have failed! I have failed."*

Russell then found himself being overpowered by the sorrow in the room as images of his own failure appeared before him. He cried out, *"God, you have failed me! You have left me alone in this world. Where were you when I needed you the most? You have failed me! And I have lost my wings! I have lost my beautiful wings!"*

With a suffocating force as their breath of life was taken, the skin of their bodies turned into wisps of dust and blew away. They were reduced to empty shells. Russell saw something else as he observed their carcasses. Their hearts had somehow managed to survive and appeared to be thriving and beating. Russell saw what appeared to be small sparks of light that clung to it and refused to leave. The small fissures of light moved upward out of their hearts and illuminated in the darkness, in The Void. Russell believed it was their life force that was determined to survive; determined to believe that hope was still in the world. Equality, understanding, and kindness that could still exist above all the terrible things that happened in the world. For this undefeated force continued to exist, beating the odds and determined to survive, no matter how difficult the struggle, knowing that love is an inextinguishable power.

And now the creatures of The Void came for Russell. He looked around. He was surrounded as they sought to attack and possess him. But something happened. A ring and a flash of light, a powerful arch of The Brilliance appeared. He fell backward into the darkness, crying out to God for mercy. In a sudden clap of thunder, a shattering streak of lightning lit up the darkness. They all emerged out of the door, gasping for air, choking, breathing hard.

But something happened and changed them for they had transformed and had become younger. They returned to a state of consciousness, a place from their past lives where nothing mattered and nothingness was an acceptable way to live. As they emerged from the darkness, dazed and shaken, they appeared to be in a large casino as the noise from slot machines and the laughter of people shouting, stirred and quickened them back into reality. The floor of the casino was covered with expensive red thick plush carpeting. The casino had a winding staircase with gold railings that went down into a luxurious room that was the size of a football field. There were hundreds of neon colored slot machines, along with an enormous bar that had hundreds of people crowding around it as bartenders worked furiously, pouring drinks into a never-ending supply of demanding and thirsty glasses. This was the room of the movers and the shakers, the opportunists, the jet setters, the captains of industry that made things happen. For there was a certain level of opulence that you could feel in the atmosphere. The ceiling of the room represented a Michelangelo renaissance style with paintings that depicted Napoleon, Caesar, and Emperors all sitting upon thrones. The ceiling also had numerous chandeliers that had large teardrop crystals that hung down and sparkled over the crowd, creating a starlight effect. The noise of the laughter in the room was deafening as the travelers forgot how they were stranded, broken, and lost in the desert.

There were waitresses, darting through the crowd with mini-skirts, dressed in fishnet stockings, and cute tiny aprons that tied around their dresses. The waitresses carried silver trays that had a variety of treats and hors d'oeuvres as they presented them to the gleeful and noisy crowd. Russell could see a multitude of different people in the crowd. Businessmen in stylish suits, sheiks in robes, mingling with movie stars, and athletes from every sport. There were presidents from different countries and even kings with their entourages that followed them. There were leaders from African, European, and Asian countries. There were even religious leaders dressed in their ceremonial robes as they appeared to be laughing and eating with the large group of people that were assembled. There were hundreds of slot machines of every description with neon colors that were constantly ringing as people from all over the auditorium were picking up their winnings from the coins falling out of all the different machines. A pleasant and an excited voice was heard somewhere over a loudspeaker that was almost speaking non-stop, **"Ladies and Gentleman, aisle** *number four has just won ten thousand dollars! And they just keep on winning at the End of the Road Casino! There is no end to the fun and the excitement! Go ahead and try your luck at one of our fun slot machines! Winners are happening all the time! Why don't you be one of them?"*

There were constant shrills from people as they cried happily over their winnings, every time a slot machine rang. *"Hey, over here! I just won! I just won! I just won! I want to cash in my winnings!"* There was a long beautiful horizontal engraved mahogany table that had engraved faces of gargoyles upon it as if it belonged in a castle. The table appeared to be over one hundred feet. It was filled with every tasty treat that you could possibly imagine. There were roasted turkeys, a large pot roast, and a humongous roasted stuffed pig with an apple in its mouth, turning on black prongs over an open grill as a blazing fire surrounded it. The enormous buffet table was covered with large gold and silver platters filled with an array of tasty dishes, and delightful casseroles surrounded by a variety of cakes and pies. There were tables of chocolate cakes, cupcakes, strawberry pastries, and heaps of cookies that appeared to be freshly baked. The aroma from the delicious buffet consumed the room as the hungry casino guests crowded the food table. In a maddening savage display of gluttony, they stood stuffing their mouths as they appeared to be snarling, growling, and baring their teeth at each other. And still, there were more platters upon the tables filled with trays of chocolates, candy lollipops, gelatin molds in the shapes of hearts, dollar signs, snakes, spiders, and other candied insects. As Russell looked at the bar, it appeared to be the largest bar that he had ever seen. There was a platoon of bartenders pouring the scotch, whiskey, rum, and beer into rows of glasses as a maddening crowd of humanity surrounded the bar, drinking down each glass hurriedly that was served to them.

Then Russell noticed something else. It was impossible. It could not have been real. Maybe it was just his vertigo from riding in the convertible for such a long time. Or perhaps it was the after effects of him passing through the darkened Void to arrive at the casino. He knew all of them were in great danger, but his mind was leaving him. His sense of what was palpable and his sense of reality was slowly being diminished. He noticed that as the bartenders poured their drinks, the bottles somehow never became empty. But it did not matter anymore to Russell, nothing mattered. The only thing that mattered right now was if he could get a drink, and if he could have some fun. A large group of businessmen was drinking together in a secluded room on the right side of the casino. They appeared to be having some sort of convention. Most of them appeared to be intoxicated. They were laughing and singing out of tune while they tried to prop themselves up. Then Russell saw a man dressed in a black tuxedo near another secluded room in the casino, calling out to guests that walked by, saying, *"YOU HAVE NEVER SEEN WOMEN MORE BEAUTIFUL THAN THIS IN YOUR LIFE! YOU COME INSIDE AND SEE FOR YOURSELVES, THE END OF THE ROAD SHOWGIRL PALACE! IF YOU ARE LONELY, THEY WILL TAKE AWAY YOUR LONELINESS. THE SHOWGIRLS WILL MAKE YOU FORGET ALL OF YOUR TROUBLES! THEY WILL BE YOUR COMPANION, YOUR PERSONAL ESCORT, YOUR PRIVATE DANCERS!"*

One extremely attractive young woman walked slowly back and forth in front of the gold door in a bouncing stride. She wore a black silk dress that molded around her body and had a long slit on the side that went all the way up her leg. Her hair was an assortment of black waves that shimmered as she paced back and forth, looking a lot like a sultry panther that had been released from its cage. Like a hypnotic fly caught in a mummified web, one of the casino guests appeared before the gold door, looking around in a nervous, panicky state as he hastily opened the door and disappeared inside the colored lights of the room. But in that brief moment, Russell was able to look inside, behind the gold door. He saw groups of women dancing on tables wearing negligees. There also appeared to be crowds of people inside. All of them were pushing and shoving each other around the tables, trying to gain a better position. And as the door opened, Russell heard the frightening sounds of their voices. It was an inhuman sound that sent frightening chills down his spine. Russell said to himself, *"It is impossible for people to scream like that. My God! It sounded as if a wounded dog is inside of there! I must be hearing things! I am desperately in need of some rest!"*

In the center of the casino, there was a large orchestra playing that was composed of an assembly of horns, clarinets, a piano, a bass drum and a group of violin players. The orchestra was playing a toe-tapping melody of big band tunes. They were all dressed in white tuxedos with black bow ties. As the dance floor slowly revolved, a tall skinny conductor wearing a white tuxedo that had long tails in the back, started conducting with his baton in a rapid pace and then called out to the crowd saying, *"IT'S TIME TO DANCE! GET ON YOUR FEET, EVERYBODY! LET'S DANCE!"*

They began playing a rendition of Benny Goodman's, "Sing, Sing, Sing!" The crowd covered the dance floor dancing in a feverish, raucous rage of drunken madness. As they danced, fights would periodically break out. The voices of people were overheard in the crowd saying, *"Don't you know how to dance? You just stepped all over my Stacy Adams shoes! You just danced in front of me! Don't you know how to say excuse me?"* And as soon as the offenders began pushing and shoving each other, they were escorted out of the room by large men in black coats.

A fat woman with large arms in a shimmering, sparkling red dress, who had a red gardenia in her hair, stood before a microphone and started singing a song about being happy and forgetting about the troubles of life. The orchestra conductor was swaying his body back and forth appearing as if he was an overcooked noodle. He shook his head like he was a salt shaker while the room continued to slowly revolve. The horns of the orchestra sounded as if they were screaming as the drums pounded and the violins echoed, temporarily transporting everyone into what seemed to be a state of bliss. The crowds started doing the Jitterbug, the Foxtrot, the Charleston, and the Cakewalk. It was as if a time machine had thrust them into another dimension as well as the casino, carrying travelers from a different world.

But Russell had been blinded as they all had been. It did not matter to them now. Nothing mattered to them anymore. They had come out of the darkness of their lives and had been made wonderfully new. That was all that mattered right now. Miss Honey Creek appeared to be twenty-two years old. Her hair had returned to its shimmering baby blonde color. The obtrusive platinum blonde color was gone, which gave her hair a fake neon glow from all her years of using hair dye in an attempt to capture its original color. The hidden strands of gray still appeared even after she dyed them many times. But now, her hair had become flawless, capturing all the light in the room, magnifying her beauty. Miss Honey Creek slowly took out a compact mirror and marveled, looking at her face which appeared to be bereft of the scars from the plastic surgery. The facelift was supposed to get rid of the wrinkles. Instead, that surgery left noticeable scars which were now completely gone. She had returned to her original Barbie doll looks. Her waistline was also transformed into a petite, flowing graceful curve; delicate in structure and motion. She no longer needed the elastic girdle that flattened her stomach and hid the unmovable layer of fat that plagued her ability to lie about her age. At times, when she wore the tight-fitting girdle, it caused her sides to ache. She smiled in front of her suitors, even though she was suffering in great pain. She no longer remembered what happened before she arrived at the casino. Furthermore, she did not care. She took her hand that had bright red fingernail polish, matching her cherry red lips, and began to smooth out her tight-fitting polka dot dress. The dress also had a stylish bow in the back that was attached near her buttocks and went upward into an open V shape that exposed a large portion of her porcelain back. As she continued admiring herself in her compact mirror, she deliberately parted her cherry red lips, licked a finger, smoothed her eyebrows, and then flashed her sea blue eyes until she created her heart stopping smile with her perfect white teeth.

Next, she focused on the group of businessmen attending their convention meeting. They appeared to be in their late fifties, laughing and drinking heavily while taking turns dancing with a woman in a yellow bikini. She appeared to be a model that was advertising suntan lotion for their company and other outdoor and recreational products. Miss Honey Creek grinned with a wide and deceitful smile as she took another quick glance at herself. A waitress darted between them, serving an endless supply of drinks and specialty appetizers from the casino. She looked at the businessmen gazing at her and said, *"Looks like dinner is being served!"* She sashayed down the winding staircase, almost gliding, skillfully walking in front of them as her perfume transfixed their attention away from the woman with the yellow bikini. She strategically dropped her handkerchief in front of a bug-eyed, drooling, fat man that stared at her as if she was a flawless angel dropped down from the sky. The businessmen scrambled over the fallen handkerchief in a mad dash as they pushed each other out of the way, trying to pick it up. The woman in the yellow bikini, who was advertising the suntan lotion for her company, was quickly forgotten. Miss Honey Creek stood there innocently, batting her mesmerizing blue eyes before the gawking, excited, weak-kneed businessmen. One overweight man with a stomach that lapped way over his belt, crowded everyone out of the way to secure the handkerchief, catching his breath as he tried to speak, saying, *"Well Howdy Miss...would you like to join our little party! We just flew in from Dallas. We are having our convention, and we could use a little more company, if you don't mind! Miss...I'm sorry, but I didn't get your name."*

Miss Honey Creek fashioned a pose, batting her eyes like she was a honeycomb and bumble bees were swarming around her. *"Well, I don't know? I am kinda new around here. I really don't know my way around, and I am afraid of strangers!"* The large man cowered, slightly, trying to make himself appear smaller, and then using a soft sneaky tone of voice said, *"Miss we are harmless as newborn kittens. We would not hurt you at all! We just want to have a good time. That is why everyone is here. Just to have a little fun! That's all!"* *"Well, I would be honored to be in your company*! Miss Honey Creek playfully said. *"I am alone in this casino. I need to have a little fun and let my hair down! I just come in from out of town myself. And I need a good man like you to show a sweet girl like me how to get around!"* Then Miss Honey Creek grabbed the elbow of the old gray-haired man and spoke to him in almost a musical tone. *"Let's go, Big Daddy! Turn on your headlights, and I will follow you anywhere, even if it's to the doors of hell!"* She continued laughing in a soft and sweet voice.

Russell believed that he was the only one that could remember how they were just outside, tired, dusty and hurting deeply for love.... for true love. Charlie came out of the door next. He had a new mat of curly black hair that was long and wavy and hung down to his shoulders, giving him the appearance of a Rockstar. Charlie's eyebrows and mustache also returned back to black. There were no longer any flecks of annoying gray hair that kept him constantly trying to pluck it out every day. He had long black Elvis Presley sideburns that came down to a point almost to the corners of his mouth. All of his teeth were now his own. They no longer moved around his mouth when he talked. And he wore a one-piece, ultra-tight elastic gold jumpsuit that clung so tightly, it could have passed for his own skin. He no longer had the large row of fat that poked out of his shirt and wiggled when he walked. His shiny gold jumpsuit only had one zipper that ran down the entire length of his body. It was zipped down the front until it stopped in the middle of his chest where a large crop of chest hairs stuck out. He wore a pair of super high, silver platform shoes that caused him to lean forward and slightly stumble as he walked along, just as if he was on the verge of falling. He wore five gold chains that dangled around his neck, and a large, tacky, neon medallion dollar sign that lit up.

He excitedly looked at all of the people in the casino until his eyes focused and locked in on the woman who was walking back and forth in front of the Show Girl Palace Club. She turned and winked at him and seductively motioned with her hand for him to come over. *"What a hot girl! I am ready to blow off some steam!"* He turned around in a quick circle and shuffled his feet from side to side, almost performing a clumsy dance move as he almost lost his balance. He then stopped and held up both of his hands and pointed his fingers at her like they were pistols and said, *"I am coming straight for you babe! It's me and you tonight!"* He slid down the winding staircase, clumsily dancing all the way down. Then he trotted over towards her, turning and twisting to the music of the orchestra like he was Fred Astaire. When he approached her, he looked at her and said, *"Hey, sweet ray of sunshine! I bet you got something that will brighten my day!"* She slowly grabbed his hand, unzipped his gold jumpsuit, and stroked the fluffy black hairs on his chest. She reached up and nibbled on his neck and said, *"I bet you got a pocket full of lightning for a lonely girl like me!"* Charlie had the face of a wild dog in heat. She then grabbed his hand again and let him stroke her long legs. *"Does it feel soft and good to you, Honey! Come inside and see me dance! I take off a lot more inside than what you see out here! Please come see me dance, Honey!" She began to kiss his face and playfully touch his long sideburns!* Charlie spun her around and carefully took her by her arm. He escorted her inside and disappeared behind the gold door.

Russell knew that this was a portal; the dangerous entrance to The Void. But he was slipping away as well. His mind was being diverted. His memories disorientated. He wanted a drink so badly, the bar served free drinks. It had been a tiring and dusty trip. Everyone else had appeared to change for the better. Russell declared in an angry voice, *"He does not care anyway! He left me in this dust bowl of the desert. God could have rescued all of us a long time ago if he really cared for anyone of us. We are doomed! It is too late for all of us! We are at the entrance of The Void. It does not matter anymore. I need a drink! And since I am dying anyway, I might as well enjoy myself before it's all over! I have been forgotten by God! I have been left out of his plans! I am desperately in need of a drink! Let me jump in the dark hole of failure after I have had a good time! That is all that I want to do; have one last good time!"* Russell slowly walked down the winding staircase. He put his cowboy hat on his head and started chewing on a straw in his mouth before heading toward the enormous bar, whispering, *"It doesn't matter anymore! Nothing matters anymore! It is just a happy time for all of us!"*

Diamond Jenkins emerged from out of the darkness wearing a white tuxedo with a French cuffed white shirt that had diamond cufflinks. He also wore a red bow tie and a red cummerbund. His suit coat had two long tails, and he wore a white top hat that was tilted to one side. He skillfully twirled a straight stick walking cane that had a large diamond attached to the top. Gone were the dirty, worn-out shoes that were on his feet. He now wore a shiny pair of black and white spats. He was clean shaven. Underneath the top hat, you could see that his hair had been cut and styled. He looked down at the slot machines giggling. His smile revealed his white teeth. One of his front teeth was capped with gold. The others were covered with diamonds. He stopped twirling his cane, nervously pulled out a brand-new brochure, and then unfolded a large roll of free play tickets for the slot machines. *"THIS IS TRULY MY LUCKY DAY! What a wonderful place this is! They even gave me a roll of free plays on their slot machines! I am so lucky to be here!"*

As he walked down the winding staircase he twirled his cane and started tap dancing as he spun around, twirling his cane. Instinctively, the orchestra started playing *"Luck Be a Lady Tonight!"* Diamond Jenkins then jumped on the railing of the golden staircase, singing and gliding all the way down, causing everyone to momentarily stop and applaud as he gracefully dismounted from the railing, spinning around in perfect syncopation to the music. He yelled out, *"MY DIAMONDS ARE SHINING BRIGHT TONIGHT!"* The great crowd of people returned their attention to the entertainment of the casino. Diamond Jenkins slowly strolled between the slot machines as the noise of people winning caused his body to tremble with joy. He had a whole row of hundred-dollar coupons, a gambler's dream come true. *"This is the place that I have been looking for! I am here! I have been looking for this place my whole life! And I have finally arrived! I have made it! Diamond Jenkins, the greatest player of all time has come to play the last game of his life! And nothing is going to stop me from cashing in my winnings!"* He started unrolling the large streamer of tickets in his hand as he pranced around and twirled his cane and tilted his white top hat to the side. He found a waitress and said, *"Hello, sweet Dear! Can you tell me where a gentleman can cash in his tickets for playable tokens!"* The happy young attendant said, *"To cash in your super roll of tickets, go directly to the cashier station."*

Diamond Jenkins found the cashier station and returned to the main floor of the casino with a heavy bag of hundred-dollar tokens. He could hardly believe that he was given so many free coins to play with. The orchestra was playing in a fury of sound as Diamond Jenkins continued to tap dance through the slot machines until he spun around and found the right one. He gently put a gold coin into the slot machine and took a deep breath. Slowly he pulled down the lever. Everyone momentarily paused to see what was going to happen next. As he pulled the handle, the spindle of the machine began to twirl and spin as three large diamonds appeared on the neon monitor. The slot machine began to ring loudly. Everyone erupted in applause when a flood of gold coins came pouring out of the slot machine, covering Diamond

Jenkins' hands and falling onto the floor. Elated, Diamond Jenkins cried out, *"LADY LUCK AND DIAMOND JENKINS ARE BACK TOGETHER!"* Diamond Jenkins picked up every coin until his bag was on the verge of bursting. His suit coat pockets sagged out of shape. Diamond Jenkins cried out again, *"LADY LUCK, MY SWEET GIRL! YOU ARE BACK IN MY ARMS AGAIN!"* Then a Casino Attendant announced over the intercom, *"LADIES AND GENTLEMEN! WE HAVE ANOTHER WINNER! THE MAN IN THE WHITE TUXEDO HAS JUST WON ON THE TEN THOUSAND DOLLAR SLOT!"*

Russell wanted to do something as he watched Diamond Jenkins reliving a deep fantasy that he had held on to for all his life. But it was all just an illusion. He sensed danger, evil, and the presence of demons disguised as humans. But why should he care about what happened to any of them? He was fighting his own battle with insanity. For why would a loving and caring God strip him of everything and leave him powerless to fight his greatest enemy, the Demon of Suicide. Now, it would be just a matter of time before he lost his Brilliance anyway. Russell looked at the skin upon his hands and arms. It had become a dark and toxic tint of green and purple. Large black veins protruded in every direction from the surface of his skin. He had become what he hated. Just like the rest of humanity, eventually becoming the darkness they despised. What a terrible world, Russell thought as he slowly swallowed a shot of a glass of whiskey, and sucked on a straw in his mouth. He wondered how far they all were from the opening of The Void.

The top of Russell's head ached. He wished that he had some aspirin or something to help numb the pain. The horns on his head had changed into two small curved horns that resembled a goat. Fortunately, his cowboy hat covered them up since he was starting to resemble something out of a horror movie. Then Russell pondered the thought of why he didn't change like the rest of the travelers. Why didn't he become an angel again? There was something that was still fighting against it. If I was going to die, he thought, it will not be an easy fight. *"If I am going to be sucked into The Void, then let me go battling and fighting the creatures that are trying to toss me in!"*, he said to himself.

A platoon of bartenders could not keep the drinks pouring fast enough while a large crowd of people was drinking in a non-stop, inhuman pace. Russell knew they had been abducted. The drinks fooled the people. It was all an illusion. He cried out to God. It took all his strength just to push his words out. He cried out saying, ***"God, give me the ability to see the truth again!"*** Russell looked and saw the glasses not only had liquor in them, but they were filled with worms. Russell felt sick. He wanted to stand up and leave, but he staggered and fell over a table. He managed to pull himself up into a chair and hoped he would survive a little longer before being swept away by the illusion. He laid his head down on a table. He felt sick to his stomach and started to weep himself to sleep.

After about an hour, Russell awakened. He could see Miss Honey Creek laughing while sitting among the group of businessmen. They all looked at her as if they were fascinated by her conversation. Russell scanned the room and recognized that he had the ability, once again, to see through a wall. That was one of the gifts he once had when The Brilliance was in full operation. Now, it was back again. Granted, its strength was weak, and the images were blurred at times, but he could see well enough through the Showgirl Palace Club to see that Charlie was in his own dreamland. He could see a young woman dancing on top of the table that he was seated at as he threw hundred dollar bills at her smiling. At the same time, another young woman stroked his long black hair and played with the hairs on his chest from his unzipped jumpsuit.

Diamond Jenkins seemed to be having the time of his life as well. He trotted through the casino while putting coins into dozens of slot machines. The slot machines started to ring loudly, signaling that he won the jackpot. So, he giddily ran to collect his winnings from each machine, picking up the coins with his top hat.

Russell then wanted a bottle of whiskey. The taste was driving him crazy. He cried out, ***"Whiskey! Bartender! I Need Whiskey!"*** A bartender instantly materialized and left him a large bottle on his table. Russell slowly poured it into a small glass that was also left by the bartender. He stared at it for a while before slowly lifting it towards his lips. Russell looked in shock as a flash of light appeared in his hands. The light beamed from his fingers and shattered the glass. Russell cried out in pain as The Brilliance started tingling and flashing across his skin. The light moved and created a glowing circle at the top of his head before dimming and disappearing. The sudden flash and the shattering of the glass caused everyone huddled around the bar to stop drinking and freeze. Russell whispered to himself, *"Oh God! This is it! The last of my Brilliance is leaving me now for good! The last glitters of truth and light are sending out a distress signal to me! Like the flare of a ship, shooting out a distress signal in the middle of a darkened sea, this burst of light is a warning to me that it's only a matter of time before I am overtaken and the essence of my existence will be extinguished forever. Your precious Spirit God, help me to hold it! Help me to maintain it!"*

As the tears ran down Russell's face, they turned into white powdery ash that dispersed and vanished away. Then Russell saw his hand holding the glass. Three of Russell's fingers had broken off and turned into ash. The joints of his body also ached and were stiff. The Brilliance had blown off his fingers as it exited his body. Russell knew that there would be just a few more bursts of light before he would be sucked into the screaming darkness like a speck of dust pulled into a vacuum cleaner without hope. Russell took the bottle of whiskey and smashed it against the counter of the bar. A bartender yelled at him in disgust, *"Hey, get away from the bar! Get out of here you freak! You are scaring off my customers!"* Russell then decided that he would make one last attempt to persuade the convertible travelers to leave the casino, even if he was considered by them to be a lunatic drifter, he had to do something. He had to take them out before the transformation was complete or they would be swept away into the loathsome darkness.

Suddenly there was a ruckus that occurred. One of the old businessmen with Miss Honey Creek had taken her by the arm and was twisting it behind her back. *"I KNOW YOU STOLE MY WALLET AND YOU BETTER GIVE IT BACK! AND YOU BETTER GIVE IT BACK TO ME RIGHT NOW! OR I SWEAR I WILL TWIST YOUR ARM OFF! DO YOU HEAR ME YOU HUSSY!"* The old man held her in place as she twisted and fought back wildly. Then another balding gray-haired man stood before both of them shouting, *"YEAH, I SAW HER FRANK! I SAW THE WHOLE THING! She stole your wallet right out of your pocket when you were dancing with her. She slipped it into her bra. She's a tricky one!"*

The man continued to hold her arm while she twisted and turned trying to break free. So, he reached around with his free hand into her bra, searching for his wallet. Suddenly, the wallet fell out of her clothes onto the floor. As the old man reached down to pick it up, Miss Honey Creek found a bottle of liquor on a table and smashed it over his head. The old man dropped like a petrified tree that fell apart and toppled to the floor. Miss Honey Creek started laughing at the old man as he struggled to regain his balance. Then she swooped down, took his wallet and held it in her hands while pulling the money out. *"Is this what you were looking for?"* She said as she laughed in a crackling scorn. *"You owe me this for the time that I spent with you! You don't think I am going to waste my time being with some old fuddy-duddy like you and not get something out of it!"* She snatched the money out of the wallet and started stuffing the bills into her purse and bra. Then suddenly, as she held the wallet in her hand, it burst into flames. She writhed in pain and immediately threw the wallet down onto the floor as her hand continued to be consumed by flames. She ran screaming wildly through the crowd of people in the casino pleading for help. Everyone stood laughing as she tried to extinguish the flickering flames. Russell leaped forward almost tackling her as he began pouring dozens of bottles of water on her burning hand. It finally went out, after Russell took out a feather from the inside of his jacket and placed it over her. Her hand was scalded. Layers of her skin were blackened and hanging off.

As Russell examined her hand more carefully, there was a hole that had been burned directly through the center of her palm. So, Russell took a handkerchief from the inside of his jacket, wrapped it tightly, and told her to press it until the pain subsided. Miss Honey Creek was whimpering on the floor crying, *"My hand has a hole in it! How did this happen? Why did we end up inside this terrible and disgusting place?"* Maybe it was the shock of the fire that jolted her memory back in place. Russell did not know for sure, but he was terrified by what had happened. She was leaking Brilliance. It was the presence of the light of God that was leaving her. And it would be very soon that the Demon of Suicide would come and pay a visit to all of them. The hole in her hand was a sure sign that it would burst out of her hand once again.

Then Russell noticed Diamond Jenkins. He was in a heated argument with a fat angry man with large arms smoking a cigar and blowing the smoke in his face. He looked like he was the manager of the casino. He also had another man with him that looked even bigger than he was who kept poking his finger against his chest. The fat man with the cigar angrily said, *"I don't know who you think you are, Mister! But you came into this casino, ran up a huge bill, and overextended your credit without paying anything back! We are going to get our money back! Even if we have to rip it out of your little white tuxedo wearing skinny hide!"* The bigger man came forward and took Diamond Jenkins' tuxedo jacket. In one quick motion, he ripped it in half. Then he took his top hat, stepped on it, picked it up again and smashed it on his head. Diamond Jenkins was infuriated. So, he reached inside his jacket and pulled out a small diamond-handle pistol. He pointed the gun at the two of them. *"They don't call me Diamond Jenkins for nothing! You two saps are going to pay the price for trying to take Diamond Jenkins down!"* Diamond Jenkins was nervously shaking the shiny pistol up and down. He started backing away from the men, but not before taking off his smashed top hat and sweeping a table clean of bills and coins as he quickly put them inside of the hat. Then he put the top hat back on his head, and said chuckling as he backed away with a wide and mocking smile, *"Gentlemen, I can't say it wasn't a pleasure doing business with you!"* He continued to slowly move backward when he suddenly cried out as a flash of light shot out of the top of his hat and then caught on fire. He took off the top hat, screaming as it appeared that his head was engulfed in a blaze of flames, all while the burning bills fell to the floor. He ran through the crowd screaming and pleading for someone to help him. *"MY HEAD IS ON FIRE! SOMEONE HELP ME PLEASE! SOMEONE HELP ME PLEASE! HELP ME!"* A trail of fire and smoke followed him as people speedily moved out of the way as he ran past them resembling a runaway train.

Russell knew now that The Brilliance was leaving them. Soon they would all be taken away. Russell watched Diamond Jenkins run by him. He saw a waiter with a bucket of ice and a towel, so he grabbed them and doused Diamond Jenkins. Both tumbled forward over a row of tables and crashed to the floor. This activity instigated a brawl among a group of people that rapidly spread throughout the casino. The casino turned into a violent pushing, shoving, fist fight. Tables were overturned, and people wrestled on the floor, fighting for their lives. Russell pinned Diamond Jenkins to the floor, covered his head with the bucket of ice, and smothered the fire with the towel. Diamond Jenkins was whimpering, *"I should have never come in here in the first place! This place is a scam! A complete joke! Every time you win, you must pay the house first most of your winnings! Help me get out of here Russell! My head is hurting so bad!"* Russell looked at the top of his head. His scalp was completely charred, and there were trails of white smoke rising from the top of it. There was also a terrible looking hole in the top of his head where The Brilliance had blown out. *"I have never seen a case this bad! The Brilliance came right out of the top of your head! You are lucky you are still alive! This is the worst case I have ever seen before!" "Yes, I am lucky alright."* Diamond Jenkins said in a sorrowful voice. Russell was able to drag Diamond Jenkins to the winding staircase. He instructed him to go back upstairs until he found the entrance to the shack. He told him to keep his eyes closed.

Russell moved through the chaotic crowd, looking for the rest of his convertible companions. He found Miss Honey Creek crawling on her hands and knees looking for the staircase while people fought all around her. He carefully helped her off the floor and led her towards the staircase and told her to pass through the open door at the top, giving her the same instructions that he gave Diamond Jenkins.

The large crowd of people turned into an all-out brawl. A man dressed in dirty overalls, dusty, brown work boots, and wearing a weather-beaten hat pushed his way through the crowd and started firing a shotgun into the air. The people stopped fighting and began dodging bullets, ducking, and running for cover. He cried out saying, *"WHERE IS SHE AT? WHERE IS SHE AT?! WHERE IS MY EMMA JEAN? I KNOW YOU TOOK HER AWAY! I KNOW YOU*

HAVE HER! IT HAS TAKEN ME A LONG TIME TO TRACK HER DOWN. AND IT HAS TAKEN ME A LONG TIME TO FIND THIS PLACE! AND I AM NOT LEAVING WITHOUT HER! AND IF SHE IS NOT RETURNED TO ME, THEN SOMEONE IS GOING TO BE SLEEPING WITH ELVIS!"

Then he started shooting at the chandeliers bringing them down in an explosive burst of exploding glass. After that, he started shooting at the slot machines that caused them to fizzle into an electronic shower of sparks. He then started shooting at bottles that were lined up on the bar, causing them to explode with flying glass. A mad stampede now erupted as people tried desperately to find an exit from the lunatic that was brandishing the shotgun. Then in the back of the casino, Russell caught a glimpse of Charlie. He appeared as if he was oblivious to all the mayhem that was taking place around him. A young woman, who Russell saw earlier with Charlie, was now sitting on top of his lap next to a small table, looking into his eyes, kissing him, nibbling on his ears, and wrapping her fingers around the gold chains on his neck. The terrified, grappling people fought each other for cover while Russell watched their facial characteristics change into what appeared to be horrendous looking creatures.

Charlie then pushed the young woman away. As she fell over the table, Charlie grabbed his own throat screaming, *"I'M DYING! I AM DYING! SOMETHING IS INSIDE OF ME! I AM ON FIRE!"* He ran towards the bar and found bottles of water. He drank them down one after another! *"MY LIPS ARE BURNING! MY LIPS ARE HURTING! OH GOD! I AM HURTING! I HURT SO BAD!"* The young woman ran back to Charlie screaming, *"MY DADDY WILL KILL YOU WHERE YOU ARE STANDING IF YOU DON'T TAKE COVER!"*

Charlie was on the floor writhing in pain as if something was coming out of his throat. He cried out as his lips began to burst into flames. The man came over and held the shotgun over Charlie's head. *"You slick playboy fooling around with my baby girl! You are twice the age of Emma Jean! Mister, you are going to be pushing up daisies!"* Russell leaped forward and pushed the shotgun away from the man as the trigger of the gun went off and shot up into the ceiling, bringing down another chandelier. Russell then took the shotgun out of his hand and threw it across the room. He then kneeled over Charlie, opened his coat, and pulled out a white feather from an inside pocket and placed it over his lips until the fire was extinguished and the smoke was rising from Charlie's lips. *"Hey, Russell man, I don't know how you got over here so fast, but I'm glad you did! I think I was turning into a piece of burnt toast!"*

Charlie watched as he observed the young girl growling and clawing at them behind an overturned table. *"I didn't know that my cologne would have such an effect on a woman like this."* He said in a weak, frightened, sarcastic voice. *"She looks like she is in some kind of trance?"* *"You sure know how to pick 'em, Charlie!"*, Russell said shaking his head. *"Yeah, I know. All of my women end up like this; sneering at me, talking fanatically, and taking me to divorce court!"* The young woman then glared at him. *"You want to come home with me, Sugar to meet the family? Well you can meet them right now!"* She burst into flames while screaming at Charlie, and then came running towards him saying, *"Take me back! Take me back! Take me out of here! Don't you love me? Don't you love me? I love you! I love you!"* The man with the shotgun also burst into flames. The flames ignited his body until his face and hair were also engulfed in flames. They both appeared to be flaming torches as they came closer toward Charlie and Russell. The old man with the gun cried out, *"I will take you home, Son! Everything will be alright! You can home with us! Don't be afraid. I will take you home!"*

The man appeared to be in agony as he was being scorched and burned alive. Russell cried out saying, *"Charlie, we have to get out of here now! There is a possibility that the flames can jump on us! The evil has overwhelmed the environment! This place is just a portal to kidnap travelers like us on the road to destruction! And I am convinced that some of these people are already dead! The brochure is just a way to recruit new clients!"*

Suddenly, all the people in the room spontaneously saw the flames jumping upon them as it created a horrible maddening panic of screaming death. Charlie who was still touching his smoldering lips as he patted them slightly while he tried to suffocate the white smoke that was rising from them. The flames were skipping like they were alive as people tried desperately to escape the nightmare they were trapped in. Russell pulled Charlie off the floor and helped him walk as they searched for the winding staircase through the dark smoke and haze that had engulfed the casino. As they approached the entrance of the winding staircase, Russell yelled out to Charlie, *"Keep moving, Charlie! Don't stop for anything until you find the exit at the top of the staircase. If you want to live man, don't you stop for anything!"* All at once, the woman that Charlie had the romantic encounter with, came charging out of the smoke, haze, and flames. Her face was almost completely burned off. Pieces of her bones stuck out of her body as she screamed at him saying, *"Hey, Baby! Don't you love me? Hey, don't you still care for me? Take me with you! I don't want to die here! Baby, please take me with you!"* She grabbed Charlie's pant legs and set them on fire. Charlie started kicking at her wildly, trying to escape as he pleaded with Russell to help.

Russell looked on in terror when he saw that they were surrounded by casino patrons with their clothes on fire. They were in a desperate situation as they were encircled by the burning casino guests, trying to overpower them. Charlie's clothes were ablaze as he screamed out to Russell for help. Russell knew that he had to do something quickly or they would be pulled back into the burning haze. Russell stood before the crowd of terrified looking people, opened his jacket and released the last of his Brilliance out over the crowd. A light moved around his jacket and turned into a bright glowing circle upon his chest as thousands of white feathers blew out in a wind storm with the fury of a hurricane that came out of his coat and covered everyone in the room. The feathers blew through the room until they became thick as an open pillow catching on fire and creating a fiery diversion for Charlie and Russell to escape.

It was a struggle to help Charlie's limp and almost motionless body up the winding staircase as he leaned on his shoulder. They forged ahead until they found the battered door that led to the entrance of the shack. Exhausted, they fell through the door and disappeared into the floor less darkness. As they emerged from the darkness, they were standing on the porch of the shack looking bewildered at the old man in the rocking chair. The old man in the rocking chair smiled at them with his rotted teeth as he swayed back and forth in his chair saying, *"Did you have a good time? Then come back again! Come back again! We are always open! Did you have a good time? We are always open! We are always open!"*

Russell and Charlie scrambled off the porch and made their way back to the convertible where Miss Honey Creek and Diamond Jenkins were already sitting inside. *"What took you so long to get out of there? We have been waiting for over an hour for you two to come out!"* Diamond Jenkins said as he looked nervously around. *"I would have driven off and left the both of you, but I didn't have a key!"* Charlie sat in the driver's seat. He looked a wreck! Half of his mustache was burned off and the skin around his mouth had peeled off. He pulled his toupee off and sat it on the dashboard as it looked burned and smoking. He grabbed it and started beating it on the seat, trying to extinguish the smoke. He tried putting it on his head again. In an act of frustration, he picked it up and threw it out of the car. Charlie's right pants leg was ripped open. His leg was burned. He found a bottle of water and poured it out on it.

"I can drive, Charlie! Looks like you need help! I can take the wheel and get us home!" Russell said as he looked at him. Charlie did his best. He tried to look composed and in control as he grimaced in pain. *"I will be alright! I will be fine! I will drive us all the way home and everything will be alright!"* *"If you say so, Charlie! But you don't look so good, Man! It looks like you're hurt"!* *"I said am alright, Russell! I am alright! Just leave me alone! I should have never picked you up! You are somehow responsible for doing all these terrible things to us! You are the one that is causing all this evil to follow us! I should have never let you in my car in the first place! I should just kick you out of my convertible!"* *"It is not me, Charlie! You have to believe me! It's not me! We have been marked and we are being chased!"* *"Don't give me none of that religious nonsense that we are being followed by the Demon of Suicide, Russell! You are a crazy lunatic! You got all of us going crazy like you! At the next exit, you are getting out of my convertible! And don't you say another word to*

me for the rest of the night! I am sick of your stories! I am sick of all of it! And I am sick of you!"

Miss Honey Creek was in the backseat sobbing, nursing her sore hand that had a terrible looking black hole in it. She was slowly wrapping the makeshift handkerchief that Russell had made for her around it. *"God this thing hurts like hell! When will my hand return to normal Russell, since you know what is happening to us?"* Russell looked at her hand and then quietly said, *"It will never return to where it once was. You have to keep it wrapped all the time. You don't want any more of The Brilliance jumping out! Just one or two more times of The Brilliance leaving you, and you will no longer exist in this world."* Diamond Jenkins called out in a weak voice from the front seat pleading, *"Keep the thing wrapped up! We have enough stress for one night!"* Miss Honey Creek tied the handkerchief tightly around her hand and wept quietly as she held her injured hand against her chest. Miss Honey Creek's dress was in shambles and covered with soot. Her hair lost all its blonde color and she had long strands of gray. Wrinkles appeared around her eyes, her mouth, and under her chin. She took out a compact mirror that she raised up with her one good hand, and slowly took out a cotton ball and patted her face.

Diamond Jenkins was sitting in the front seat. It appeared that he looked the worst. From his chin to the top of his head, it looked as if the skin had all peeled away. It looked as if he had suffered second and third-degree burns, and there was a large burned hole at the top of his head. *"That really must hurt like hell!"* Miss Honey Creek said as she found a bottle of water, and poured it on the top of Diamond Jenkins head. Diamond Jenkins started screaming out saying *"WHAT ARE YOU DOING TO ME? THAT HURTS! JUST LEAVE ME ALONE! I WILL BE ALRIGHT! YOU JUST NEED TO MIND YOUR OWN BUSINESS, AND LEAVE ME ALONE!"*

His white suit was a wreck. It was covered with dirt and ripped on every side. One of the sleeves was only attached by a group of exposed threads. Diamond Jenkins reached into his shabby coat and found the long roll of coupons that said, *"Free Play"*. He ripped them up into small pieces as they blew out of his hand. Charlie hit the gas and they spun out into the darkness, leaving the blinking lights of the shack of the casino behind.

Russell sagged in the back seat with his old cowboy hat on his head. For a long while, no one said anything. Then Miss Honey Creek spoke in a whisper to Russell saying, *"Hey, Russell, were those things back there real?"* Russell thumped his cowboy hat up for a second and said, *"What is real? It is only in your mind. Is it in your thoughts? It is what you have within you. You have a hole in your hand that is burned all the way through! And that sure looks real to me!"*

"I knew I should have gone to Jersey City. They say that the slots down there are winning big! This has been one big disaster!" Diamond Jenkins said as a trail of smoke came seeping out of the top of his head. Charlie put in a CD and started to play a song by Frank Sinatra. *"The summer wind came blowing in from across the sea. It lingered there to touch your hair and walk with me. All summer long we sang a song, and then we strolled that golden sand. Two sweethearts and the summer wind!"*

Then he looked in his rear-view mirror, and caught a glimpse of himself and said, *"I look like crap! It was a good thing Russell that you pulled me out when you did! I would have been totally deep fried by now! My leg is really hurting! I think I can feel a bone sticking out of the side of my knee! I will be glad when we come to a rest stop! I need a break. I am tired from running. I am tired from running away from everything. I just need to rest!"*

As Charlie continued driving through the blackness of the night with only the headlights and the road before them, Russell noticed that the convertible was going off the road. Charlie had nodded his head and closed his eyes for a moment when Russell shouted, *"CHARLIE, KEEP YOUR EYES ON THE ROAD, MAN! WHAT'S WRONG WITH YOU?"* *"Oh, I am so sorry! I almost fell asleep. My body is still shot from what happened to us in that casino. I need some rest! There must be a Budget Motel around here somewhere? There has to be someplace around here, so I can rest. We have been driving around for hours and there is nothing!"* *"Look, I told you I could drive! You don't have to put yourself through this! Why don't you stop and give me the keys and let me take over?"* Russell said.

But Charlie ignored him and continued to drive through the deserted blackness when the convertible started to drift away, but this time way off the road. Russell moved his hat upward as the car bounced along on the desert floor. ***"CHARLIE, WAKE UP! YOU ARE ABOUT TO GET EVERYONE KILLED!"*** Charlie tried to take control of the wheel as the convertible verged off the road. At that instant, there was a loud crash against the front bumper of the convertible. While everyone else screamed, Russell yelled, ***"CHARLIE, MY GOD MAN, I THINK YOU HIT SOMETHING!"*** The convertible came to a sliding stop as it spun around in a cloud of dust. *"I told you to keep your eyes on the road! Charlie, you fell asleep again! You fell asleep! Are you trying to kill what's left of us?"* Russell said while wiping the dust from the brim of his hat. *"You hit something, Charlie! It sounded like you hit something!"* Diamond Jenkins said in a fearful voice. Miss Honey Creek then spoke as her voice trembled, *"It sure sounded like you hit something to me too! Hey, why don't we get out of the car and look around?"*

Russell was the first to get out of the car. He slowly walked around it and did not see anything. *"There is nothing out here but darkness, dust. and sand."* Then Charlie leaned forward, peering into the darkness. He saw something. It was crumbled on the ground, and one of its legs was extended straight up. *"Hey, look over there, by the ravine! You hit some kind of dog or something!* "Russell cried out. Miss Honey Creek then got out of the car and followed slowly behind Diamond Jenkins who was looking around as if someone was stalking them. They all converged on the dead animal that looked twisted and mangled on the roadside. *"Charlie! It looks like you killed a coyote!"* Diamond Jenkins shouted. Charlie found a stick and poked it as its lifeless body stared back at them. *"Yeah, you crushed it with your bumper! That is one ugly looking thing!"* Diamond Jenkins said in disgust. *"The poor thing was just looking for something to eat. Why did you have to kill it?* Miss Honey Creek said compassionately.

Then the dog's eyes rolled back in its head. It started breathing hard as its chest noticeably moved up and down. *"Looks like you just knocked the wind out of it!"* Diamond Jenkins said as he slowly started backing up. The dog tried standing on its hind legs unsteadily and wobbled as its body was shaking, and its head moved back and forth as it tried to regain its balance. *"The dog is coming back to himself again. I am glad you didn't kill that poor creature."* Miss Honey Creek said as she genuinely seemed to care. Then the dog's bones started snapping as it twisted its body in different directions. Then its breathing turned into a terrible growl as saliva started foaming at its mouth. Then its eyes turned a bright yellow. *"Its bones are snapping back together! That thing is coming back to life!"* Diamond Jenkins started slowly moving back to the convertible. Then its jaws started snapping at them as a set of glistening pointy teeth appeared in its snarling mouth. *"Hurry, get back into the car! This dog is from the underworld!"* Russell warned rubbing his hat in his hands.

Miss Honey Creek then noticed the long curled looking horns that had begun to grow out of Russell's head. *"Talking about something that looks from out of this world! Russell, you really look scary!"* *"I know. I had a bad cup of mocha, that's all!"* Then the dog then started snarling at them more viciously, snapping and threatening to attack. The dog appeared to have sparse hairs that hung off its body. It had a broken tail, and one of its ears had been chewed off. *"What is this dog doing in the middle of nowhere Russell?"* Miss Honey Creek asked with a trembling voice. *"I don't know, but we need to move quickly into the convertible right now! This thing is coming alive and looking for a snack!"* The group scrambled towards the car, jumping over the doors into their seats. *"LET'S GO CHARLIE BEFORE THAT DOG WAKES UP!"* A great fear shook up the group when Charlie started to turn the ignition switch. Nothing could be heard but the numbing sound of the clicking of the battery. *"HEY CHARLIE, THAT'S THE BATTERY! YOU NEED A JUMP START! I DON'T THINK THAT CRAZY LOOKING DOG IS GOING TO WAIT AROUND FOR THE TOWING SERVICE BEFORE IT ATTACKS US!"*, Diamond Jenkins said almost in tears. *"CHARLIE DARLING, THAT TERRIBLE MONGREL HAS NOT EATEN IN DAYS! AND MISS HONEY CREEK DOES NOT WANT TO BE ON THE BRUNCH MENU! HURRY HONEY AND MOVE THIS CAR!"* Miss Honey Creek exclaimed while nervously powdering her face in a state of panic. *"CHARLIE, MAN! START THE ENGINE OR ELSE IT IS GOING TO BE THE END OF US ALL!"* Russell cried out.

Suddenly, the dog jumped on the hood of the convertible and lurched its head over the windshield, snapping dangerously at Charlie as Diamond Jenkins pushed himself down into the front seat crying, *"RUSSELL THAT CRAZED DOG IS TRYING TO TAKE A BITE OUT OF ME! DO SOMETHING!"* Charlie said in a hysterical, pleading voice. Charlie was able to dodge the snapping and lunges of the dog as it opened its jaws of razor teeth appeared only inches away from his face. They noticed that even the saliva from the dog's mouth was made from an acidic, burning fluid that dripped and burned holes into the interior of the convertible. *"RUSSELL THAT DOG IS PUTTING HOLES IN THE SEAT OF MY CONVERTIBLE! THIS IS A SEVENTY THOUSAND DOLLAR CAR! HELP ME RUSSELL! HE IS SCRATCHING UP THE PAINT AND BREAKING THE WINDSHIELD!"*

Russell moved forward took off his hat, and put it over the face of the dog which blinded it momentarily. That gave Charlie a few seconds to find his briefcase which survived the casino as he blocked the attacks of the dog by pushing the briefcase into the face of the raging and snapping dog. The dog's teeth were so sharp and powerful that they started to chew through the case. When it gnawed the case and barreled through it with its sharp claws, a large hole formed, and all of Charlie's life savings fell out, covering the front seats. In frustration, the dog turned furiously towards Diamond Jenkins who had pushed himself down on the floor of the car near the front seat, crying. The dog snapped at him, lunging for his throat. Diamond Jenkins searched his tattered jacket pocket and found a deck of cards and shuffled them in its face. The dog was distracted and started biting the flying cards. Russell covered the dog's face with his cowboy hat and hit the dog on the side of the head with his fist. To that end, the creature collapsed on top of the hood, looking dead and motionless. *"I think that did it! That thing is out for the count Russell!"* Charlie said as he checked his neck for any bite marks.

"What is going on Russell? I can't take this anymore! What kind of dog was that?" Diamond Jenkins said peeking up and looking over

the dashboard at the dead creature on the hood. *"That was not a dog! That was a creature from the outer darkness. One bite and you will slowly morph into one of them. That is a soul enslaved in madness!"*

Russell peered out into the desert. Everything appeared to be quiet once again. Diamond Jenkins examined his hands and his throat for bite marks. *"Thank God I am alright! There are no bites on my neck. I just have a hole burned through the top of my head. I can easily cover that up with my top hat! I am just fine!"* Diamond Jenkins said while his hands were shaking as he put the broken hat on the top of his head. *"And everything else appeared to be shining with diamonds!! Diamond Jenkins is back on top! You can't keep a man that sparkles with diamonds down! Lady Luck is riding with me again!"* He said while displaying a nervous smile as he looked around. Miss Honey Creek fumbled with her cotton balls while trying to pat her face with powder. Angrily she said, *"I should have never let you fruitcakes pick me up! I should have taken my chances walking in the desert! Well what are we going to do now? Just sit here away from the conveniences of civilization. I need a hot shower and a pedicure. What a nightmare, being stranded and attacked by a rabid dog"!*

Russell got out of the convertible, followed by Charlie. *"Let's see if we can get this thing going Russell, and get the hell out of here!"* Russell came near the dead dog that was lying on top of the hood with its tongue hanging out. The hood had large burn marks where the dog's saliva had leaked out. Russell found a long hard stick and pushed it off the hood. *"What a disgusting looking thing!"* Russell popped open the hood and started adjusting the battery cables. *"Charlie go back and start it again. Looks like one of the cables was burned through with that stuff that came out of the dog's mouth!"* Charlie started to gun the engine as it sputtered to turn over. *"Charlie, take your time. You don't want to flood the engine!"* *"I am just trying to get it started Russell, so we can get out of here!"*

Diamond Jenkins was peering over the front seat from his cowering position on the floor of the convertible when he saw a large group of yellow eyes in the darkness rushing towards them. Stuttering,

Diamond Jenkins cried out, *"That dog has a lot more friends! We better hurry up or we will become their Scooby Doo Snacks!"*

Russell looked on the left side of the convertible. He could see a group of dark shadows coming towards them with yellow eyes glistening in the darkness. *"RUSSELL MY GOOD MAN! GET THIS CAR MOVING! THERE ARE TOO MANY OF THEM TO FIGHT OFF! MAYBE YOU CAN DO SOME SERIOUS PRAYING!"* Russell thought to himself for an instant. *"Prayer was a force that I depended on at one time. Now, I am afraid to pray. I am afraid if God will ever hear me again."*

His mind shifted back and he could see the dogs on the verge of surrounding them. He knew that he had used up all his Brilliance, and there was nothing left inside of him. He was so weakened that just one bite from these hellhounds would transform him into one of the creatures that he despised. Russell reached up and felt the small curved horns that had protruded from out of his head. They had risen higher signaling his ever-present shame and disgraceful fall.

Russell cried out *"Charlie it's the battery! We need a jump start! This thing is dead!"* *"Just like us!"*, Diamond Jenkins said in a whimpering whisper. *"Please, Mr. Russell, you have to do something! Don't you have a little bit left of that stuff you call The Brilliance to jump-start a little old battery!"*, Miss Honey Creek said pleading as she went down onto the floor of the convertible peeking out over the side of the door. The dogs appeared to be coming from every direction, and there was no way to escape, but to start the convertible. *"Can't you do something, Mr. Russell? I am not ready to die. I am afraid now that I should have never left my wife! All because I received some stupid free coupons in the mail. I left everything!"* Diamond Jenkins cried out.

Russell looked at all of them and said, *"There is something that we can do. Let's pray!"* Russell now made one last plea to heaven as if he was shooting a flare gun out of the darkness into the sky on a sinking ship, he cried out to everyone saying, *"Quickly now, say a prayer to yourself! Please try to pray. For this may be the last time, the last opportunity that we can!"* Everyone silently whispered, praying for help. Even Charlie reluctantly muttered a quick prayer over his trembling lips. And then suddenly, Russell's hands started aching as electrical sparks jumped from off them. A flash occurred, and a wave of light appeared moving through his hands that caused his fingertips to spark. *"Russell your hands have some kind of electricity moving through them!"* Diamond Jenkins said excitedly. Russell pressed two of his finger together and sparks jumped from them. *"Yes, I still have a little of The Brilliance left in me!" "Well just don't stand there! Jump start this car before these dogs eat us alive!"* Russell jumped over the side of the door, and ran towards the opened hood, almost sliding on the sand. He pressed his fingers together again, and sparks jumped out as he touched the positive and negative posts of the battery. *"CHARLIE START THE ENGINE! DO IT NOW! START THE ENGINE! DO IT!"* The convertible's engine roared in a thunderous sound as Charlie called out, *"HEY, RUSSELL! IT'S READY TO GO! JUMP IN NOW! RUSSELL FOR THE LOVE OF GOD! RUSSEL JUMP IN!"*

The dogs were almost upon Russell. They were just a few feet away. Russell slammed the hood down, picked up a piece of driftwood, spun around, completely knocking out one of the leaping dogs. Charlie hit the gas as Russell jumped on the hood holding on to the windshield with all his might, hoping that he would not be tossed off. One of the dogs jumped on Russell's back trying to bite him. Diamond Jenkins came out of his hiding place took off his shoe and stood up looking over the windshield, smacked the dog in the face, knocking him off Russell's back. It tumbled in the darkness, making a whelping noise as if it was hurt.

Charlie weaved back and forth as he drove, trying to find the road that had now vanished. Smoke was rising from the spinning tires as the convertible bounced upon sand dunes, and moved through rocky trenches. Russell bounced on top of the hood as he held on to the windshield for dear life. Suddenly, one of the mad dogs came out of nowhere from the darkness, and jumped into the front seat, right next to Diamond Jenkins. The dog grabbed his neck, and tore into it with his teeth, causing his head to shake violently. Russell still had the large piece of driftwood in his hand, so he climbed over the windshield, knocked the dog in the head, and tossed it out. Screaming, Diamond Jenkins said, *"HELP ME MR. RUSSELL! IT HURTS SO BAD! MR.*

RUSSELL MY NECK IS BURNING! MR. RUSSELL IT HURTS SO BAD!"! Russell moved back Diamond Jenkins hand to look at the gaping hole that sizzled with green liquid oozing out of it. Russell was shocked that Diamond Jenkins was still alive. Russell stood motionless, horrified as he took out a handkerchief and wiped away some of the terrible looking liquid. *"MR. RUSSELL, AM I GOING TO DIE? MR. RUSSELL, AM I GOING TO DIE? I STILL HAVE TO PLAY SOME MORE SLOTS IN ATLANTIC CITY! MR. RUSSELL, I AM NOT READY TO DIE! I AM NOT READY TO DIE, MR. RUSSELL! PLEASE, MR. RUSSELL! HELP ME!"* Russell tore off a large piece of his shirt, tied it around his neck, and told him to hold on to it as the dogs were converging around the convertible. *"RUSSELL! THAT DOG BIT ME! THAT NASTY DOG BIT ME! IT HURTS, MR. RUSSELL! IT HURTS BAD, MR. RUSSELL"* *"Just be quiet and lay down. You are going to be alright! Just be quiet and lay down. Everything is going to be alright!"* Diamond Jenkins curled up in a fetal position on the floor of the convertible as Russell took what was left of his ripped tuxedo and draped it around him. He appeared to be shivering and whimpering.

Out of nowhere, another dog leaped on the back of the trunk and jumped into the seat next to Miss Honey Creek. It bit through her chest as she screamed in horror. The dog bit two large pieces of padding that were stuffed inside of her bra, shaking its head wildly, trying to tear it apart. Russell took the piece of driftwood that he had left, and swung at the crazed animal, knocking him out completely. *"CHARLIE, CAN'T YOU DRIVE THIS CAR ANY FASTER?! WE CANNOT SURVIVE ANOTHER ATTACK!"* Charlie stepped on the gas and gunned the engine. The car picked up speed and started to fishtail, creating a cloud of dust. Without warning, there was the loud smashing sound of a dog crashing through the windshield, breaking it apart. The dog's head penetrated the broken pieces of the windshield, snapping at Charlie while he did all he could to avoid being bitten. Russell climbed over the front seat and kicked the dog in the face, causing it to roll off the hood into the darkness of the night.

The convertible was moving extremely fast. Russell looked at the speedometer. The needle had moved way past 100 mph. *"Charlie, my man, what are you trying to do, kill us?! Slow down!" "Well, you said to speed up, and that is what I was doing! I am trying to get us out of here!" "Well, don't you kill us before we leave!" "Well, I am not getting bitten by no infected dog! I still want to live my life and have some fun before I die!"*

Russell stooped down and touched Diamond Jenkins on the shoulders as he laid motionless on the floor. Russell slightly moved the handkerchief to peek at his neck. There were no signs of blood, but the handkerchief was completely burned and had turned black as pieces of it fell apart in his hands. *"How are you doing Diamond Jenkins? Are you ok?" "I'm alright, Mr. Russell. I am just hot and sweating like crazy. I need some water really bad. When are we going to stop so I can get some water?" "It won't be long Diamond Jenkins. You just hang in there. You are going to make it! "I hope so Mr. Russell. I am afraid that I am going to die Mr. Russell!"* Russell could feel the heat coming from Diamond Jenkins' body and he wondered if he was going to make it out of the desert alive.

Next, Russell climbed into the backseat beside Miss Honey Creek as she attempted to mend the pieces of her torn dress. *"Did it bite you? Did it bite you? You have to let me know! Did it bite you Miss Honey Creek?" "I checked Mr. Russell. I'm ok! It did not bite through the skin. Thank God that horrible creature did not break the skin!"* Miss Honey Creek said as she patched up her dress and found her compact mirror. *"I really look a mess!"* She opened her purse and found a cotton ball and begin to pat her face as the rest of her cotton balls flew out of her purse into the darkness. Miss Honey Creek screamed, *"That was the last of my cotton balls! This must be the end of the world!"*

Russell looked at his hands. He was shaking with fear. *"I am too human too weak too sinful to fight the forces around us! God, I cannot save these people. I cannot save myself!"* He whispered. He looked at his hands and there was no more light. The Brilliance was completely gone. *"I have failed! I have truly failed. Our fate is sealed!"*

Russell was tired, and he sensed a great presence of evil around them. The darkness was thick. The sky and the ground had seemingly disappeared. The convertible moved with neck breaking speed, even though Charlie was trying his best to slow it down. The car was moving too fast, and Russell was afraid that they would crash and die. *"CHARLIE, I TOLD YOU TO SLOW DOWN! WHAT ARE YOU TRYING TO DO TO US?! SLOW DOWN MAN! YOU ARE GOING TO KILL US! SLOW DOWN CHARLIE!"* Charlie tried to downshift the convertible. He gripped the steering wheel and slammed his foot on the brakes, *"HOLD ON EVERYONE! I AM STOPPING THIS CAR!"* Charlie panicked while pressing his foot down on the brakes. *"RUSSELL IT'S DRIVING BY ITSELF! I DON'T KNOW HOW TO STOP IT!"* Everyone looked at Charlie in shock as he took his hands off the sterling wheel while the stick shift changed gears by itself.

Diamond Jenkins was still curled up in a ball on the floor of the convertible, holding his injured neck when he said in a whimpering voice, *"I should have never left home. I was such a fool leaving my family."* Charlie looked amazed at the convertible as it continued to shift gears moving with frightening speeds creating a storm of dust in the darkness. Diamond Jenkins stood up in the car and in a crying voice, *"I am getting out of here! This is too much for me!"* He was starting to climb out of the convertible when Russell caught him and pulled him back. *"Diamond you will kill yourself if you climb out of this car!"* *"It doesn't matter! I am dead anyway! It doesn't matter! My life is over!"* Then Charlie cried out, *"This is really wild! The convertible is driving by itself!"* Diamond Jenkins said in a terrified voice, *"Russell my neck is burning I feel like I am on fire! And Russell look at my skin, look at my hands!"* Diamond Jenkins reached up and showed everyone his hands that had large purple veins that had broken out, and his fingernails had turned black. *"Russell, if I can't go home again, then let me die!* Diamond Jenkins went down onto the convertible floor again in the front seat and started whimpering.

The car charged forward and the engine roared as the speedometer started shaking as the convertible reached its highest speed. Charlie was panicking as he cried out, *"RUSSELL THE CONVERTIBLE IS GOING TOO FAST! WE ARE GOING TO FLIP OVER ANY MOMENT!"* Miss Honey Creek was screaming so loudly that Russell wished that he had some of her cotton balls to put in his ears. Shockingly, Diamond Jenkins had stopped whimpering, and started laughing hysterically, *"I still got a few more free plays on the slot machines! We need to turn this car around and go back! I want to finish my game! I still got some free plays! I still got some game left! Diamond Jenkins is coming back! Yes Sir! Diamond Jenkins is coming back to roll the dice again!"* He turned around and looked at Charlie grinning wildly. *"He looks crazy as hell and his eyes have turned yellow!"* Charlie exclaimed.

Charlie moved over towards the far side of his door and put his legs safely up on the seat. The convertible continued to shift and move forward at neck breaking speeds. Charlie looked at Diamond Jenkins cautiously as he watched the steering wheel turning back and forth by itself. The wind and the dust were becoming intense as Miss Honey Creek lowered her head down behind the front seat as pieces of her hair blew off. *"RUSSELL IF YOU KNOW GOD! STOP THIS CAR! WE ARE ALL GOING TO DIE! RUSSELL PLEASE DO SOMETHING! ONLY YOU CAN HELP US NOW!"* Russell tried to move forward, but his whole body was numb and paralyzed as if an invisible force was holding him. *"I CAN'T MOVE! SOMETHING IS HOLDING ME IN THE SEAT! SOMETHING IS STOPPING ME FROM MOVING FORWARD!" "WELL IF YOU DON'T STOP THIS CAR, THEN I WILL, MR. RUSSELL!"*, Miss Honey Creek said in an alarming voice. She tried to move, struggling with the seatbelt, and tried to maneuver out of her seat. But she was also held tightly in place. Charlie also tried to move, but he was stuck as well. *"WE MUST TRY TO DO SOMETHING!"* Charlie said in a weak and petrified voice as he watched the speedometer bouncing erratically at the far end of the display. Charlie started beating on the steering wheel with his fist trying to stop the convertible. He hit his fist on the dashboard, banging on it until small cuts appeared on his fingers. Diamond Jenkins appeared to be the only one that could move around freely. But he was laughing insanely on the floor of the convertible as if nothing else mattered to him anymore.

Russell started praying. But now, he felt weak as though he was being overpowered by fear. He tried to move, but he felt exhausted and could do nothing but brace himself and hold on as the car drove with breakneck speed. Then the car spun in a complete circle in a cloud of dust and came to a heaving stop. Once again, the engine was dead.

Everyone was quiet, and just grateful to be alive. Charlie reached out and tried to turn the key in the ignition and nothing happened as the battery made a clicking noise. *"LET'S GET OUT OF THIS CAR NOW! LET'S GO WHILE THERE IS STILL TIME! WE WILL ALL DIE IF WE GO ON ANOTHER RIDE LIKE THIS AGAIN!"*, Russell said as he fought trying to remove his seat belt. Charlie struggled to open the door and said, *"Let's be grateful the convertible stopped. I thought for sure we would flip over and that would be the end of us!"*

Miss Honey Creek was also trying to remove her seat belt and pull on the handle of the door. *"I had enough of this traveling nightmare! And I have had enough of all of you psychopaths! I would rather walk home now than be with any of you!"* She said as she struggled with the door. *"My God I broke a nail! What is wrong with this door!"* She shrieked as she tried kicking the door with her foot.

Diamond Jenkins was still on the floor laughing in a whisper. His hands were shaking when he touched the hole in his head. Then their fear was once again renewed. They could not leave the convertible; something had enclosed them. It was something evil that choked their breath and gripped them from every side. *"Russell, I'm afraid! I can't get out! I can't run away! Russell, what are we going to do?"*, Miss Honey Creek said while sobbing in her seat. Charlie then spoke out, *"Russell, I am afraid too! I have never been through anything like this! Something is holding us, Russell. I just wanted to have a little fun! I wanted to spend the last of my retirement savings, and go out with a bang! That is all that I wanted to do! Have a little fun and go out with a bang! But nothing like this!"*

Then suddenly the headlights came on, shining brightly in the utter darkness all around them. *"TURN THE KEY, CHARLIE! TURN THE KEY! THE POWER HAS COME BACK ON! LET'S GET OUT OF HERE! TURN THE KEY, CHARLIE! TURN THE DOG GONE KEY!"* When he turned the key in the ignition, everyone heard the clicking of the battery. The headlights dimmed, then went out. Once more, they were surrounded by the darkness of the desert.

An engulfing quiet had taken over the landscape. Only the whispering laughter of Diamond Jenkins could be heard. Then out of the darkness, the voice of a woman was heard in the distance. Her voice sounded unearthly as if it was part of the wind. She cried out in hurt and in pain. *"Diamond Jenkins, this is your wife and your son! We came to visit you! We have come to visit you! Don't you love us? Don't you want to come back home?"* And then out of the darkness, a shocking pale-faced woman appeared walking with a limp. Her eyes were only two black sockets. She did not have any pupils, and she wore a dirty, tattered, white-laced wedding dress that matched her blowing, white, stringy hair. Her white wedding dress was splattered with blood as if she had been in a terrible accident. She had rows of broken teeth, and the ones that remained were stained and crookedly arranged in her mouth. As she came closer to the car, her lips and tongue were decayed and black. And from out of the black sockets of her eyes, one of them was hanging on a string of membrane. Her face was mangled and was pushed in on one side. Also, there was a large hole atop of her head, and a portion of her brain was exposed. She was carrying a silver platter that was covered with a silver top. And as she staggered towards Diamond Jenkins near the side of his door, she spoke saying, *"I made dinner for you, Honey! I have been waiting all night for you to come home from the casino! Where have you been all this time? Can't you see that my heart is aching? I am your darling wife, Susan. Don't you remember me? You have been gone so long. And I have been hurting so bad!"*

As she limped closer towards the car, Diamond Jenkins' mind came back to him. He started peeking over the side of the door looking at her talking. Then out of the darkness emerged a young boy who appeared to be about eight-years-old with pale colorless skin, and who also had black sockets for eyes. He cried out to Diamond Jenkins, *"Daddy, when are you coming home? I have been waiting for you to come back home. You promised me that you would play catch with me in the front yard. Don't you remember what you said?"* He was holding a silver platter as well. When he came closer to Diamond Jenkins, he took the lid off the silver platter. There was a beating heart inside. Then the young boy stood in front of Diamond Jenkins. *"DADDY, YOU BROKE MY HEART! MY HEART IS BROKEN, DADDY! YOU BROKE MY HEART, DADDY!"* Diamond Jenkins tried to escape the convertible as he struggled to get out of his seat. Then he cried out, *"TAKE THEM AWAY FROM ME, RUSSELL! I DON'T WANT TO SEE THEM! TAKE THEM AWAY FROM ME, RUSSELL! I DON'T WANT TO SEE THEM ANYMORE!"* The woman drew closer towards Diamond Jenkins. When she opened the lid of her silver tray, there was his diamond pistol on the platter. She started screaming fiercely, *"TAKE IT, JENKINS! TAKE IT, JENKINS! TAKE THE GUN AND SHOOT YOURSELF BECAUSE YOU HAVE NOTHING TO LIVE FOR ANYMORE! TAKE THE GUN BECAUSE YOU HAVE ALREADY KILLED ME! YOU KILLED ME! YOU KILLED ME! TAKE THE GUN AND SHOOT YOURSELF BECAUSE YOU HAVE KILLED ME!"*

Diamond Jenkins was crying and shouting as tears rolled down his face. *"PLEASE, GET AWAY FROM ME! I DON'T WANT TO LOOK AT THEM! I DON'T WANT TO LOOK AT THEM ANYMORE! TAKE THEM AWAY FROM ME!"* The woman continued screaming at Diamond Jenkins, *"TAKE THE GUN JENKINS AND SHOOT YOURSELF! YOUR LIFE MEANS NOTHING NOW ANYWAY! YOU HAVE NOTHING LEFT! TAKE THE GUN AND DO WHAT IS RIGHT! SHOOT YOURSELF!"* Diamond Jenkins took the gun, held it in his hands while his eyes filled with tears. His hands were shaking as he held the gun, wondering what he should do next. He looked at them sadly, and then spoke softly saying, *"I am so sorry! I am so sorry!"* Slowly, he lifted the pistol to his temple. The boy stood looking at Diamond Jenkins saying, *"GO AHEAD, DADDY! GO AHEAD, DADDY! SHOOT YOURSELF AND END YOUR PAIN! PULL THE TRIGGER, DADDY!"*

Russell reached over towards Diamond Jenkins and tried to grab his arm. He jerked away as Russell cried out, *"DIAMOND JENKINS! DON'T LISTEN TO THEM! IT IS THE DEMON OF SUICIDE! IT HAS FOLLOWED YOU! MY GOD MAN! PUT YOUR HANDS OVER YOUR EARS! CLOSE YOUR EYES!"*

Diamond Jenkins appeared to come to himself as he slowly lowered the gun back down on the silver tray. The woman in the wedding dress quickly took the gun from the silver tray and started screaming at him, sneering, and laughing wickedly. *"THIS IS THE WAY YOU DO IT JENKINS! YOU TAKE THE GUN AND YOU*

PULL THE TRIGGER!" The gun fired in an echoing bang. A small waffle of smoke escaped from the barrel as she shot herself in the temple, and fell down dead in the darkness. The walking dead boy started screaming at Diamond Jenkins saying, *"DON'T YOU EVER COME BACK HOME, DADDY! DON'T YOU EVER COME BACK! I NEVER LOVED YOU ANYWAY! DON'T YOU EVER COME BACK AGAIN! I NEVER LOVED YOU!"* He turned, looking at him with a menacing grin before walking off into the darkness. It was quiet for a few moments in the convertible. No one uttered a word. Only the voice of Diamond Jenkins could be heard muttering to himself, sobbing. *"I KILLED THEM! I KILLED THEM! THEY WOULD STILL BE ALIVE NOW, IF I HAD NOT KILLED THEM!"* Russell then reached forward over the seat and grabbed Diamond Jenkins by the shoulders. *"It's alright. They were not real. What we witnessed was the consciousness of evil that was pulled out of our fears! For when we hurt others, we will eventually see and feel the manifestation of that hurt. For God is only asking us to search inside of our hearts and ask for forgiveness for those people we have hurt!"*

Charlie spoke up in an angry voice, hitting his fist on the steering wheel, *"I am sick of you Russell! You have turned my fun trip into some kind of sermonized revival! There is no god Russell! It's just us, and these crazy dogs in the desert trying to eat us alive? There is no god Russell! Just us trying to live, and make it one more day! Just shut the hell up Russell! There is no god!"* In that moment, the convertible was hit on the driver's side full force by an old rusty looking metallic Buick. The convertible was hit so hard on its side that it almost tipped over sideways balancing on two wheels for a moment. A woman appeared to be driving the large vehicle as its tires began screeching while she circled around driving off into the darkness.

Charlie's door was crushed. His arm was dangling as though it had been broken. *"OH MY GOD! I THINK MY ARM IS BROKEN! SOMETHING JUST HIT THE SIDE OF THE CAR AND CRASHED INTO THE DOOR!"* Charlie's arm was black and bruised and hanging from his shoulders and protruding oddly. Miss Honey Creek also cried out, *"MY LEG IS HURT! I DON'T THINK I CAN MOVE IT!"* Diamond Jenkins returned to his crouching position on the floor of the convertible and peeked over the door shaking. Trembling, he said, *"Let's try to get out of the car before that woman comes back!"*

Once again, they tried leaving in a desperate panic, but found that they could not move any further than the interior of the convertible. Then suddenly, without warning, there was another crash from the back. A dark blue Buick slammed into the back bumper and the trunk, pushing Russell and Miss Honey Creek's seats forward. Again, the woman driving the Buick swung around and disappeared into the darkness. Russell felt a pain that ran from the base of his neck all the way through his spine from the impact of the crash. Russell cried out *"WHO IS DOING THIS? WHO IS USING US FOR TARGET PRACTICE?"* Miss Honey Creek, holding her leg screamed, *"RUSSELL, I THINK MY BACK IS BROKEN! I NEED MEDICAL TREATMENT! RUSSELL, I NEED HELP! PLEASE, I NEED A DOCTOR!"* In the dark, dusty night, a set of headlights once again appeared in the distance. The roar of a car's engine, moving at a high rate of speed, could be heard approaching them in the darkness. *"OH GOD! IT'S COMING AGAIN, AND IT LOOKS LIKE THERE WILL BE A HEAD-ON COLLISION THIS TIME!"*, Charlie cried out as he tried to start the convertible. Turning the key in a panicky state, his hands were shaking. Then in the distance, above the roar of the engine, a voice was heard, the voice of a woman. *"CHARLIEEEEE! CHARLIEEEEE! I HAVE COME BACK TO YOU! I DIED THAT DAY IN A CAR CRASH! THE DAY I LEFT YOUR OFFICE, I WAS FILLED WITH SO MUCH HURT THAT I DID NOT SEE THE RED LIGHT, SO I HAD A HEAD-ON COLLISION! I HAVE COME BACK TO YOU! DON'T YOU LOVE ME CHARLIE?"*

The woman propelled her car through the darkness. Suddenly, her car crashed into the front of the convertible, shattering the windshield. Pieces of glass went airborne into Charlie's face. Diamond Jenkins was crushed between folded metal and tangled seat covers, but miraculously he was still alive. Miss Honey Creek was furiously trying to leave the convertible, but found it was impossible as she cried, *"I CANNOT TAKE THIS ANYMORE! I WANT TO GO HOME NOW! I WANT OUT OF THIS CAR! PLEASE, GOD! HELP ME! OH GOD! HELP ME PLEASE!"*

The crazed female driver spun around and disappeared into the darkness. For a moment, everything became quiet as they cautiously peered through the darkness that surrounded them. Then the sound of a car engine starting was heard in the distance. She was coming back again. Out of the darkness, the huge Buick slammed into the side of the small convertible. The car rocked from one side, almost tipping over on two wheels again. But this time, Charlie looked at the driver. He could not believe his eyes. It was his wife Mildred, but half of her face and body had been crushed on one side. It was a horrible sight. She slowly backed up the Buick, screaming at Charlie as he appeared dazed and shocked. *"LOOK WHAT YOU DID TO ME! LOOK WHAT YOU DID TO ME! YOU AND YOUR PLAYING AROUND! I DIED THAT DAY! AND IT WAS ALL BECAUSE OF YOU! YOU AND YOUR HUSSY MISTRESS! THE BUS CAME THROUGH AND IT CRUSHED ME AND IT TORE ME IN HALF! I DIED THAT DAY! AND IT WAS ALL BECAUSE OF YOU!"*

Immediately, the woman reversed the huge dark Buick, tearing off pieces of the metal of the convertible. Charlie cried out to her, *"YOU ARE TEARING UP MY CAR!"* The woman yelled back, *"THAT IS ALL YOU CARED ABOUT ANYWAY! IT WAS JUST ANOTHER ONE OF YOUR TOYS!"* She sped off into the dusty darkness as everyone heard the engine in the distance.

Everyone tried desperately to leave the convertible while scrambling in their seats. *"OH, DEAR GOD, WE ARE TRAPPED!"*, Miss Honey Creek said as she put her hands over her face sobbing. Russell had his cowboy hat over his eyes praying in another language. Diamond Jenkins had freed himself from his tangled seat and was crouched down, peering over the side of what was left of the door into the darkness. Charlie was in the front seat. His hands were shaking as he gingerly touched all the pieces of glass that were embedded in his face. Then in the distance, the roar of the engine started again as an uncanny quiet consumed the convertible. Only Diamond Jenkins spoke out, saying, in a shaky frightened voice. *"Can't you tell her that you love her or something?"* The headlights brightly shined as the engine roared directly coming in front of them. The woman was coming towards them full speed for another head-on collision. They were trapped. None of them could escape. It seemed inevitable that they would be crushed to death. As the woman was accelerating at full speed, a swirling cloud of dust surrounded the Buick as it came closer towards them. They all braced themselves for the terrible impact.

Then out of the darkness, a little, frail, old man emerged who appeared to be over eighty years of age. He was wearing a white hospital gown and had nothing else underneath. He wore long socks that covered his bare legs and floppy house shoes on his feet. He only had a few wisps of white strands of hair that stuck out on the sides of his head. He was holding what looked like a glass of milk in his hands. He pushed a rickety wheeled walker as he tottered along in front of the convertible in the distance, calling out, *"IT'S ME, MISS HONEY CREEK! IT'S ME, MISS HONEY CREEK! IT'S ME, YOUR LOVER BOY! LITTLE DARLING, YOU CAN'T FORGET ME! IT'S YOUR LOVER BOY!"*

He staggered in the darkness as the headlights from the deranged driver flooded brightly behind him. He was holding a glass of milk in his hand as he pushed his rickety wheeled walker with his other hand. *"You remember Little Darling when all of those lawyers showed up around my bed? I was feeling really sick and terrible, lying there in my bed. I loved you so much that I signed everything you told me to. That night you gave me some milk! It made my stomach hurt so badly; I just fell asleep. I didn't think that I would ever wake up again! But guess what! YOUR LOVER BOY IS BACK! I AM BACK HOME, HONEYBUN! BACK TO YOUR LOVING ARMS! AND I BROUGHT YOU A DELICIOUS GLASS OF MILK!"*

Miss Honey Creek was terrified, trying to find a way to escape from the sickly looking old man, holding a glass of milk, walking towards the convertible. *"LEAVE ME ALONE! GET AWAY FROM ME! YOU ARE DEAD! YOU ARE SUPPOSED TO BE DEAD! I WATCHED YOU DIE! LEAVE ME ALONE!"* Miss Honey Creek was trapped, just like all the rest of the travelers in the convertible. The little old man tottered closer towards them holding a glass of milk calling out to Miss Honey Creek. *"LITTLE DARLING, YOUR LOVER BOY IS BACK! LITTLE DARLING, YOUR LOVE BOY HAS RETURNED TO YOU!"*

The engine of the speed demon, woman driver could be heard roaring as it made its final approach towards another head-on collision. The old man tottered with his rickety cart in the glaring headlights of the Buick carefully carrying a glass of milk.

"HEY, LITTLE DARLING! I HAVE BEEN KEEPING THIS MILK FOR YOU FOR A LONG TIME! WHY DON'T YOU TAKE A LITTLE SIP?"

The Buick was right on top of them when the old man turned in front of it. While taking a sip of his glass of milk, he held it up and said, *"IT'S STILL DELICIOUS!"*

He pushed his cart underneath the front wheels of the Buick. It rolled over on top of him as the Buick turned on its side and came to a sliding stop. The little old man slowly got up and brushed the sand and dust from off his hospital gown. Miraculously, he was unscathed, still holding his glass of milk that was still intact. *"Well, looks like I still have my milk, Honey Bum! They say milk does a body good!"* He put his glass of milk on the ground, untangled his broken cart, picked up the glass of milk, and tottered towards the woman that was trapped in the Buick lying on its side. The crazed woman with the mashed-in face was struggling, trying to get out of the Buick. She was growling loudly and snapping her teeth. Her arms and legs were trapped by the crushed metal that had collapsed in around her. The old man approached the woman trapped in the car. *"This won't hurt a bit! This will not hurt, not a bit! Just a spoon full of sugar helps the medicine go down!"* The old man went over and quickly dodged her snapping teeth, and pinched her nose. Tilting her head back, he poured the milk into her mouth. At once, she cried out, and burst into flames, along with the Buick creating a huge firestorm in the darkness. *"Well, little Darling! My lovely Miss Honey Creek, it is all forgiven! It's me, your Lover Boy! I will bring you a fresh glass of milk next time! Well, I have to go now! And all of you good folks, have a wonderful day!"* He waved as he tottered into the darkness with his walker squeaking as he disappeared.

"Who? Who? Who was that?" Diamond Jenkins asked as he peered over the side of the door, shaking with fear as broken pieces of glass from the windshield fell off of his suit. *"That looked like my last*

husband Wendell. He died right after I left. He was lying in the bed not feeling well so I gave him a warm glass of milk. The next morning, I went to his room and found him dead! The police and everyone else blamed me! They put out a warrant for my arrest after I decided to leave. I had to leave in a hurry! They thought I had poisoned the old coot. I wonder how he found me. OH GOD PLEASE FORGIVE ME! OH, GOD, PLEASE FORGIVE ME!" She cried as she held her hands in her head sobbing loudly.

Suddenly, the convertible started up again and began shifting gears. As the headlights came on, the engine roared and the wheels started spinning in the sand as it bolted forward in the darkness. The convertible was a wreck. It was smashed and dented on every side. Surprisingly, it was able to drive with amazing speed. Charlie watched in horror as the steering wheel turned back and forth. He could do absolutely nothing but brace himself. Then in a horrific burst underneath the convertible, the wheels caught on fire. The flames moved around the racing convertible and then danced inside the interior. As the travelers fought to put the flames them out, Charlie cried out, *"FOR THE LOVE OF GOD RUSSELL, HOW DO WE PUT THESE FLAMES OUT? HOW CAN WE STOP THIS CAR FROM TURNING INTO A FIREBALL?"*

Russell shouted back at Charlie, *"I THOUGHT YOU DIDN'T HAVE ANY LOVE FOR GOD!"* Russell noticed that Miss Honey Creek's dress had small flames that were dancing on it as well. He quickly took off his jacket and smothered the flames on her dress as she screamed in terror shaking her hands. *"OH GOD HELP US! WE ARE NOT GOING TO SURVIVE THIS NIGHT!"* The flames were on the steering wheel while Charlie tried his best to put them out as they continued to reappear.

The dashboard suddenly erupted in flames also and flew upon Charlie and Diamond Jenkins, covering their clothing as they shrieked in horror. Diamond Jenkins cried out, *"MY CLOTHES ARE ON FIRE! THE FLAMES WON'T GO OUT! HELP ME RUSSELL! RUSSELL I NEED HELP!"*

Russell found some bottled water on the floor of the convertible and poured it over Diamond Jenkins and Charlie. That is when Russell heard Charlie praying for help. The convertible was now engulfed in flames on all sides, blazing like a comet in the darkness. They were all fighting for their lives as the flames reappeared and started jumping inside of the interior of the convertible. *"IT IS USELESS RUSSELL! THE FLAMES KEEP REAPPEARING!" "KEEP PRAYING CHARLIE GOD WILL BRING US THROUGH THIS!"*

Russell looked at Diamond Jenkins. He had his head down and his jacket was covered with flames. He heard him praying. Russell started swinging his coat wildly putting out all the flames inside the convertible. When Diamond Jenkins peeked over the side of the car door, he saw a horrible creature running alongside the convertible. The creature was looking directly at him smiling wickedly as it was running along the sides of the convertible, kicking up a cloud of dust and sand with its clawed feet. It had long black leathery wings that flapped out over its hulking shoulders, which helped it propel forward. The creature looked to be a cross between a corpse and a bat. It had pale leathery skin with large black veins covering it. Its face was twisted, and he had black sockets with white luminous balls for eyes. He stared at them in utter hatred. He screamed at them ferociously saying, *"YOU OLD HAG! MISS HONEY CREEK, NOBODY WANTS YOU NOW! YOU OLD HAG! WHO WANTS YOU?!"*

Then he looked at Charlie smiling, and then started laughing and said, *"AND LOOK AT YOU! YOU CAN'T EVEN FIND YOUR TOUPEE TO COVER UP YOUR BALD HEAD!"* Looking at Diamond Jenkins he jeered, *"POOR LITTLE DIAMOND JENKINS YOU HAVE LOST EVERYTHING! AND NOW YOU WILL LOSE YOUR LIFE AS WELL!"*

As they came in close proximity with the creature, they were instantly gripped in its mental consciousness. As they were being drawn closer towards it, they were temporarily freed from their confinement in the convertible. The creature appeared to be a mass of decay and sores. It mocked them while running and lifting its wings and gliding on the sides of the convertible. Then from underneath its pale membrane skin, there were faces that appeared merged and fused together, speaking in a continuous chatter of insults at the travelers.

The faces of all of the travelers appeared to be in a state of panic and consumed with fear. Diamond Jenkins peeked out from the side of the vehicle *"I think....I think...I think...it is here! The Demon of Suicide has found us!"* In one quick and startling motion, the creature lunged forward, reached over and grabbed Diamond Jenkins' head, like it was a grape in its hand. Diamond Jenkins howled in pain as the creature sunk its long black fingernails into his skull and into his face, tearing off a flap of his skin. Diamond Jenkins still had some life in him, so he began to punch the creature wildly and started screaming, *"I WANT TO LIVE! I WANT TO GO HOME AND SEE MY FAMILY AGAIN! GET AWAY FROM ME! I WANT TO LIVE!"* He then went down on the floor of the convertible trying to cover himself up with his tattered jacket.

Out of thin air, the creature started materializing Free Play Casino coupons and began dumping them on Diamond Jenkins. *"Come back with me Diamond Jenkins! You know you want to come back and try to win again! You don't want to go back home as a loser. You are Diamond Jenkins! The greatest player that has ever lived, that ever played the game! Diamond Jenkins you don't want to go back home as a loser!"* Diamond Jenkins removed his tattered jacket and grabbed some of the casino coupons. His expression looked happy as he paused for a moment before releasing them out of his hand while they blew away out of the convertible.

Russell then stood quickly up and kicked the creature with his boot. It fell over backward tumbling away from the convertible upon the desert floor. *"YOU ARE NOT TAKING ANY OF MY FRIENDS! YOU SICK CREATURE! YOU ARE GOING BACK TO THE VOID, EMPTY!"*

The creature arched its body and flung itself forward. With amazing speed, it flew and caught the speeding convertible driving itself in the darkness. The creature then took hold of Charlie and pulled him free out of his seat. His legs were dangling in the air when Russell reached out towards him and tried to pull him down into the convertible. Charlie was screaming! But he was able to wrap one of his legs around the steering wheel to keep himself from being taken by the Demon of Suicide. *"SOMEBODY HELP ME! FOR THE LOVE OF GOD! HELP ME!"*

Diamond Jenkins also emerged from his hiding place. He shed his tattered jacket as he tried to help Russell pull Charlie back into the convertible. The strength of the creature was shocking. Russell and Diamond Jenkins were momentarily lifted out of the convertible with Charlie before he was finally brought back down. Then the creature swooped down again on the sides of the convertible. The faces underneath his skin were exposed and shouted insults as they heard the voices saying, *"I know you are tired and you have been traveling all night. You need to come back with us to the casino and get a hot meal and get some rest!" "And some of you need medical attention and if you continue like this you will die!" "Why do you continue to suffer like this? Come back with us we are here to help you!" "You should be tired of the day by day battles. Rest yourself. Let us free you!" "Come back to the casino! Come back and have a good time! Why do you fight to maintain your suffering on the earth?!"* One of the faces smiled and spoke to Diamond Jenkins sincerely in a friendly manner. *"It would be such a waste not to use all of these coupons that I have for you. It is time for you to win big! You don't want to go back home as a loser!"*

Another one of the faces spoke to Charlie. *"And why waste a good night? Let the party begin! You have been working long enough Charlie! Don't let your retirement be wasted! Have some fun and do it your way!"* The face said as it started laughing hilariously.

Fear once again overpowered the passengers inside of the convertible as they were engaged in an internal battle. For a moment, Diamond Jenkins thought about jumping into the creature's arms. Diamond Jenkins slowly started to climb over the blazing door of the convertible as the creature called out to him, *"Diamond Jenkins come to me! Come and you can become a winner! Come to me Diamond Jenkins and you can be a god!"*

Russell cried out to Diamond Jenkins as he pulled him down into his seat. *"DIAMOND JENKINS WHERE ARE YOU GOING? YOU DON'T WANT TO BE LOST FOREVER! DIAMOND JENKINS WAKE UP!"* Diamond Jenkins acted as if he was totally oblivious to what Russell was saying to him. He replied, *"I am tired of all of this. I need some rest and food. And I….I….I… want to use my free plays back at the casino. I had enough of living in this world. I can play and have a good time and enjoy my life. I never did fit in this world. I am leaving. Goodbye everyone! I want to be happy again! I want Lady Luck to talk to me again!"*

The creature had its hands open in a benevolent manner as Diamond Jenkins was preparing to jump. Russell reached out to grab Diamond Jenkins, but it was too late. One of the faces under the skin of the creature opened its mouth screaming as a chain flung out, slithering and wrapping its chains around his neck while he struggled to breathe. Then the Demon of Suicide jerked its head backward as Diamond Jenkins was pulled out of the convertible and started dangling on the back of the trunk. The force knocked him backward as he was attached to a chain out of the mouth of one of the creature's faces. He started bouncing up and down on the trunk of the convertible choking to death. Even though Diamond Jenkins was gagging, he managed to speak a few garbled words as he fought for air. *"I AM DYING DON'T SAVE ME! LET ME DIE! LET ME DIE!"*

Now the creature began flying on the side of the convertible, hovering above the travelers as another flaming chain slithered out its mouth wrapping itself around Charlie's leg. He fought wildly kicking and screaming, *"I WANT TO LIVE! LEAVE ME ALONE! THERE IS NOTHING BACK THERE FOR ME! THERE IS NOTHING BACK THERE BUT GHOSTS OF MY PAST! I BELIEVE THERE IS A GOD WHO LOVES ME! AND DOES NOT WANT ME TO DIE! NOT NOW! NOW LEAVE ME ALONE!"*

Charlie quickly pulled off the jacket and tried smothering the flames that kept reappearing. Then one of the horrid faces of Suicide focused on Russell. *"We have the great Arc Angel Zachary reduced to a pitiful representation of humanity. We shall take off your head and place it at the entrance of the city of the damned!"* He said laughing wickedly.

Russell was in a battle that he appeared to be powerless to win. He no longer had his luminous burning sword to fight back. Fire reignited the chains and alighted on Charlie's arms while Russell held him down in his seat, just seconds from being lifted out of the convertible. Then one of the faces of Suicide spoke sympathetically to Charlie. *"You have wasted your life. Why continue to live in such a world of pain! And you trust this drunken vagabond angel to help you now?"* Snarling as he wickedly laughed. *"Your God is dead! There is no one to help you! He doesn't care about you! You pathetic little humans are alone in this world! Come join us! I have come to bring you treasures and wonders that you have never seen before!"* The faces of the Demon of Suicide opened their mouths. Gold coins began to pour out of them, landing inside of the interior of the convertible. *"Can't you see that you are alone? There is no God. I offer you true treasures! A chance to have anything you want, and live forever as your own god!"*

Miss Honey Creek was cradled up in a tight ball on the floor of the backseat of the convertible, crying in a continuous wail of sorrow. She was in her own battle, fighting off one of the chains that snapped at her and tried to attach itself to her arm as she was in a kicking match of survival. She cried out *"I DON'T WANT TO DIE! MY HANDS ARE BURNING! PLEASE HELP ME, GOD! PLEASE, GOD, HELP ME! I DON'T WANT TO DIE, NOT LIKE THIS!"* One of the chains did manage to attach itself to her arms. She pulled on it screaming, *"MY HANDS ARE ON FIRE! OH GOD! MY HANDS ARE BURNING!"*

Diamond Jenkins was still bouncing along the top of the trunk with the chain fastened around his neck. It was not certain if he was still alive as his body bounced lifelessly on the trunk. Then Russell looked and saw Diamond Jenkins was still trying to fight and free himself. He slowly moved his arm towards his neck. Diamond Jenkins looked a mess. Some of his fingers were gone, and his face was almost burned beyond recognition. Russell cried out to him, *"KEEP FIGHTING, DIAMOND! KEEP FIGHTING, DIAMOND JENKINS! NO MATTER WHAT, KEEP FIGHTING!"*

In an instant flashback, in a moment of time, Russell saw the victories and the past battles that he had experienced. He believed that it was his name and his power that was feared among the savage horde that he had once fought and defeated. His warrior sword had now been broken, and he had transformed into the last broken state before being consumed and taken into The Void. He was now as weak and fearful as Diamond Jenkins. He was also just as manipulative and prideful as Charlie. And he was just as empty and self-serving as Miss Honey Creek.

Like a bat out of hell, two chains from the creature wrapped themselves tightly around the arms of Russell, causing his clothes to burst into flames. The creature laughed jeeringly as one of the faces said, *"What a pitiful sight the great Arc Angel Zachary or should I say the weak alcoholic Russell Crowfeet now reduced to a sinful addictive struggling human! Welcome to a terrible reality, Russell! You were created to be a hero! Oh, how we did fear you! And just look at you now! Are you hot and thirsty, Russell? Don't you want a drink? I know you do! We can feel it! You want a drink. Let go of this love for God? God and his love have abandoned you, Russell!"*

Russell cried out as the fire ate through his clothing and he watched his skin burning. *"And now you are going to learn how to die like one of the weak ones, like the weak and miserable humans! And you are empty of your precious Brilliance! I will hang your head on my trophy wall in the city of the damned! Why do you struggle? Give in to the darkness. Why do you believe in the old concept of sin? There are no sins! Believe that. you are a god Russell! For your soul will be torn apart and consumed in nothingness! Look at you now Russell, weak and powerless, forgotten by the God you serve."*

Russell was indeed powerless as he watched helplessly as one of the terrible looking faces of Suicide opened its mouth as another fiery chain quickly wrapped around Russell's neck while he fought just to breathe. And then out of the darkness, the little old man reappeared, still holding a glass of milk in his hands while pushing his rickety, squeaky walker. He stood in the path of the fiery moving convertible as Suicide held on to the broken windshield while the limbs of his blazing tentacles were seconds away from taking the breath out of the travelers. The convertible was moving directly towards the old man who was smiling brightly with a wide grin on the road while still holding the glass of milk in his hands. The convertible collided into his body. As he collapsed to the ground, his walker twisted under the axle, bent the right front wheel, and flipped, causing it to slide on its side. It created a trail of fire, smoke, and dust as it appeared to be a flying comet, moving in the darkness of the night. The vehicle then came to an abrupt smoking stop as a few flames lingered inside of the interior.

Suicide had tumbled off the hood, and broke one of its wings. Its many faces appeared shocked and stunned by what happened. Diamond Jenkins tumbled off the trunk, which broke the chains from around his neck that had become frail and had turned to rust. His difficulty breathing could be heard in the midst of the darkness. Miss Honey Creek also realized that the chains had become fragile and rusty as she pulled them off her legs and watched them disintegrate away. Charlie untangled himself from the chains that were around him as well. They also became fragile and easily broke away.

The old man was crumpled and broken on the sand appearing to be motionless. He then started to reconfigure his body as he stood up and walked slowly and found his walker. Then he opened his robe, adjusted his checkered shorts, and pulled up his long white socks that were connected to tiny suspenders on his legs. Next, he found the glass of milk. Which still had not spilled over, and was completely intact, standing upright on the ground. In a giddy and happy sounding voice, he began to say, *"NO HARM DONE! NO HARM DONE! NO HARM DONE! SWEET DARLING, I AM ALRIGHT! NO HARM DONE! YOUR LOVER BOY IS ALRIGHT! NO HARM DONE!"* Then he unfolded the twisted metal of his walker, balanced himself, and tottered off into the darkness. The wheels squeaked as he disappeared.

The Demon of Suicide was furious as it hurled insults at the travelers while they were scrambling trying to get out of the overturned convertible. But it was to no avail as a long fiery chain came spiraling out of the chest of the Demon of Suicide, and attached itself to the bumper. The body of Suicide was smoking like a furnace. His hands and his arms were covered with flames as he began to drag the convertible in the darkness. Suddenly, the ground began to shake and a large crater appeared as the surrounding landscape of sand, vegetation, and rocks were spiraling slowly being pulled into it. The travelers did their best to try to escape out of the convertible, but they were confined in its perimeter, trapped by its inescapable force. Only Diamond Jenkins was free, but he was too hurt. He could be heard gasping for air in the darkness. It was a mad struggle of fear as the travelers watched helplessly trapped in the convertible. Suicide jerked its body as the long flaming chain flipped the convertible on its front as he dragged it towards the open crater in the desert.

Russell felt something on his cheeks. He was crying, which was impossible for an angel to do. To express something as simple as a tear, was exclusively a human emotion. For tears are the essential ingredient that defines the uniqueness of the human soul. Tears are the purest elements inside of humans. For tears are formed when the soul is illuminated and virtue can transcend and be touched with such power that even the hems and the garments of clothes can be made brilliant. For it was the Son of God who released his tears on the earth. Nothing could be more brilliant than that, Russell thought.

Russell looked down as the tears rolled down his cheeks, sparkling in the darkness. Suddenly he started glowing as his body started transforming. His arms and legs began to grow out and became larger. The horrid, twisted, green horns that protruded from out of his cowboy hat broke and crumbled apart. Russell's face began to crack and then break apart like an old clay pot. As he pulled away the pieces, new skin glowed underneath. Then a long white streak flashed, illuminated the darkness, and came spiraling from out of the skies, shattering the desert floor. The light was so intense that everyone momentarily shielded their eyes.

When Russell regained his sight, he saw a white, glowing sword sticking out of the ground in front of the convertible. The Demon of Suicide also saw the sword as he continued to drag the convertible towards the opening of the crater that had now turned into twirling sand storm pulling everything into its howling darkness. Suicide screamed at Russell, ***"WHAT IS THIS WORD TO YOU! IT WILL NOT HELP YOU! YOU ARE TOO EMPTY, TOO WEAK, TOO LOST, TOO BROKEN, TOO DESTROYED!"***, Taunted the faces of Suicide with an air of insanity. Then something extraordinary happened. Two large burning wings ripped out from Russell's jacket tearing it apart. The wings were magnificent and shimmered with such intensity that Suicide stumbled with fear for a moment. That is when Diamond Jenkins appeared out of the darkness and ran into him full force knocking him over and then running away laughing hysterically. But not before throwing away the coupons from out of his pockets saying, ***"YOU CAN KEEP YOUR FREE PLAYS!"***

Suicide fell backward and became disorientated. Russell instinctively knew what to do next. He leaped over the broken windshield, and in one swift and graceful blur of motion, he grabbed the sword and spun it around cutting the Spirit of Suicide in half. An unearthly, ghastly sound of voices came out from the body of the Spirit of Suicide. Suicide instantly transformed into a cloud of gruesome, squeaking bats that scattered terrifyingly, disappearing into the blackness of the night.

All of the travelers quickly exited the convertible, and for some time, they stood looking out as the light of the morning slowly covered the horizon and flooded the desert in an array of beautiful colors of light. Russell was on the ground praying and weeping almost in a whisper. The convertible had become shiny and brand new again without any dents or damage as if nothing had ever happened.

Miss Honey Creek's hand had completely healed; even the skin on her face. The wrinkles reappeared, but she was grateful that she was still alive.

Charlie slowly checked himself. He touched his lips and noticed that his mustache had returned. It was no longer burned in half. His toupee also instantly appeared on his head. He pulled it off in disgust and tossed it out of the convertible saying, ***"This thing has been with me for too many years! It is time for me to like who I am!"***

Diamond Jenkins had on his old dirty suit once more, and there was no longer a black gaping hole in the top of his head. His skin had returned to his face. His fingers also returned and were not burned away.

The shiny sword wielding angel had disappeared, and Russell Crowfeet was left on the ground praying. Russell was wearing his patched, faded jeans, and frayed jacket. He held an old stick where the sword had once been. Russell looked at himself, weeping softly, ***"I am human again! Why have I been left like this? Why have I been left so miserably weak?"*** Diamond Jenkins kneeled beside him and helped Russell off the ground and said, *"When we are weak, that is when God makes us strong!"*

Russell Crowfeet had returned looking like an impoverished farmhand. He entered the convertible along with everyone else. He placed his boots on the window ledge, and put his cowboy hat down over his face and said, *"It's been a real long night! I think I will get some sleep!"* Charlie then said, *"Rest and sleep sound good right now my friend! Let's get back to civilization. There is nothing back there for any of us!"*

Charlie pushed a button on the dashboard. As the music played, he said, *"This has been the best vacation of my life!"* When he pressed his foot on the gas, the engine roared, the car jerked forward, and the wheels spun in the sand and accelerated. The music of Frank Sinatra resounded in the desert as everyone started singing, *"I Did It My Way!"*

When they returned to civilization, Charlie became a sex addiction counselor for a treatment center. Miss Honey Creek became a Motivational Speaker and started a halfway house to empower women and improve their self-esteem. Diamond Jenkins became a minister and created a rescue recovery team to help people with gambling addictions. The only time Diamond Jenkins went back into the casino was to do a rescue intervention.

It was just a few days later and Russell was preparing to ride the bus again across the country. He was standing in line with the people waiting to board in front of the Greyhound bus station when a man in a long white trench coat with white hair and wearing dark sunglasses approached him and said, *"We have another assignment for you Russell. Is that the name you call yourself now? You know you can always change back anytime you want!"* Russell looked at him and said, *"I kind of like being like this! It makes me realize how much I really need God!"*

Now let's take the test.

1. *Can you recall a time when God required you to go into a deeper level of prayer and fasting and meditation? And because of a great difficulty that you would be facing, God required you to quiet yourself and seek His spirit. And you found yourself arguing with God saying that you could handle it and that his intervention was not needed. Can you write down what happened when you entered the situation without God in your life? What were the results?*

2. *God is a personal God and he interacts with us on every personal level of our existence. Can you tell me how does God speak to you on your purpose, destiny, and vision?*

3. *Do you believe that you came into this world to do something so important, so extraordinary, so meaningful that everything in your life, even your failures, your challenges, your successes, and even your secret sins are to prepare you for the place where you can impact the world? What is your extraordinary gift that if you were given the opportunity, it could change and bless the world?*

4. *Have you ever considered suicide as an option? And in that moment of your greatest crisis, how did God intervene and change the situation?*

5. *Have you ever seen someone close to you go through a horrifying crisis? How did God use you as an instrument of his love?*

6. *Can you explain a time in your life when prayer really worked for you? Can you explain how prayer, even a small prayer broke through a terrible barrier in your life?*

7. *The Demon of Suicide had faces that insulted the travelers. What would it say about you?*

8. *Have you ever been so addicted to something and you knew it was destroying you?*

9. *What brought you to the realization that it was a problem? How did you recover from this addiction? And are you still fighting the addiction? What are the tools you are using to fight the addiction?*

10. *Diamond Jenkins had a gambling addiction. Have you ever known someone that was addicted to gambling?*

11. *Did you ever help someone recover from an addiction? Have you ever watched someone die from an addiction? Were you too afraid to intervene? And did you believe it was none of your business?*

12. *Charlie Strickland had a sex addiction have you ever saw someone who was ruin because of a sexual addiction?*

13. *Have you ever had a pornography addiction? Have you ever believed you were lost and broken because of adultery and fornication? Have you ever felt lost and far away from God during the times when you participated in inappropriate sexual acts?*

14. *Miss Honey Creek lived her whole life in deceit but had a measure of wealth. Wealth is the standard of success in our society. If given the choice of poverty or great deceitful success, which one would you choose? Can you make a list of successful, but deceitful people nationally, and in your community? Can you make a list of people that you consider honest nationally, and in your community? How would others perceive you?*

15. *Why would Russell Crowfeet want to remain a human after he had regained his Brilliance? What could Russell give to others after living as a fallen human and finding God again?*

~Holding On To Your Green Patch~

Willa Mae Ernestine Johnson stood, looking over her garden. Everything this fall came up far beyond her expectations. She had just turned ninety-two years old, and her dark-skinned face had a tiny patch of gray hair growing underneath her chin, which she considered a proud emblem of her age. As she looked out over the huge garden and orchard with her thick bifocals, everything appeared to be growing amazingly wonderful this year. The giant size mellows, cantaloupes, squash, turnip greens tomatoes, sweet potatoes, green beans, cabbages, and sweet corn all appeared perfectly ripe, and ready for canning, baking, and sharing. She also had a most lovely orchard that had the biggest, reddest, juiciest apples in the whole county of Evergreen, California. Her apples were so delicious that one bite would cause a delightful stream of sweet juice to run down your chin in a happy sensation of joy. Willa Mae's apricots, pears, and cherry trees filled the air around her house and land with a sweet and intoxicating fragrance. And every fall, she would allow the children of the neighborhood to run happily wild in her garden and orchard with their straw baskets picking out anything they wanted. Despite her age, Willa Mae's hands were strong. The protruding veins that covered them from the years dedicated to hoeing, planting and carefully making sure her garden were given the very best effort she could offer.

Willa Mae's husband Andy was long dead after building the little house in the 1930's with his own hands. They both worked hard buying the land that surrounded their small house. But everything in her life had slowly been forgotten, swept away by time. Andy died over forty years ago, leaving her with the responsibility of taking care of the land, and the garden that surrounded the old, tattered house. As time developed, the land surrounding her became a suburban, upscale community of professionals that looked at her dilapidated shack as an eyesore that needed to be destroyed. But every year Willa Mae made sure she gave away most of her tasty fruits and vegetables from her garden to everyone in the neighborhood. She would create beautiful baskets of vegetables and fruits and pick the flowers that she planted in her front yard. And she would leave the baskets on the doorsteps of the exclusive homes that surrounded her tiny shack.

As time went by, a large gated community was created around her little shack until it became an undeniable eyesore. The shack became a symbol of everything that the residents around her hated. Mrs. Hayworth Vanderbilt looked out of her window and stared in disgust at the little run-down shack that greeted her every morning when her maid opened her large living room bay windows. Her husband Wilbert Phillip Vanderbilt was one of the major bankers and financial movers and shakers of the Shady Green development subdivision. Mrs. Vanderbilt spoke in a loud and angry voice, *"Wilbert can't you do something! Every morning I have to glare at that little filthy shack! It is destroying everything that we have tried to build in Shady Green! That poor little crippled Black woman needs to go back to the mud hole of Mississippi or whatever god-forsaken place she came from, and leave our community alone! We don't have to live looking at her little rusty shack every day! Wilbert! Can't you do something? We had everyone in the neighborhood, from the Development Improvement Association, sign the petition to have the old woman moved out, but somehow, she still manages to stay here! It is all so appalling! I can't take it anymore!"* She paced around her large front room, and then dramatically put her hand up to her head and flopped in a histrionic fall on her long white sofa that stretched endlessly around the room as if she was on the verge of fainting.

Her husband was drinking his morning cup of coffee at the breakfast table when he heard her crying out like that. In fear, he rose, but not before slamming his morning newspaper down on his long vertical table, all while the maid was serving him. The long napkin underneath his chin somehow became caught and dragged across the table, causing his breakfast to go crashing down onto the floor. The house maid looked at the broken dishes on the floor, and whispered silently, saying, *"Oh my! I have seen two-year-olds in their high chairs behaving better than this!"* She quickly tried sweeping everything up in a dust pan. Mr. Vanderbilt ran into the room as if he was in a terrible panic with the long napkin still tugged underneath his chin. *''Darling I heard you crying out for help! Are you alright? Please tell me that you are alright?"*

Mrs. Vanderbilt stood holding her hand against her mouth, biting down hard on it, trying not to scream. Then she blurted out, *"I can't take it anymore Wilbert! It is just too much for me to endure! What a tragedy this is! Our dream house; everything that we worked so hard to acquire has been destroyed. All because we have been forced to live next door to a farm!"* *"Oh, I know darling. This is such a heartfelt situation for you. And every day you have to endure looking at this horrible view. I am surprised that you have not had a cardiac arrest from the entire trauma that this old lady has put you through!"* *"She is a menace to our property values! They are going to hit rock-bottom if we don't get her out of our community!"* She moaned in a tearful voice. *"That old woman got some kind of grandfather clause over her property. I have tried everything in my power to get her removed, and nothing has worked so far. I believe, if we pull the right strings, and talked to some high-power people downtown, we can annex her property, and get her removed once and for all!"* Mr. Vanderbilt said in a most sympathetic voice *"I refuse to live like this any longer! This old woman's house is an eyesore, a pitiful disgrace! She is an example of how people refuse to better themselves. We cannot live next to people like her, and expect to keep our lifestyle, and our standard of living!"* Mrs. Vanderbilt said coughing and sneezing as she took a handkerchief out of her expensive Louis Vuitton handbag, and covered her mouth. *"And I can smell those apples and apricots from her orchard over here. I bet she has some cows, chickens, and other farm animals living over there as well."*

Mr. Vanderbilt came over and patted her on the head, spilling his coffee on his hand, then shaking it painfully, saying, *"Honey, Cupcakes, are you feeling alright? Everything is going to work out. That old woman cannot hold everyone hostage in our community because she wants to live on a farm. I promise you that old lady will be removed this month. I will make sure of it!"* *"Please, Wilbert I beg of you. It is too much for me to bear at times just to see her over there working in that humongous garden of hers. It makes me think that I am living next door to a country squatter! I am overwhelmed by all of this. I need a nice and relaxing latte!"* She stood up and clapped her hands furiously, *"Lucia where are you? I need my relaxing latte! I need you to come right now!"* Lucia came trotting into the room, almost out of breath. *"I was cleaning the broken dishes from the morning breakfast that Mr. Vanderbilt had spilled all over the floor."* *"Well, you need to move faster girl, if you want to keep this job! You know you can always be replaced! Listen to me, Lucia! When I clap my hands, I want you to be here without excuses!"* Lucia stood still, not moving a muscle as if she was made of stone. *"At least we don't have to look at her over there anymore!"*, Mr. Vanderbilt said as he hurriedly shut the curtains and blinds of the windows so hard that they broke and fell, crashing to the floor. Once again, the maid looked at what had happened. Startled, she whispered to herself, *"Oh My! What a nightmare!"* Lucia ran over to the fallen curtains and blinds. Carefully, she tried to reattach everything to the front windows again.

Mr. Vanderbilt spilled some more of his hot coffee on his hands, crying out in anguish, *"That old woman is driving me crazy! It is causing this whole house to fall apart! We are an upscale community! It's time that she is removed from off her land!"* Mrs. Vanderbilt was still sitting on the sofa when she snapped at her maid, *"Lucia, you lazy thing, can't you move any faster? I am having a stroke over here and you have done nothing to help me! Go and get me a damp towel, and a bag of ice, so I don't pass out!"* *"Yes, Madam, but I was trying to repair the broken window blinds that Mr. Vanderbilt had broken!"* *"You better move fast girl or you won't have a job!"* *"Yes, Madam!"* *"And where is my latté? Wilbert, you are one of the leading bank presidents of this city, surely you can do something?"* *"I have researched her land and title. She owns nothing over there! There is nothing signed or legally binding keeping her on that land but a grandfather clause. But I do have a good friend with the County Attorney's office. I think that I may be able to persuade him to annex her land. And we will be done with the old woman once and for all! I have a good plan that will remove her. So, we won't be forced to look at this eyesore every day!"*

On a beautiful October morning, a large group of children could be heard laughing outside of Willa Mae's white picket fence that surrounded her neatly trimmed lawn. She had everything ready for them. They had been waiting all year long to go through her garden and enjoy themselves. She had about fifty straw baskets that had handles so the children could gather and carry as much fruit and vegetables as they liked. She had also canned an ample supply of preserves and jellies to give to everyone in the neighborhood. It was a lot of hard work, but she knew that the nutritional value of her toxin-free organic fruits and vegetables was becoming more difficult to find in the grocery store.

When Mrs. Vanderbilt heard the voices of the children, she quickly rose from off the sofa, and opened her curtain in a huff and said, *"This is unbelievable! Not again! Every year these children gather from everywhere in the city to come to her garden, and run through it, like a bunch of wild rabbits eating everything in sight! This is a total disgrace! These people should be ashamed allowing their children to come from every part of the slums to run through her garden. This situation is getting out of control! Wilbert, we have slum children in our neighborhood running around in that old woman's garden! This has become too much for me to handle! They will be stealing from us soon?"*

Mrs. Vanderbilt was almost shouting, *"LOOK AT THIS! HAVE THE PEOPLE IN THIS COMMUNITY LOST THEIR MINDS? How can they allow their children to gather in the old woman's garden to have their yearly fruit picking session? This is a gated community! How did the slum children get through? And look at this? There is also a television news crew over there, interviewing the old hag. I am at a loss for words."*

Mrs. Vanderbilt ran to her sofa clapping her hands screaming furiously, *"LATTE! LATTE! I NEED MY LATTE!"*, collapsing on the sofa in a dramatic fall once again as if she had sustained a serious injury. Lucia came running into the room with a tray and a tea cup! *"I heard you crying, Mrs. Vanderbilt! I have your latte for you!"* Mr. Vanderbilt clumsily took the little tea cup and saucer off the tray and tried to quickly give it to her when it slipped through his fingers and drenched her with the drink. Mrs. Vanderbilt and her white sofa were covered with streams of chocolate. The chocolate started dripping down her face as she started crying and sniffling. Mr. Vanderbilt hands were shaking as he nervously tried to wipe the chocolate off her face. *"Look what is happening to us, Wilbert! We are losing our sense of civilized living! We have to get her kicked off that land or we are destined for ruin!"* Mr. Vanderbilt continued wiping the splattered drink off her while speaking in a reassuring voice, *"I have everything in the works! She will be removed from that land! We will not lose our way of life. For her time of being in our community will be over soon!"*

It was a special day for Willa Mae. She stood in her yard, smiling with a large grin, watching the throng of inner city children, and the children from Shady Green. They were laughing and running through her garden, eating the large apples, the other fruits, and just enjoying themselves. They were experiencing firsthand how special it was to protect and preserve the environment.

The news crew from Action 7 City News had arrived and began to set up cameras around her house, recording videos of the children running through the garden. They also requested an interview with Willa Mae. Willa Mae had never been on television before. She was frightened, at first, when the microphone was placed before her. The reporter asked her what was the most important reason she allowed the children of the city to come to her garden? Willa Mae raised her bifocals off her nose, and patted down any wild streaks of gray hair that covered her head. Incipiently, she nervously started speaking, soon after, she found her voice, and calmly said, *"It is important to understand that children have a relationship with their environment. They must recognize that their food supply doesn't just come from the grocery store they come from out of the earth, from the ground. Look at my hands they don't look as pretty as they should because I have been hoeing, planting, and digging for over forty-five years. But you know something, my melons, apples, cabbage and butter beans are the tastiest fruits and vegetable you will find anywhere. There is something sacred in understanding our role as the caregivers of the earth. And in a sense, we are the guardians that God has chosen to protect his sacred green patches that are still struggling to survive upon the earth."*

The news reporter was overwhelmed by the old lady's answers. It took the reporter by surprise that Willa Mae spoke so elegantly about something that she did not expect from a woman her age. Soon Willa Mae became the talk of Shady Green, and the city at large. News spread about the old black woman, her beautiful garden, and how she allowed the inner-city children to eat natural organic fruits and vegetables for the first time in their lives. One organization that directed their efforts towards environmental issues asked her if they could use her image as a symbol of the earth when they saw what she was doing for the community.

Soon t-shirts with pictures of Willa Mae walking around her garden as the sun was setting behind her house, started to be seen everywhere. There were also billboards around the city with her face on them that read, *"All it takes is one person to touch the earth with love!"*

Willa Mae's garden became a symbol of a community that had given children the opportunity to experience an intimate relationship with the earth. The children would participate in the living practice of understanding that the food that they ate was not grown in the grocery store, but real hands must take the necessary time, and patience to bring it forth with dedication, and struggle out of the earth. More large billboards dotted the landscape of the city with Willa Mae's picture on it with more heartfelt words that said, *"The Earth can still be saved! One Woman did it!"*

It was all too much for Mrs. Vanderbilt as a daily group of people came from the city into Shady Green to take pictures of the old black woman, rocking on her porch. They came to buy some of her fruits and vegetables, and delicious jelly preserves. Mrs. Vanderbilt knew she needed to take action against Willa Mae or she would never be rid of her or her shack. Therefore, Mrs. Vanderbilt started her own campaign with a community improvement associate. She went from house to house in Shady Green, trying to get people to sign a petition to remove Willa Mae off her land for not following the community's resident bylaws. Mrs. Vanderbilt was flabbergasted when none of the residents of Shady Green wanted to sign her petition. They only talked about Willa Mae's delicious fruit, vegetables, and the colorful flowers that she would leave on their doorsteps as well as how their children loved to run happily through her garden every year. They also conceded that the experience was worth any monetary cost. Mrs. Vanderbilt tried to explain to the residents how their property values would be destroyed, and that the resale value would be highly diminished by Willa Mae's garden, and her little country shack. But none of that appeared to matter anymore. It was all too frustrating to Mrs. Vanderbilt as she returned home distressed without any names on her petition.

One day Willa Mae sat on her porch with a bowl of snap beans, breaking them in half as she rocked back and forth in her rocking chair. An official looking car pulled up to the white picket gate of her front yard. A tall looking man with an impressive uniform, got out of the car, and walked down the sidewalk, and stopped in front of her porch. Willa Mae did not know what to make of the official looking gentleman that appeared before her. She squinted, adjusted her bifocals, and could see a star pinned to his shirt with the word Sherriff on it. She stood up nervously while he spoke, saying, *"Are you Willa Mae Ernestine Johnson?"* Willa Mae replied, *"Yes I am!" "I am serving you official papers from the city of Evergreen Grove Country. All your land has been officially annexed, and you have thirty days to removed yourself from your property or you will be in contempt of court, and can possibly face imprisonment or a fine!" "What do you mean Sir?! My husband and I bought this land over fifty years ago, and it is ours! He worked hard to buy this land, and I helped him. So how can we be removed from something that we own?" "I am sorry Madam. I am only doing my job! All I know is that you have thirty days to move off your property or you could face jail time."* The Sheriff said as he handed her the official looking papers. *"I will not move anywhere! Do you hear me, young man?! My late husband, Andy, bought this land,*

and every piece of it is ours! And I don't care what this paper says! This is my land, and I am not going anywhere!"

Willa Mae started reading the paperwork as the tall man in the uniform jumped back into his vehicle, and drove away. It was another beautiful morning, but fear filled her tiny frame as the dread of her leaving her garden and her house was too much for her to take. Tears filled her eyes, steaming her bifocals. Large teardrops fell upon the paper she held as her hands trembled. She whispered to herself saying, *"Oh Lord Jesus, what am I am going to do?"*

Mrs. Vanderbilt watched the whole scene as she peeked out from her large windows, behind her front room curtains. *"He did it! Wilbert finally found the right solution to get the old woman kicked out of our community!"* She said laughing with a wicket howl. *"I am quite sure she can rent or relocate to a public housing facility where she will be more comfortable with her kind of people. And besides, it is not good for a woman of her age to be living by herself. She would be better off sewing or knitting in a nursing home. That is where she belongs! Wilbert told me that today would be the day of her undoing. He did say that she would be served by the Sheriff and the construction crew will be out to crank up their bulldozer for demolition. That old, dirty shack is going to be torn down and there will be nothing that she will be able to do about it!"*

Thirty days later, a demolition crew arrived, walking through Willa Mae's garden, stomping the pumpkins, and the cantaloupes with their boots, and leveling rows of cabbage. They walked around the house trampling through the flower patch and destroying large groups of them until their petals were scattered about the yard. The Foreman and other official looking men stood in the yard discussing how to tear down the shack and bulldoze the garden the most expeditious way.

Willa Mae could not believe what she was seeing. She could hardly restrain herself when she met them with a broom held high in her shaking hands. *"Young man, just look what you are doing to my garden with your boots! And you destroyed a whole group of tulips! You should be ashamed about the destruction you caused today. Do you know how hard it was to grow these wonderful vegetables that you just destroyed in a matter of minutes? You have no right to be here.*

And you have no right to be on my property!" "Well, we are sorry Madam, but they told us no one would be here. They said that the land owner would be gone by now! Didn't you receive the official notice that this land has been taken over by the city, and you had thirty days to move out before the final demolition?" "I saw those papers and I threw them out! This land is mine! My late husband worked hard for it, and I don't care what you fancy dancy downtown people have said. I am not moving off my land!" "We are so sorry but my crew will be here tomorrow, and they will be bringing the heavy equipment to tear everything down." "You better leave here right now! You see this broom? I am not afraid to use it!"

Mrs. Vanderbilt saw the commotion and came over snickering uncontrollably as she stood in front of Willa Mae's white picket gate. *"I thought I would give you a going away present. We need to make up since you won't be here any longer. So, I came over here with a peace offering for you."* She opened the gate and walked up to her handing her a beautiful box with a big bow tied on the top of it. Willa Mae stood silent for a moment and then said, *"I have always believed that it is important to try to heal broken relationships while we are still living upon the earth. I know we had our differences, but maybe, just maybe, we can work and live together!"* Willa Mae slowly opened the beautiful little box and slowly untied the big red bow on the top. Inside the box was an old, beat-up, brown shoe. *"I thought you needed a present that would identify with your going away! You are getting the boot old lady!"* Mrs. Vanderbilt laughed with a terrible howl, turned around, and started walking back home without looking at Willa Mae again.

Willa Mae stood in front of her gate, raising her trembling voice, and said, *"You are a wicked woman Mrs. Vanderbilt! You are going to need someone one day! And all of your money will not be able to help you!" "Well, that day is not today and there is nothing you can do to stop the legal proceeding of you being moved off this land. My husband knows the people that work for the County Attorney, and your land has been officially taken away. You are moving back to the sticks where you belong!" "Mrs. Vanderbilt, you got some nerve to even come over here! You already own a lot of property, and this is all I have! And now you are trying to move me off my land!" "I am tired of looking at your country bumpkin house destroying my view in the morning. You are leaving old lady, and there is nothing you can do about it. And in a few days, there will be nothing left of your house or your garden but an empty field."*

Mrs. Vanderbilt reached down and found a flower growing by her picket fence, pulled it apart, and threw it down to the ground. She wiped her hands as if she had been contaminated. *"In a few days, I won't have to look at your old face or your beat-up shack anymore!",* She scowled as she quickly flung her hair backward, prancing back to her house.

Willa Mae took the box and threw it angrily down to the ground. *"That woman is a curse to this community, and God is still going to turn everything around! She is going to see!"* Willa Mae stood holding the letter in her hands saying, *"My God is stronger than all of those folks downtown! The heavens are going to break open!"* One of the foremen spoke softly and said, *"Madam, I am so sorry for what has happened to you. I hope things will work out for you. But we have our job to do."* Willa Mae was shaking as her tears dropped upon the land that she had labored and loved for over fifty-five years.

Later that day, after the construction crew left, Willa Mae walked around her garden. She felt the strength, and all that she loved, being drained from her. She heard the birds flying above her head, and then flying down into her garden, plucking some leaves and bits of apricot to take to their nests before the darkness of evening had completely covered everything. *"This cannot be!"* she said as she looked at the beautiful garden, and the house that she and her husband had built. She looked around. She could still see Andy when they were first married. He brought her to sunny California. She was young then and had just graduated from high school. She was swept off her feet by the dashing young man with his black and white shoes, his plaid zoot suit, and his sleek hotrod-looking Studebaker. They traveled together over a thousand miles from Greenwood, Mississippi loaded with everything they could carry in the Studebaker until they came to this beautiful valley in California. There was nothing around back then; no houses, just trees everywhere, and the beautiful mountains where the land sits between them.

Times were tough for her and Andy. There were few opportunities for colored people back in the thirties, but somehow with strength and determination, they made it. Andy soon found a job laying down tiles for the railroad. Eventually, he became a brakeman. Willa Mae worked hard as a seamstress. Together they dug the soil around the land creating an orchard and a garden that had the most delicious fruit in the whole county. Word soon spread among the neighbors about the wonderful and delicious produce. People came from miles away every year to buy them. They started to save every penny and finally had enough to purchase the land around the house. They worked hard hoeing the land and digging up the roots of trees. They worked until their bodies were exhausted, and they achieved their dreams. Now, it did not seem right that one little piece of paper had that much power to take everything away in less than a few days. She looked around the little beautiful house. Her mind flashed back. She saw Andy building the foundation of the house, and how they marked off where each room would be. The men from Andy's railroad job came and helped raised the walls of the house into place. People helped each other through the tough times back then. Willa Mae looked out over the large beautiful homes that surrounded her little tiny house. She silently whispered, *"People just don't seem to help each other anymore. And they just don't take the time to get to know each other."*

Instantly, her mind went back to that terrible storm that occurred in 1954. The humidity had become so high that day, circles of dust were seen swirling upward in a vertical motion and blowing across the valley. A severe storm took place that night as the lightning flashed in striking bursts across the sky. The sound of thunder boomed and echoed throughout the valley, causing the ground to tremble and shake. Back then, everything around was all farmland. There was no Shady Green gated community. The people survived in a communal relationship with nature. And during that terrible storm, Willa Mae remembered huddling together with Andy, surviving only with the power of love. That morning when they had awakened, there were trees down everywhere, and crops and fields had been badly destroyed. They quickly jumped in their truck and went to check on their neighbors and saw Elisa Stubblefield's house and that a large oak tree had crushed it in half. Elisa lived by herself. Her husband, John, was long dead after she found him lying in the field from having a stroke. It was a tragic death. So now, she had been living alone for years. Therefore, she and Andy thought it was best to check on Elisa first. For Andy sometimes helped her if a fence needed mending or if some of her livestock had gotten out of their pens. Andy quickly stopped the truck and ran toward the mud and tree covered house. He climbed over a thicket of branches and found the door and called out. *"ELISA, ARE YOU ALRIGHT? ELISA, ARE YOU ALRIGHT? DO YOU HEAR ME? DO YOU HEAR ME? THIS IS ANDY! ANDY JOHNSON! WILLA MAE AND I HAVE COME OVER HERE TO HELP! ARE YOU ALRIGHT?"* Somewhere in the darkened house, a weak voice called out, *"Please help me, Andy. I am trapped in a room, and there is no way out!"* Andy looked inside and saw a large tree branch that had covered the entrance. He quickly ran to his truck, and took out his chainsaw, and began to cut through the branches until it sputtered, stopped, overheated, and refused to work anymore. He then attached a chain to one of the large branches and secured it with his truck and pulled it out until Elisa was freed. There was such a sense of community; of being connected with one another. And now it seemed like those days were long gone forever.

Willa Mae stood outside and gazed at the sky above. She could sense that it was going to rain; maybe a terrible storm, she now believed. One of her toes was tingling, and the bunion on her left foot was sore, which was a sure sign that a big storm was coming. As she looked at the thunderstorm clouds overhead, she sighed, *"Everything back then is gone. All of it is all gone. All the people, everything that I believed was sacred, is now all gone. I am the last one to remember what happened. I need to let it all go. This house, the land, and even my life, I need to let it all go."*

As she continued to walk through her garden, it was cold, chilly, and the wind was, swirling. *"I am an old woman now. I need to give up my land and let them put me in one of those nursing homes. I have nothing to live for anymore."* She quickly returned to her little house and noticed that the storm had knocked out all the power around her house. It appeared that no one had any power in the large community of Shady Green that looped around her. She was grateful as she sat in her rocker and started to knit a sweater before falling into a deep and peaceful sleep.

At that moment, the thunderstorm began breaking out windows in the Shady Green community. It was a terrible storm, and the wind started to blow all around. But amazingly, the sun continued to shine, and the wind was calm around Willa Mae's paltry, little shack.

Mrs. Vanderbilt looked out of the window of her front room as one of her windows shook with so much force, it knocked a lamp over, causing it to crash to the floor. *"Wilbert, can't you do something about this storm?"*, Mrs. Vanderbilt said in a terrified voice. *"There is nothing I can do about this storm, Dear. We just have to go through it!"* *"The storm is shaking the house apart! Wilbert, what are we going to do?"* She screamed as a tree limb suddenly crashed against the window pane and cracked it. *"WILBERT, DID YOU SEE THAT? A TREE LIMB JUST HIT THE HOUSE!"* *"We might have to go to a safe place; maybe in the basement, Dear until the storm is over!"* Then suddenly, all the lights went out in the house. Mrs. Vanderbilt screamed out, *"WILBERT, ALL THE LIGHTS ARE OUT IN THE HOUSE? WE ARE IN THE DARK! I'M AFRAID! WILBERT! WHERE ARE YOU? CAN'T YOU CALL THE POWER COMPANY? CAN'T YOU DO SOMETHING?"* *"I am quite sure they are doing all they can, Dear, with all the power going off all over the city. We just have to ride through this storm. We have to go downstairs to the basement. I will go and find the flashlights so we can take cover!"* *WHAT? WE HAVE TO GO INTO THE BASEMENT! THAT IS WHERE THE MAID KEEPS ALL THE BROOMS AND MOPS! I AM NOT GOING DOWN THERE! THAT IS WHERE LUCIA, THE MAID, TAKES HER BREAKS! I AM NOT GOING DOWN THERE, WILBERT! JUST LET ME DIE UPSTAIRS! FOR THE LOVE OF GOD, PLEASE, WILBURT, CAN YOU DO SOMETHING ABOUT THIS STORM?"* *"There is nothing I can do about it, Dear. I am just a human being. We have to go take cover now!"*

Mrs. Vanderbilt peeked out the window and saw the lights on in Willa Mae's little house. *"WILBERT! THE OLD LADY STILL HAS HER LIGHTS ON IN HER SHACK! HOW IS THAT POSSIBLE*

WHEN EVERYONE ELSE HAS THEIR LIGHTS OUT?" "I don't know Dear, but maybe we are on a different power grid. I don't know how she has her lights on, but we need to go to a place of safety right now!" "DID YOU CALL THE POWER COMPANY, WILBERT?" "Yes Dear, but they are working, trying to restore lights everywhere in the city." "Well, that old Colored lady still has her lights on!" "I don't know how, Dear but we need to go now before something terrible happens to the house!" "We have a million-dollar house and we are in the dark, Wilbert! I don't understand it!" "Please, Dear, we have to go downstairs to the cellar right now."

Mrs. Vanderbilt decided to go outside to see how the old lady still had her lights on. Her husband tried to stop her as she stood outside with her hands on her hips as if she was angry at the skies above. When the wind suddenly became so strong, she felt as if she was being lifted off her feet as she held on to the door handle while her legs went upward into the air. Just then, her husband grabbed her, just in time, and pulled her into the house. *"HAVE YOU LOST YOUR MIND? YOU COULD HAVE BEEN SWEPT AWAY BY THE STORM! CAN'T YOU SEE HOW DANGEROUS IT IS?" "I JUST HAD TO SEE FOR MYSELF. SHE REALLY HAS HER LIGHTS ON! HOW CAN THAT BE IN THAT LITTLE SHACK OF HERS?" "YOU COULD HAVE GOTTEN KILLED! AND IF YOU DON'T STAY IN THIS HOUSE, I WILL DRAG YOU DOWNSTAIRS MYSELF!" "WILBERT! YOU HAVE NEVER TALKED TO ME LIKE THAT BEFORE!"*

The storm shook everything around the city, and the wind was so strong and furious that the trees were being uprooted, while lightning illuminated the skies. It was in the cool of the morning when Willa Mae awakened. She looked out of her door and saw the destruction that surrounded her little shack. She slowly strolled outside. Many of the roofs had been blown off the houses of the Shady Green community. Willa Mae looked frightened and adjusted her bifocals, *"Oh my, what a terrible storm it was last night. So many homes of the Shady Green community were destroyed. I pray that no one has been hurt from this terrible storm."*

Willa Mae walked around her house. Not one shingle was missing from the roof. It appeared as if the storm had totally missed her house.

She inspected her garden. All of the wonderful plants had survived, completely untouched.

Willa Mae noticed a cool mist in the air that created a white fog which appeared to be floating over the garden. She looked out over the community of Shady Green. Everything seemed to be in total chaos. The sound of fire trucks and police cars could be heard as they arrived with their loud sirens and blinking headlights surrounding the community. Several tree companies arrived and started cutting down large branches that had become tangled around the houses of Shady Green. The sound of their buzz saws was heard as power company trucks also arrived trying to untangle the whole mess of wires that were pulled down into the streets.

The power was out in the Shady Green community. Groups of people stood outside their homes and looked at the devastation that took place overnight. The destruction was unbelievable. Cars were overturned, and some houses were split in half. Confusion and fear overcame everyone. Only Willa Mae's house was completely intact. She sat on her rocker looking at the devastation, and she knew that this was not a normal day.

A gas company truck arrived and immediately, danger and warning signs were constructed all over in front of the homes. A news crew helicopter was heard hovering overhead taking pictures of the devastation. The catastrophic scene appeared as if it was right out of a disaster movie. A family stood in front of their house weeping, not knowing what to do. The police blocked off the entrance to Shady Green, preventing the public from entering. Many of the residents were not able to leave their homes and were trapped in the Shady Green community. For the residents that made the hazardous decision to leave, it was a real challenge to navigate through the confusion and chaos that had transformed the landscape. And now, food, water, and basic human needs became a physical challenge for survival. Most the residents were stranded. They were informed by the power company that their services would be turned on in a day or two depending on the severity of the damage. Until then, everyone in the Shady Green community was trapped. Obtaining the basic needs was now a real concern.

Willa Mae could see the disaster and the devastation surrounding them, so she decided to act. She quickly gathered baskets of fruits and vegetables for the residents of Shady Green. It was a daunting task for a woman of her age, particularly with all the dangerous conditions with downed tree branches, and live wires on the street. But she was determined to go from door to door with her baskets of fruits and vegetables. She prepared a basket with her homemade canned jellies, fruits, and vegetables delivering them to the residents of Shady Green. The residents were so happy with the gifts because the lack of refrigeration left them in dire need.

The last house she approached was Mrs. Vanderbilt. She was afraid to go there. Then she decided that she was not going to walk away if the Vanderbilts needed help. Willa Mae said to herself, *"Yes forgiveness is what every disciple of God must have."* She stood at the door and then tapped lightly. The maid peeked out of the door, and then quietly whispered, *"Oh My! It's you!"* She shut the door again and called out to Mrs. Vanderbilt. Willa Mae could hear Mrs. Vanderbilt yelling at her husband, *"Wilbert, when will we get the power back on? This is an embarrassment to our affluent community. We are groping around in the dark like mice! Can't you go downtown and talk to someone from the power company and threaten to fire someone if they don't turn the lights on soon. And I am hungry! When are we going to eat? All the food in the refrigerator has spoiled. This is a terrible situation for people like us to be in!"* *"I have done all I could, Honeybun to try to speed this matter up. They are outside working around the clock, trying to restore everyone's power in Shady Green. There is nothing we can do, but go through this emergency until everything is restored!"* *"Well, can't you go out and get us something to eat? I am turning into a refugee in this house with nothing to eat."* *"I tried, Dear but there are so many tree branches down, and power crews working on the streets, we cannot even leave the neighborhood. We are stuck, Dear and there is nothing we can do about it right now!"*

Once again, the maid called out to Mrs. Vanderbilt, *"There is someone at the door for you, Mrs. Vanderbilt!"* Mrs. Vanderbilt thought it was the power company at the door to inform her that they had restored the electricity in the house. She swung open the door gleefully saying, *"It's about time you got everything turned on! I have been waiting all day cooped up in this house!"* And then her face turned into a disgusting frown when she saw old Willa Mae Ernestine Johnson with her basket of fruits and vegetables standing outside of her door. Willa Mae pushed her large glasses upward upon her nose, and opened her large picnic basket and said, *"I thought I would bring you something to eat out of my garden, seeing that everyone's power is out all over. And I thought you might be in need of some fresh fruits and vegetables."* Mrs. Vanderbilt was enraged when she looked at Willa Mae saying, *"You got some nerve coming over here! We don't need a handout from some field worker like you!" "I thought I would do the neighborly thing and help you out until everything is up and running again. You never know how long the power might be out." "Well, we don't need a handout from an old degenerate like you. And who knows what contaminants are lurking in those fruits and vegetables of yours! You people don't even wash your hands. And with you living in that shack, it has to be totally unsanitary. I am not eating anything you have grown from that toxic wasteland over there." "Well, I was just trying to be kind. Please forgive me for wasting my time coming over here. You know things turn around quickly in this world. And I have seen a lot of situations when those who thought they never needed anybody had to ask for help. So, you just better watch your mouth." "Are you threatening me? You old bag of bones! In a few days, you will be living in a nursing home, knitting a sweater, and waiting to die. The bulldozers should be over there any day now to wipe your whole life off the face of the earth. So if you don't mind, please remove your country toxic food off of my property! I will call the police if you ever set foot over here again!" "Well, Mrs. Vanderbilt as long as there is a God in heaven, I will not be removed from my land!" "Well, if he is in heaven, he can't help you on the earth! So please get off my property or I will be forced to call the police!" "I am going to hold on to my sacred patch, and you better find yours before it is too late!" "What is going to happen to me? Nothing is going to happen to me, you old woman? Is God going to strike me down?"* She mocked as she stood looking up at the skies, and started laughing in a crackling voice. *"You need your soul re-adjusted!"* Willa

Mae said looking at Mrs. Vanderbilt. *"I don't have a soul you old hag! I have a bank account and a trust fund with plenty of cash! Now get off my property!"*

As Willa Mae walked back to her little shack, she looked around the neighborhood of Shady Green. It was in shambles. It was nearly impossible to drive out of the community with so many trucks blocking the streets, downed power lines, and people working in a state of frenzy, trying to restore everything back to normal. Willa Mae also noticed that some of the workers were yelling about a pipe being broken in the middle of the street as tall gushers of water spurted into the air, creating a spectacular fountain in the neighborhood. *"Oh my, this really looks bad!"* Willa Mae said as she cautiously and safely made her way to her porch, looking at the mayhem that was occurring all around her.

Willa Mae sat on her porch in her rocker and started to snap some beans for her lunch. Sitting there, she saw something curious that bubbled upward from the ground, creating a tall tower of dark water that poured out over Mrs. Vanderbilt's front yard. In the distance, she could see workers scrambling around, calling out to everyone, *"HEY, THE MAIN WATER LINE HAS JUST BROKEN! SOMEONE NEEDS TO TURN IT OFF QUICKLY!"*

The water spilled out all over Mrs. Vanderbilt's front yard. A terrible, reeking, brown sludge came spurting out of the pipe. She could see Mrs. Vanderbilt waving her arms in a hysterical motion. Then she proceeded to yell at every person that had a construction hat on. Willa Mae could not figure out what was going on as the sludge covered the streets, and moved rapidly through the neighborhood of Shady Green. It was a chaotic scene. Shady Green had transformed into a mud-soaked pit as groups of people came out of their homes to see their once beautiful community with its carefully professionally groomed lawns, now covered in a flood of mud, and sludge. And to make matters worse, a terrible sewage smell consumed the atmosphere of the entire neighborhood. Willa Mae could hear the construction workers yelling, *"TURN THE MAIN WATER PIPE OFF! HURRY OR THE WHOLE COMMUNITY WILL BE FLOODED!"*

Willa Mae continued rocking back and forth. She sat on her porch snapping her beans, and then she started to pray for the people and the mayhem overtaking the community. *"Lord, please help these poor people! For everything has turned into such a horrible and terrible situation. I don't know how they are going to make it!"*

Mrs. Vanderbilt had turned into a screaming, frantic hurricane. She even picked up some of the sludge and started throwing it at the power and city street workers. *"I AM GOING TO SUE YOUR POWER COMPANY FOR EVERYTHING YOU HAVE! JUST LOOK WHAT YOU HAVE DONE TO OUR LOVELY COMMUNITY OF SHADY GREEN! THIS IS INTOLERABLE!"* She continued picking up handfuls of the sludge and started flinging it at the supervisor before she was restrained by her husband. The sludge had quickly covered most of the streets of Shady Green and created a putrid smell that overtook the upscale community. It was a maddening scene. The residents tried to pack their bags, and drive away from their homes. But the sludge now made it impossible for them to drive away. Many of the residents tried walking out of the community, but even that was proving to be a daunting task as the sludge appeared to be everywhere; almost knee deep in some places.

The construction workers quickly found the shut-off valve and stopped the horrific sludge from overtaking the community. But in the process, the water valve was also shut off, so there would be no water in the community. The Power Company and the Maintenance Crew informed everyone about the lack of water for the next two days or more. Everyone went gasping, searching for fresh, breathable air, due to the stench in the air from the sludge. All of the residents had been affected by this terrible disaster, except the small, little shack of Willa Mae Ernestine Johnson for she still had water and electricity in her home. Also, there was a wonderful fragrance of flowers, the ripe produce of apples, plums, apricots, and orchard trees that surrounded her land and garden.

It was late in the evening. The residents of Shady Green still had no water. The city workers had worked tirelessly, trying to restore everything back to normal. But repairing the broken pipe, and cleaning the massive wave of sludge, would take another day. Mrs. Vanderbilt was infuriated. She screamed at the Power Company Supervisor.

Her voice could be heard all the way across the modest valley that separated the shack and Shady Green. *"That woman is going to lose her tonsils with all the screaming that she did today! Some people just don't know how to go through a crisis without making themselves and others even more miserable!"*, Willa Mae lamented.

It was a most heart-wrenching day. Willa Mae watched the whole chaotic scene play out from her porch. It was as if she was watching a disaster movie from a Hollywood production company. *"I wish there was something that I could do to help them."*

Willa Mae saw a falling star twinkling in the atmosphere as the night gradually began to fall over the suffering residents of Shady Green. Suddenly, Willa Mae's eyes squinted behind her bifocals. She saw someone standing outside of her gate. It was the new young Doctor, along with his wife, and their small child that recently moved to Shady Green. He had what appeared to be a tent in his hand and some sleeping bags. He approached her humbly saying, *"I don't want to leave my house tonight, but everything over here looks to be so comfy. I think this might be a good opportunity to teach my young son how to camp out for the night. And it is such a lovely night with all the stars out all over the sky." "You are always welcome to come and spend the night with me anytime! I am so happy you decided to come over to my place. You can spend the night inside the house if you like. I have plenty of room for guests!" "Please, that will not be necessary. It is good for all of us to get back to the earth, sleep outside, and appreciate the land that we all came from."*

They began to set up their little tent. He brought a little lantern to see with. The young Doctor began to point out the different stars to his son, who looked on in amazement at all the wonderful things that he could not see before, during the daytime sky. Then Willa Mae noticed that another family appeared at her front picket gate. They also had a tent and some camping equipment. They pleaded with Willa Mae asking her if they could spend the night in her front yard. Suddenly, Willa Mae's front picket fenced yard was filled with groups of residents from Shady Green, wanting to spend the night in her front yard. It appeared as if they were all moved by an internal, intrinsic spirit that caused them to leave their homes; leave the failed comfort of their possessions, and to leave that which they thought gave them life. And now if they could find the rest, the quiet, the sacred place, even if it was only for a moment, it would renew and replenish their ability to love. For the greatest thing to know, amidst a disaster, is that love is the greatest, indestructible force forever renewing itself.

Willa Mae watched as her entire yard, and property became filled with the residents of Shady Green, happily talking, laughing, and camping out around her little shack. Willa Mae knew that many of the residents had not eaten a hot meal in over a day, so she started cooking a huge pot of tasty, and nutritious vegetable stew. She also stewed some cabbage, and she had an ample supply of cornbread and sweet potato pies that she had made a few days ago. She was angry at herself for making so many pies. Aware of the fact that she lived alone, she pondered why she made so many pies. Now she was delighted that the pies were ready for her numerous guests that had arrived.

The night turned into the most fun and amazing time that many of the residents of Shady Green had in years. For it was the first time that many of the residents of Shady Green actually talked to each other. They introduced themselves and shared wonderful stories about their lives, experiences, and how they came to live at Shady Green. And they found new deep, life friendships that were created as they bonded together.

Then Willa Mae started singing. She had an old banjo that she had brought back from Mississippi. She had not played it in years. The last time she played her banjo was when Andy was alive. It was on a night like this one. All the stars were out, and neighbors had filled up the yard for Andy's birthday, so now she decided to sing again. She sat on the porch and started strumming the strings of the banjo. In a clear, crisp, happy voice, she started singing, *"SHE WILL BE COMING AROUND THE MOUNTAIN WHEN SHE COMES! SHE WILL BE COMING AROUND THE MOUNTAIN WHEN SHE COMES! SHE WILL BE COMING AROUND THE MOUNTAIN WHEN SHE COMES!"* Without trepidation, an overwhelming display of joy had everyone clapping their hands, and lifting their voices until it filled the nighttime sky. Many of the children started dancing and laughing as their parents danced with them in a jubilant celebration as families happily learned how to come together as one. Then in a spontaneous act of jubilation, the residents of Shady Green took off their shoes and started dancing barefoot on the soft grass in Willa Mae's yard.

Mrs. Vanderbilt walked in front of the yard with her husband; both wearing gas masks watching the spectacle in disgust. Mr. Vanderbilt then noticed that the tables in front of Willa Mae's porch were covered with dozens of sweet potato pies, and another table had a large, steaming pot of stew, and plates of black-eyed peas and cornbread. Mr. Vanderbilt looked astounded at what he saw. Slowly, he took off his gas mask. Overjoyed, he threw it to the ground, and said, *"I can finally breathe again!"* Appearing oblivious to the loud, blurring demands of his wife questioning his actions, he happily found a bowl, and spooned out a generous helping of the stew and sat down contently eating while stuffing his mouth with the stew and sweet potato pie. *"WILBERT! WHAT ARE DOING? YOU ARE EATING THE FOOD OF THE ENEMY? DON'T YOU BETRAY ME LIKE THIS, WILBERT!" "I am eating, Dear!" "I WILL DIVORCE YOU!" "But I am hungry, Dear!" "I WILL TAKE EVERYTHING YOU HAVE AWAY!" "But Dear, I am hungry!" "Wilbert, you come back here right now! You are a traitor if you stay on her property!" But Dear, we have no food or water at home." "Wilbert, if you don't come back home, I will divorce you! And I promise you that I will take everything that you have! "But Dear, we have not had a good night's sleep in two days! And her property is not mud soaked! I think I will sleep over here tonight, on the grass." "Ok, you can stay over here! As a matter of fact, you can live over here! Don't you ever think about living in Shady Green again! You can stay over here and drop dead with your banjo strumming neighbor."*

One of the neighbors came to Mr. Vanderbilt and gave him an extra backpack. He placed it near a soft green patch in the yard, sat down on the grass, and joined in the singing of the folk songs while eating a big slice of sweet potato pie. He then softly spoke out to his wife, saying, *"Please Dear, come sit down and stay over here tonight. That sludge is unbearable around the house. We can't do anything until the city gets the water pipes fixed and restores all our services. Please, Dear, come back and get a good night's sleep!"* Mrs. Vanderbilt turned around, looked at him and said, *"I will come back when hell freezes over! Or when they put that old woman in the ground! For whatever comes first is alright with me!"*

It was a clear and beautiful night. With all the electricity that was out all over the city, the stars were easily seen in their magnificent beauty. The singing and dancing continued as the people held hands in the yard creating a ribbon of the human spirit, overcoming their fear, and being determined to survive together. It was a celebration of life, a celebration of enduring together, a celebration of believing that love truly conquers all. For as the stars were perfectly aligned, so were the people of Shady Green as they held hands and sang together. Mrs. Vanderbilt interrupted the celebration when she screamed out at everyone, *"IN HEAVEN'S SWEET NAME'S SAKE! WHAT ARE ALL OF YOU DOING OVER HERE? You have turned Shady Green into a migrant camp! Just look at all of you!"* Then one of the neighbors spoke out, *"It is still better over here! I don't care what you say! You need to calm down and eat some of this delicious sweet potato pie."* Mrs. Vanderbilt continued her scathing rage, *"We are a community of professionals. You are one of the premiere Doctors of the city, and you are over here eating rabbits and drinking moonshine. And you are dancing around her yard just like a common field hand!"*

Then the Doctor said, *"No! You are the one who should be ashamed. Mrs. Johnson has been so kind, allowing us to come over here and spend the night in her yard. We have been so busy with our careers that we lived together and did not know each other. And now, through this terrible storm, a great gift has been presented to us. We have been taken out of our homes to enter the hearts of each other. We have created Shady Green into an inseparable community of families that found each other. Now we have friendships that will last forever. Go home Mrs. Vanderbilt and be a lonely snob isolated from what is real. For we are having too much fun to let a gossiping musty, moldy, biddy like you stop us!"* The yard was filled with a sudden roar of laughter as they began clapping their hands as the music and the dancing commenced again. Mrs. Vanderbilt screamed at her husband, *"WILBERT! ARE YOU COMING HOME WITH ME RIGHT NOW? DO YOU HEAR ME SPEAKING TO YOU, WILBERT? YOU NEED*

TO COME HOME WITH ME RIGHT NOW?" Mr. Vanderbilt was sitting in the yard obviously enjoying a huge plate of vegetable mash and sweet beans and cornbread. *"I will be over there in the morning, Dear! Mrs. Johnson is really a great cook you should try some of her cornbread? It is truly unbelievable!"* "ARE YOU GOING BACK WITH ME WILBERT? IF YOU DON'T COME WITH ME THIS INSTANT, YOU WILL BE GETTING DIVORCE PAPERS TOMORROW! AND YOU CAN STAY ON THIS FARM AND EAT YOUR CORNBREAD AND BLACK-EYED PEAS!" *"But Honey, it has been a long day and it is so peaceful and relaxing over here. I will see you in the morning." "Wilbert, you are one of the leading bankers of this community! Please come back home! Don't do this to me! Wilbert, my God, where is your dignity?"* Willa Mae then started singing loudly again as everyone joined along, *"SHE WILL BE COMING AROUND THE MOUNTAIN WHEN SHE COMES! SHE WILL BE COMING AROUND THE MOUNTAIN WHEN SHE COMES!"*

Mrs. Vanderbilt's voice sounded like she was growling. She stormed back to her house and put her gas mask back on her head. When the darkness of the night settled upon the yard, the residents of Shady Green huddled together with their families preparing to sleep looking in awe at the starry nighttime sky. A glittering mass of fireflies floated silently through the yard creating a dazzling display of wonder until sleep consumed the residents of Shady Green.

It was late in the evening when Mrs. Vanderbilt crept back over towards the yard, hoping that no one saw her. The smell of sludge coming from her house was intolerable. She could no longer stomach the smell and dropped down beside a large oak tree outside Willa Mae's yard and fell asleep. Willa Mae was on her porch silently rocking with a soft quilt around her shoulders when she saw Mrs. Vanderbilt creeping silently in the yard and then falling asleep by a tree. She quietly walked towards her. Kneeling down, she placed a warm quilt around her and then left a large slice of sweet potato pie on a dish next to her.

Early the next morning, the sound of construction machinery could be heard in Shady Green. The construction workers promptly fixed the broken pipe and quickly restored order to the residents of Shady Green. Mrs. Vanderbilt had awakened before everyone. Her voice could be heard ferociously screaming at the construction crew for taking so long to repair everything. A mass exodus now ensued as the residents of Shady Green slowly began to pack their items and return to their homes.

It had been a spectacular night. A deep bond of care had been formed. The word neighbor now truly stood for something important. Even the children had a deep awakening with nature. The children now understood that they were not outside of everything that existed, but they were participating in creating the beauty that surrounded their lives. One little boy was skipping along as he was holding the hand of his father saying, *"Dad we have to do this again! It was so much fun! And did you see the fireflies that came out last night? This was better than our last vacation! Let us come over here and go camping again!" "We will if Mrs. Johnson will allow us to come back to her yard."* Willa Mae overheard their conversation and said, *"Look you two! I will be more than happy to have you back in my yard anytime you want. Please come back! I would love to see you and your little cute pumpkin anytime, sleeping in my yard."*

Willa Mae had plates of vegetable mash, and sweet potato pie prepared as a going away present. For the fun that everyone had last night was like the great harvest festival that Willa Mae remembered when she was a little girl. Willa Mae looked at her tiny house surrounded by the large houses of Shady Green and she said, *"This little green patch may be little, but it sure is mighty!"* She felt the sunlight on her skin and watched the white clouds moving silently in the sky above her house. Tears fogged her bifocals as she silently said, *"I guess it is enough now. That was one last goodbye party you gave me God. I guess you wanted me to go out with a bang!"*

As she laughed to herself, Willa Mae decided that she would give in to the demands of Mrs. Vanderbilt. She was old now and perhaps it was time to give up this earthly fight. She walked around the yard and cleaned up a few paper plates that were left behind. She was tired, yet happy, and wanted to rest. She felt the cool breeze surrounding her as she walked back to the porch, sat in the rocker, and put the warm quilt around her, and then fell asleep.

The next morning, she awakened to the sound of a large bulldozer that was being unhooked from a truck. It immediately started to plow through her garden. Willa Mae was shocked at what she was seeing and quickly trotted towards the bulldozer. She had not moved that fast in years. She stood in front of the bulldozer, out of breath, and thought for a moment that she might faint. The bulldozer had plowed up a whole row of cabbage and had destroyed a patch of beans before she stopped the noisy, steel beast by standing in front of it. A large fat man with a stomach that lapped over his belt called out to her angrily, *"You could have gotten yourself killed, lady, running in front of my rig! I don't know what you were doing! You must have a death wish or something lady, but it was a good thing I stopped when I did or you would have been flatter than a pancake!"* Willa Mae yelled at him as she tried to catch her breath, *"WHO DO YOU THINK YOU ARE, COMING ON MY LAND DESTROYING EVERYTHING? YOU HAVE NO RIGHT TO COME HERE! DO YOU KNOW HOW LONG I LABORED TO GROW THAT ROW OF BEANS THAT YOU DESTROYED? YOU GET OUT OF MY GARDEN RIGHT NOW! OR I SWEAR I WILL TEAR THAT MACHINE APART WITH MY BARE BLACK HANDS!"*

"Look lady, I have a job to do! The boss said that there would be no one here and that the place would be vacated. I don't know why you are still here. They said I could come today and bulldoze everything!" Something intense moved in Willa Mae. A sense of justice, and right, and holding on to that which was sacred. *"My late husband Andy and I worked and tilled until our fingers blistered to cultivate this land! He built this house with his own hands! While you were still in your diapers, we were growing food that we sold to the grocery stores for your baby food. And I will not allow you to come on my land with your tractor and destroy a lifetime of work and sweat! I will die before I let you plow over my life! I will die first! Do you hear me, young man?"* *"I am not putting up with this lady! I have a job to do!"*

The man in the rig then pulled out a cell phone and started arguing with a supervisor over the situation. *"Yeah, she is standing in front of my rig! What am I supposed to do? Run over her? I can't do anything until she gets out of the way! I don't think she understands that she is breaking the law!"*

Mrs. Vanderbilt saw her standing in front of the rig and came scampering over aggressively demanding Willa Mae to get out of the way. In defiance, Willa Mae laid down in front of the bulldozer in a horizontal position. It was her last act of protest. She and Andy had worked too hard to let it be destroyed like this. The bulldozer driver now could not do anything as he pleaded with her to move out of the way. *"Please, lady, I have a job to do! Everything is legal. I have a right to destroy everything on this land. Will you please move out of the way?"*

Then Mrs. Vanderbilt stood in front of the driver of the rig demanding action. *"Why haven't you started your tractor back up? She will get up off the ground when she knows that you mean business?"* *"Well, I can't do that, Madam! I am not in the business of running over old ladies!"* *"Well, you are leaving off this land today!"*, Mrs. Vanderbilt demanded as she rushed towards her grabbing Willa Mae's arm, attempting to drag her out of the way of the rig. *"You are breaking the law, Mrs. Johnson! Your time of turning Shady Green into a haystack has come to an end! You are getting off this land if I have to drag you off by myself!"*

A struggle now developed as Mrs. Vanderbilt tried to pull Willa Mae out of the path of the bulldozer. Mrs. Vanderbilt could not believe that Willa Mae was still so strong for a woman that was ninety-two years of age. *"You are not pulling me off my land! You will get a boot in the face if you try to touch me again!"*

The struggle engaged for several minutes before a police officer arrived. *"I heard there might be some trouble today. The City Planning Commission notified us to make sure the eviction process went smoothly."*, the Policeman said. *"She is breaking the law! Everything is legal and in order. She has no right to be on this property right now! The city owns her land now. It is all legal and binding!"* Mrs. Vanderbilt quickly unfolded a legal looking paper from out of her purse. The Police Officer looked at the legal papers and then kneeled down next to Willa Mae, and said, *"I am so sorry, but you will have to* *leave. There is nothing I can do about it. She is right. It's all legal. The land is no longer yours. It belongs to the city."* "I am not moving off my land. I have lived on this land for over sixty years and I am not going anywhere!" "Please Mrs. Johnson, you must leave. I will have no choice but to remove you from your property!"*

"Well, what are you waiting for? Take her away! Take her away, so I won't have to look out of my window at this terrible eye sore looking shack again!" "I am not going anywhere young man! This is my land. My husband and I paid for it in the thirties and I am not leaving now!"* Then Mrs. Vanderbilt shouted back saying, *"You don't know what you are saying! My husband Wilbert could not find any records or deeds that you own anything over here! You have been squatting on this land all of this time! You own nothing over here! You own nothing at all!"* Mrs. Vanderbilt attempted to drag her again by one of her arms, out of the path of the bulldozer. The Police Officer stepped in front of her and spoke to Willa Mae. *"Please Mrs. Johnson, I can take you anywhere you want to go but you don't have any legal right to the property."* "I demand that you do your job! Drag her away! I have been waiting a long time for this day!"*, Mrs. Vanderbilt insisted.

One of the residents of Shady Green saw what was happening and called a local news station to report the commotion that was taking place in front of Willa Mae's little shack. The news crew arrived on the double. They came out of their truck with cameras turned on and immediately started reporting the chaotic scene that had developed. Mrs. Vanderbilt sidestepped the Policeman, pulled up a row of beans near Willa Mae and said, *"Is this what you are trying to protect? This is as worthless as your life!"* That is when Willa Mae reached up and hit Mrs. Vanderbilt in the face and busted her lower lip. *"I HAVE BEEN ASSAULTED! I HAVE BEEN ASSAULTED! I'M HURT!"* Mrs. Vanderbilt fell down on the ground sobbing and shaking, *"I AM BLEEDING! OH MY GOD! LOOK AT THIS! I AM BLEEDING!"* Mrs. Vanderbilt started shaking and wiped a trickle of blood from her mouth with a handkerchief.

Then the officer pulled Willa Mae out of the path of the bulldozer. As he handcuffed her, a reporter started speaking into a microphone,

"You are watching it for yourself, ninety-two-year-old Willa Mae Johnson, better known as Mother Earth in this community, has been arrested and pulled off of her land. It is a terrible scene that is taking place right now! This is a sad and terrible day for the community of Shady Green for the beloved mother of the earth has been dragged off of her land! This is Action News reporting, giving you the news as it happens!"

Mrs. Johnson reluctantly gave in to the officer's demands. She walked to the cruiser, handcuffed, sat in the backseat and broke down crying. Mrs. Vanderbilt stood next to the vehicle, waving at her, laughing and saying, *"Finally, you are gone for good! And I hope you rot inside of that jail!"* as the officer drove her away.

When Willa Mae arrived at the station, she was kept in a room by herself. A Social Worker arrived and began questioning her about her plans after leaving her house. The Social Worker informed Willa Mae that she met the requirements for several nursing homes in the city. Willa Mae then said, *"I have plenty of help! And my personal attendants will be coming to help me. So, you just mind your own business! And I will mind my business! I am not leaving my house or my land! I will leave when God tells me to leave!"* *"Well, maybe these relatives of yours will come and help you move. Seeing that you are up in age and have nowhere to go. And you are being evicted from your land today!"* *"I told you before I am not going anywhere! I will leave when the time comes! And that time is not today! So you can go back to your office and leave me alone. I will be alright!"*

No charges were filed. So, Willa Mae was released with one stipulation. She had to promise not to hit or harass Mrs. Vanderbilt again. Consequently, she decided perhaps it was time to leave everything. After all, she was ninety-two years old; way too old to be fighting the whole city of Evergreen County. When she walked out of jail, she decided to withdraw what money she had left from the bank. She had relatives down South that would take her in. She took a taxi that night back to her property.

It was almost dark and a misty white fog was settling in and hovering over the ground. When she arrived home, she was speechless.

She did not recognize anything because everything that she loved was gone. Everything that was her life was piled up in a large heap of dirt, broken boards, and trees. Willa Mae walked across the ground in a daze, staring at the emptiness of her land. She fell down on the dirt and started crying asking God for help.

All of her photographs with Andy when they were young had been destroyed. Her marriage certificate, her pots, and pans that she cooked food in, her secret recipes, everything was destroyed. Even her large family Bible trimmed with the beautiful gold edges with her family history and the names of her ancestors were destroyed. Everything that she breathed life into, loved, trusted, and believed was on the far side of the land plowed over in the pile of dirt. Every leaf and tree were now gone, the rows of cantaloupes, the sweet corn, cabbage, pumpkins, sweet potatoes, green beans, and strawberry patches had been plowed over. Even her sturdy old rocker had been broken up into pieces as she saw traces of it scattered in the empty field. The beautiful orchards and garden. It was all gone as if it never existed. Willa Mae laid prostrate in the middle of the empty field with her hands outstretched, communicating and praying on the dirt as if it was an altar to God. She could not utter a sound. The sorrow was too deep. She now had become empty as the land itself. And in her silent spirit, she spoke to God because there was no one else that could enter that space that could touch her pain. *"It is over, God. I am an old woman. You can take my life now. Just let me die! I had enough of this world. I have nothing left."*

Just as she finished uttering her last word, a flurry of fireflies twirled and darted in the darkness, illuminating the fog that hovered above the ground. The fog had become increasingly dense as large white pillars tumbled on the ground as the fireflies darted within. Willa Mae was too overtaken with grief to see the supernatural phenomenon that was taking place. Then she saw them. There appeared to be people walking in the fog. There were people walking that were made out of mist. Willa Mae looked for her bifocals that she had dropped on the ground. And when she found them her eyes squinted as she tried to adjust to the sight. There were people not having real bodies but were made of mist, the wind, and fireflies. Then she noticed that there were hundreds of them moving through the clouds. Some appeared to be flying around her touching her hands as Willa Mae fearfully reached out to them. Willa Mae noticed that she felt a heaviness. The people in the mist appeared to be talking and having conversations as they walked and hovered above the ground. She did not know for sure if she was still dreaming or wide awake. But the people were all over her land as if observing, studying, measuring, and taking notes. Willa Mae stood up. Her body weak and shaking in fear, she called out to them *"Who are you? Who are all of you? What do you want?"* Then one of them approached her. His face and his body were entirely covered with the mist of the ground that disappeared and reappeared as he spoke. *"We are your personal gardeners. We have come to help!"* *"I have nothing left. How can you help me when there is nothing left of my life!"* *"It is your heart that is most sacred. It is your sacred patch."*

Willa Mae tried to stand up, but she was too weak. She looked at the beings moving through the white misty fog and saw that they were working. The beings were working without making a sound. She saw walls being erected, hammers, saws, screwdrivers, nails flying in the air, boards, frames, and millions of pieces connecting, twirling in the wind, the fog, and the fireflies. Willa Mae saw her little shack take form, little by little. As the clouds hovered above the ground, hands came out of the mist and gently swept across the ground as plants, bushes, and flowers started growing and bursting out of the barren soil. Willa Mae could feel the grass covering her bare feet as she knelt and touched the once desolate ground. Then Willa Mae saw her rocker moving through the wind. She adjusted her bifocals and took a deep breath as she watched all of the broken and damaged parts reconnecting and reassembling into place. Even her pots, pans, and dishes came floating around her until they moved inside of the house and started to fill the shelves of the cabinets. The beings then playfully flew down from the mist and lifted Willa Mae off her feet as her toes drifted above the ground.

Willa Mae found herself laughing for a moment and then stretched her foot down towards the earth to reassure herself that she was still alive. Then Willa Mae watched the pages of a book flying in the air around her when she realized that it was her Bible. She watched the pages stacking themselves together to form a book. Her Bible gently floated down from the wind and fog to return by the side of her rocker that was on the porch. Willa Mae stood up trembling as she walked through the fog calling out to the beings. *"I just want to say thank you for what you have done! Are you still there? Where did you go?"* She reached her hands out into the white fog that was all around her as the fireflies illuminated the darkness of the night.

It was morning when she awakened on a carpet of thick green grass surrounded by a group of children that nudged her on her shoulder. They had large straw baskets in their hands as they spoke saying, *"Is she alive? It looks like she is just sleeping!" "Mrs. Johnson, are you alright? Please wake up! Mrs. Johnson, are you alright? Please wake up!"* They continued to deliberately try and wake the sleeping woman on the ground. Willa Mae stirred and started crawling across the grass until she found her glasses. *"What are you children doing over here this morning?" "We have come to pick some of your fresh strawberries!" "There is nothing for you, children to pick. Now you go back home! Most likely, your parents are looking for you. Please go home before you get into trouble." "Can't you see? Mrs. Johnson, you have a whole row of strawberries that look like they are ripe! And look how big they are!"* One of the children held up a vine of strawberries that looked as big as his hand. Willa Mae looked around. She could hardly believe what she was seeing. It was as if nothing had been destroyed. She stooped down and ran her hand across the carpet of green grass that surrounded her. She was stunned and speechless as a little boy pulled on her dress saying, *"Can we pick some strawberries, Mrs. Johnson, please? You promised. Remember that you said as soon as they became ripe we could come over and pick some of them."* Willa Mae found her voice again and patted the child on his forehead saying, *"Yes! Yes! Yes, you can!"*

Willa Mae looked out over the land and saw the garden and everything had returned with vibrant, beautiful colors. The children grabbed her hands as she ran across the green carpet of grass laughing. The garden, the orchard, and the fruit trees now appeared to have deeper colors and had grown to amazing enormous sizes. The large heads of cabbages, melons, cantaloupes, and cucumbers also appeared as they had erupted from out of the ground. Some of them looked like they weighed over one hundred pounds! It was an utterly fantastic experience as Willa Mae ran with the children in the garden, eating strawberries. They turned around in circles, creating a merry go-round as they held hands, falling down laughing.

The apple, peach, plum, and pear trees were covered with so much fruit that their branches hung down because of the weight. Then she saw her house in the distance. It had transformed and was made new, just like when Andy first build it. It had been freshly painted. Each board had been renovated into a small architectural masterpiece. She ran to her house and stood on the porch in awe and screamed in delight. She saw her old rocker which had not changed. For that, she was grateful because certain things needed to remain the same. As she walked on the porch to her amazement, everything had been restored. She held her bible. Every page was repaired and even the names of her family members and their history were all intact. She tenderly picked up her bible. As tears steamed up her bifocals, she wiped them away to see more clearly.

Then she walked inside the house and stood dazed in astonishment. The floors had a beautiful mahogany finish that glimmered before her. Every picture was mounted in gold frames on the walls, along with her wedding certificate. It was all there; the pictures of she and Andy, eating their wedding cake when they were young. Everything had been replaced, but somehow, they knew how she would design the house if she had the money and the capability. All of her old furniture was gone. It had been replaced with new like it had never been used.

The children gathered inside the house and pulled her by her hands as she walked from room to room, laughing and looking with excitement at everything around her. All of the wonderful things that had happened in her life had all been captured and put in gold frames all throughout the house. It was as if someone had recorded all of her meaningful experiences in her life and saved them. In each room, everything had been replaced down to the minute details of how she had planned to design each room.

Mrs. Vanderbilt had her housekeeper Lucia open her large bay windows in her front room to see Willa Mae skipping in the yard with a large basket of strawberries.

Mrs. Vanderbilt let out a distressing scream. *"THIS IS IMPOSSIBLE! I WATCHED THE BULLDOZER KNOCK DOWN HER LITTLE SHACK! I SAW IT BEING LEVELED TO THE GROUND! AND THERE WAS NO WAY IT COULD STILL BE THERE! THERE WAS NOTHING LEFT BUT A PILE OF BROKEN BOARDS! WHAT IS GOING ON OVER THERE?"* Mrs. Vanderbilt was terrified as she looked at the little house. It looked amazingly new as it glistened in a yard surrounded by green grass. Then she saw the garden. It had been replaced with rows after rows of large hefty plants and vegetables. The large spacious orchards that circled the garden on the land had all been replaced. Mrs. Vanderbilt was shaken with fear as she pulled the curtains down and tried to close them.

Willa Mae returned to the house to pray. For a while, she stood on her porch and watched the children in the trees, picking the fruit, and running around the green patch of her property laughing. Mrs. Vanderbilt left her house in a huff. She was so angry that she did not care that her hair was in a cluster of rollers or that she had on her sleeping robe, which women of her stature, would have never left her house dressed like that.

Mrs. Vanderbilt roamed around the yard as if she was in a trance from what she was seeing. The children were in the garden. Some of them were still in the apple and pear trees picking the fruit. Their laughter could be heard throughout the property. Willa Mae sat in her rocker watching Mrs. Vanderbilt walking around the field distraught and in fear as she approached the yard. Willa Mae remained on her porch in her rocker humming a song and snapping some beans when Mrs. Vanderbilt approached her and spoke in a petrified voice, *"I don't know how you did all of this! I don't even want to know! I don't know what powers you have, old woman! But all of this will be gone again by the afternoon! You can count on it! I will destroy everything that you have on this land! I will not be defeated!"* Willa Mae did not utter a single word to her as she continued snapping her beans. Mrs. Vanderbilt continued her outburst, *"I saw the bulldozer destroy everything over here! I saw it with my own eyes! What powers do you have? How did you do this? This is impossible!"* She looked around afraid as if something was going to jump out and attack her. *"I don't know how you did all of this, old woman! I don't know who has helped you put everything back! But you can be assured of this, it will be destroyed! The bulldozer is coming back today! When I am done, you will be left with nothing!"*

"You know it would not be neighborly of me to not ask you to sit down and rest in the shade of the porch, drink a cool glass of lemonade, and have a slice of sweet potato pie.", Willa Mae said. This infuriated Mrs. Vanderbilt. She raised her voice, *"DON'T YOU PATRONIZE ME, OLD WOMAN! YOU ARE LEAVING OFF THIS LAND BY THIS AFTERNOON! SO, DON'T YOU GET TOO COMFORTABLE FOR YOU WILL BE GONE TODAY! YOU ARE GOING BACK TO THE COUNTRY WHERE YOU BELONG!"*

"Well, it's all left up to God! All I know is I am still here; still making sweet potato pies and corn mash. Then I am going to take a nap on the porch and maybe go for a walk in my beautiful garden in the afternoon. Don't you think everything came up so wonderful this year? I really have some wonderful caretakers that have helped me with my garden." Mrs. Vanderbilt turned around and stormed back to her house in Shady Green.

Later that day, a construction crew arrived on the far outskirts of Willa's Mae land. Willa Mae could see men arguing with one another. Subsequently, Mrs. Vanderbilt returned and Willa Mae could hear her arguing with someone that looked like the foreman. And even from this distance, on her porch, she could hear Mrs. Vanderbilt's conversation. *"Look at this fiasco! You assured me there would be nothing here but an empty plot of land this morning. And what happened? Your crew has done nothing! Everything is still in place. That old woman is still here sitting on her porch and snapping her beans!"* The foreman spoke angrily to another man whose stomach lapped over his belt with an unlit cigar in his mouth. *"Well, Boss, I don't know what happened! I knocked everything down yesterday evening. It was flatter than a pancake before I left. This stuff is scary!"* *"If I find out you have been drinking again, you are going to be fired! You will never drive another rig again with this company! You better finish this job, and you better get it right this time!"* The fat man moved quickly and sat inside a large yellow bulldozer. He turned on the noisy machine and moved the shovel up and down a few times. Then the foreman said, *"We have to take the old woman out of the house before we can finish the job!" "NO! You are going to complete this job right now! It was your construction crew that did not do it right the first time! I am not waiting another day for her to be removed. My husband has connections with the people that run this city. And your company will lose a big contract if you don't get this job done right!"* Mrs. Vanderbilt sternly said. *"Well Madam, we need to get the Sheriff here first to remove her from the property before my boys can start the job." "I am not waiting another day! You and your crew better do something to fix this! You will never get another contract from the city again! Be rest assured of that!" "I don't know what happened. I don't know how everything is still here. The whole thing is scary, but we will knock everything down when the Sheriff arrives!" "Well, you better do something! This whole experience is a nightmare! It is too stressful for me! I thought she would be gone, and she is still here!" "Well Madam, I cannot bulldoze a house with her still living inside of it!" "At least you can start at the garden. I will get the Sheriff to remove her out of her house!"* The man in the rig called out, *"I don't know boss! I don't want to start this rig with an old woman and a bunch of kids that are still on the property!" "Get this rig moving and plow through the garden or you will be fired today!"*

When he started the engine up, a loud roar was heard throughout the community as he prepared to go through Willa Mae's garden. He started shifting a row of levers in the rig. The large shovel came down and it started tearing through a row of pumpkins! Willa Mae put down her bowl of snap beans and quickly ran and stood in front of the shovel of the massive rig. The driver immediately turned the rig off and called out to the foreman. *"I have had enough of this? Fire me! This is way too much for me to continue!"* The foreman looked at the situation and said, *"We can't do anything, Mrs. Vanderbilt, until she is completely gone from the property! This situation is way too dangerous for us to continue!"* Willa Mae stood silently before the large bulldozer with her hands folded in a final act of defiance. People from the Shady Green community saw the commotion from Willa Mae standing before the big rig. They started coming out of their houses. Eventually, everyone from the community silently stood in front of the bulldozer with their children, and Willa Mae. The large man on the rig opened the door, jumped out, and said, *"I am not moving this rig any further!"*

Mrs. Vanderbilt was screaming now at the people standing silently in front of the bulldozer. *"All of you people need to move and get out of the way! You are breaking the law! All of you are going to jail! This is not her land! She does not own anything on it! She is going to be removed as soon as the Sheriff arrives! This is official business, and this does not concern you! How can you allow one old decrepit woman to deceive you all? Because of her, all of our property values have gone down. All because she continues living in this shack! She is bringing us all down!"* Mrs. Vanderbilt went towards Willa Mae and tried to grab her arm and pull her away. But Willa Mae stood firm. Finding a tree root in the ground, she moored herself down. Mrs. Vanderbilt was enraged and started screaming, *"GET UP, OLD WOMAN! GET UP OFF THIS LAND! GET UP! I HAVE HAD ENOUGH OF YOUR DEFIANCE!"*

Suddenly, the engine of the bulldozer turned on and the large gears moved as the rig started coming towards the crowd of people. The crowd started screaming as parents moved their children out of harm's way to safety. Everyone moved out of the path of danger, except Willa Mae. She resolutely held on to the root of the tree in one last act of strength and determination. Silently she whispered and thanked God for her life as she folded her trembling hands together in prayer.

Mrs. Vanderbilt's heart was pierced as she stood still beside Willa Mae. Mrs. Vanderbilt was paralyzed in fear, not knowing what to do next. She knew it would only be a few seconds before they both were killed. She knew that Willa Mae would face death rather than give up her land. But it was something deep that she sensed. An overwhelming power consumed her as a rainstorm of tears flooded her face. It was impossible to ignore. For the first time, she saw her hatred. And she saw how that hatred plowed over the land and destroyed every leaf and tree because of her own selfishness.

Willa Mae held on to her little patch of green, even if it cost her last breath, she was determined to hold on. For each leaf, each tree, each blade of grass, held the memories, and the promises that love endures, despite the struggles and despair. Love shall return no matter how often it is plowed over and oppressed. In silence, it shall return. It shall return in its blossoms, in its budding, in its golden fruits, in its nourishing seasons of wonders. If you can believe and endure, love will hold you, breathe through you, and restore you to its sacred dream and its sacred space.

Then Mrs. Vanderbilt called out to Willa Mae, *"Please get up off the ground. You will be killed! Please get up off the ground!"*

"This is my spot? I am not going anywhere!

This is my land and this is where I will die!"

"You are going to be killed any second if you don't get up off the ground!

What is wrong with you?"

"I will die before I leave my land!"

"What are you trying to do to yourself?"

Please don't do this? Please don't do this?

Please, please, I beg of you, don't do this!"

Mrs. Vanderbilt tried pulling Willa Mae away as she continued to hold on to the root of the tree with all of her strength. And then in a flash, in a futuristic moment of time, Mrs. Vanderbilt saw Willa Mae's house being torn apart; the walls being pulled down, her rocker broken into pieces, her bible, and the memories of a lifetime, all plowed over because of her hatred. Then she saw Willa Mae's funeral, and her fragile, broken body being carried back to her land. She watched it being lowered into the ground as thousands of people came from miles around to dance and celebrate with the old black woman one more time in her yard. Mrs. Vanderbilt returned home and opened the curtains of her front room's large bay windows. She saw herself living as a terrified recluse. She was divorced and trapped in a house covered with clutter and afraid that her loneliness had become a way of life.

Then it was all gone. The vision had vanished and she saw the bulldozer moving closer towards Willa Mae. Mrs. Vanderbilt cried out saying,

"Please God, she doesn't deserve to die like this!
Please God, she doesn't deserve to die! No, not like this
No not like this! I don't want to live if she must die!"

Mrs. Vanderbilt quickly moved closer towards Willa Mae and covered her body with her own and whispered, *"Please forgive me."*

The bulldozer continued to come closer. In a mind-boggling moment, it stopped, just inches away from hitting and killing them both.

One week later, Willa Mae was on her porch snapping beans. It was a bright and cool morning when a young man arrived in an official looking city vehicle. He was dressed in the uniform of a Deputy Sheriff. He promptly showed her his credentials as he opened her white picket gate and spoke to her politely

"Are you Willa Mae Ernestine Johnson?"
"Why yes, I am!
"I have a letter from the City County Office that I need you to sign and authorize." Willa Mae put on her bifocals and wondered if this was the official eviction notice for her to leave. It was a long journey and the eviction process had finally come. The young man, after receiving her signature on a receipt, jumped back into his vehicle and drove away. Willa Mae stood in the yard. The sun formed a bright and glowing circle in the sky as a group of white clouds appeared to be drifting around her little shack.

Willa Mae took a deep breath and started reading the letter out loud.

"It has been brought to our attention that the City of Evergreen California owes you an official apology. A deed of records has been found with the names of Andy Benjamin Johnson and Willa Mae Ernestine Johnson registered owners and beneficiaries of all of the land pertaining to the Shady Green County and community. The deed was found in a file cabinet in a basement where old records are kept. You own all of the land fifty miles west, north, south and

east of the Shady Green community. And you are duly entitled to compensation for the property from the City of Evergreen County and from the Shady Green community for the use and benefit of your land. It has been determined that rightful funds will be calculated and immediately put into your designated bank account. Until additional compensation has been met for the use of your land and surrounding property. As a demonstration of the good intentions of Evergreen Country, we are giving you ten million five hundred thousand dollars for the use of your land and surrounding property.

Sincerely, The Country Assessor's Office of Evergreen County

Also, please note the annexation of your land has been dismissed.

There was a large facsimile check with Willa Mae's name on it for ten million five hundred thousand dollars, along with the deed of records of her land. Willa Mae could not believe it. Her eyes welled with tears and blurred her glasses. She cried out so loud that even the clouds circling in the sky around the house could hear her.

Later on that day, Mrs. Vanderbilt came through the gate and called out to her,

"Hey, Willa Mae! Do you have any more of that delicious sweet potato pie?"

"I sure do!" Willa Mae said with a smile. *"Come on up and get a slice!"*

Both of the women sat on the porch. It was a quiet, wonderful day. The kind of day that you don't want to do much talking.

Sometimes it is enough to let God talk, and everyone else should just shut up.

~*Epilogue*~

It was some years later, the day before Willa Mae died that somehow, amazingly, strength returned to her body. She left her bed and walked outside to let her feet touch the green grass. That is when she saw a beautiful blue bicycle parked next to a tree in her front yard. To everyone's amazement, she jumped on the bicycle and started riding it.

It is time to answer the last questions of The Test.

You have been on a journey, a pilgrimage of your soul, and you were given the opportunity to examine your life. And there, in the silent rubble of the ashes of your mistakes, there was something still beautiful that still sparkled that refused to give up. There was something so wonderful that it refused to die. It refused to wither and crumble away. For when this life is over, when your body has become a shell that is buried under the earth, I shall remember the power of your love. A day will occur when Heaven and Earth has been joined together and you shall have a picnic lunch with me the Creator of the Universe on a sunny, grassy hill. And I will tell you personally, how wonderful it was for you to realize that love overcomes all your mistakes!

Now you must finish the last part of The Test.

1. *Have you ever been in a position like Willa Mae, where you had to hold on to the spiritual beliefs and principals of your life?*
2. *How did you hold on to your life when things were falling apart all around you?*
3. *Can you explain the significance of the tree root that Willa Mae was holding on to as it related to the tree? What things in your life can be identified as a tree root? What things can be identified as a tree?*
4. *Can you describe a time in your life when you had neither money nor success? What was the motivation that kept you moving forward, despite all the odds against you? And after you had attained a certain measure of success, what was the motivation that kept you moving forward once again? What motivates you when you wake up each day?*
5. *If Mrs. Vanderbilt did not have an expensive house or wealth, how do you think she would have related to Willa Mae?*
6. *Does success and wealth make you different from other people?*

7. *In your opinion, what makes all of humanity the same?*

8. *Can you think of people in your life that had nothing and suddenly came into great wealth? How do you relate to them now? If you won the Powerball, would you have the same friends? What things would be different? What things would remain the same?*

9. *Have you ever been in a situation where your beliefs and your integrity influenced others around you? How has your lack of integrity influenced others around you? Can you explain?*

10. *Have you ever been in a situation where you saw someone purposefully make a determined effort to destroy someone because of their culture, race or what they believed? And what did you do to help them positively or negatively to impact the situation?*

11. *What are the things you believe that would survive if you lost everything? And what makes these survivable things so important?*

12. *Does having wealth make you automatically evil?*

13. *Does being poor make you more aware, more spiritual, and more conscious-minded?*

14. *Do you believe God is dead?*

15. *How is God alive in your life?*

16. *What is spiritually and powerfully alive in you each day?*

17. *What truly gives you spiritual meaning to wake up each day?*

18. *Have you ever survived a terrible failure in your life, such as a divorce, an addiction, the loss of a job or the death of a loved one? What were the steps that brought you back to life? And how were you able to function in the world again? Can you make a list of ten steps that brought you back to life?*

19. *Did you believe that God creates interventions and events and circumstances in your life so that you can participate in them?*

20. *Have you ever been so hurt and humiliated that you did not want to leave your house or leave your bed? What was that situation about?*

21. *Who was the person or what was the situation or the spiritual connection that made you realize that your life truly meant something?*

22. *What makes God real to you?*

23. *Have you ever heard the voice of God?*

24. *Have you ever heard God speak to you through other people? Have you ever heard God speak through your circumstances? Can God speak to you when you are silent? Can you explain these experiences?*

25. *Have you ever been in a situation where you had to deny God? Have you ever been in circumstances where you denied God to keep the necessities of food, shelter or employment? Has God ever spoken to you to help someone when there was an injustice? Or when someone was hurting and humiliated and you watched the events unfold, and yet you turned away? Can you explain the events and how God spoke to you after the event?*

26. *Have you ever been angry at God for taking something away from you?*

27. *Have you ever discovered later that which God had taken away, turned out to be a blessing for you?*

28. *Do you believe in every situation in your life that God is trying to speak to you?*

29. *If you had a week or six months to live, what would be the most important things you would do? Make a list!*

30. *Make a list of people that you have truly hurt in your life and write letters to each one of them apologizing for your behavior. And please include a small gift with your letter. And if you believe that they will receive the letter and the gift, then please take it to them personally. This exercise will take some time and there is no hurry to complete it. This task can be done when you have awakened!*

31. *Now with your immediate family members, I want you to write a second group of letters to your wife, your husband, your children as well as the closest people in your life and simply tell them that you love them. This is a most difficult exercise*

for many people since love is so often taken for granted. And please include a small gift with the letter. This task can be done when you have awakened!

32. *Are you fearful and despondent? Do you have thoughts of suicide because you are in debt, from a bankruptcy or a divorce? Regardless of where you are spiritually or financially, develop a daily routine of talking to God. Pray in the morning. Rehearsing the good qualities that still exist in you offers the opportunities for you to experience new doors of healing and prosperity. Please remember in all impossible situations you will find God's power working for you. Before the light of day has touched the earth pray alone in your room and see great results throughout your day! You must pray every day in the morning for the next 30 days and write down the results of what has happened during the day. This task can be done when you have awakened.*

33. *Willa Mae's garden was a place where she could walk and sense the presence of God. Willa Mae's garden was her place to have a real conversation with God about her life. Do you have a quiet garden or a sacred place where you can speak to God? If not, start today to find your sacred place.*

34. *How will Mrs. Vanderbilt's relationship be now with people of a different color, income, and culture?*

35. *What is failure to you? What is success to you?*

36. *What does it take to be successful in our modern world today? And what are the positive skills necessary to be successful? Make your own list of ten things necessary to be successful?*

37. *Mrs. Vanderbilt made her house and possessions a god. What have you made a god in your life? Make a list of ten things in your life that you have made a god? This will be difficult for most people to do.*

38. *Has the god you made and worshipped ever turned, attacked or even tried to destroy you?*

39. *Willa Mae's garden required time and patience to develop and grow. A true and loving relationship takes time to nourish and grow. Have you ever hurt someone so badly you thought*

that the relationship could never be repaired? But as time developed, it gradually healed. Can you recall how the relationship was restored? Have you ever sinned so terribly in your life that you thought and believed that your relationship with God could never be restored? What circumstances or what person, did God use to bring you back into a loving relationship with Him? And are you still struggling to repair your broken relationship with God? Is a relationship ever broken with God?

40. *Willa Mae had a truly organic, spiritual, natural relationship with the earth and the people that lived around her. All of us are growing something in our garden, our truth, our life mission, our accomplishments, and every day we are creating the fruits of our life. Make a list of ten things you have grown positively in your garden of life. Here are examples: your integrity, your honor, your respect for others, your ability to help others.*

41. *Make a list of ten things you have grown negatively in your garden. Here are examples: Your addiction of holding on to things that keep you bound and depressed. Your lack of empathy for others. Your selfishness and unresponsive attitude when people need your help. Your running away in fear when confronted to make truthful decisions.*

42. *Have you ever known someone that was poor? Someone that was so poor that they did not have enough money to eat or pay their bills. What was your response, attitude, and relationship with them?*

43. *If someone moved into your community, your neighborhood, or next door to you that was poor. What would you do differently than Mrs. Vanderbilt?*

44. *When Willa Mae was holding on to the tree root what does the tree root mean to you in the spiritual sense as it relates to your family and your beliefs?*

45. *Remember when all the residents of the Shady Green community were in Willa Mae's yard looking at the stars, preparing to go to sleep, and the fireflies instantly appeared*

and illuminated the evening skies? Have you ever witnessed a natural phenomenon or a supernatural miracle? Is there a difference between a miracle and a natural phenomenon or are they the same? What is your definition of a miracle? Can acts of kindness be considered a miracle?

46. *Have you ever believed that at least one time in your life, God interceded with an Angel to help you in an emergency? Can people take the place of Angels upon the earth?*

47. *If you died today, who would speak at your funeral and what would they say? Be extremely honest. Most people have difficulty with this question.*

48. *If you died today and saw the whole spectrum of your life, and if God restored you to come back to the earth to finish one important task, what would that task be?*

49. *On the very last day of your life, God will speak to you. He will not say much. He will only ask if you love Him? And if you say "Yes" that will be enough. And now this is the last question of The Test. For only you can say the words. For only you can speak them out! What do you have to say?*

50. *On the very last day of your life, an Angel will arrive at your house, the nursing home, the hospital, or the place where you will stand outside of your body. That Angel will be riding a blue bicycle, and then he will ask you to hop on. What will you do?*

Now that you have finished "The Test" let us pray before you wake up!

For my living voice will wake you each and every morning. It is the voice of my inner loving spirit. It covers you as the morning light that washes you in the warmth of my healing strength preparing you for the day. And you will know that I love you. And even before your feet touch the floor, I will speak my promises into your mind and cover you in the quiet of my love. And I will appear in your life and reward you ten times more for not doubting and for trusting my incomprehensible, eternal personal embrace.

For you will know I am alive when you breathe and stretch forth your hands in the wind. I will give you a plan, a place of safety. For I will build you a Sanctuary when you are unsure and when you are afraid for this is my promise to love you forever.

For you have known me your entire life. From the moment that you took your first steps. You have felt my loving invisible spirit pull you out of your mother's womb. For it was I who told you how to suck the milk between your quivering lips when you were cold and shaking, struggling for life. For I was with you when the training wheels were taken off your bicycle. You heard me the "FIRST TIME" crying out in your inner Spirit saying, "DON'T BE AFRAID! TURN THE PEDALS OF THE WHEEL! RIDE WITH ALL OF YOUR MIGHT AND DON'T LOOK BACK!" You rode your bicycle with all of your strength and fury until you could keep your balance and do the impossible!

Whenever you failed, and no one believed in your dreams, and you were left abandoned, humiliated and broken, you felt me breathing out of your lips reassuring and resuscitating your gifts and your abilities to begin once again. Your failures are just an opportunity to demonstrate an even greater love for you. I prepared your bandages from the skin of my broken body. When I was killed, my beating heart was taken out and placed inside of you. For I have applied the ointment of grace and mercy to fortify your bones when you were afraid to move and felt defeated. And I shall call out to you a "SECOND TIME" when you were lying on the bed of regret and doubt. I shall call out to you saying, "DON'T BE AFRAID! GET UP!"

And I saw you unsure, afraid to leave your room, shaking in the darkness while putting on your clothes as you prepared to face the world once again. But when you went outside, you did something wonderful for you believed anyway and took a deep breath and reached your hands upward and touched the sky.

When the time comes, when you are old and frail, and you are suddenly swept out of the world into the darkness, I will call out to you again a "THIRD TIME" in a voice that will calmly sing to you, and will compel you to come forward. I will call out to you as you step out upon the stars of space saying, "Come to me, don't be afraid and you shall live forever!"

The alarm clock is ringing you have been given the power to breathe once again!
You have been such a marvelous student, such a magnificent learner and you have passed this most difficult and yet rewarding test. You have graduated with honors.

Now wake up! And go forward and live forever!